DARK SPACE IV: Revenge

(3rd Edition)

by Jasper T. Scott

http://www.JasperTscott.com

@JasperTscott

Copyright © 2014 by Jasper T. Scott
THE AUTHOR RETAINS ALL RIGHTS
FOR THIS BOOK

Reproduction or transmission of this book, in whole or in part, by electronic, mechanical, photocopying, recording, or by any other means is strictly prohibited, except with prior written permission from the author. You may direct your inquiries to JasperTscott@gmail.com

Cover design by Thien A.K.A "ShooKooBoo"

This book is a work of fiction. All names, places, and incidents described are products of the writer's imagination and any resemblance to real people or life events is purely coincidental.

Table of Contents

Copyright Page 1
Acknowledgements 4
THE ENEMY IN OUR MIDST 6
   Chapter 1 7
   Chapter 2 17
   Chapter 3 35
   Chapter 4 51
   Chapter 5 67
   Chapter 6 80
   Chapter 7 97
   Chapter 8 110
   Chapter 9 126
   Chapter 10 144
WHERE THE DARKNESS FINDS US 158
   Chapter 11 159
   Chapter 12 173
   Chapter 13 183
   Chapter 14 195
   Chapter 15 209
   Chapter 16 228
   Chapter 17 246
   Chapter 18 257
   Chapter 19 271
AVILON 286
   Chapter 20 287
   Chapter 21 302
   Chapter 22 318
   Chapter 23 340
   Chapter 24 350

Chapter 25	364
Chapter 26	376
Chapter 27	388
Chapter 28	403
Chapter 29	416
Chapter 30	435
Chapter 31	447
Chapter 32	454
Chapter 33	465
Chapter 34	473
Chapter 35	480
Chapter 36	493
Chapter 37	502
Epilogue	508
DARK SPACE CONTINUES IN FALL 2014 WITH	516
PREVIOUS BOOKS IN THE SERIES	517
KEEP IN TOUCH	520
ABOUT THE AUTHOR	521

Acknowledgements

This book comes to you thanks in large part to my wonderful wife, who endured many a lonely night and weekend to help me finish on time. The quality of the story is thanks in large part to my editor, Aaron Sikes, whose remarkable feedback helped me to see the big picture through all the little details. Thank you, Aaron for helping me make this story shine. Also, a big thanks to my very talented cover artist, Thien "Shookooboo," for artwork that far surpassed my expectations.

Finally, I have to say an extra special thanks to all my beta readers, without whose feedback this book would be far less polished than it is. Many thanks go to Andrew de Mora, Bill Gallacher, Carmen Romano, Daniel Eloff, Damon Trent, Dave Cantrell, David Brotchie, Davis Shellabarger, Gary Watts, Ian Jedlica, Ian Seccombe, Jay Gehringer, Jeph Yang, Jim, John H. Kuhl, John K. Nash, John Parker, John Rowles, Kedd Burmeister, Mark Tindall, Marten Ekema, Maurizio Cattaneo, Patrick Blenkinsop, Randy Mills, Raymond Myers, Sandra Roan, Steven Shapse, and Wade Whitaker.

To those who dare,
And to those who dream.
To everyone who's stronger than they seem.

"Believe in me /
I know you've waited for so long /
Believe in me /
Sometimes the weak become the strong"
—STAIND, *Believe*

THE ENEMY IN OUR MIDST

Chapter 1

Master Commander Lenon Donali dropped out of superluminal space (SLS) for the tenth time. The bright streaks and starlines of faster-than-light travel disappeared with a flash, persisting only as an afterimage burned onto his retinas from staring too long into that mesmerizing swirl of light. Ghostly patterns floated across the diamond-bright sparkle of the void. Fuel was running low from so many stops. He hadn't travelled more than twelve light years away from Dark Space, but entering and leaving SLS were the most fuel-expensive parts of space flight.

Donali checked the grid for enemy contacts, just as he had

done at each reversion point since leaving Dark Space. He wasn't expecting to see anything, and he wasn't surprised. Apart from the spreading wake of radiation from his corvette, there was no detectable trace of tachyon radiation. Donali waited a minute longer, watching the grid without blinking, but his scopes were clear; he hadn't been followed.

He sighed with relief, and his thoughts went to the alien implant which he'd left in the corvette's med bay to be analyzed by the ship's computers. Whatever it was, it had finished calling home long ago, and now it couldn't be bothered to tell the Sythians where it was. The last time that mysterious alien device had transmitted anything at all had been at the entrance of Dark Space. Donali hoped it hadn't given away the location of the sector. Dark Space was humanity's only refuge from the Sythians, and it was only safe because it had been kept hidden for the last ten years after the invasion.

But now that refuge was in jeopardy. If the alien implant they had discovered while dissecting High Lord Kaon's brain had managed to call home, then for all Donali knew Dark Space was already overrun with Sythians.

Donali unbuckled his seat restraints and pushed out of the pilot's chair. It was time to finish studying the alien device and then jettison it out the nearest airlock. He had a rendezvous with Admiral Hoff Heston coming up in just five days, and that was precious little time to study the Sythian device.

When he arrived in the med bay, he was gratified to find the implant still sitting inside the holoimager where he'd left it. He'd been half expecting it to have walked off by itself. Donali keyed the machine for the results of its analysis and a hologram flickered to life above the imager.

The inside of the implant was organized into a crystal lattice structure, and the outside hadn't responded to any probe of any kind ... except for ... the electrical conduction test. When the device had been exposed to low level electrical signals, it had begun to respond with the same. That made sense, since it would have to interact with the Sythians' brains somehow. Donali stared at the screen, wondering what purpose the implant served.

If the Sythians had known Kaon was going to be captured, or if they had allowed him to be captured, then the device could be a tracker of some kind, but if that were so, then why wasn't it transmitting now? The fact that it responded to electrical stimulation seemed to indicate that it still had power.

It's a pity I don't have someone to implant this in ... he thought. It was much larger than the average human implant, and would require surgery to insert—not that he had a test subject for that, anyway.

Unless....

Donali's eyes turned to the stasis room adjoining the med bay. Abruptly he turned and walked toward it. He waved his hand over the door controls, and the door slid away with a *swish*. The lights came on automatically for him. This was Donali's own personal transport, and it knew him well.

He walked to the back of the room to the pair of empty stasis tubes there. The room held twelve stasis tubes in all, one for each of the corvette's standard crew. When Donali reached the pair of empty stasis tubes, he stepped up to the control panel of the leftmost one and keyed in a code which only he knew. He heard a *clu-clunk* of duranium bolts sliding away and reached out with both hands to grasp the sides of the heavy stasis tube. It pulled away from the wall easily enough, rolling on wheels that it shouldn't have had. Behind that, lay another stasis tube, the transpiranium cover glowing blue and active. Donali saw a stranger staring back at him from the other side of the transpiranium. That stranger was his escape plan—a clone of a long dead fleet officer.

Serving under someone like Admiral Heston, Donali had to be careful. The admiral had been betrayed so many times that he would betray his friends and family preemptively just to keep it from happening again, and that meant Donali needed to keep a few secrets of his own—just in case the admiral should ever decide to preemptively betray his own XO.

Already fitted in the clone's wrist were all the credentials Donali would need to get away and make a new life for himself without the admiral ever being the wiser. Being a senior member of the *Tauron*'s medical staff had its advantages. Any bodies which passed through the morgue were his to examine if he so chose. He'd stolen the identichips from more than a few of them and subsequently erased the record of their deaths. Then he'd cloned them and left their cloned bodies in stasis until they were needed. Using the Lifelink implant in his brain, Donali could transfer his conscious self from his current body to any one of the clones. Like that, he could effectively disappear. So far Donali hadn't needed that backup plan, but it gave him a unique opportunity now.

He walked into the dark crawl space and keyed the control panel to release the clone. The cover of the stasis tube opened with a hiss and the clone opened its eyes for the first time. It saw him and began to cry pitifully. It fell into Donali's arms, unable to even stand up on its own. Donali backed out of the crawl space, half dragging and half carrying his clone.

He tried to ignore its wailing cries while it clung to him like a baby to its mother.

Clones grown for immortals spent their entire lives in an induced sleep, growing to maturity at an accelerated rate until they reached the right age, and then they were frozen like that until they were needed. All a clone ever had a chance to experience was a cloning tank and the endless dreaming of accelerated aging, and after that—another tank and the near perfect metabolic suspension of stasis. They could last in stasis for a thousand years and only age ten. What they dreamt about while they were in there was a mystery, but the most likely answer was nothing. They had never experienced anything, so how could their brains imagine something? They never learned to walk, talk, eat, or do anything else that a regular adult took for granted. They were full-grown newborns until the Lifelink implants in their brains received the flood of information which they would use, along with a billion little nanites, to sculpt their brains into the mirror image of their creators'.

Clones were never woken like this, without their Lifelink implant being activated first. Donali tried to ignore the pinprick of guilt which he felt over that and over what he was about to do. "I'm sorry," he whispered. "It's okay. Daddy needs your help." Donali set the clone down on the cold deck and its cries intensified. The man curled into a fetal ball, while Donali fumbled with his grav gun. He aimed the gun at the clone and gravved him off the deck to carry him into the med bay.

An hour later, Donali had his subject strapped down on the examination table, still crying, but more softly now. The clone's eyes flicked from side to side, darting and wide. Donali put him out of his misery a moment later with a sleep-inducing anesthetic.

Now the operation could begin. It took just over an hour to open the clone's skull and delicately tuck the alien implant inside his brain. Then Donali sealed the clone's skull once more. Another hour passed while he cleaned up his surgical instruments and waited for the clone to wake.

Suddenly, there came an alien warbling and Donali spun around to look. His patient was awake. He hurried back to the clone's side, his heart pounding, his eyes wide and filled with wonder. The clone had been a blank slate, dumb and mute, and now he was speaking in some facsimile of Sythian. There was only one explanation for that. The alien implant was more than just a tracker. It contained information from the Sythian they'd taken it from. Perhaps it was the Sythian equivalent of an immortal human's Lifelink implant.

"Hello, Kaon," Donali tried, testing his theory. He was almost unable to contain his excitement.

The clone turned to look at him, and warbled something else. Donali wasn't wearing a translator, so he didn't understand. Then the clone appeared to notice that he was strapped down to the table. He raised his chin to his chest and saw that he was a human. Seeing that, he turned back to Donali with a hateful glare. "Where am I? What you do to me?" he demanded, now speaking in Imperial Versal.

Donali blinked and his red artificial eye winked in tandem with his real one. "You can speak our language?" He shook his head incredulously, still trying to catch up with everything. This confirmed Admiral Hoff's suspicions. Humans and Sythians *had* met before, and they were both doing the same thing—using implants and clones to live forever.

"Answer my questions, human," Kaon demanded.

"You're on board my corvette, and I put your implant in a human body to see how it would react. . . ." Donali shook his head. "But I never imagined this."

The clone hissed again. "So I am your experiment? You pay for this, human."

Donali raised one eyebrow. "I don't see how."

Kaon closed his eyes and Donali watched his lips move. He heard whispers coming out, but they were alien warbles, not human speech. "What are you doing?" he asked, frowning.

Kaon turned to him with an ugly smile. "You will sssee."

Donali cocked his head and raised his eyebrows. A moment later, the ship shuddered, and Kaon's smile broadened.

"No," Donali said.

"Yess," Kaon whispered.

Donali ran back to the bridge. He arrived, out of breath and panting all of a minute later, but he was too late.

The entire forward viewport was filled with the shining hull of a Sythian warship. It was bigger than any ship he'd ever seen, and it wasn't firing on him—it was drawing him toward it with some kind of grav gun.

"How?!" Donali demanded as he sat down at the controls and powered up the drives. He'd made ten jumps! They couldn't have followed him through all of that.

Then he noticed that the grid was painted with the yellow vector of a tachyon trace. That radiation was just over an hour old, meaning Kaon's implant must have called for help almost the instant it had been inserted in the clone's brain. For the Sythians to be here now, they had to have been very close when they'd received the transmission. They *had* been following him, then.

Donali pushed the throttle up past the stops into overdrive, trying to escape the grav gun which had seized his ship ... but nothing happened. The ship wouldn't turn, and the drives just pushed him faster toward the alien cruiser. He shut down the drives with a scowl and sat back to consider his options.

There weren't any. He could armor up and go down fighting, or he could let the Sythians capture him. What kind of choices were those? Donali settled for the dubious third option of holding Kaon ransom in the med bay.

* * *

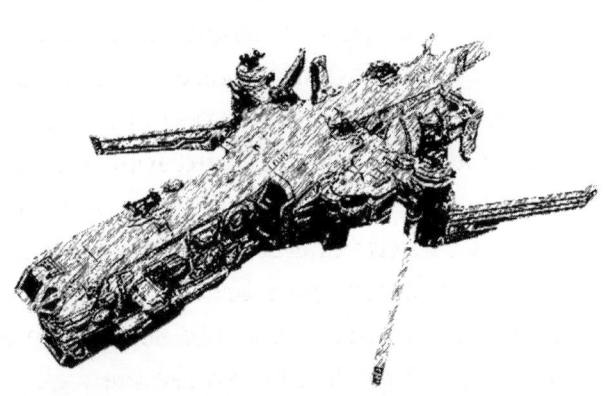

Less than half an hour later, a pair of hulking Gors burst into the med bay in their glossy black armor. These were the Sythians' slave soldiers—carnivorous monsters with gaunt, skull-like faces; slitted yellow reptilian eyes; thick, rippling muscles; and ashen gray skin. Armored as they were, Donali was spared the horror of seeing them in the flesh, but that was a small comfort. He knew that these two would happily eat him alive if they had the chance.

Holding Kaon at gunpoint, he told the Gors not to take another step—not that he thought they could understand him. Kaon smiled up at him and warbled something. At that, the Gors shot them both.

In the dark, Donali had no concept of time. His artificial eye helped him to see and pick out details of his surroundings which a regular human wouldn't be able to observe, but all he saw were the usual glossy black walls and floor of a Sythian ship. He also noticed strange, hulking shadows moving around him. He felt like he was trapped in a bad dream. All he knew was that he wasn't dead. The Sythians had kept him alive. But why?

Why . . .

At last, he was awake and conscious enough to think clearly, but his thoughts were different now. He knew where he was and why. He wasn't frightened. And the cold, unfeeling darkness was a comfort to him—a touch of home.

A moment later, a dim light snapped on, and now Donali could see better. He tried to sit up and found that he could. There was no longer any need to restrain him. He looked around and saw more beds like the one where he lay, each of them occupied by another man or woman of his species. There were thousands of them, and the room where they lay was so large that Donali couldn't even see the walls or ceiling, just endless rows of humans, disappearing to all sides of him.

A voice spoke into the darkness, warbling at him in a language which he now knew and understood. "Arise," it said. Donali did as he was told and stood up. "Walk toward the light."

A pale yellow light appeared in the distance, shining through the darkness, and Donali strode toward it, his footsteps eager, driven, and purposeful. When he reached that light, he found someone waiting for him. It was High Lord Kaon. Donali recognized him by the subtle pattern of lavender freckles on his translucent skin, as well as by the gills in the sides of his neck.

"My lord," Donali warbled.

"We have a special purpose for you, Lenon Donali."

"I await the honor of hearing it."

"You are to meet the admiral at the entrance of Dark Space as planned."

"As you wish, My Lord."

"You must get close to him."

"Yess—" Donali hissed, anticipating the rest of his mission. "—and kill him!"

"No. Capture him and bring him to us. We use him to find the lost sector of humans, and then we kill him."

"It will be done, My Lord."

Chapter 2

Admiral Hoff Heston stood on the bridge of the *Valiant*, watching from the captain's table as the *Intrepid* coasted toward them from the Dark Space gate. Even as he watched, the gate shut down and the glowing blue wormhole it maintained disappeared, sealing the entrance of the sector. It wouldn't be enough to keep out another Sythian invasion, but at least it would slow them down.

"Gravidar, magnify the *Intrepid* 400%. Comms, put me through to the captain."

"Yes, sir," Lieutenant Hanz said from the comm station.

The gravidar officer said nothing, but Hoff saw the *Intrepid* suddenly swell to four times its size, filling a much larger section of the forward viewports. A moment later, it shimmered, replaced by a head-and-shoulders view of

Captain Loba Caldin. She had striking indigo eyes and short blonde hair which framed a deceptively delicate-looking set of features—button nose, small jaw, smooth alabaster skin, and a narrow, unlined forehead.

"Admiral Heston," Caldin said.

"I trust your mission was successful," Hoff replied.

"It was. Commander Donali was already waiting at the rendezvous when we arrived."

"Any sign of Sythian pursuit?"

"None sir. We stayed cloaked for fully ten minutes, checking the area before we revealed ourselves."

There had been a time when cloaking technology had been an enigma to humanity, but now, thanks to their Gor allies, it was no longer exclusive to the Sythian invaders.

"You were wise to be cautious, Captain," Hoff replied. Not that it would matter if Donali had been followed. The Sythians knew where Dark Space was now. "You may proceed to dock, Captain. Tell Commander Donali to meet me in the Operations Center as soon as you set down. I'll debrief you right after him at 1600 hours."

"Yes, sir."

"Dismissed."

The captain's face disappeared, replaced by a now-much-closer view of the *Intrepid*. It was one of two 280-meter-long venture-class cruisers which berthed inside the *Valiant*. To the *Valiant*, a five-kilometer-long gladiator-class carrier, those cruisers were gnats, but at over 20 stories high, with 18 decks, the venture-class was hardly small—just not a mobile fortress like the *Valiant*. Thanks to heavy automation those cruisers had a crew of only 128 men and women. That included gunners, engineers, pilots, sentinels, medical staff, and bridge crew. Most of the deck space was devoted to weaponry, power, fuel, storage, and an ample living space. The venture-class had been designed to go for a decade or more before needing to resupply.

Hoff admired the rugged lines of the *Intrepid*, the broad bow and bristling beam cannons. It wasn't an elegant warship, but what it lacked in elegance it made up for in brawn. For its class and size, the venture-class was unparalleled in a fight. Sure the *Valiant* could squash dozens of them by herself, but she was also a thousand times the size. Big, impressive warships like the *Valiant* were intimidating, but not efficient. They were safe for important political figures and high-ranking fleet officers to sit behind the lines, but they were not the real engines of war, and they were not nearly as emblematic of the Imperium. Just six gladiator-class carriers had been requisitioned for the Imperial Star Systems Fleet (ISSF), while over a thousand venture-class cruisers had been in service at the height of the Imperium.

That was before the invasion. Now there was just one gladiator-class carrier and six venture-class cruisers. Hoff worried his lower lip, the skin around his gray eyes tensing. Shadowy, half-remembered memories of death and unspeakable destruction across countless worlds drifted through his mind's eye on a sea of blood. The mind was a capricious warden, at times holding captive all of the worst memories, while at others, letting them all out in a dire free-for-all. Hoff remembered. . . .

Ten years ago, the Sythians had come boiling into the Adventa Galaxy from the neighboring Getties Cluster and stormed across the galaxy, wiping out everything in just nine months. Trillions of people had died in that war. Humanity had been woefully unprepared.

The Sythians had come with almost two thousand

cloaked warships filled with millions of slave soldiers—vicious, two-meter high monsters called Gors. Even the foot soldiers were cloaked, and they'd always had the element of surprise—*always ripped our throats out before we could scream,* Hoff thought with a grimace.

The war had come to be known as *The Invisible War,* and the Gors—with their glossy black armor and skull-like helmets—had been the ugly face of that war. They crewed the Sythians' warships, piloted their fighters, drove their spider tanks, and did all the Sythians' dirty work. They'd done such a fantastic job of keeping their Sythian masters out of harm's way that for almost a decade, no one even knew the Sythians existed. Even after meeting one of them, Hoff had continued to believe that the Gors were the real enemy.

That suspicion had almost cost humanity everything they had left.

Near the end of the war, a few million wealthy and important people, including Supreme Overlord Altarian Dominic, had managed to flee to Dark Space. Once a place of exile for the Imperium's worst criminals, it was now the last refuge of humanity. The sector was surrounded by black holes and had just one safe way in or out, which was hidden by a sensor-disrupting nebula. No one except for a few high-ranking officers had even known where it was. Officially, Dark Space didn't exist, and for ten long years, that had been enough to keep it safe.

During that time, Hoff had been almost 1,000 light years away, having been cut off from the retreat. He'd used the remnants of his Fifth Fleet to rescue survivors from the war and bring them to his Enclave. Much later, he'd found out about the survivors hiding in Dark Space, and he'd learned that the sector had suffered a criminal revolt. The criminals had come to him with a stolen warship—none other than the overlord's flagship, the *Valiant* herself—and Hoff had chased them back to Dark Space, thinking he would defeat the rebellion with just one captured Sythian cruiser and his own flagship, the *Tauron*. That plan would have worked flawlessly, too, were it not for the fact that he'd unwittingly brought a Sythian tracking device with him.

"Hangar bay controllers have a grav lock on the Intrepid," Lieutenant Hanz said from the comm station, interrupting Hoff's reverie.

Hoff acknowledged that with a nod. "Bring them in."

"Yes, sir."

Waiting on board that cruiser was Hoff's XO, Master Commander Lenon Donali. He'd missed a lot in the week that he'd been away. When they'd parted ways, Donali had been leaving to take the alien tracking device they'd found with him, hoping to lead the Sythians away from Dark Space. Before that tracking device had been found, Hoff had suspected that the Gors had betrayed them. In retaliation for that, he'd broken the alliance and had thousands of them slaughtered at a human-run Gor training facility on Ritan. Not long after that they'd found the alien tracking device and realized that the Gors had been innocent all along, but by then it had been too late. Thanks to the tracking device, the Sythians knew where Dark Space was, and they had ignored Commander Donali's diversion to rather follow Hoff into Dark Space with an entire fleet.

Suddenly it had no longer mattered whether the legitimate government or a gang of criminals would be in control of the sector. There was no way that a dozen human starships were going to fight off several hundred Sythian ones. There wasn't going to *be* a Dark Space.

Yet when all had seemed lost, Hoff had found a way to detect the Sythians' cloaked command ship. . . .

And destroy it.

His eyes turned from the approaching *Intrepid* to the drifting ruins of the Sythians' thirty-kilometer-long behemoth-class cruiser. The red eye of the Firean System's sun glinted brightly off the distant halves of the giant alien warship. The dark speck beside it was what was left of Hoff's flagship, the *Tauron*. He'd crashed his kilometer-long battleship into the Sythians' command cruiser, slicing it in half before they could raise their shields. With that killing blow, the Gors had shown their true colors—

And stopped fighting.

With the command ship disabled, the Gors were no longer afraid of what their Sythian masters would do to them if they disobeyed, and like that, the battle was over.

Hiding behind the cloaking shields of a captured Sythian warship, Hoff's men snuck aboard the *Valiant* and took it back from the criminal insurrectionists. The remainder of the outlaw fleet surrendered, and the Gors agreed to maintain the alliance in exchange for mutual asylum in Dark Space.

The legitimate government was still shattered, however. As the last surviving admiral from the ISSF, Hoff was the closest thing they had to a legitimate leader, and as such, he had assumed the title of supreme overlord. His first act as overlord had been to offer a onetime, unconditional pardon for all of the criminals in Dark Space if they would agree to work with the fleet defending the sector. Most of them had welcomed that opportunity, though whether they would actually mend their ways remained to be seen.

For the first time in a long time it seemed like humanity had a chance. It seemed like they were finally safe.

But things are not always what they seem. Hoff frowned as the *Intrepid* disappeared in the shadow of the *Valiant*. The Sythians had invaded the Adventa Galaxy with seven fleets. Just less than a whole fleet had been destroyed during the war, and the Gors had surrendered with one recently, leaving the Sythians with the equivalent of five full fleets and six surviving command cruisers. He estimated that left them with over a thousand capital-class vessels—more than enough for them to return and get their revenge. Dark Space had been a wonderful safe haven when the Sythians didn't know where it was, but now that they did, it was a death trap. Humanity was holed up in a sector with just one way in or out. They were outnumbered and backed into a corner.

"Admiral," Lieutenant Hanz said from the comm station.

Hoff looked over at the young man. "Yes?"

"The *Intrepid* has successfully docked, sir, and Master Commander Donali is already aboard."

Hoff nodded. "Good. I'll be in the operations center if anyone needs me. Deck Commander Akra—" Hoff waited for her to look up from the helm. Her pale blue eyes contrasted eerily with her honey brown complexion.

"Yes, sir?" she asked.

"You're the acting CO. I'll be back at 1730 hours."

"Yes, sir," Akra replied.

With that, Hoff stalked down the gangway to the entrance of the bridge. Heads turned, the crew watching with frowns and curious eyes as he left. The doors swished open and then shut behind him. No doubt his crew was wondering what he was going to discuss with Commander Donali, if it were important, and whether or not it affected them.

Hoff strode up to the bank of lift tubes outside the bridge and slapped the call button. He heard a quiet shuffling of feet and turned to see that two of the four sentinels standing guard at the entrance of the bridge had peeled away from the doors and were now flanking him at a discreet distance. Hoff nodded to them. Major Rekan, the ranking officer of the two, nodded back.

Turning away, he waited for the lift tubes with a frown. *Bodyguards. A necessary evil these days.* He thought back to a time when he could walk around his flagship without fearing for his life. It felt like forever ago. Those days were long gone, and they weren't likely to return.

One of the lifts opened, and Hoff stepped inside followed by his guards. He selected the deck marked OP. The operations center was one of 12 decks inside the *Valiant's* bridge tower, which in turn sat on top of another 142 decks. The warship over half a klick high—so big that it had to have its own gravlev train system just so that people could get from one end to the other in a timely fashion.

It was like a city in space, and it required a skeleton crew of over 10,000 officers just to keep it running properly. Unfortunately, the criminal revolt had wiped out the original crew of the *Valiant*—more than 50,000 officers, and Hoff had had to strip crews from stations and warships all over Dark Space just to get half the people he needed. To fill the rest of the ship's skeleton crew he'd pulled newly-recruited criminals from the outlaw fleet, and he'd even allowed more than a thousand Gors to come aboard as navy sentinels and ISF (Imperial Security Forces) in training.

Hence the bodyguards. Between the Gors and the ex-cons, Hoff had to watch his back wherever he went. The irony was, though, he was more worried about the criminals than the Gors. The Gors had surrendered when they could have won, but the criminals had only done so when their backs were to the wall. That was a big part of why Hoff had agreed to have the Gors come aboard. Besides the fact that they were unparalleled soldiers and better suited to be sentinels than any human, they were the one thing that might keep the ex-cons in line. *You'd have to be a stim-baked skriff to mutiny against a ship full of Gors.*

The monsters were everywhere, their heads scraping the ceiling in their glossy black armor, the glowing red optics in their helmets seeming to follow Hoff with malicious intent. Despite his rationalizations that the ex-cons were more likely to stab him in the back than the Gors, those aliens still haunted his dreams, leaving him with dark circles under his eyes, and a perpetual sense of impending doom.

This is my punishment for exterminating them at Ritan. To Hoff's amazement, the Gors had decided to forgive that atrocity and call it even for the trillions of humans they'd killed in the war. Hoff doubted the alien soldiers were as forgiving as they seemed, but so far none of them had tried to rip his throat out. . . . He considered that a good sign.

A golden rain of light streaked by the transpiranium sides of the lift tube as it fell past the lower decks. Hoff forced himself to stop worrying about internal threats and rather focus on what they were going to do now about the looming *external* threat of another invasion.

The lift tube stopped and the doors slid open. Hoff strode out and around a curving corridor with a wall of real viewports. His gaze wandered to the stars, taking in the bright red orb of the Firean System's sun, and the frigid blue-white ice ball of Firea herself—the Gors home away from home. They liked the cold, the darkness, the dangerous predators and challenging prey. Gors were hunters at heart, which was ironic considering that now they'd chosen to join the hunted.

Hoff reached the broad double doors of the carrier's operations center. He stepped up to the doors and waved his wrist over the identichip scanner to provide his credentials. The doors slid open with a *swish* and Hoff saw his XO already seated at the long rectangular table beyond. Donali rose and offered a brisk salute.

"Admiral," he said.

"At ease, Commander. I'm glad to see you're still in one piece."

"I could say the same about you, sir."

Hoff offered a tight smile and moved to the head of the glossy black table. His guards had taken up positions outside the doors, leaving them to speak in private. Pulling out his chair on the articulated arm which attached it to the deck, Hoff sat down and folded his hands on the table, taking a moment to eye his XO. Lenon Donali was a middle-aged man of about 40, though middle age was a misnomer since the average human life expectancy with good medical care was around 140 years. Nevertheless, Donali's face was lined and his dark hair was receding noticeably at the temples. The man's most striking feature was his artificial eye which glowed red like a Gor's. Donali could have had a new eye grown to replace the one he'd lost, but cybernetics were far cheaper.

"Did Captain Caldin fill you in on anything that's happened?"

Donali shook his head. "She didn't want to speak with me. Said she wasn't going to tell me anything until I had a full body scan. I have the feeling she doesn't trust me."

"I see. And why would that be, Commander?"

Donali shrugged. "She said that I could have been

captured and released in the time I was gone, and she'd already been caught by that trick once. She mentioned Captain Adram. I assume from what she said that he . . ."

"He was a Sythian agent, yes."

"Was he the source of the signal radiation we detected?"

"No. As far as I can tell, Kaon's implant called home before Adram could give us away, but it does seem that no matter what we did we were going to give Dark Space away."

"We never should have come."

"Perhaps, but it's too late now." Hoff's brow furrowed, and he pursed his lips. "So, are you?"

"Am I what, sir?"

"A Sythian agent."

"Not that I know of, but would I know if I were?"

Hoff smiled. "I'm not sure how to answer that. Would you be willing to submit to a body scan?"

"I already have."

"And? Clean I suspect."

"Yes, but since we know that Sythians have cloaking implants . . ."

"You're afraid that you might have one."

"I don't know how we could find it if I did. Perhaps you could find some way to test me yourself. . . . Tell me some particularly juicy bit of classified information and wait to see if you detect any signal radiation leaking from me."

Hoff laughed and gave a tight smile. "Relax, Donali. We'll have our medics run a few more tests on you to be sure, but something tells me that if you were a Sythian agent, you wouldn't be discussing the possibility of that with me, much less giving me ideas about how I might discover you. Now, tell me what you found out about Kaon's implant."

"It was some type of Lifelink, sir. It stores the host's

memories and an eidetic map of their brain. I can only assume it serves the same purpose as our own Lifelinks. Add to that the fact that Kaon was a clone and it becomes even more obvious."

"So you think the Sythians have been doing the same thing as immortal humans—copying themselves to cloned bodies in order to live forever." Immortals were mythological beings to most people. They'd been in hiding for so long that only a few even knew of their existence, and Hoff could count those few on one hand. Hoff and Donali knew better because they *were* immortals, or at least Donali was. Hoff's wife had recently convinced him to deactivate his Lifelink and live a normal life.

Donali nodded and his artificial eye winked in tandem with his real one. "The question is, is that specific type of immortality a natural progression for any sentient race which becomes sufficiently advanced, or is it an idea which the Sythians stole from us?"

"I wish I didn't have the answer to that question, but I do."

Donali cocked his head to one side, and his real eye narrowed thoughtfully. "You discovered something?"

"More than one something."

"I'm listening."

Hoff took a deep breath. "They didn't steal the idea from us, Donali. They *are* us. And we are them."

Donali slowly shook his head. "What? You're saying I'm a Sythian?"

"Not quite. Humans are their evolutionary ancestors. Origin, the lost world where humanity supposedly began, isn't in the Adventa Galaxy, Donali. It's in the Getties Cluster, and its real name is Sythia."

Donali's jaw dropped and his real eye grew wide and round. "That's not possible. You're making that up."

"I wish I were. We're not fighting aliens at all. We're fighting a more evolved version of the human race. A genetic experiment in longevity." Donali's mouth began moving, but no words came out. Hoff went on, "That's not all. Our resident traitor, Captain Adram, was implanted with a cloaked Lifelink implant like the one we discovered in Kaon's brain. He was, for all intents and purposes, another iteration of Kaon himself. He revealed the Enclave to the Sythians, Donali, meaning Dark Space is the last surviving refuge of humanity, and now that the Sythians know where it is, time is running out. We are facing extinction."

Donali clamped his mouth shut and pursed his lips. After taking a long moment to process that his head jerked suddenly into a nod, as if he'd just decided something. "There is one way out, sir."

Hoff's eyebrows elevated slowly. "Evacuate?"

"No. Get help."

"There is no help, Donali. We're all alone. We've already recruited the Gors and the ex-cons in this sector, but it won't be enough. Before he died, Adram told me that the Sythians are making slaves out of *us* now. In all likelihood when they return we'll see the refugees from the Enclave, all of them turned into Sythian slaves like Adram. We're badly outnumbered, and what's stopping the Sythians from sending reinforcements from the Getties? Adram told me there are quintillions of them, Donali. What they sent to conquer us was probably just meant to test the waters. By a happy coincidence it was enough to wipe us out."

Donali sighed. "It does look grim, but we aren't alone. You're forgetting Avilon."

"The Immortals?" Hoff sat back in his chair and considered it.

"Why not? There are trillions of them, too. You said it yourself. And their technology is more advanced than even the Sythians'."

"I haven't been to Avilon in over 30,000 years. They would execute me if I went back."

"Would they even remember you?"

"Yes. Besides, what makes you think they would help us now, after they stayed out of the entire war? If they'd wanted to help, don't you think they would have helped when they could have saved trillions of us with their intervention rather than just the few million survivors hiding out here? No, in all likelihood they thought it was justice that the Sythians wiped us out—justice for the war we started which drove them into hiding."

"They can't seriously hope to stay hidden forever. The Sythians will find them."

"I wouldn't be too sure about that."

"Admiral." Donali's artificial eye bored into Hoff's brain with the pinpoint accuracy of a laser sight. "It's our only hope."

Hoff spent a moment drumming his fingers on the armrest of his chair before giving his reply. "I'll give it some thought. Meanwhile, you should go hit the rack. I'll schedule some tests in the med bay for you just to put your mind at ease."

"All right," Donali nodded, rising from his chair. "Ruh-kah, sir," he said with a salute.

"Ruh-kah." *Death and glory.* Hoff returned the salute and watched his executive officer (XO) leave the operations center. When Donali was gone he slumped back into his chair with a sigh.

Donali was right. Making an alliance with Avilon was their only hope. Failing that, perhaps the Immortal Avilonians would accept a few million refugees. . . .

Something told Hoff that even if they would, he wouldn't make the cut. *Immortals have a long memory.* He told his family that he'd left because he could make a better life for himself in a society where he didn't have to compete with other immortals, but the truth was he'd been forced to leave for advocating the *heresy* that people should be allowed to choose whether or not they wanted to live forever. Ultimately, he'd been forced to flee Avilon before he could be executed for his beliefs.

"Perhaps things have changed in the last 30,000 years?" Hoff wondered aloud. Based on what he had seen from the Avilonians when they'd agreed to provide aid to the Enclave, a lot had changed. They were now employing *mortals* in their fleets, for one thing, a fact which suggested that perhaps the societal change which Hoff had been lobbying for all those years ago had finally come to Avilon. For all he knew, he was responsible for those changes, and they'd hail him as a hero. *Either that, or they'll give me a nice public execution. . . .*

I suppose there's only one way to find out.

* * *

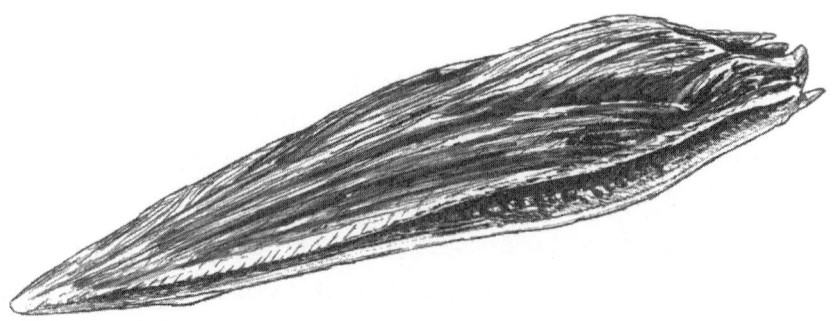

Master Commander Lenon Donali sat undergoing rigorous scrutiny in med bay. He was busy playing the part of a loyal officer who was horrified by the possibility that he might have been captured and turned into a Sythian agent without his knowledge.

The truth was, he was fully aware, and he was equally aware that these tests would reveal nothing. No technology known to either man or Sythians could pierce a cloaking shield, and the only mark the Sythians had left on him was in the form of a small, cloaked implant. The rest of their tampering could only be discovered with a mind probe, and the admiral would never authorize something that dangerous unless he had proof that his XO was a Sythian agent. Mind probes could kill a person in under five minutes, fifteen at most.

"I'm going to inject a hunter probe. It will travel through your bloodstream, looking for foreign objects," Doctor Elder said.

Donali turned to offer the younger man a smile. "Of course. You should know I do have one cerebral implant. It's to help me with my memory after the accident which took my eye." He reached up to tap his glowing red optic. The implant he was referring to was actually his Lifelink implant. The cloaked *Sythian* implant would not be revealed by a hunter probe or any other."

"I see," Doctor Elder replied.

"The admiral can confirm that if you like."

"No, that's all right. Whatever we're looking for, I'm sure it won't be hiding in plain sight."

Donali nodded and watched the doctor prepare the hunter probe, filling an implanter syringe with a clear solution that no doubt contained billions of nanites. Donali switched his focus from the syringe to the doctor himself. Doctor Elder was young, perhaps thirty human standard orbits old. His smooth, youthful features and his startling magenta eyes must have made him a hit with women.

Donali's own face was marred by an artificial eye and the faint tracks of old scars from the accident that had taken the real one. That glowing red optic had earned him the nickname "Bug Eye" while in med school.

The sharp prick of a needle yanked him back to the present as the hunter probe was injected into the back of his neck.

"There, now just relax while I take readings from the probe," Doctor Elder said.

He did as he was told. A few minutes later he passed the hunter probe test with a clean bill of health. Over the course of the next two hours, he passed a dozen more probes and tests, all of which came back negative for signs of Sythian tampering.

Three hours after he'd walked through the med bay doors, he left by those same doors with a smile on his face. Humanity was now convinced that he was not working for their enemy.

They couldn't have been more wrong.

When Commander Lenon Donali reached his quarters he locked the door behind him and immediately cloaked himself to send a message to his handler, High Lord Kaon.

"My Lord, the humans suspect me, but there is no test they can perform to reveal what I am."

"Good. Do nothing to make them suspicious. You have one month to find the location of Avilon before we come."

"You are coming?" Donali asked, surprised that he hadn't been told about that before the Sythians released him.

"Our human crews are trained and ready. The Lords are decided. Dark Space has a resource we now require urgently—slaves."

"I see. . . ."

"If we are to conquer Avilon, we must be able to bring all our forces to bear with reliable, human crews, not rebellious Gors."

"Yes," Donali nodded. "You are right."

"Of course we are," Kaon replied. "Now hurry and find what you are there to discover. Do not disappoint us, human."

"I won't," he replied, but Kaon had already broken the telepathic connection. Donali de-cloaked himself and stood staring out the viewport in his quarters at the distant gray clouds of the Stormcloud Nebula. The Sythians were coming, but this time they wouldn't come to kill and destroy; they would come to establish a new order with humans feeding them crew for their fleet. The day was coming where he would no longer have to hide; he would be but one of many millions of human slaves serving the Sythians. Donali smiled, and the Stormcloud Nebula flashed with a spark of lighting.

That day couldn't come soon enough.

Chapter 3

One month later . . .

The stars shone with a dazzling brilliance, like glow bugs trapped on the other side of the Nova Fighter's cockpit canopy. Atton Ortane stepped on the left rudder pedal, causing his fighter to slew in that direction as its triple bank of thrusters vectored and maneuvering jets fired.

A gray veil swept across the stars as the Stormcloud Nebula came into view. That nebula lay shrouding the entrance of Dark Space, keeping the way hidden from passersby. Unfortunately, the Sythians already knew where it was.

"Form up, Guardians. Line abreast formation, stagger 50 klicks."

A handful of acknowledging *clicks* came over the comms, along with a, "Roger that, Commander," from his wingmate, Gina "Tuner" Giord. Atton looked out the side of his cockpit to find an amplified representation of her Nova flying right beside him. He watched her fighter arc away until it reached the specified 50 klicks from his own, becoming little more than a magnified speck which glinted in the distance like an oversized star.

The Guardians were lined up one beside the other as they approached the nebula, cutting a wide swath with their sensors, such that they'd have an extra 600 klicks sensor range from one end of the formation to the other. While inside the nebula their sensors had a 65-klick range, meaning that each member of the squadron would only be able to see at most two of their squad mates on gravidar—his or her wingmate and the fighter immediately on the other side. To get around that, they had chain-linked their comms to periodically ping the fighters beside them, conveying coordinates. Upon receiving the ping, each Nova would automatically add its coordinates to the transmission and then pass it on until all 12 members of Guardian Squadron had reported in to each other. That would happen every five seconds, allowing them to see each other's positions on gravidar with a five second delay. If one link in the chain went missing, however, then the two sides of the formation would be completely cut off from each other.

It was a dangerous formation, but as one of 12 recon squadrons, their job was just to find the enemy and report back to the *Valiant*, not to find and engage them. Hopefully, if they ran into any trouble, at least one of them would escape to report back what they had found.

Atton's fighter plunged through the leading edge of the

nebula and the nose of his Nova was swallowed by wispy gray clouds. The stars disappeared behind those clouds, and a flash of discharging static caused the star map on the main holo display (MHD) to shudder and turn to snow. Atton heard the simulated *boom* of thunder rumble through his cockpit a moment later, and he gave a wry smile. The SISS (sound in space simulator) could be a little too realistic at times. He didn't need misleading audio cues right now. Between the appearance of clouds and the sound of thunder, he was apt to start maneuvering like he was in atmosphere rather than space.

A heavily distorted commcast came through the dash speakers. "SC . . . I think I'm picking something up out there." It was Gina again.

Atton frowned and keyed his comm with a mental command. Not everyone had a command control implant (CCI) to access thought-activated software suites, but not so long ago Atton had been using a holoskin to pose as the Supreme Overlord of the Imperium, and the ability to control computer systems without needing to touch them had been a part of that role.

"I don't see anything on my scopes," Atton replied.

"It was just a brief blip," Gina said. "Showed up for maybe half a second after that burst of static."

"Probably just distortion, but mark the spot on your nav to be safe. Attach coordinates to the ping and we'll investigate."

"Yes, sir."

Second Lieutenant Gina Giord was Atton's XO and his only friend in the recently-reformed Guardian squadron. It was hard to make friends with half the squadron senior to him in both rank and experience. His only legitimate claim to lead the squadron was his unusually high 4A pilot's rating. But whatever legitimacy his skill gave him, it was overshadowed by the fact that his stepfather was Admiral/Overlord Heston. Atton could almost hear his squad mates whispering about him behind his back. He was probably the youngest squadron commander in the history of the fleet, and there was no doubt in anyone's mind that the only reason he was the SC was because of his connections.

Atton frowned. Even Gina wasn't immune to thinking that way, but at least she didn't try to hide it. *"You've got to earn their respect, Atton,"* she liked to remind him. *"Prove that you're the right man for the job and they'll fall on their swords for you. Until then, you're going to have to pretend you're hard of hearing."*

The warning screech of a siren jerked Atton back into the moment. It was his enemy contact siren, a part of the fighter's threat detection system (TDS). Atton's eyes dropped to the glowing blue star map, searching the grid for whatever had triggered the siren. There was nothing there.

Activating his comms, he said, "Be advised, Guardians, something just set off my TDS."

"My scopes are clear, are you sure?" Guardian Seven said as soon as Atton's message had been passed down the comm chain.

"I'm sure. There's definitely something out there."

Atton kept his eyes glued to the three dimensional grid, searching for even the faintest glimmer of a red enemy blip.

Boom. Thunder rumbled through the cockpit speakers once more, and Atton looked up reflexively to make sure that it was thunder and not one of his squad mates exploding. When his gaze reached the horizon, his jaw dropped. The gray clouds of the nebula were flashing almost continuously with discharging bursts of static electricity, and through the luminous tendrils of that lightning Atton saw the dark, ovoid outlines of Sythian ships in the distance. Not one or two of them, but an entire fleet, with countless capital-class vessels. At the center of the formation, like the queen bee in a hive, lay the Sythians' command cruiser, a 30-kilometer-long behemoth-class cruiser.

"Motherfrekkers . . ." Atton whispered. The Sythians were everywhere.

"Contact, contact!" Guardian Three screamed from the other side of Atton's Nova. His TDS wailed in the next instant with another enemy contact siren.

"Contact confirmed," Atton said into the comm. "Break and run, Guardians!"

"I've got incoming!" Gina screamed. Atton saw what she meant an instant later. Just now appearing on the gravidar were two squadrons of Sythian Shell Fighters. The Guardians were coasting toward them at a modest one klick per second, while the approaching Shell Fighters were barreling on at over three and a half klicks per second. With 80 klicks between them, Atton's rangefinder indicated that the nearest Sythian fighter would reach them in under 20 seconds. Nova Fighters were considerably faster than Sythian Shells, but even if they turned around now and accelerated in full overdrive in the opposite direction, it would take the Guardians more than 24 seconds to match the Sythians' current vector and velocity, and that was *if* the alien fighters didn't ignite their own thrusters to speed up.

Atton didn't need to get his Nova's AI to crunch the numbers for him to know that they would be forced to engage the enemy.

"All right, listen up, Guardians," Atton said as he

stomped on his right rudder pedal to head back the way he'd come. He pushed his throttle up past the red lines and into overdrive. "Reduce stagger to five klicks, inverted *V*. We're going to redline it all the way back to the *Valiant*. I want to see you all racing out ahead of me. Guardian Two and I are going to hang back at the tip of the *V* and cover your retreat."

Static hissed through the comm, followed by, "You can't cover our retreat against 24 Shells! We're better off sticking together, SC. We can take 'em!" that from Guardian Seven, Horace "Hawkeye" Perkins, the resident hot shot and smart mouth of the squadron.

"And what about the thousands waiting behind them?" Gina, Guardian Two, snapped. "The commander wasn't making a suggestion, Hawk."

Atton heard a sullen *click* as Horace acknowledged that order in as trite a way as possible.

"Are you ready, Gina?" Atton asked, now on a private comm channel with his wingmate.

"Hoi, if you want to see the netherworld so badly I could always put a ripper round between your ears when we get back. You don't have to go all heroic on me."

Atton smiled. "What if I want some company in the afterlife?"

"*Commander* . . ." Gina's tone filled with mock astonishment. "Are you asking me on a date?"

"Sure, why not," Atton chuckled. "We can order some flaming cocktails and follow them down with brimstone chasers."

"Sounds delightful."

Atton's eyes dipped to the star map. He eyed the nearest red blip on the grid and watched the pair of numbers beside it. The number on the left put his range to that Shell at 26 klicks, while the number on the right put time to reach it at seven seconds. It would probably be just five before they reached firing range. Atton peripherally noted Gina's fighter boosting along right beside his, while the rest of the squadron arced out on either side of them, forming the two sides of the V.

"Ready?" Atton said.

"Ready," Gina replied.

Atton disengaged his thrusters in order to maintain his current vector and velocity, and then pulled up hard until the red bracket pairs of enemy fighters crowded into view. He targeted the nearest enemy and thumbed over to Hailfire missiles. The muted *beep-beep-beeping* of a target lock began to sound. An instant later, the targeting reticle turned red and emitted a solid tone.

"Ruh-kah!" Atton roared as he pulled the trigger twice in quick succession, firing two Hailfire missiles one after the other. He watched the warheads jet out on hot orange contrails, dwindling to bright specks in a matter of seconds. Peripherally, he noted Gina's warheads join his. Then the TDS sounded with the more urgent beeping of an *enemy* missile lock alarm, and Atton grimaced.

"They're locking on to me!" someone wailed.

"Likewise," another added.

"You know the drill," Atton said. "Wait until they're close and jink hard." Sythian missiles were impossible to shoot down, but they had poor tracking, so the best way to counter them was to pull a sudden maneuver at the last possible second.

Sirens wailed as the enemy missiles locked on and jetted out toward them in a shining purple wave. Sythian Pirakla missiles looked like purple stars—bright and mesmerizingly beautiful. Death in a pretty package.

"Get ready to dance, Guardians!" Atton said.

"Roger that!"

A handful of affirmative clicks rippled through the comms, and Atton sent a private comm to Gina. "Time to turn tail, Two."

Click.

Atton followed his own advice, pulling up hard to face in the direction of his fighter's momentum. He reengaged his Nova's thrusters and toggled his left holo display to show him a rearview of space. With all the nearby gravidar contacts magnified to 500% by his fighter's *visual auto-scaling system* (VASS), Atton was able to watch the action as if it were happening just a few hundred meters away. His and Gina's Hailfire missiles reached 500 meters to their targets and then abruptly blossomed like fireworks, with each warhead splitting into four smaller ones in order to track their targets from multiple angles at once. The Sythian fighters opened fire on those warheads with bright lavender pulse lasers, but only two of the Hailfire shards turned to fireballs before reaching the enemy formation. The remaining shards converged and a pair of Shell Fighters flew apart in a spectacular burst of light. Atton heard the distant rumbles of their explosions and almost mistook the sound for more simulated thunder. Then the nebular clouds flashed around them, and real thunder boomed through the SISS.

"Two down," Gina said.

"Twenty two to go," Atton replied. His eyes dipped to the grid to watch the enemy missiles closing on them—fourteen Pirakla missiles, one for each of the Guardians, with a couple extras for good measure. His hand tightened on the flight stick and his palms began to sweat beneath his gloves. He waited until the last possible second and then pulled up hard, stomping on the right rudder pedal and throwing the flight stick to one side for a defensive spiral. He broke the missile lock almost instantly. Other Guardians pulled similar maneuvers, going evasive until the enemy warheads skipped by them and lost their tracking solutions.

Guardian Four wasn't so lucky. Two Pirakla missiles had locked on to him, and while he managed to evade one, the other one was coming in from a different angle. It slammed straight into his starboard thruster. The rear half of his fighter flew apart in a messy hail of molten alloy. Then came a flash of light as the fighter's dymium reactor exploded, and Atton flinched away from the glare. No ejection seat appeared on the grid in the wake of that explosion.

"Motherfrekkers!" Four's wingmate roared.

"Keep your head in the game, Three! You'll have your chance to get even," Atton said.

No reply. Atton couldn't blame him. Three and Four had been good friends, and now one of them was just gone, without even the chance to say goodbye.

The flashing gray clouds of the nebula thinned and parted to reveal glittering stars. Atton's eyes skipped back to the grid to watch as pursuing Shell Fighters began turning back the way they'd come.

The engagement was over, and all but one of the Guardians had made it away. Atton let out a breath he hadn't realized he was holding and then commed the *Valiant*.

"Control, this is Guardian Leader reporting, be advised we have confirmed enemy contact. Repeat, confirmed enemy contact."

The comm crackled with a reply, "Acknowledged. How many are there, Guardian Leader?"

"It looks like a whole fleet. Stand by to receive log data now."

"Standing by . . ."

Atton punched the button to transmit his flight recorder logs and waited.

"Transmission received. Give us a moment to analyze the data, Guardian Leader."

"Roger that."

It wasn't even a full minute before the *Valiant* replied, and this time it was the Admiral's voice rather than that of the *Valiant's* comms officer. "Attention all vessels, this is a red alert! A Sythian fleet has been found hiding in the Stormcloud Nebula. Current estimates suggest in excess of 100 capital-class vessels. Stand by for further orders."

"Ruh-kah!" Hawkeye put in.

Death and glory. The old Rokan battle cry sounded more like a pronouncement of doom rather than a rallying call.

"A 100 cap ships—that's it?" Let them come. We've got more than that with just the Gors."

"Hoi, don't get cocky, Seven," Atton commed back. "We don't know the full extent of their forces yet."

Atton was far less optimistic about the Sythians' arrival and what that meant. Just one month after the last battle, the Sythians were back. As far as he was concerned there could be no doubt about their intentions—

They were back for revenge.

* * *

After four hours of posturing at the edges of the Stormcloud Nebula without so much as a glimmer of the Sythian fleet which had caused all the fuss, Hoff had dropped the fleet's readiness from a red to yellow alert, and he'd retired to the *Valiant's* operations center to discuss recent developments with a few of his officers.

Hoff watched as footage from Guardian One's nose cam played out above the long, glossy black table in the operations center. In addition to that footage, he had the footage from dozens of recon drones which he'd subsequently sent out to probe the nebula.

Footage from those drones only mirrored what the Guardians had gathered. Hoff froze the nose cam recording just as the nebular clouds flashed, revealing the enemy fleet, and then he keyed the table's built in holographics to display the most recent drone footage. He paused it in a similar place so they could visually compare the size and disposition of the enemy forces over the past four hours. Nothing had changed.

"I don't get it," Donali said, gesturing to the pair of holograms. "Why haven't they moved? They have to know they're not fooling anyone by hiding out there."

Hoff grimaced and turned to his XO. "They don't have to fool anyone. We're already foolish enough without them having to do anything." Out of the corner of his eye, Hoff noticed his stepson, Atton, fidgeting. He turned to the boy with his bushy eyebrows raised. "Is there something you'd like to say, Commander?"

Hoff saw the boy's eyes skip sideways to the Gor commander who sat watching the humans from the far side of the table. Following his stepson's gaze, Hoff studied the Gor. She had her thick arms planted on the table. Her glossy black armor reflected the blue glow of the holos, while the glowing red optics of her helmet turned first one way and then the other, looking from one human to the next as if trying to decide who she should eat first.

That Gor was none other than High Praetor Tova. Hoff didn't completely trust her, but he had allowed Tova into the operations center to discuss the latest developments with the Sythians for the simple reason that she was currently commander-in-chief of the human-allied Gors, and technically right now she held more power in her icy hands than Hoff did. If the alliance broke down, the Gors had enough ships in the sector to wipe out the Imperial Star Systems' Fleet in a matter of minutes. So, Hoff had to make nice and show the Gors that humanity could be trusted.

Atton turned back to Hoff and nodded. "Well, sir, it occurs to me that for all we know, the enemy fleet could have arrived days or weeks ago, and this is just the first we've seen of them. Our nebular patrol only started a week ago."

"If that's true, why wait in the nebula? Why haven't they attacked us yet?"

An alien warbling answered from the far side of the table and was conveyed a second later by the simultaneous translators they each wore in their ears. "They wait to catch us when we try to leave," Tova suggested.

All eyes turned to her, and Hoff asked, "What do you mean when we try to leave?"

"They expect us to run, not to stay and fight."

"You're suggesting that this is a blockade ..." Hoff mused, steepling his hands beneath his chin. "I agree. Based on what we know about the Sythians and their aggressive nature, the only reason they're not attacking us is because they're not sure they can win."

Hoff noticed his XO begin nodding slowly, and a light of understanding dawned in his one good eye. "They're waiting for reinforcements."

"Yes. That's exactly what I am afraid they're doing, and that's why we're all assembled here now. Humanity can't hope to stand against the Sythians in a straight fight. If they manage to bring all five of their remaining fleets to bear, we are finished."

"Not if we help you," Tova said.

Hoff forced a smile. "We appreciate your people's support, Tova, but even with your people, we are little more than a match for just *one* of the Sythians' fleets. Even if we assume that we can turn some or all of the Gors aboard their ships to our cause, we have to consider the additional problem that Sythians have begun to crew their ships with *human* slaves, and we are apparently much more loyal than Gors."

Hoff allowed a moment for that to sink in before he went on. "Besides all of *that*—there's still a whole galaxy of Sythians waiting in the Getties Cluster. Based on the reported size of their population and the fact that they came here just to find more room for that population, the fleets they sent to conquer us were likely just the tip of the serpent's tongue."

"That's a pleasant thought," Atton said.

"Our reconnaissance efforts have been non-existent until only very recently, thanks to Sythian cloaking shields and our lack of the same. For all we know there could be more than a hundred fleets on their way to Dark Space right now."

Grave silence followed that statement.

Tova was the first to break that silence. "You speak death upon us. Do you say then that we do not survive this?"

"No. Commander Donali has recently brought it to my attention that we *do* have one hope of survival. It's a long shot, but it might just even the odds."

Tova cocked her large, armored head. "And what hope is that?"

"We have to go to Avilon for help."

"Avilon?" Tova asked.

"It's a lost sector of humans that the Sythians overlooked during the invasion. Humanity hasn't had direct contact with Avilon for millennia, although they did provide some aid to my refugee enclave before the Sythians wiped it out. Not much is known about the Avilonians, but what we do know is that they are numerous, they are immortal, and their technology is far more advanced than either the Sythians' or ours."

"These ... *immortal* humans know of the Sythians and the war?" Tova asked.

"They do."

"Then they do not care for your people or their fate. They watch you all die, and they do nothing. They are no longer your créche mates."

"Perhaps they didn't care enough to get involved during the war," Hoff agreed, "but now we have to change their minds. We need to make them realize that their survival is also at stake. If the Sythians have hundreds of fleets just like the initial seven that destroyed us, then even the Avilonians' superior technology won't be enough to save them when the

Sythians find out where they are hiding." Hoff turned to his stepson. "I'm sending you as my envoy, Atton. You will go alone, out of respect for the Avilonians' desire to remain hidden, and you will go to their forward base, not their actual location. If they know that their secret is safe with us, they might just trust us enough to listen to what we have to say."

Atton was silent for long seconds. For a moment Hoff was afraid his stepson was going to refuse the mission or raise the obvious objection that someone else more suited to the diplomatic role should go as his envoy instead, but all Atton said was, "When do I leave?"

"In a few hours. We're sending you aboard the *Intrepid*. She'll be cloaked so the Sythians don't see her leave. The *Intrepid's* official mission will be to look for survivors in the Enclave. As soon as you get there, Atton, you will leave aboard an assault recon-class transport which I have prepared for you. No one else on board except for Master Commander Donali will know the details of your mission, and even he won't know the coordinates of your destination. Nevertheless, he will be standing by with a team of Gors, and you will be able to contact him for extraction if you need help. I don't expect the Avilonians to greet you with violence—that is not their way—but we'll be prepared either way.

"Tova—no offense, but your people who will be going along for the mission will have to stay in stasis until the *Intrepid* jumps to SLS. We don't want them to accidentally give us away." Hoff could have sworn Tova's eyes narrowed, but of course he couldn't tell what her naturally-slitted eyes were doing behind her helmet's glowing red optics. Something about the way she became so abruptly *still*, however, set Hoff's nerves on edge.

"Accidentally?" she asked.

Hoff smiled thinly and keyed off the holograms hovering between him and Tova so he could watch her more carefully. "Of course. My understanding is that your créche mates can detect one another telepathically, even through cloaking shields."

"That is correct."

"I am also given to understand that your people cannot always control when they are sending telepathic signals to each other, and that as soon as a telepathic signal is received, both the sender and recipient can locate one another."

Tova was silent for a long time—so long, that Hoff thought perhaps the silence only seemed long to him. Then he heard Donali clear his throat and finally Tova spoke, "That is correct," she said. With that she looked away to the far corner of the room, as if Hoff had just offended her so deeply that he was now *unworthy of her sight*. In Gor culture that meant he'd fallen out of favor with her.

Hoff frowned, but he decided to ignore the tension between them for now. Turning back to Atton, he said, "Any questions?"

"Just one—what if the Avilonians don't want to help us?"

"Then . . ." Hoff hesitated. "We're all going to die here."

Chapter 4

Ethan Ortane stood on a grassy field behind the Vastras' house, watching the rolling green hills of Forliss ripple in the wind. The long grass came alive wherever the wind touched it, making it seem to flow from the foothills of the Astral Mountains like a river. Now setting above those mountains was the bright blue orb of the Alissan System's sun. The setting sun had turned the planet's usually misty blue sky to a cold turquoise shot through with glowing ribbons of gold that were high-flying wisps of cirrus clouds.

Ethan stood there, mesmerized by the beauty of it, lost in

his thoughts. A lot had happened in the past few months. Ten years after the war and his sentence to Dark Space had separated him from his wife and son, he'd found them both again. Now his son was grown, and his wife, Destra . . . she had remarried and given birth to a daughter who was already seven years old. Ethan frowned. It was ironic. He'd waited for his wife—mourned her loss for ten years, thinking that she had died in the invasion—but she hadn't waited more than three years for him.

And she had married Admiral Hoff Heston of all people. As fate would have it, Hoff was now the Supreme Overlord of Dark Space, and Ethan was forced to admit how much better off Destra was without him.

It had been a bitter pill to swallow, but he had done all right for himself. During the years he'd spent mourning for the family he thought he'd lost forever, his copilot, Alara Vastra, had stood by his side helping him through the darkest of those days. She'd been waiting for him to recover enough to notice her. Years had passed like that, with him too blinded by his grief to notice much of anything.

Finding Destra alive and married to another man had been just the slap in the face he'd needed to snap him out of it. Not long after that he'd proposed to Alara and she'd accepted. He was just glad that it hadn't been too late to return her affections. Now that he looked back on all those years he'd spent feeling sorry for himself, he realized just how much time he'd wasted longing for an idealized version of his old life.

Now he was about to start a new life, and tonight was the night before it would begin—the night before the wedding. Ethan smiled. It seemed like a dream. Alara was beautiful. With her flowing dark hair, wide violet eyes, slender hourglass curves, and porcelain skin she was the envy of any man, but aside from that superficial appeal, she was also the sweetest and most faithful woman he'd ever known. *Of course she has to balance that sweetness by being a hot-blooded firebrand.*

Ethan sighed. In times like these, he had to force himself to remember all the good things. It was easy to forget those things when she was freezing him out with a stony silence or going on the attack with flashing eyes and barbed tongue. He'd known she was an emotional woman when he'd met her, and all through their tension-filled partnership as freelancers he'd seen that side of her, so he'd known what he was getting into. He suspected that fire was part of what attracted him to her—she didn't take krak from anyone.

"Hoi, are you trying to get away from me out here?"

Ethan started at the sound of Alara's voice. He slowly turned to face her. She stood a dozen feet away with her hands planted on her hips, her violet eyes narrowed, and her dark hair glowing gold in the light of the setting sun. He forced a smile and shook his head. "No, Kiddie. You're not *that* scary," he said with a wink, and then turned back to watch the sunset.

Alara replied with a snort of laughter, and Ethan heard the grass rustling against her black leggings as she came to stand beside him. "You know . . ." she began. "You're going to have to stop calling me that when we have kids."

"Hmmm?" Ethan turned to her with a dumb look. "Oh—the nickname. Well I'm sure I'll get at least a few more years' use out of it," he said, slipping an arm around her shoulders.

"A few years? You want to wait that long to have kids?"

"Well . . . yes. Just because we've got our own ship now doesn't mean we're rich." Hoff had given them that ship—perhaps because he felt guilty for stealing Ethan's wife, or perhaps because Destra felt guilty, and she'd convinced Hoff to do it. Whatever the reason, Ethan didn't care. A seraphim-class corvette was nothing to sneeze at. It was exactly what he and Alara needed to start their life together. Of course Alara's father thought it was exactly what they needed to *sell* in order to start their life together.

"You don't need to be rich to have kids, Ethan, and the last time I checked a corvette like ours is worth a small fortune, so technically, we *are* rich."

"It's an asset, Alara. We can't eat it. We have to use it to make some profit before it'll be of any use, but don't worry, we will, and in a year or two we'll have enough saved up that we'll be able to buy that house we talked about, or maybe a habitat on a station if you prefer. Once we have that, then we can think about starting a family."

"That's one option. . . . Another option might be for you to consider my father's offer."

"What, sell the ship and go work for him in the agri corps as a freighter pilot? I'll just be a glorified babysitter for an AI. Those freighters are almost entirely automated. Not the most exciting job in the world. And where does that leave you? Stuck on some planet raising our kids all by yourself, waiting patiently for me to return once or twice a week and spend some time with you?"

"It's not ideal, I agree, but maybe after a few years you could transfer to a desk job. I'm sure my father could help you with that. Then you would be home every night."

Ethan snorted. "A desk job. That sounds even better than babysitting an AI."

"It would pay the bills, and the money from our ship would give us enough to buy a mansion, let alone a house."

Ethan rounded on Alara. "Please tell me you didn't come

out here just to convince me that your father's right. What happened to you? I thought we were on the same page, Kiddie. We've always dreamed of having our own ship, of freelancing together and making our living between the stars. That's been our dream for as long as we've known each other, and now suddenly you want to change it."

It was Alara's turn to sigh. "Look, just don't close your mind to the idea, okay? There's nothing wrong with settling down."

"No, there's nothing wrong with settling down, Kiddie, but there *is* something wrong with settling."

Alara recoiled from him as if he had slapped her. "Are you sure you're still talking about our ship?" she asked quietly.

Ethan frowned and shook his head. "What are you talking about?"

Alara crossed her arms over her chest. "Maybe you're having second thoughts. Maybe you've got cold feet and you're just too much of a frekking coward to say it to my face."

"I'm not talking about *you,* Alara! And I'm not having second thoughts. I love you, Kiddie, but you can't expect me to give up my dreams just because now we're getting married."

"*Just because.*" Alara smiled bitterly. "I thought *I* was one of your dreams, Ethan. Isn't that why you proposed to me?"

"You are! Frek it—Alara, listen to me . . ." Ethan took a quick step toward her and grabbed her by her shoulders before she could storm away. The smoldering look in her violet eyes warned him to choose his words carefully. "You *are* my dream. Marrying you is a dream come true. People don't get to live twice, but here I am, living my life over with you. All I'm asking for is a chance to prove to you that my way could be better. I know it seems riskier than your father's idea, but *trust me*. I can make this work. The corvette we have is ten times the ship our old rust bucket was. We don't owe any debts on her, and now we can command a much better fee for our services."

Alara frowned and let out a deep sigh. "I *do* trust you, Ethan, but security is not as overrated as you seem to think it is." Alara uncrossed her arms and he took the opportunity to give her a hug. She pulled away all of a second later and looked him in the eye. "Just don't say no without talking to me first, okay? We're a team, remember?"

"I know."

"We're at my parents house, my father is trying to help us, and rather than being polite and saying you'll think about it, you just refused and got all defensive. You didn't even give me a chance to say what I thought about it."

"I felt ambushed, but I'm sorry. Next time we'll talk about it and decide what to do together."

"So does that mean you'll think about it?"

Ethan's eyes narrowed. "Wait a minute—I already have thought about it, and now we *have* talked about it. Look—there's one thing you're forgetting in all of this. You're right—security isn't overrated—but being tied down to a home on a planet like Forliss might not be as secure as you think. Ten years ago all the people with so-called security died because they didn't have the freedom we have right now. Right now, if the Sythians come back, we'll be among the lucky few who can escape—but only *if* we keep our ship."

Alara crossed her arms again. "And where do you think we'll run to after this? Dark Space is humanity's last hope."

"It might be humanity's last hope, but it isn't ours. We are just you and me, and as long as we're alive and together we can always find somewhere else to live. I hope it doesn't come to that, but at least we can run away if it does."

"Seems like you already have everything all figured out," Alara said, turning back to look at the sunset.

"Alara ... you have to admit what I'm saying makes sense."

"Hoi, Ethan, you're complaining that I'm asking you to give up on your dream, but have you ever thought to ask me about mine?"

"Well, I thought I already knew what it was, but I guess I was wrong..."

"You do know, but it's not the one you're thinking of. Do you remember what I told you aboard the *Valiant* before we left? About the dream I had?"

Ethan's brow furrowed. "You dreamed of a cabin on a lake, of two kids running around it and their father chasing them. You said the father was me."

"Exactly. I didn't dream of you chasing our kids around on a starship, Ethan. I dreamed of a home and a family, on a *planet*—a real life. You seemed to want that, too. You asked me to marry you already knowing what my dreams were. *Now* you're asking what happened to me? I'll tell you what happened: you led me to believe you were ready to settle down—to start a life with me—and now you don't seem so sure."

"Alara ..." Ethan reached for her hand, but she jerked it away and turned to leave. Once she was a few paces away, she stopped and turned back to him.

"I'm going to leave you here to think, Ethan. Maybe you'll find the answers you came out here for. Just promise me you'll let me know what they are before we're standing at the altar tomorrow." With that, she turned and walked away once more.

"Alara!" he called after her, but a sudden gust of wind drowned him out. He shivered in the growing cold, and reached a hand up to run it through his salt and pepper hair as he watched his fiancée pick her way back along the trail to her parents' house. The Vastras were a wealthy family, one of a very few such families in the entire sector. Their home was a mansion, with thick, black marble columns and an imposing façade of transpiranium and white duranium siding. The home had its own hangar, a greenhouse, and even a pool with a retractable skylight. There were more rooms in that mansion than Ethan had seen in most hotels.

This was what Alara had come from. He should have known she wouldn't be happy with a spacer's life. Maybe she was right. Maybe he was getting cold feet. What if he couldn't make her happy? What if they wanted different things and couldn't build a life together without one of them being forced to give up on their dreams? Would she do that for him, or would he be forced to do it for her?

Something told him if she were willing to do that for him, then she wouldn't have left him all alone out here *to think*. Ethan sighed and his brow furrowed in thought.

Would he be able to give up on his dreams for her, or would he just end up resenting her for it? Was there a compromise where he could have his freedom and she could have her security, or would they just fall apart trying to find that middle ground?

Suddenly Ethan realized that Alara had already tried to find that middle ground. She'd had her father offer him a steady job piloting freighters for the agri corps. That gave him his freedom and her the stability she wanted. *Frek*, Ethan thought. *She's busy compromising and I'm being just as stubborn as ever.*

The problem was, compromise or no compromise, he finally had his own ship—he was so close to everything he'd ever wanted! He wasn't ready to give up on his dreams of being an independent trader just yet. That was the ultimate freedom. Alara could have her home on Forliss, and he would have his ship. She could have the security she wanted. In fact, he would even do one better by giving her the added security of knowing that if they had to flee Dark Space in a hurry, then they still could. It was the best of everything. It gave them both what they wanted.

She just has to be patient, Ethan thought. *We don't have to start a family right away. What's her rush? She's twenty-three, not forty!* The same wasn't true for Ethan. He was already 46, and without longevity treatments which he'd probably never be able to afford, he wouldn't make more than 100. His life was already half over, and if he couldn't make his dreams come true now that he had everything going for him, then chances were he never would.

Ethan nodded to himself and turned back to watch the dying rays of the Alissan sun. Alara just needed his reassurance that he really was sure about marrying her tomorrow, and that he could make both their dreams come true. All he needed from her was a little bit of time and some faith in the man she'd agreed to marry.

Just be patient, Alara. You'll get that cabin on a lake and the family you've been dreaming about.

* * *

Atton Ortane waited in the concourse between the *Valiant's* port and starboard venture-class hangar bays. All of his gear and personal effects were stuffed into an 80 pound grav bag and slung across his shoulders. Thankfully the bag's grav field generator made it weigh little more than 10 pounds. Atton stepped up to the bank of viewports which lay between him and the port hangar bay. He spent a moment looking up at the skyscraper-sized *Intrepid,* feeling suddenly very small. It didn't help remembering that the 280-meter-long *Intrepid* was actually berthed inside of the five-kilometer-long *Valiant* where he now stood. Sometimes it was hard to remember he was living on board a starship, rather than some immense space station.

Atton watched the milling crowds inside the hangar bay. Most of the *Intrepid's* 128 crew members were already aboard, so the crowds were ground crew. Here and there a mechanized load lifter could be seen carrying plastiform crates of supplies and munitions up the five-story high boarding ramps of the warship. Giant fuel hoses snaked out from the aft section of the ship. Her standard gold dymium fuel was being pumped and replaced with the much rarer and more potent red dymium which would enable the *Intrepid* to fly nearly 10 times faster through superluminal space. They would be able to travel the almost 1,000 light years to the admiral's Enclave in just over a week. Due to the extreme distances involved when travelling across the galaxy, red dymium fuel was necessary for any fleet operations outside of Dark Space. However, due to the scarcity of red dymium, ships within the sector were restricted to the use of the less potent gold variant. That restriction had almost spelled the end for the Imperium a few months ago when local crime lord, Alec "Big Brainy" Brondi had captured the *Valiant* and forced the surviving crew to flee aboard another venture-class cruiser, the *Defiant*. That cruiser had been fueled with nothing but gold dymium, and under-fueled at that. Under those circumstances they had barely managed to fly 30 light years away from Dark Space to get help from Admiral Hoff's fleet. Atton sighed. At least this time they wouldn't have to worry about fuel problems.

"Atty!"

Atton turned with a smile to see his little sister, Atta, running toward him. Walking at a more measured pace behind her were her parents, Admiral Hoff Heston and Atton's own mother, Destra Ortane. Atta collided with Atton's legs and he staggered back a step. She locked her arms around his waist for a breath-stealing hug. He smiled and tousled his sister's dark hair. She looked up at him with Hoff's gray eyes and their mother's button nose.

"Take me with you!"

"I'm sorry, Atta, I can't, but I won't be gone long."

"Promise?" She squeezed him harder, and he gasped, pretending to suffer.

"Okay, okay, I promise!"

"Good!" She let go of his waist, and he tousled her hair once more. Atta was his half sister. Not long ago he'd hated her for replacing him. He hadn't seen his mother for ten years and then suddenly he'd found her married to the admiral with a daughter whose name sounded suspiciously like his.

"Atton!" Destra said as she drew near. "What is this Hoff tells me about you going on a secret mission in Sythian Space?"

Atton smiled. "It's classified, Mom."

"I don't care." She shot her husband a dark look. "I told Hoff no more secrets, and I meant it."

Atton's gaze slipped sideways to find the admiral. "What did you tell her . . . ?"

"She doesn't know the details."

"I know enough," Destra said. "You can't go, Atton. What if you don't come back?"

"He'll come back," Hoff replied.

"How can you be so sure?"

"Hoi, guys, I thought you were coming to say goodbye, not convince me to stay."

"He'll be fine, Destra," the admiral reassured. "With that Sythian Fleet here watching our every move, he'll be safer than us."

"Maybe we should all go, then," Destra said.

"Are you suggesting we abandon everyone here and save ourselves?"

Destra frowned. "I suppose not." She took another step toward her son and stopped within arms' reach of him. She just stood there, her blue eyes staring into his green until he was forced to notice the sadness lurking in her gaze. "I'm going to miss you," she said.

"I'll miss you, too, Mom, but I'll be back in a few weeks."

His mother pulled him into a hug and whispered, "You be careful out there."

"I will."

"And don't hesitate to call for help. Promise me, Atton."

"I promise."

"Good. If you don't come back I'm going to go get you myself."

"He won't be in any danger, Des," Hoff said. "I give you my word, if I thought they would harm him I wouldn't send him."

Destra pulled out of the hug to turn to her husband. "I know, because if something happened to him I'd never let you forget it."

Hoff chuckled. "Like you haven't let me forget that I made him a squadron commander?"

"Because it was an incredibly stupid thing to do."

"That was my choice, Mom. My choice to accept this rank, and my choice to accept this mission. I wouldn't have it any other way. I wasn't going to sit by and watch everyone else fight the Sythians. Why should I let them have all the fun?" he added with a wink and a smile, hoping to lighten the mood.

Destra blinked a tear onto her cheek and shook her head. "You really are your father's son. Adventure and excitement were all he cared about until he lost everything that really mattered. Make sure you don't make the same mistakes, Atton."

"I won't. Besides, the admiral is right; I'll be safer out there than I will be in Dark Space. That's why I have to go. We need to get reinforcements or else no one is going to be safe."

Destra held his gaze for a long moment, as if hoping he'd change his mind. When he didn't so much as blink, she sighed. "Okay."

"Well! Now that that's out of the way ..." Admiral Heston stepped up to Atton and held out his hand for shaking. Atton accepted the handshake, but the admiral pulled him close. Under the guise of giving him a hug, he whispered in Atton's ear, "Whatever you do, don't tell the Avilonians I sent you." Then he withdrew with a smile and said, "Good luck, son. Hopefully by the time I see you again, you'll have a whole fleet with you."

Atton replied with a quizzical frown. "Hopefully more than one . . ." His eyes flicked to his mother, but if she had noticed Hoff's whispered warning, there was no sign of it on her face.

"You'd better get aboard," the admiral went on. "They're launching in half an hour."

"Right." Atton felt an insistent tug on his sleeve, and he looked down to see Atta smiling up at him with her doll-like face.

"Don't forget to bring me something."

Atton smiled. "Like what?"

"I don't know," she shrugged. "Something pretty."

Atton laughed, already backing away from his family to enter the hangar bay. "Okay, Atta. Something pretty it is."

"Come home safe!" Destra pleaded.

Atton met his mother's gaze one last time and nodded. "I will." Turning to the admiral, he gave a quick salute and said, "Sir."

"Make the Imperium proud, Commander."

"I will, sir." And with that, Atton turned and passed his wrist over the door scanner to open the broad double doors of the hangar bay. The doors parted with a *swish,* and Atton broke into a light jog, angling for the *Intrepid's* nearest boarding ramp.

As he ran, his comm piece buzzed in his ear, and he sent a mental command to answer it.

"Ortane, what's taking you?" Master Commander Donali asked. "You're the only member of the crew who hasn't reported in yet. Captain Caldin is asking for you."

"Sorry, sir. Do you know what the captain wants?"

"She wants you to come aboard so we can get under way."

"Right. I'll be aboard in five."

"Good. One more thing, Ortane—"

"Yes, sir?"

"I'd like a word with you in my office once you've reported in. There are a few things the admiral didn't tell you about where you're going."

Atton frowned as he reached the foot of the boarding ramp. On his way up he passed a pair of load-lifter mechs carrying cold-storage crates full of freeze-dried rations. "If the admiral didn't tell me, I'm sure it can't be that important, sir."

"He feels the importance of your mission outweighs the risks you'll be exposed to, but I believe in full disclosure. If this mission is going to succeed, you need to know what you are getting yourself into."

Atton was gasping for breath by the time he reached the top of the five-story boarding ramp. He shook his head and walked to one side of the *Intrepid's* cargo hold to lean against the bulkhead and rest. "What do you mean? What am I getting myself into?"

"We'll discuss that in my office. For now report to the captain, and I'll see you after we make the jump to SLS, at thirteen hundred."

"Yes, sir," Atton said. He blinked spots from his eyes and set off at a run for the nearest bank of lift tubes. The loud, *clanking* approach of mechanized footsteps called his attention back to the top of the boarding ramp, and he saw the pair of load-lifters he'd passed on the way up. Turning back to the fore, he was just in time to sidestep another load-lifer on its way out. The pilot shook a mechanical fist at him and yelled in an amplified voice for him to watch where he was going. Atton smiled and waved an apology.

Then he did run into something. He bounced off and landed on the deck to sit blinking up at nothing but empty space. The air shimmered, and a pair of two-meter-high Gors de-cloaked right in front of him.

The Gor Atton had run into turned to him, and the glowing red eyes of its helmet seemed to burn a hole straight through his chest. The creature warbled something, and Atton shook his head. "I'm not wearing a translator, sorry."

Warble.

The Gor held out a giant hand. Atton eyed that hand for a long moment before he decided to accept it. The creature's cold armor closed around his wrist in a vice grip, and then came a sharp jerk on his arm as the Gor yanked him roughly to his feet. He had to bite his lip not to cry out as his shoulder threatened to pop out of its socket.

"Sorry about that. I didn't see you there," Atton said, rubbing his shoulder. The alien turned and walked away without another word, and Atton frowned, thinking back to what he'd told his mother about the safety of this mission. They hadn't even left Dark Space yet and he'd already cheated death twice—once almost getting crushed by a load-lifter mech and again by almost becoming breakfast for a Gor. Besides that, there was Donali's ominous warning about his mission being more dangerous than he thought.

What haven't you told me, Hoff?

Chapter 5

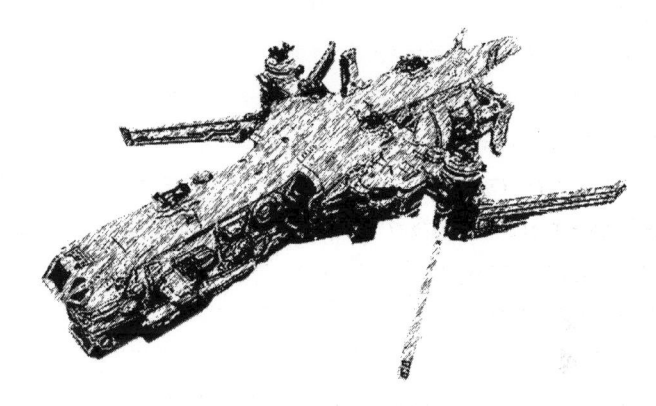

Ethan stood waiting in the hangar of Alara's parents' home. He wore a glossy black suit complete with a shiny white crystal flower corsage. Looking down at the glossy petals of that flower, he found it drooping, as if peering down from his breast pocket, getting ready to leap back to the ground from which it had been plucked. Ethan adjusted the corsage so that it could droop from a new angle.

His bride was busy getting ready, leaving him at a loose end. The wedding was set to take place in the Vastras' garden, all expenses paid generously by Alara's father. Of course, Ethan didn't have any family to invite besides his son, who would be unavailable on such short notice, and he didn't have any friends besides Alara, so the wedding really wasn't for him. It was just a formality, and a painful one at that. Over the last month he'd spent with Alara's family while planning the wedding, tensions had been running high. Alara's father, Dr. Kurlin, disliked him with a passion due to some ... *history* they had together, and while Alara's mother wasn't against him, she wasn't really for him either. Both parents were quick to point out Ethan's shady past. He was an ex-con who'd been exiled to Dark Space before the invasion—a sol-scraping *grub*, as Kurlin liked to call him.

A grub. Kurlin would have been hard-pressed to think of a more insulting, pejorative term for his soon to be son-in-law. *Why do the rich always try to make the poor feel like krak? They think they're better because they're rich, but they're just lucky; most of them were born into it. Show me a poor man who clawed his way to the top despite all the odds being against him, and there's a man I'll look up to.*

Ethan had been struggling to make a living for his loved ones as long as he could remember, and he didn't need some upper-class snob without so much as a single callus on either of his bony hands to tell him that he wasn't good enough to marry his daughter.

Now, the morning of the wedding, Ethan felt like his blood was just about to boil, and he was sorely tempted to go find Dr. Kurlin and break his bony, upturned nose. Ethan let out his frustration in a sigh. He wasn't sure how he'd managed to keep his cool all this time. He couldn't wait to get away with Alara for their honeymoon. That was the only thing that had kept him sane these past four weeks—the thought of another four spent in a romantic getaway on Karpathia, just the two of them. After that, they could fly off and start their lives together. They'd see her family once or twice a year, and Ethan wouldn't feel the constant need to murder her father.

He smiled wryly as he stepped up to the side of his corvette. It was a relatively large ship, and it dwarfed the Vastras' own transport, taking up the bulk of their hangar. At five stories high and almost 50 meters long, it towered over Ethan, looking like a structure in its own right. *Alara wants a home, but she's already got one—a mobile home with more rooms than most mansions.* Granted most of those rooms would have to be converted to extra cargo space, but they would still be left with ample living area.

A fresh coat of white and blue paint made the ship look clean and new. That had been his side project for the past four weeks—painting their corvette. Alara had convinced her father to let him use the paint they had set aside for the house, and Ethan had bought a heat sealer to protect the substandard paint during re-entry. Now the ship was looking like a real slick devlin. Every time he saw it his chest swelled with pride. It was the same way he felt when he saw Alara. He smirked, wondering if that meant he was in love with his starship. Reaching out to stroke the duranium side of the corvette, he whispered, "Just don't tell Alara about us. She wouldn't understand. . . ." He followed the gleaming lines of the ship, walking beside it and looking for imperfections. There weren't any. The corvette had been given a complete overhaul by the admiral's greasers, and now she was practically fresh off the stardocks. Ethan stopped walking when he reached the amidships section of the starship, and then he took a few steps back to get a better look at it as a whole. He stared up at the empty space on the hull where the vessel's name was meant to go.

"I haven't even had a chance to name you yet, have I girl?" Ethan reached up to stroke his chin. "What am I going to call you?" He thought about it for just a moment before the perfect name popped into his head. "How about the *Freedom?*" Ethan smiled. It was perfect.

"Freedom from what?" A familiar voice called out, wiping the smile from Ethan's face. "Not me, I hope."

Ethan turned to see Alara standing in the open doorway to the hangar, already wearing her wedding gown. His heart began beating suddenly faster and his grin returned. He gave a long, slow whistle.

Alara started toward him, the train of her figure-hugging white dress swishing across the floor as she walked. "How do I look?" she asked, stopping just a few paces away from him.

Ethan shook his head and covered the remaining distance between them in a few quick steps. "Amazing," he breathed. His hands found her waist and pulled her close, while his lips drifted down to hers.

She smiled and put a finger to his lips, pushing him away gently. "Not yet."

"Right. Hoi, isn't it bad luck to see the bride before the wedding?"

"I think it would be bad luck not to see her, don't you? Might be because she's making a run for it."

Ethan laughed. "Good point."

"What are you doing out here? It's almost time for the ceremony to begin."

Ethan shrugged. "I needed to clear my head."

Alara's eyes flicked to the corvette, and she nodded slowly. "I see."

"Hoi, not because of you, okay? I was thinking about our fight, and . . . look, Alara . . . I'm sorry."

"No, *I'm* sorry." Alara turned back to him with a faint smile. "You're right. I can't expect you to give up your dreams for me."

Ethan blinked. "Well . . . apology accepted, I guess."

"I'm just scared. Being a freelancer is dangerous work, especially here in Dark Space, and it's only getting worse now with all the criminals pardoned, and with the Gors taking refuge here, too . . . I don't want anything to happen to you, Ethan, and I don't want us to get into debt again just to keep our ship running."

"This time it will be different, Kiddie."

"What if it isn't?" Alara's wide violet eyes searched his, and he felt an echo of her concerns ripple through him as he remembered how they'd struggled to make a go of it with their last ship, the *Atton*.

That glimmer of self-doubt blossomed just enough that he was willing to compromise. "I'll tell you what. Give me six months. If we haven't managed to make enough money to keep our ship running and *save* at least 10% of profits for the future, then I'll sell the ship and take your father up on his offer."

Alara's eyes widened. "You'd do that?"

Ethan nodded. "I will."

"Six months isn't much time . . ."

"It's enough. You can start counting after the honeymoon."

"Either you're very in love with me, or you're just *that* confident in yourself."

Ethan grinned. "Why can't I be both?"

"Ha ha. All right, it's a deal, Ethan."

"Good. I *love* you," he said, dropping a quick kiss on her lips before she could push him away again.

"I love you, too...." Alara said as they broke apart. She turned away to stare up at their ship, and a faraway look crept into her eyes. "The *Freedom*..." she said, as if trying out the name to see how it sounded.

"What do you think?"

"Mmmm..."

"I could always name her after you," he suggested.

Alara smiled and shook her head. "What about ... the *Trinity*."

Ethan frowned and shook his head. "Why *Trinity*?"

Alara turned back to him with a hesitant smile. "Well, we're not going to be just the two of us forever, Ethan."

"I know *that*, but it's not like we've got a baby already."

Alara bit her lower lip and her eyes filled with tears. "Are you sure about that?"

He took an involuntary step back and shook his head. "How ... I mean ... never mind. When did you find out?"

"The day before yesterday. I wanted to tell you, but after you shot down my father's solution without even a second thought—"

"Hold on—Kurlin knows?"

Alara gave a tremulous smile. "My mother does, too."

"I can't believe this. You told your parents before me!"

"I had to talk to someone!"

Ethan sighed and squeezed the bridge of his nose until it felt like it was about to break. "You should have come to me first. What made you think you couldn't talk to me about it?"

Alara gestured to their ship. "That did. You just spent a whole month giving her a fresh coat of paint. It's all you could talk about—how we're going to have such a great time piloting her together. I didn't know how to tell you that your dreams were about to take a sudden turn in a different direction. You can't raise a child on a starship, Ethan."

"Why not?" he shook his head. "What's wrong with that?"

"Do you remember how many missions we took that went sour before we could even get paid? I remember at least a half a dozen where we ended up working for some offshoot of Brondi's organization without even knowing it. We carried more contraband than legitimate cargo, and we waltzed through at least a dozen pirate bases to make our deliveries."

Ethan frowned. "It's not our fault if they don't tell us what's really in the cargo crates."

"No, it's not our fault, Ethan, but who are you going to blame when outlaws hold your family ransom for a shipment that got confiscated by an ISSF patrol? It's not going to matter whose fault it is. It'll be yours for not listening to your wife and finding a safer job."

"Look, I'll make sure we only take jobs with the Freelancers' Guild, and we'll check the cargo ourselves before we agree to move it anywhere. We have a much bigger ship this time, so we'll qualify for regular trade runs, not just courier."

"So how's that any different from being a freighter pilot for the agri corps?"

Ethan sighed and pressed two knuckled fists to his temples as if to beat away the encroaching headache he felt pulsing there. "Trust me it is. We can't run from the Sythians in an agri corps' freighter."

"Okay," Alara said in a small voice. She reached up and pulled his fists away from his temples. "Look, I don't want to fight on our wedding day."

Ethan shook his head. "Neither do I."

"Good. So, let's be thankful for what we have and not

worry too much about the future just yet."

Ethan let out his anxiety and frustration with a shaky sigh. "All right." Suddenly he understood Alara's change of heart about freelancing together. He glanced back over his shoulder and this time he winced to see his freshly-painted corvette. Something told him it wasn't going to be *his* much longer. "The *Trinity* it is," he said, nodding to himself.

"Six months, Ethan. Prove to me that this is a safe move for us, that we can stay out of trouble and make a living while we're at it."

"I will," Ethan said, turning back to her. He found her hand in his and squeezed it tight.

Alara smiled and stood on tiptoes to kiss him. "I believe you," she said, reaching up to smooth away the wrinkles on his forehead. "Now, come on, the future's waiting for us."

Ethan let her lead him away by the hand. They walked to the other side of the hangar and through a pair of doors to find both Kurlin and Darla Vastra waiting for them in the hall.

"What took you so long?" Kurlin demanded, his gaunt features making him look sinister in the low light of the corridor.

Alara smiled and answered for both of them. "I told him."

"Oh, darling!" Darla exclaimed, her eyes skipping from Alara to Ethan. "How do you feel? You're going to be a father, Ethan."

"I already am a father," he said.

Kurlin frowned. "Yes, well, let's hope that *this* time you're around to raise your child. Perhaps you'd like to reconsider my offer."

Ethan turned to the old man with a frown, but Alara answered before he could.

"Actually, Father, we've agreed to give freelancing one

last try before we sell the ship."

"I see. That was the grub's idea, I presume."

"Father!"

"What? Being a grub is nothing to be ashamed of, not if you recognize it and do what you can to change your lot in life." Kurlin turned to Ethan with a thin smile. "You don't have to struggle. Sell your ship and you'll have enough to buy a home—cash. After that you can get any old job to pay the bills. You'll be better off than almost anyone."

"And when the Sythians return, we'll be just as dead."

Kurlin snorted. "I'm afraid if the Sythians come back to finish us, it won't matter how far you run, it will never be far enough. The admiral understands that, which is why he hasn't ordered an evacuation of the sector. Where would we go that they won't find us?"

"Can we *not* talk about this now?" Alara said, her eyes smoldering with barely contained fury. "It's our wedding day, not a time to discuss the end of the human race."

"I'm sorry. You're right, my dear. I don't know what I was thinking."

"And one more thing—Ethan and I have already made up our minds."

"But, Alara . . ." her mother began.

"No buts. It's our decision."

"Be sure that it's not your mistake," Kurlin said.

"Your concern is duly noted," Alara replied. "Now, if you'll excuse us, I believe the guests are waiting for us in the garden. I'll see you both there."

Ethan shot Kurlin a smirking look as they walked by. Kurlin glared back. Ethan and Alara turned a corner and passed through an open door into her father's library. "Where did that come from?" he breathed as soon as they were out of earshot.

Alara shook her head. "I almost forgot why I left home. They want to control everything I do!"

Ethan smiled, thinking to himself, *now you know how it feels,* but he couldn't blame her for considering her father's offer. She was pregnant and afraid for the future of her child. That was enough to make any woman rush to put down roots. They reached the garden and Alara stopped beside the doors and turned to him, taking both of his hands in hers.

"No regrets?" Alara asked. Ethan smiled and shook his head. "Even if we do have to sell our ship?"

Ethan hesitated, but again he shook his head. "It's just a ship, Kiddie."

"It's your dream."

"Not if it means losing you. Then it's a nightmare."

Alara's features softened and her eyes filled with tears.

"Hoi," Ethan chuckled. "Don't smudge your make up. I don't want people to think you're unhappy to be marrying me."

Alara shook her head and smiled broadly. "Nothing could be further from the truth."

"Good."

"I'll meet you at the altar," Alara said, nodding to the doors.

Ethan nodded back and pushed through those doors into the garden. All of five minutes later he was standing at the altar under a wooden arbor overgrown with hanging white crystal flowers and looking out at the sea of faces watching him. Over a hundred people had been invited—friends of Alara's from her youth on Forliss, and friends of her parents. One or two distant relations of the Vastra family were also there, but no one had much extended family these days—not since the invasion had killed all of them.

Then the band began to play an old classical piece and Alara came walking down the aisle on her father's arm. Ethan's breath froze in his chest and all conscious thought came to a grinding halt. All he could think about was how beautiful his bride was, and how happy they were going to be together. All three of them.

Three.

I really am starting my life over, Ethan thought, smiling. Alara reached his side, and Ethan took her hand as they turned to the priest. The music stopped playing, and a nearby fountain began to make itself known, splashing down into the swimming pool which lay behind the altar. A pair of blue birds flitted by overhead, chirping out a pleasant tune.

"We are here today to celebrate the union of Alara Vastra and Ethan Ortane. In these uncertain times, after humanity has lost so much, we can only thank the Immortals for two such as these who remind us that no matter how much we've lost, life does indeed go on. Love, faith, and hope for a better tomorrow, these endure no matter whether we are a multitude or just two." The priest spread his hands. "Ethan is there something you'd like to say to your bride?"

Ethan nodded and turned to Alara. "Forever isn't long enough for us, Alara. I'd need to live the lives of a thousand men to even begin to do justice to the love I feel for you. You are everything I have, and everything I want. Thank you for marrying me. I promise I'll do everything in my power to keep you safe and to make you happy. You are my dream, Alara. A dream come true."

Alara's lower lip began to tremble, but she clamped down on it with a smile. "After all the years we spent working together, with you insisting you couldn't ever be more than just my friend, I thought this day would never come. I'd contented myself with that and accepted that, and now ..." Alara shook her head as a pair of tears spilled down her cheeks. "Now I'm afraid that I'm the one who's dreaming, but if I am, I don't ever want to wake up. I promise to love you and support you, to be there for you in every circumstance and every trial. I'll be there the way I've always been there, Ethan. I love you more than I love my own life."

Ethan felt a suspicious warmth begin coursing through his veins, and his eyes began to itch with the threat of tears.

The rest of the ceremony went by in dreamy haze. They put on each other's rings and kissed. Before he knew what had happened, he was grinning from ear to ear and rushing down the aisle, back to the hangar where he and Alara had been only half an hour ago.

Ethan led his bride toward their waiting ship and keyed the boarding ramp to open with the keycard in his pocket. Alara poured on a sudden burst of speed, leaving him to wonder how she could run so fast in that dress.

"Slow down!" he said, breathless as they ran across the hangar floor.

"Can't blame a woman for wanting to be alone with her husband," Alara said, angling for the boarding ramp now hissing open at the back of their ship.

Ethan sent Alara a wry grin as they reached the foot of the ramp. They stopped there to turn and wave goodbye. The entire wedding party had followed them into the hangar.

"Should we wait to say goodbye to your parents?" Ethan asked, scanning the crowd for their faces.

Alara shook her head. "We'll comm them from orbit. Come on."

Ethan allowed her to lead him up the ramp. "After you,

Kiddie," he said through a smile.

All aboard the Trinity, *he thought. Next stop—us.*

Chapter 6

Atton stood in the XO's office aboard the *Intrepid*, watching the stars blur by in whirling streaks of light as the cruiser travelled through superluminal space. Most of the next week would be like that, travelling between the stars at hyper light speeds. They'd left Dark Space less than an hour ago, using their cloaking shield so that the Sythian fleet wouldn't see them go. By now they had to be halfway out of the Stormcloud Nebula and Dark Space itself.

"Sit down, Commander. Make yourself at ease," Donali said.

Atton turned from the viewport with a frown. "Sir, how am I supposed to be at ease when you've called me here to tell me that my mission is more dangerous than I think, and the admiral hasn't told me everything I should know about it."

Atton noticed the glowing red iris of Donali's artificial eye grow smaller to match his real one as it narrowed. "Very well, you can hear about it standing up. You've been told that the immortals in Avilon won't harm you, and while that might well be true, you should know that they're not going to welcome you either."

"With respect, sir, I already know that."

"But do you know why? Did Admiral Heston tell you why he left Avilon all those years ago?"

Atton hesitated. "He said something about it being easier to compete with mortals. He could make something of himself more easily when he had the hidden advantage that he was immortal and no one else was."

"Yes, that is true, but that's not why he left. He left because they would have executed him if he'd stayed."

"So he's a fugitive."

"Immortals have no patience for those who don't conform to their society. To their rules. Admiral Heston advocated that people should be allowed to be mortal if they wished to be. He wasn't an advocate of mortality for himself, although apparently your mother has since changed his mind about that. Back then, however, all he wanted was a freer system, where people could choose to live however they wanted in Avilon."

"And I'm guessing the Avilonians didn't like that."

"No, they didn't, and for good reason. Mortals and immortals have fought many times in the past, and twice the immortals were forced to flee—once to our galaxy, and once again to Avilon."

"You know about that?" Atton asked, not sure why he

was surprised that the admiral had told his XO what he'd discovered aboard the Sythians' command ship.

Donali nodded. "I know the Sythians were human once, and I know that history has repeated itself enough by now for the Avilonians to be very wary of us. Why should they come out of hiding to help mortals when mortals were the ones who forced them into hiding in the first place? They must have felt like our demise was justice for what we did to them."

"Where are you going with this?"

"The admiral has sent you on a mission that you can't hope to achieve. You're not the right man for the job."

Atton crossed his arms over his chest. "So who is the *right* man?"

Donali gave a slow smile. "We shouldn't be sending a mortal to speak with immortals. We should be sending someone who is just like them—another immortal."

"You just said that the admiral is a fugitive."

"I'm not suggesting we go back and convince him to go."

"Then . . ."

"Have you forgotten that I have a Lifelink implant, too, Squadron Commander? I also have clones to revive myself when I die. I'm just like them, and because of that, they'll be far more willing to listen to me."

Atton's eyes narrowed. "With due respect, sir, if that's true, then why *didn't* the admiral send you?"

Donali shrugged. "Who knows . . . the admiral has been distracted lately," he said as he stood up from his desk and walked over to the viewport to stand beside Atton. "There's political unrest in Dark Space. The fleet tax is higher than ever, and food is being funneled to the frontlines so fast that the agri corps can't keep up. There's the very real danger that having over a hundred thousand Gors to feed is going to push us all to the brink of starvation. And now, with the appearance of a Sythian fleet, the admiral knows that we're running out of time. Perhaps the Sythians are content to wait at the entrance of Dark Space because they know we're in trouble, and that given enough time, we'll self-destruct."

Atton frowned. "So, what are you saying? That I should give you my mission and what ... stay on the *Intrepid* with the Gors in case *you* need extraction?"

Donali spread his hands and smiled. "It would be the wiser move. Besides the fact that you're a mortal, you are also a particularly *young* mortal. What makes you think the Avilonians, who are by now thousands or millions of years old, will listen to a boy who is only seventeen?"

"Eighteen," Atton corrected. "I celebrated my birthday a week ago."

Donali looked like he was about to laugh. "Of course—I apologize—eighteen."

"The admiral believes I'm the right man for the job."

"He believes you're the only one he can *trust* for the job. Remember his mistrust of the Gors and what that nearly cost us? The admiral does not trust anyone easily. One can hardly blame him, but that doesn't mean we have to let his mistrust usher in another catastrophe. He very nearly alienated the Gors, and right now they are the only thing standing between us and utter annihilation. Ironic, isn't it?"

Atton pursed his lips and shook his head. He turned back to the dizzying swirl of light beyond the viewport, considering everything Donali had said.

"I understand this is a lot to process. You have to think for yourself, to think beyond your orders. It's the opposite of what a good soldier does, but it is the *essence* of what a good *leader* does. You played the part of the Supreme Overlord for a time, Atton. You know how to think for yourself, and deep down, you know that I am right."

Atton sighed and turned back to Donali once more. "We have a week's journey ahead of us. There's no rush for me to decide anything."

Donali nodded. "Of course, take your time. You know where to find me. Until then, Commander."

"Yes, sir." Atton gave a curt salute before turning to leave the office. The door swished shut behind him, and he let out a breath he hadn't realized he was holding. As he stalked down the corridor from Donali's office, Atton had to work hard to control his indignation. The commander was telling him he couldn't hope to succeed in his mission, that he was too young. That was a sore point. His entire squadron thought he was too young to be in command, and apparently so did the admiral's XO.

Atton heaved a sigh. With the survival of the human race at stake, he knew better than to make it about him, and when it came right down to it, Donali was right. He was the more logical choice for the mission. So why *hadn't* the admiral sent him?

Now it was his call to make—follow his orders or let Donali go instead. Atton reached the lift tubes at the end of the corridor and punched the call button. One of the lifts arrived a moment later. He stepped inside and rode it up to level 17, the *Spacer's Rest*. It was an officer's lounge, located conveniently just below the bridge deck. The first leg of the *Intrepid's* journey was over 12 hours straight, so he wouldn't be back on duty until the scheduled reversion to real space at 0200, and even then, the chances that they'd been followed were fewer than zero. All of which meant that right now he could afford to knock back a few drinks and enjoy some downtime with his squadron.

The lift tube slowed to a stop at the 17th floor and Atton strode straight out into the lounge. A cacophony of merriment assaulted his ears—laughter, clinking mugs and bottles, the not so distant mechanical *clanking* of robots as sentinels played their favorite game—*Mech Rally*. It involved using a pair of miniature assault mechs to battle each other remotely in a ring. Nova pilots and assault mech pilots—known as *stompers* by the former—would usually stand around taking bets on the winner. More often than not the games would devolve from simulated to real as sore losers resorted to climbing into the ring themselves to beat live opponents senseless.

A week ago, while celebrating his birthday with the squadron, Atton had to jump into the ring to stop Gina from knocking Horace "Hawkeye" Perkins unconscious for an ill-advised comment he'd made about *wanting a piece of her*. He hadn't meant the comment quite the way Gina had taken it, and he'd ended up spending half the night in med bay for his trouble.

Atton smiled. He spotted Gina now, sitting by herself on one side of the bar counter, and he angled her way. He walked up beside her and laid a hand on her shoulder while waving his other hand to get the bartender's attention. "Hoi, Kerk!" The bartender turned his head. "Can I get a Black Maverick over here?"

"Coming right up, sir."

"So," Gina said, "you finally decided to join the common people."

Atton's drink came sliding across the counter in a shatterproof mug and he caught it with a nod of thanks. He raised the mug for a quick sip and turned to Gina. The strong, bittersweet flavor of the beer drew a sigh from his lips, and he hopped up on the barstool beside Gina. "I was in a meeting with the XO."

"Which one—Delayn or Bug Eye?"

Atton smiled. The ship's regular XO was also her chief engineer, Deck Commander Cobrale Delayn, but Master Commander Donali outranked Delayn, making him the XO for the time being. "Bug Eye."

"Mmmm," Gina said, taking a sip of her own beer.

"How's everyone taking it that Four is gone?"

"You mean Lieutenant Thales, right?"

Atton winced. "Right."

"You're going to have to stop thinking of them as numbers, Atton."

"Sometimes it's easier that way."

"Easier for you."

"Hoi, take it easy on me, okay? I barely knew him."

Gina shrugged. "We *all* barely knew him. There's a memorial planned at 1900. You might want to say a few words."

"You think it will help?"

Gina turned to him with her eyebrows patiently raised. "A commander with heart is the only kind worth following. It might not help Thales, but it *will* help you."

Atton frowned. "I'm not heartless, Gina. I'm just trying to keep some distance."

"Distance is one thing. You're as cold as a skull face."

Atton winced at the racial slur. "We don't call them that anymore," he whispered, looking over his shoulder and half-expecting to find a Gor de-cloaking behind them, waiting to vivisect them for their disrespect.

"Maybe *we* don't, but *I* do, and you are cold."

Atton frowned and took another sip of his maverick. He became peripherally aware of Gina sidling closer to him, then he felt her breathing in his ear and heard her whisper, "If you're interested, I'm sure I could think of a way to heat you up. . . ."

Atton's heart rate sped up suddenly, and his skin prickled as he felt Gina begin rubbing his knee. Her hand trailed slowly higher, up to his thigh, and then across to his—

He grabbed her hand and removed it slowly. "I'm your commanding officer, Gina."

"And?"

He turned to her with what was meant to be a serious frown, but his cheeks had flushed bright red. "And ... we need to keep things professional between us."

"Some would say I *am* a pro," Gina said with an accompanying wink.

"You know what I mean."

"What's the matter, are you afraid you won't know what goes where? I bet you haven't even been with a woman before, am I right?"

Atton hesitated and she grinned at him, her dark amber eyes sparkling with glee. "That's what I thought. Hoi, there's no shame in that. I think it's sweet."

Atton shook his head and scowled, trading his embarrassment for annoyance. "Look, Gina, you can save your acerbic wit for someone else. I'm not in the mood."

"Apparently you never are."

Atton raised his hands in mock surrender and stood up from the bar stool. "That's it. I'm leaving."

"Tucking it between your legs and running is more like it."

"You realize that I'm your superior officer, right? Those remarks could get you court-martialed."

"Aww, come on, Atty. You know I don't mean any harm by it. Besides, no one is getting court-martialed for anything short of murder these days. There are few enough officers in the fleet as it is."

Atton shook his head and stormed off to a deserted sitting area that lay along one side of the lounge, beside a bank of real viewports. He flopped down into an armchair and sat sipping his beer and contemplating the mesmerizing swirl of SLS—that, and his insubordinate first officer. It was no wonder Gina was alone. She couldn't stop insulting anyone long enough for them to get to like her.

So why are you alone? asked an annoying voice in his head.

"Hello, sir. Do you mind if I join you?"

Atton turned toward the unfamiliar voice and saw that it was Guardian Four's replacement, Ceyla Corbin. She was young like him, pulled out of flight training a year early to help fill a desperate need for officers and pilots. Atton nodded to the armchair opposite his. "Go ahead."

She flashed him a winning smile. "Why are you over here all by yourself?" she asked.

Atton turned from the viewport to study her. Marksman Corbin was a generally quiet, unassuming woman. She had long blonde hair, bright blue eyes, an almost angelic face, and a unique ability to somehow fade into the background of whatever room she entered—not because she was unremarkable—but because she had a way of sinking into the shadows and shying away from attention. Ceyla was almost the polar opposite of Gina, and right now, that was like a breath of fresh air.

Atton released the remainder of his annoyance with a sigh

and returned Ceyla's smile. "I'm not the most popular commander you'll ever meet," Atton replied.

"Why not? You seem likeable enough to me."

Atton shrugged. "Well, for one thing I'm about eight years younger than I should be to be commanding a Nova squadron."

"I know the feeling," Ceyla said. Atton saw her bright blue eyes skip sideways, and he followed her gaze to watch a cluster of their squad mates playing a game of chance at a nearby table. Among them were also some of the pilots from Renegade Squadron, the *Intrepid's* other Nova squadron. "I think they feel the same way about me."

Atton's eyebrows elevated above the rim of his beer mug as he took another sip. "Young doesn't have the same negative connotation for a marksman, particularly not for a *female* marksman. I would have thought a young, pretty girl like you would be very popular with the squadron."

Ceyla shook her head and shot him a rueful smile. "I was—at first."

"What did you do, get on the wrong side of a debate about whether or not stompers are real pilots?"

"No, sir. Everyone knows stompers aren't real pilots."

Atton chuckled. "Good girl. So what is it then?"

"I'm an Etherian."

"Oh," Atton sat back, momentarily stunned. Religions had all but ceased to exist before the Sythian invasion, but they'd seen a resurgence in Dark Space now that humanity was no longer so sure of itself. He tried to recall what Etherians believed.... He knew they believed in an afterlife and immortal souls, which they simply called Immortals. If he wasn't mistaken they also believed in a god of some sort.... but he couldn't imagine why people wouldn't like her because of her beliefs. "What's that got to do with it?" he asked.

"Well, among other things . . . I don't believe in sex before marriage."

"Oh," Atton said again. "I think I know what you mean now."

"Women don't like me because I'm . . . well, I guess because I'm beautiful and I get too much attention, and men don't like me because I don't respond to their attentions."

"By women you mean Lieutenant Gina."

"And Tails."

Atton smiled. "Don't worry about it. Tails doesn't like anyone who can turn a man's head away from her, and Gina doesn't like anyone—period."

"You want to know what they're calling me?"

"I'm not sure I want to know what they're calling *me*, but sure, why not, let's have some scuttlebutt."

"They're calling me Green V. As in greeny, but . . ."

"What's the V stand for?" Atton asked with a furrowed brow. Ceyla raised her eyebrows patiently, waiting for him to catch on. Then he got it and his cheeks turned red again. "Oh." Atton tried not to smile. A greeny was a rookie pilot who hadn't seen much action. *Green V* . . . well, it was phonetically similar, but it didn't refer to a lack of experience in the cockpit. "Well, Corbin, it could be worse."

"How?"

"You could be me."

"How's that worse?"

"I'm just as green as you, but I'm a guy, and I don't have any religious reasons for it."

Ceyla smiled. "Well, I think that's—"

"Sweet?"

"Yes."

"That's what Gina said."

"Being sweet isn't a bad thing."

"Maybe not, but it's not smart either. Last I checked, wearing sheep's clothing in a wolf den is a good way to get eaten alive." Atton's eyes left Ceyla's face and travelled around the room. He caught Gina stealing a backward glance at the two of them. When she saw him looking, she blew a kiss, and he looked away with a grimace. "You want my advice about the nickname, Corbin?"

"Why not? You know them better than me."

"Don't let them use anything to get to you. *Green V* is only an insult if you think the way they do, that a lack of experience somehow means you're undesirable or strange. For you, believing the way you do, that nickname should be a point of pride, not shame. So own it. Make it your call sign and rub it in their faces. The men will respect you for it, and the women . . . well, women are more complicated. If you act like them they'll call you a sclut, and if you hold to your values they'll say you're an ice princess."

"So how am I supposed to make any friends?"

"You already have one. I'd say that's a good start for your first day with the squadron." Atton stuck out his hand. "Put it there, Green V."

Ceyla smiled and took his hand. "Thank you, Commander. That means a lot."

"Hoi, us greenies need to stick together."

"I suppose we do," she replied.

They spent the next hour by the viewport talking. Atton found out that Corbin was a war orphan who'd been raised in a government institution for children without parents and children whose parents couldn't afford to provide for them anymore. Ceyla fell into the former category, having been rescued by a shuttle pilot during the exodus. She'd become an Etherian in the orphanage, and when she turned 16 she joined the fleet for a chance to get back at the aliens who'd taken her parents from her. Now, two years later, she was already a Nova pilot with a training rating of 2A over 12. That meant she had an average of two kills per sortie across 12 officially rated training missions. It wasn't the highest kill score Atton had seen, but her *A* letter grade put her right at the top of the squadron along with Atton and Hawkeye. It meant she was likely an even better pilot than Gina, who had a 2B rating—although hers was combat, not training.

"Well, Corbin," Atton said, rising from his chair with an empty beer mug. "I'd better get some rack time before Lieutenant Thales' memorial service."

"Right, I almost forgot about that. I'd like to go, too . . . even though I didn't know him."

"I think that would be a good idea," Atton said. "After the service maybe we can meet up here again, and this time, who knows, maybe I can convince my squadron to play nice."

Ceyla winked at him. "Sure, it's a date. I think I'm going to hit the rack, too. You mind walking with me?"

"Not at all."

They made their way to the lift tubes and Atton punched the call button.

"We're on the red-eye patrol, aren't we?" Ceyla asked while they waited for the lift.

"Technically, but we won't be launched unless there's trouble at the reversion point, and there won't be. We should be clear all the way to the Enclave. All the same, I expect to see you seated in the ready room at zero one thirty."

"I'll be there," Ceyla said.

The nearest lift opened and Atton and Ceyla both tried to walk through at the same time. They bumped shoulders and both stopped in the open doorway, looking embarrassed. "Where are my manners," Atton said, and gestured for her to go ahead of him.

"No, you're the SC; you should go first."

"Beauty before rank."

"Well . . . okay," Ceyla said, blushing.

"Hoi, wait up you two lovebirds!"

Atton turned to see Gina jogging toward them with a broad smile.

She reached them a moment later and Ceyla started to object. "We're not love—"

Gina stopped her with an upraised hand. "You don't have to explain anything to me Green V. I saw you two sitting over by the viewport."

Atton punched in their destination—deck 7, the flight deck—and the lift doors slid shut with a *swish*.

"Jealous?" Ceyla challenged, crossing her arms over her chest.

Gina turned to her with an incredulous look. "Jealous? No, girlie, you can have the Iceman all to yourself."

Atton began chuckling. "So *that's* what they're calling me?"

"They who?" Gina asked as the lift slowed to a stop all of a moment later. "That's what *I'm* calling you. Now if you'll excuse me, I need to go get some sleep." As she left the lift tube, Gina shot him a leering grin and said, "I'll leave my door open, just in case you'd rather not sleep alone, *sir*."

Atton frowned and shook his head, gesturing for Ceyla to go out next while he held the doors open for her.

"Don't pay any attention to her, Commander," Ceyla said

as they walked down the corridor to the pilots' quarters.

"I could say the same to you—you just called her jealous."

"Because she is."

Atton laughed. "Come on, we both know that's just her way of getting under my skin."

"No, it's her way of getting into your pants," Ceyla replied.

They reached the pilots' quarters and Atton stepped up to the door to wave his wrist over the scanner. "You think so?"

"Come on, sir . . . you're not *that* young," she said as they walked through the doors. "Tension between two people is often a sign of unexpressed attraction. It's obvious she likes you, and from what I heard, she's not even bothering to hide it. *I'll leave my door open, just in case you'd rather not sleep alone?* What does that sound like to you?"

"Hmmm," Atton rubbed his chin. "I just assumed because she's always so defensive with the other guys that she's not interested in that type of relationship inside the squadron."

"Maybe not with them. She's probably wary because she's been hurt before, but it's obvious you're not like the others, sir. You're a gentleman, and if I had to guess, I'd say that's why she likes you."

Atton ran a hand back through his short dark hair. "I suppose it's possible."

Ceyla stopped walking and turned to him with a small smile. "It's more than possible. Trust me. She likes you for the same reason I do."

Atton did a double take. "You like me?"

Ceyla shrugged and averted her eyes. "Of course. You made me feel welcome when no one else did, and you praised me for my values instead of making fun of them." She looked up again. "Who wouldn't like that?"

Atton smiled, understanding what she meant now. "Well I'm glad I could be a friend."

Ceyla nodded and smiled back. "So am I." She turned to the door she'd stopped beside and waved her wrist over the scanner. The door opened and Atton realized that they'd reached her quarters. "Sweet dreams, Miss Corbin," he said as she walked inside.

"To you, too, sir." Ceyla turned and waved from inside her room, and then the door slid shut between them with a quiet *swish*.

Atton continued on to his quarters with a thoughtful smile. A few minutes later, he was lying in bed. As he drifted off to sleep, Gina popped into his head out of nowhere, half naked, wearing only her underwear, and smiling at him in that wry, taunting way of hers.

"What's the matter, Commander?" she said as she slipped off her bra straps. "Never seen a naked woman before?" With that, she crawled on top of him and stole his reply with her lips and tongue. He felt her warm body pressing against his in all the right places, and a wave of desire washed over him. Then he rolled her over, and he was on top, kissing her. When he withdrew for air, he realized it wasn't Gina at all, but Ceyla. Atton smiled as he gazed down on her, somehow unfazed by the fact that she'd abruptly morphed into someone else. "You're beautiful," he said, admiring the way her long blonde hair fell across her naked breasts.

But Ceyla shook her head in dismay. "What have you done?" she asked, her blue eyes wide and full of horror. "You seduced me! How could you? I thought you were a gentleman!"

Atton woke up to the buzzing of an alarm. He rolled over to the comm suite beside his bed and smacked it until it shut up. Then he sat up with a frown and shook his head, wondering what that dream meant—if anything. "It's just a dream," he whispered to himself. But as Atton got up, showered in the room's vaccucleanser, and washed his face, he realized that maybe it meant something after all. He'd enjoyed the dream, and not just for the obvious reasons.

So what did it mean?

"It means I like them both," he decided, watching in the mirror as water dripped from his chin to the sink. "The question is, Iceman, what are you going to do about it?"

Chapter 7

"I want to know what we're going to do about it! For frek's sake, Admiral! Do you think we're all stim-baked skriffs?"

Admiral Hoff Heston folded his hands on the glossy black table of the operations center and met Captain Ocheron's blazing brown eyes with a calm look. "We're not going to do anything," he said.

Ocheron blinked. "We have a Sythian Fleet on our doorstep—Gors eating all of our food—" Ocheron gestured to Tova, who sat at the foot of the table, glaring unblinkingly at Hoff. "—the Hydroponics Guild is raising prices on all shipments from food to caf and salves, and you want us to do *nothing*?"

"I have the situation in hand."

"How exactly do you have it in hand?" Ocheron demanded, his thick black mustache twitching as he loomed across the table. Hoff eyed the man's shiny bald head, and wondered absently if he might be able to see his own reflection there. Ocheron was a big brute of a man, the former Outlaw Captain of crime lord Alec Brondi's fleet, now one of Admiral Heston's own captains in the legitimate Imperial Fleet. Ocheron had been pardoned along with everyone else after Brondi had been defeated, but like virtually all of the outlaws in Dark Space, he wasn't adapting well to the level of discipline and structure in the Imperial Fleet.

"Unfortunately, that information is classified."

"Of course it is," Ocheron said drily. "One question, Admiral, how do you expect us to trust you if you won't tell us what you're planning? I think I can speak for the skull faces on that, too—right Tova?" Ocheron turned to the High Praetor of the Gors, and Hoff was relieved to see her finally break her death stare with him. She turned the glowing red optics of her helmet on Ocheron and began warbling at him. A moment later the translation came through Hoff's ear piece.

"We ... *skull faces,* as you call us, are aware of the Admiral's plan."

Hoff winced at that revelation. Captain Ocheron hadn't been present for the initial strategy meeting which had led them to the conclusion that they needed to get reinforcements from Avilon. Few people in Dark Space even knew Avilon existed, and for good reason. If they knew that a lost sector of humanity was out there somewhere, untouched by the war, then there would be more unrest than ever. The people would demand to know where Avilon was, and insist that Hoff take them there.

But it's not that simple, Hoff thought. Even if the Immortals agreed to take them in as refugees, few would meet up to the Avilonians' strict standards for humanity, and those who didn't would be turned away.

Captain Ocheron turned slowly back to Hoff, his pale skin having turned an ugly shade of purple. "The skull face knows and we don't?" Ocheron jerked a thumb over his shoulder to Tova.

Hoff shrugged. "The Gors were required for my plan to work."

Ocheron breathed a deep sigh and turned to the man sitting beside him, his XO, Master Commander Leskin. That man had more bright and glowing tattoos than visible skin. He was a quiet man with a frightening appearance, and in Hoff's experience, it was the quiet ones you had to watch. "I think we're done here, Commander, don't you?" Ocheron asked.

Leskin turned to look at Hoff. He wore a pair of glowing blue contacts which contrasted sharply with the pulsing red tattoos that whorled around his eyes. Leskin nodded once and rose to his feet in tandem with his captain, while Ocheron turned back to Hoff with a scowl. "I had thought we'd learned to trust one another, Admiral. Apparently I was wrong."

"I'm sorry you feel that way, Captain." Hoff watched Ocheron and Leskin leave the operations center, leaving him alone with his bodyguards and Tova. Turning to the alien, he raised his grizzled eyebrows. "Are you going to storm out of here, too, Tova?"

"Be thankful I am not the one you leave out of your meetings."

Hoff regarded Tova quietly for a moment. "Is that a threat?"

"No," she said, rising from the table. "It is wisdom."

Hoff nodded slowly and regarded her with a small smile.

Tova stepped up to the doors. The pair of bodyguards standing there eyed her for a moment, looking nervously between themselves, and then to Hoff. He nodded, and they opened the doors for her. She stooped to get through the doorway. The doors swished shut behind her, leaving Hoff alone with his thoughts. He wondered about the uneasy alliance he'd constructed. *Criminals, ISSF, and Gors—all forced to work together for the common good.* It was a recipe for disaster, but none of them had a choice. They had to stand together if they wanted to have even a scant hope against the Sythians. *And soon we'll be adding Immortals to that alliance. . . .*

Hoff's thoughts were interrupted as his comm piece trilled insistently in his ear. *Incoming call from Councilor Destra Heston,* the comm piece declared. Hoff was grateful for the distraction. After the tension-filled meeting he'd just had, it would be nice to hear his wife's voice.

"Hello, darling," he said.

"Hoff, we have a situation developing."

"What kind of situation?"

"The kind where the council just declared an emergency session. We have riots on Karpathia, Etaris, Forliss . . . basically everywhere, and almost all of the guilds are on strike. The entire economy just ground to a halt."

"What?" Hoff sat suddenly straighter in his chair. "Why? What happened?"

"They know about the Sythian Fleet."

"Ah . . . that does explain things. How did they find out?"

"Someone leaked recon data to the commnet. It's everywhere, on all the news nets."

Hoff frowned. It had been inevitable that people find out

about the Sythians, since the whole fleet knew about them, but what was harder to imagine was how highly classified recon data had been leaked to the commnet. His thoughts went straight to Captain Ocheron and the rest of the outlaws. "This is the price we pay for bringing a gang of ex-cons into the fleet. The press probably bribed one of them to leak the data."

"Well, whoever's responsible, they've forced our hand. We need to make a formal statement about this crisis, and you need to give the people a reason not to be afraid."

"Yes, you're right. Get a holo conference together with the press. I'll start preparing a statement. Let me know when my audience is ready."

"I will. . . . and Hoff?"

"Yes?"

"*Should* we be afraid?"

He was about to dismiss his wife's concerns with an empty platitude, but the worried tone in her voice gave him pause. She was worried, not just as a councilor, responsible to millions of citizens on the planet she represented, but also as a mother and a wife, and she deserved to know the truth. Hoff's eyes went to his bodyguards, who were watching him discreetly from the doorway. "Fear is wasteful, Des. What we need right now is hope. I'll see you soon."

"I'll be waiting in the press briefing room."

Hoff nodded and ended the comm call. As he left the operations center, his bodyguards took positions flanking him. He stalked down the corridor, heading for the nearest rail car tunnel, his mind twisting and turning over recent events. He considered what he was going to say to the press, briefly toying with the idea of telling them the truth, but that only led to visions of even greater unrest as the people demanded he lead them to safety in Avilon. Hoff shook his head.

No, the time hadn't yet come for something as dangerous as the truth.

* * *

Ethan and Alara waded into a heated infinity pool, passing through gauzy white curtains of steam which rose perpetually from the surface of the water and into the chilly air. This was the Vermillion Palace on Karpathia, a ski resort built high on the near-vertical cliffs of White Cap Mountain. Guests staying at the Vermillion had the best of both winter and summer activities. While staying on the mountain they could enjoy gravboarding, ice skating, and skiing, while just a short gondola ride away was the small seaside town of Ostin where guests could make their way to the waterfront to enjoy sun, sand, and surf, along with fresh seafood. There was something for everyone at the Vermillion. They'd arrived on Karpathia and checked in to the honeymoon suite just a few hours ago, and now—finally—Ethan could relax. No more Kurlin Vastra, and no more wedding plans—just him and Alara in paradise.

"What do you think?" Ethan asked as they walked up to

the edge of the pool. Upon reaching it Ethan slipped his arms around Alara's waist and propped his chin on her shoulder. Alara gasped as they took in the view together. Between the infinity pool, which seemed to run endlessly into the abyss, and their high, cliffside vantage point, they had the illusion that they were at the top of a waterfall, about to plunge three kilometers straight down. Far below, the bright turquoise waters of the Argyle Sea sparkled in the sun beneath a clear indigo sky. Islands overgrown with opalescent vegetation peppered the middle distance between them and the pale white line of the horizon.

"It's amazing," Alara breathed, sounding short of breath. Whether that was from the altitude or a touch of vertigo, Ethan wasn't sure. The air was much thinner at the palace than it was on Forliss where they'd been staying with her family. Here they were over three kilometers above sea level. Altitabs were offered to all the guests upon arrival as a courtesy of the resort. Ethan and Alara had taken theirs as soon as they'd checked in, but it would take a few more hours before those pills boosted their blood counts enough for their lungs to get more out of the thin air.

"Excuse me," a gender-neutral voice asked. Ethan turned from the view to see a hovering metallic sphere with a quartet of articulated arms. "Would either of you like a hot beverage?"

"Hmmm ..." Ethan pursed his lips, focusing on the bright blue iris of the bot's photoreceptor. "How much?"

"It's free, sir. My records indicate that your package gives you unlimited access to our facilities, which includes your fill of food and drink."

"Well, it seems like your old man spared no expense," Ethan said, sending Alara a sidelong glance.

"Why do you sound surprised?"

"I'm not sure, maybe because a part of me is still expecting someone to hand me the bill."

"You're not very good at accepting gifts, are you?" Alara whispered. Turning to the hovering server bot, she smiled and said, "I'll have a cup of hot chocolate."

"And for you, sir?"

"What do you recommend?"

"The palace is famous for its selection of vermillion ice wines. The wine is fermented from fresh snow berries, and it comes highly recommended if you're in the mood for a cold beverage."

Ethan took a moment to feel the chill around his ears and weigh that against the steamy heat of the pool. If anything he was too warm, rather than cold, so he decided to risk it. "Bring me a glass of that, then."

"Very well, sir," the bot said. Ethan watched it buzz away, skimming low over the surface of the pool. It stopped to take orders from another couple just now entering the shallow end of the pool.

"You know," Alara began, while Ethan absently studied that couple. "You don't have to be so defensive. Just because my father's paying doesn't mean he expects something in return."

Ethan was about to reply to that when a flash of light drew his attention to a holoscreen floating above the bar. It was a local news channel, showing scenes of fires burning, stores and marketplaces being looted ... and the most frightening thing of all, Gors in shiny black armor being dispatched right alongside ISSF sentinels to deal with the riots. In one particularly disturbing scene a Gor was shown hefting a man over his head. A mob of angry citizens had backed the alien into a corner with makeshift clubs. As Ethan watched, one or two citizens opened fire with handheld ripper weapons, but the shells bounced harmlessly off the Gor's armor. Then the Gor threw the man he was holding and promptly disappeared, cloaking to get away from the crowd.

"What the . . ."

"My father's generosity doesn't make you any less of a man." Ethan ignored her and went on gaping at the holoscreen. "Are you listening to me, Ethan?"

"Hold on a second . . ." he said, and with that, he swam across the pool to get a better look at the holoscreen. When he got close enough to focus on the news ticker, he read: *Riots storm across Dark Space as Sythian threat looms. 59 dead, 420 injured.*

"Frek . . ." Ethan whispered.

"What's going on?" Alara asked, swimming up behind him.

He turned to her and shook his head, his face ashen. "They're back."

"Who?"

Ethan left that question unanswered as he watched the screen. Now it switched to a different scene. There was a podium with a lectern, and behind that, the golden emblem of the Imperium emblazoned on a shiny black wall—six stars surrounding a clenched fist. As Ethan watched, none other than Admiral Hoff Heston stepped up to the lectern, wearing the trademark white uniform of the supreme overlord. Ethan called out to a nearby bartender who stood watching the news with them. "Could you raise the volume, please?"

The man turned to them with a vacant look. A second later his brain seemed to process what was being asked of him, and he waved his hands at the screen to raise the volume.

Ethan heard, "... the people of Dark Space need to understand that this civil unrest is more threatening to our security than any Sythian Fleet. If we are to mount a proper defense, and indeed repel the invaders as we have recently proven we can, then we need you, all of you, to keep doing your jobs. Don't stop living your lives just because the Sythians have returned. The very fact that they've already been here for more than 24 hours without making a move to attack us is a sign that they know we can beat them if they do. Rest assured we are preparing for an attack, and our defenses are stronger than ever before. This is not a time to give in to despair; it is a time to fight on, and to remind ourselves of the real reason the Sythians are here: they're here because *they* are afraid of *us*. That is why they have worked so hard to exterminate us, and we have proven that they are right to be afraid, because they have thrown their best at us and we are still here. Trust us to protect you. We will not fail in our duty to humanity."

Applause followed that statement, followed by a question from someone off screen. "And what if you do fail? Humanity has been defeated before."

The camera shifted to cover an assembled group of reporters, their features flickering and glitching ever so slightly, indicating that they were not actually there with the admiral, but rather pre-recorded holograms for the benefit of the viewers. Even with comm signals travelling at superluminal speeds, time delays from one solar system to another meant that it could take as much as an hour for a signal to get to a neighboring solar system.

The man who'd asked the question had his hand raised and appeared to be waiting for an answer. Hoff's voice returned and the camera angle shifted back to the podium where he stood.

"We were defeated because we were not prepared. We didn't even see them coming. This time, we know where they are, and not even their cloaking shields can hide them from us. We also have an entire fleet of theirs now fighting for us, complete with the Gor crews. The ease with which we captured and turned the Sythians' own fleet against them must now give them pause. They don't attack us because they are afraid we will turn another fleet to our side."

"If they're not here to attack us, then what *are* they doing here?" another reporter asked.

The admiral spread his hands. "Our best guess is that they are watching us, waiting for us to panic and do exactly what we are doing now—weaken ourselves with infighting."

"How can you be certain that they're not waiting for reinforcements?" a third reporter asked.

"If their intention was to overwhelm us, they could have waited until their entire fleet was assembled before moving into Dark Space. Instead, it is apparent from their attempt to hide in the Stormcloud Nebula that they are not seeking a direct confrontation."

"Admiral, where is the *Intrepid*?"

The Admiral smiled thinly at the camera. "The whereabouts of fleet vessels is classified. Rest assured, all available forces are being rallied on the frontlines to respond to whatever the Sythians throw our way."

"What do you have to say about recent reports of violence between Gors and humans?"

"Gors are an official part of the Imperium, and they serve in the same capacity as regular sentinels. I have not heard any reports of undue violence initiated by Gors, so they will remain in effect as a peacekeeping army on human-colonized worlds. It is time for us to set the prejudices of the past aside in the interests of moving forward. Thank you, no further questions." With that, the admiral stepped down from the podium and a local news reporter appeared on the screen.

"So far riots on Karpathia alone have taken over 37 lives, with more than 300 injured. Now two hours after the press conference first aired, there is no sign of the riots abating, and no sign of the Overlord softening his response. There are now more than 5,000 Gors and 2,000 human sentinels documented to be on the planet's surface, and those numbers are expected to double before nightfall with the arrival of another garrison."

Ethan shook his head and turned from the screen to look at Alara. "So much for our honeymoon," he said.

Alara turned to him with wide, terrified eyes. "What are we going to do?"

"For now? Nothing. We're going to wait and see what happens."

"What about the Gors? They're all over Karpathia!"

"They're all over Dark Space. If they meant to betray us, they could have done so a month ago when we took out the Sythians' command ship and our forces were in disarray. You saw what that Gor did in the newscast—he was surrounded and being attacked by an angry mob, but rather than fire back, he simply cloaked to get away."

Alara reached out to hug Ethan. "What if the Sythians really are just waiting for reinforcements?"

Ethan's brow furrowed. "It's possible. Still think it's a good idea to sell the *Trinity*?"

"No," Alara admitted.

"For now we're going to do exactly what Admiral Heston

suggested. We're going to pretend everything is fine—and keep a close eye on the news channels," he added, turning back to the holoscreen above the bar.

He was just in time to see the breaking news. "This just in from an anonymous source . . ." a pretty young reporter said, putting a hand to her ear-mounted comm piece to listen as someone else communicated the news to her. "The Sythians have made contact with our fleet," she said, her celadon-green eyes widening. "And they have . . . requested an audience with our leaders." The reporter shook her head and looked up at the camera. "This is unprecedented news . . ."

Ethan tuned her out and turned back to his wife. She asked the question that was already on the tip of his tongue. "What do they want?"

He slowly shook his head. "I don't know."

Chapter 8

Admiral Hoff Heston stood on the bridge of the *Valiant*, gazing out at an impressive array of Sythian warships, their gleaming lavender hulls glinting in the distance against the hazy gray clouds of the Stormcloud Nebula. The 30-kilometer-long Sythian command ship stood in the middle of the enemy formation, surrounded by half a dozen one and two-kilometer-long battleships. They'd come just far enough out of the nebula to communicate without interference, and there they'd stopped to send the first comm signal humanity had ever received from the Sythian invaders. When translated, the message had simply said, *we must speak with your leaders.*

That had been two and a half hours ago.

Admiral Heston had sent a reply almost immediately via

his current XO, saying that they would need time to get their leaders together. After that, they had waited through several tense hours, watching the Sythians and waiting for them to snap. They hadn't so much as twitched. Making the Sythians wait was a risky gamble on Hoff's part, but it sent an important message—the message that humanity was not running scared, they were not desperate, and they were not defeated.

The Sythians had waited patiently, and now Hoff, Tova, and Captain Ocheron were assembled on the bridge of the *Valiant,* standing in front of the captain's table and waiting to hear what the Sythians had to say. Hoff nodded to his comm officer. "Make contact again, Lieutenant, and get us a visual if you can."

"Yes, sir. Should *we* transmit a visual?"

"If they can receive it."

The comm officer nodded and turned back to his control station. A moment later he gave a thumbs-up sign and said, "Connection established. Transmitting in three ... two ... one."

The main holoscreen faded from stars and space to a view of a dark, circular room with a glossy black floor. All around was a dome-shaped canopy showing an unobstructed view of space. Beneath that dome, control stations were arrayed in concentric circles, glowing with lavender, yellow, and red lights. In the weak glow from those consoles, Hoff could just make out the blurry faces of aliens hunched over their controls, but it was impossible to tell whether they were Gors or Sythians. Standing in the center of the holo feed, however, was a creature unlike any Hoff had ever seen before. He had to stop and remind himself that the Sythians were all subtly different from one another, having been genetically-engineered to live in the diverse environments of the worlds which they came from in the Getties Cluster.

The creature standing before them wore a suit of glossy black armor, much like a Gor's. His breastplate was festooned with colored bars of light and a few glowing symbols, which Hoff assumed to be some type of rank insignia. The creature was humanoid, but his face was a nightmare of jagged black teeth, and sharp, bony ridges protruding along his prominent brow and nose. His eyes appeared to glow white in the gloom of his bridge, but whether his eyes were naturally phosphorescent or the effect was a product of some technology, Hoff couldn't tell. The Sythian's pallid gray skin reminded him of a Gor's, but while Gors were hairless, this Sythian had a mane of pure white hair which fell from a topknot on his head down to his shoulders. As they watched, the Sythian opened his mouth in a grimace that was probably meant to imitate a smile—or perhaps a snarl.

The creature began warbling at them in its native language and Hoff held his breath. None of them were wearing translators, but one had been wired into the comm station so everyone could hear what the Sythians said. All of a moment later, the translation came booming across the bridge speakers.

"You make us to wait. Now you listen, and do not speak. You have the honor of hearing from Shondar, High Lord of the Sythian Fourth Fleet, and commander of the *Gasha*. You may bow to offer your respect, humanz . . . and *Gor*."

Hoff smiled. "No thank you, Shondar. What is it your people want?"

Tova hissed and warbled her own reply. "This Gor does not bow to Sythians."

"We ignore your disrespect, but soon you see our

supremacy and know that we are your masters."

Hoff squared his shoulders and crossed his arms. "If you could have conquered us, you would have done so by now. Instead, what happened? We turned your fleet against you, and we will do the same with the next one that attacks us."

"You speak far too much for one who knows so little. Observe."

The visual abruptly disappeared, and the main viewscreen went back to showing stars and space. Hoff turned to his comm officer with a frown, but Lt. Hanz shook his head. "We're still connected, but they've cut the visual feed from their end."

Hoff turned to look at the ceiling where the bridge speakers were hidden. "Shondar? Why are you hiding from us?"

Shondar gave no reply.

Hoff turned his frown upon the viewports, and suddenly he understood. Space was shimmering all around the alien warships which had come to make contact with his fleet. More Sythian warships were de-cloaking by the dozens. They were everywhere. Hoff heard a few of his bridge crew gasp. In seconds several fleets had de-cloaked in front of them in a terrifying wall of gleaming lavender hulls. Hoff's jaw dropped open and he turned to Tova with an accusing look. "Why didn't you warn us they were there?" he demanded.

Tova turned to regard him quietly, the glowing red eyes of her helmet drilling into his.

High Lord Shondar replied before she could, "She did not warn you because she could not sense them. These ships are not crewed by Gorz; they are crewed by humanz."

More gasps rose from the crew. They were hearing for the first time what Hoff had already known—the Sythians were making slaves of humans now. What he hadn't known, however, was the extent of it. *Where did they all come from?* he wondered. An instant later, he had the answer. *The Enclave.* Hoff had assumed the Sythians killed the over 100,000 refugees in the Enclave, but the reality was they'd suffered a fate worse than death. "So now you have us fighting your battles for you. Shall I take that to mean you'd be willing to release the rest of the Gors to us?"

The visual returned and back was a life-sized view of the *Gasha's* bridge. Shondar's mouth hung open in a very human-looking expression of dismay. "Oh, yes . . . we could free them and send them to you . . . but they are not alive. Do you want the bodies?"

Tova hissed loudly and warbled at the screen. "I rip the intestines from your belly and hang you with them! Then I eat you while you suffocate on your own krak!"

"And that is why you no longer serve us," Shondar replied. "You should know your people on Noctune are also dead, Tova. The Gorz in Dark Space are now the only Gorz anywhere."

Tova hissed so loudly that Hoff felt like his ears were about to explode. Her hissing turned to a keening wail and she sunk to the deck with a heavy *thunk* of armor meeting duranium.

Hoff scowled as Shondar gave another fierce display of jagged black teeth. "I'm running out of patience, Sythian. Tell me why you contacted us, or I'll end this transmission before you get the chance."

"Yesss . . . we contacted you to make a deal."

"We don't make deals with Sythians."

"This deal isss special," Shondar hissed. "It is in your best interestsss. You can see the fleets arrayed before you are far stronger than yours, yes?"

"I don't agree, but go on."

"We want but one thing. Release the Gorz to us so that we may punish them for their rebellion, and then join the Sythian Coalition. Then we agree to leave your people in peace, and you have our permission to exist in Dark Space as long as you please."

"Join you? Why would we do that, Shondar?"

"Because that way you do not die."

"I see."

"The decision is yours."

"You are asking us to surrender," Hoff clarified.

"Yesss, we are giving you that opportunity. It is generous of us."

"Very generous," Hoff replied. He shot Tova a sidelong glance, but she hadn't reacted to Shondar's demands; she was still slumped on the deck, apparently in shock. Her people had been summarily wiped out. It was ironic that after the Sythians had used them to exterminate humanity, they had then turned around and done the same thing to the Gors.

Captain Ocheron chose that moment to add his two cents. "My fleet would happily agree to your terms, Shondar."

Hoff sent him a scathing look. "You do not have a fleet, Captain! *I* control the fleet, and you are subordinate to *me*. You would do well to remember that before I have you court-martialed for insubordination."

Ocheron glared back at Hoff, his thick black mustache twitching as his pale head began to turn an angry shade of red. "We did not join your fleet willingly, Admiral. We joined it because we had no other choice, and you need us just as much as we need you."

Hoff turned back to the main holoscreen with a dark look.

"Your proposal will need to be discussed, Shondar. I will meet with my commanders and inform you of our decision as soon as possible."

"Of course," Shondar hissed. "Do not make us to wait too long. Your time is running out."

With that, the transmission was cut on the Sythians' side; back were stars, space, and the overwhelming display of force which the Sythians had mustered to back up their threats. Hoff shook his head and turned to Tova. "Get up. We have a lot to discuss."

"What's to discuss?" Ocheron demanded. "Return to frekking sender! The Gors are their slaves, so why should they be our problem? They're eating all our damn food anyway."

"Ocheron—" Hoff didn't have a chance to finish his intended rebuke. Tova flew off the deck and reached out to seize Captain Ocheron by the throat. She lifted him high off the deck with one arm, and Ocheron's face turned an ugly purple. Veins stood out on his forehead, and his cheeks bulged. He beat his fists against Tova's armored forearm, but to no avail. Hoff stood frozen, watching everything happen as if in slow motion.

"You worry how to feed us? *I* have an answer! We eat humanz. Starting with *you*."

A part of Hoff was tempted to let Tova do exactly that, but instead he stepped up beside her and laid a hand on her arm. "Tova. This is not the way. He does not speak for all of us. Put him down."

Tova's head turned and her glowing red eyes drilled into his once more. "Do you take his side, then?"

"I do not agree with him, no."

"He must die for his treachery."

"He will be punished."

"Is not good enough!" Tova roared, her warbling speech almost loud enough to drown out the simultaneous translation which came across the bridge speakers.

"Tova. You will not win this fight by killing him. You will lose, and your people will lose, and I will not be able to stop it. Humanity must never again see you as the monsters who slaughtered us. Do you understand? Put him down."

Tova's broad chest heaved with fury, air hissing in and out of her helmet, but at last she responded. "I do what you ask ... for now." With that, Tova flicked her wrist and Captain Ocheron, a man of some two hundred and fifty pounds, went flying. He landed several feet away with a *thud* and a grunt of pain.

"Good. Now, as I said, Tova. We have much to discuss ..." Hoff's gaze found Ocheron as he rose from the deck. The outlaw captain stood rubbing his throat and his lower back. "And we will discuss it without *him*. Follow me, Tova. Guards! Kindly show the captain to the brig."

"What?" Ocheron rasped. "You can't lock me up! *Heston!*"

"No?" Hoff turned away with a smirk. "I believe you're about to be mistaken."

A soft *click* sounded somewhere behind him, and he felt the hair rising on the back of his neck.

"Stop right there, Admiral."

Hoff froze and slowly turned back to the captain, his smile still in place. "This is treason, Captain. Are you ready to die for your pride?" Hoff nodded to Ocheron's sidearm, which was drawn and pointed at his chest. All of the crew on the bridge had abruptly frozen at their stations and turned to watch the confrontation. Hoff heard the clanking of armored sentinels approaching from the entrance of the bridge.

"Are *you*?" Ocheron countered, clucking his tongue. "You're real skriff-krakking special, Admiral. You think you can take us all down to the netherworld with you? You're wrong. By a show of hands . . ." Ocheron said, waving his own free hand in the air. "How many of you think the Gors should go and we should accept the Sythians' offer?" No one moved a muscle. "Come on, don't be shy," Ocheron said.

Hoff heard the sentinels' clanking footsteps draw near, followed by, "Drop your weapon!" The voice was distorted by the sentinel's combat helmet. "You are under arrest."

"Am I?" Ocheron looked surprised. "All right," he said, raising his sidearm along with his other hand. Just don't shoot me, okay? I have a sensitive stomach. He used his empty hand to pat his protruding belly, and Hoff's eyes abruptly narrowed on the outlaw captain's uniform jacket. The captain was a heavy man, but not because he was overweight.

Hoff held up a hand to stop the sentinels from advancing any further. "Halt!" he said, just as they took up flanking positions on either side of him.

Ocheron smiled slowly. "You're not as dumb as you look, Admiral."

"That man's wired with explosives," Hoff said.

Officers began rising from their control stations in a hurry, but Ocheron called out, "Stay where you are!" And with that, he used the hand which wasn't holding his sidearm to rip open his vest, revealing three belts of WDX4 explosives. "The detonator is tied to my pulse. If I die, so do all of you — and don't think you can stun me either. I've wired in an electrostatic sensor which will detect a stun blast and detonate the explosives either way."

"What do you want, Captain?" Hoff asked.

"What do I want?" Ocheron turned in a slow circle to

address everyone on the bridge. "I want you all to think about this very carefully. Are the Gors worth it? They nearly wiped out the human race! I say we cut the dumb freks loose and join the Sythians. What do we have to lose?"

"Besides liberty?" Hoff asked.

Ocheron turned slowly back to face him, and in that moment Hoff became aware of something important—

Tova was missing.

The admiral looked around suddenly, his eyes wide. "Tova?" Then he noticed Ocheron's expression become abruptly confused. The outlaw's head jerked backward, and blood spurted from his nose. Screaming, he whirled around with blood pitter-pattering to the deck in fat droplets as he searched for whatever had hit him. "Frekking skull face! Show yourself!"

Then Ocheron's face contorted once more as his knees buckled the wrong way with a sickening *pop*. He toppled to the deck, his screams going on and on. "I'm going to kill you!" he roared, fiddling with something on his belt.

"Everybody down!" Hoff yelled, flattening himself to the deck and crossing his arms over his head. He heard a loud *whump*, followed by something heavy landing on top of him. A superheated rush of air roared past his ears like a hurricane, followed by muffled screaming, and then . . . ringing silence.

When Hoff's ears recovered enough for him to hear through the ringing he heard a violent crackle of flames eating away at whatever they could find. Acrid smoke reached his nostrils, and his head spun with the fumes. The weight on his back felt heavier than ever, and he wondered if some fragment of the captain's table had landed on top of him. He risked lifting his head off the deck to check . . .

And saw the gunmetal gray armor of a sentinel's arm,

lying in a puddle of blood beside his head. He reached out to prod the sentinel, but the arm moved independently of its host. Hoff twisted around in horror to find that the sentinel lying on top of him was maimed beyond recognition. With a monumental effort he managed to roll the body off of him. Then he himself off the deck to stand swaying on his feet in the middle of a scene straight out of the netherworld.

Control stations had been shredded, and some of them were on fire; the captain's table was reduced to a charred stump. Crew members lay here and there at their stations below the gangway where the bomb had detonated. Some were unmoving, while others were only now climbing to their feet to survey the carnage. Captain Ocheron was a bloody smear on the deck, and Tova . . . Tova lay to one side of the ruined captain's table, her glossy black armor shredded to a poor reflection of its former glory. Her helmet had been carved open on one side, but the skull-like face beneath it seemed relatively intact. She was, however, lying in a puddle of pale blood. It caught and reflected flickering orange light from flaming debris that had landed around her.

The bridge was decimated, the thick transpiranium viewports striated with fractures, but thankfully still intact. The deck was scuffed and charred and a few of the bulkheads had been gouged with shrapnel. Hoff gazed down upon his savior, the sentinel who had given his life to shield him from the blast. *Sergeant Arconin,* Hoff thought, remembering the man's name. His armor was shredded even worse than Tova's; there could be no doubt that he was dead. "Frek," Hoff growled. Looking up he turned to the nearest officer he could find standing on the deck with him. It was his comm officer, Lt. Hanz. "Comm the medbay!" Hoff barked at him, but that command came out more like a wheeze for air than an urgent order.

"Yes, sir!" Hanz nodded and touched the comm piece in his ear to make the call. His comm control station was far too damaged to send the message.

Hoff hurried to Tova's side and dropped to his knees in a sulfur-smelling pool of the alien's blood. His nose wrinkled, but he forced himself to focus. "Tova."

She hissed softly, but said nothing.

Hoff grimaced. "Help is on the way, Tova."

"Do not . . . waste time, Woss."

He shook his head and grabbed her upper arm. "You're stronger than this, Tova! Fight!"

"I fight . . . long enough. Now I leave my mate to do what I cannot."

"Frek it, Tova . . . we need you! Your créche mates need you!"

"No, Woss . . . my créche mates already have what they need. They have freedom." Tova's real eye, a yellow reptilian slit now exposed by the missing half of her helmet, turned from the ceiling to stare at Hoff. She seemed to be looking past him, but then her eye narrowed still further to focus squarely on his face, and she hissed once more. "Do not let them . . . take that from us."

Hoff shook his head. "I won't."

"Give me your word, human. Swear it before your gods. . . ."

Hoff shook his head. "I have no gods, but I swear it, Tova. I will not let the Sythians enslave your people again."

"Good." Tova's chest heaved, and she released her breath in a sigh. With that, the light went out of her eye and she went back to staring past him. A moment later, the red glow of optics in the other side of her helmet also faded, and just like that . . .

She was gone.

Hoff stood up, but some type of a disruption in his inner ear almost caused him to fall over.

Strong hands took hold of him, and Hoff turned to see the surviving sentinel of the two who had been standing beside him when Ocheron had detonated his bomb. "Are you okay, sir?" the sentinel asked.

Hoff gave the man a weary frown. "Yes, thank you." He turned to look around the bridge, and now he saw officers moving all over the deck, tending to one another's injuries. One of them had pulled out a fire suppression hose and was spraying it over the flaming sections of the bridge.

"Listen up!" Hoff yelled. "Those of you who are injured too badly to move, stay where you are; med teams will be here to tend to you soon. As for the rest of you, follow me; we're heading to the auxiliary bridge." Hoff clapped his hands together for emphasis just before doubling over with a hacking cough. "Move out!" he croaked. With that, he jogged toward the double doors of the bridge. The surviving sentinel kept pace beside him, limping from a shrapnel wound in his leg. Along the way Hoff considered what he was going to say to Tova's mate, Roan, and how he would convince the alien that he'd had nothing to do with Tova's death.

Hoff grimaced. The Sythians' *deal* had unraveled the tentative alliance in Dark Space in a matter of minutes. Something told him that was exactly what they had hoped to achieve.

Divide and conquer. Hoff hoped the Sythians didn't find out how fast their plan had worked until he had regained control of the situation. He needed to call an emergency meeting between Ocheron's second-in-command and Roan in order to apprise them of recent developments and devise a strategy to deal with the Sythians' demands.

Based on what he'd seen of the Sythian fleet, outright refusal was not an option. Dark Space couldn't win a straight fight, so they needed to at least appear to acquiesce, and that meant trouble for more than just Dark Space. Even if the Sythians honored their deal, there was something much more important at stake. Hoff had an invaluable piece of information which the Sythians were after—he knew the location of Avilon. A month ago when he'd gone aboard the Sythian command ship and spoken with High Lord Kaon, the Sythians had offered him a similar deal—they would agree to leave Dark Space alone in exchange for the location of Avilon. Something told him that they hadn't simply forgotten what they were after.

The Admiral felt a pang of dread, but not for *his* life. His thoughts went straight to his wife Destra and his seven-year-old daughter, Atta. If he refused to tell the Sythians where Avilon was, they would torture his family until he cracked, and he knew he wouldn't be able to resist that.

No. He had no choice; he had to tell the Sythians where Avilon was. *But they can hardly blame me if my memory is off by a few thousand light years,* Hoff realized with a burgeoning smile. *After all, it has been a long time since I was there.*

It wouldn't be enough to lie. The Sythians surely had mind probe technology the equal or better of what humanity had. They would dig around inside his brain until they either found exactly what they were looking for or killed him in the process. The only way to fool them was to make the lie true, and for that he would have to physically alter his memories.

Hoff touched his comm piece to make a call just as he reached the rail car tunnel which would take them down to the auxiliary bridge.

"Call med bay," he said while waiting for the ambulatory members of his bridge crew to catch up. A few saluted as they walked past and into the waiting rail car. Hoff nodded back, but made no move to follow them.

"Admiral!" someone answered. "This is Doctor Elder, I've just sent three teams to the bridge."

"Good, but I need something else from you. I need you to prep a mind probe and have it waiting for me."

"Of course, sir . . . does that mean the saboteur survived?"

"No, I'll explain when I get there, Doctor."

"Yes, sir."

"I'll be there as soon as I can," Hoff said, ending the call.

He caught his nav officer's eye as she approached the rail car tunnel. She was limping and clutching her side, but otherwise fine. He was relieved to see that she had survived the explosion more or less in one piece. Deck Commander Teseray Akra was the highest ranking officer on the bridge besides Hoff himself. He stepped in front of her before she could enter the rail car, and she stopped to offer a quick salute.

"Commander," Hoff said.

"Sir!"

"You have the bridge until I get there. I have to attend to some urgent business. Have Lieutenant Hanz contact Commander Leskin of the outlaw fleet and Praetor Roan of the Gors. Tell them to come aboard ASAP and to wait for me in the operations center."

Commander Akra nodded. "It will be done. Immortals be with you, sir."

Hoff smiled wanly at the irony of her words. "Let us hope they are with us all soon."

"Yes, sir . . ." the commander said with an accompanying frown. Like almost everyone in Dark Space, she didn't understand that immortals existed in more than just the stories that parents told their children about their ancestors — powerful beings who never die and keep watch over humanity from Etheria.

Hoff stepped aside for Commander Akra to enter the rail car. As soon as she was through the door, he turned and hurried down the corridor to a nearby bank of lift tubes.

It's time to give the Sythians what they want.

Chapter 9

Hoff entered the operations center for the third time in as many days. This time he sat down behind the glossy black holo table with a sense of impending doom rather than the feeble hope that everything was going to be okay. Humanity's chances had gone from slim to none. He had thought they'd have more time before the Sythians arrived with a fleet strong enough to overwhelm their defenses, but he'd been wrong. The only reason the Sythians hadn't already attacked was because humanity had something they were looking for—according to them that something was revenge on the Gors, but Hoff suspected they were really after the location of Avilon.

He just hoped his gambit would work. He was about to take a big risk with his allies, but ultimately that risk was in the spirit of protecting the alliance. He couldn't accede to the Sythians demands without alienating the Gors forever, and he couldn't let the outlaws know his real intentions without knowing that he could fully trust them.

The doors to the operations center *swished* open and in stepped Master Commander Leskin. His glowing blue eyes found Hoff and there they lingered for a long, silent moment.

Hoff cleared his throat and gestured to the chair to his left. "Take a seat, Commander."

Leskin's glowing facial tattoos chose that moment to pulse a brighter red, making his features stand out in the devlinish light radiating from his own skin. He gave no sign that he had heard Hoff, but moved to take his seat nonetheless.

They spent several tense moments waiting for Roan to arrive. Leskin eyed Hoff carefully, but said nothing, as if expecting his deadly silence to unnerve the admiral.

For his part, Hoff stared right back, smiling smugly and basking in the man's silence. Under any normal circumstances a thug like Leskin wouldn't be allowed anywhere near an ISSF vessel, and he certainly wouldn't be made privy to a highly sensitive battle plan.

All of five minutes later the doors *swished* open once more, and in stomped a two meter-high Gor, fully armored in his glossy black exoskeleton, the glowing red multifaceted eyes of Roan's helmet found Hoff almost immediately. He wiped the smug smile he'd been using on Leskin from his face out of respect for Roan's loss. Rising from his chair, he gestured to the table. "Please sit down, Roan."

The Gor made no move to take a seat, but instead warbled something unintelligible at Hoff. The translation reached his ear a moment later via the translator he wore. Hoff had never heard a Gor's voice boom before, but Roan's did.

"Tova is dead. How?"

He wasn't surprised that Roan had found out about his mate's death. Gors were telepaths, and as his mate, Tova would have contacted him before she'd died.

Hoff shook his head sadly. "She died trying to stop a traitor who threatened to detonate a bomb on the bridge of this ship. He succeeded, killing her and several others in the process."

For a long time, Roan said nothing. He didn't so much as twitch. Hoff felt a flicker of dread begin worming through his gut, and he turned to look at the pair of sentinels standing inside the entrance of the operations center. Normally they wouldn't be allowed to listen in on a meeting like this, but they were a necessary precaution since Hoff wasn't sure he could trust either of the other attendees.

"I understand that this is a shock," Hoff said carefully, "and I am sorry for your loss. I can only imagine if it were my mate, but there is more, and I'm afraid we need you to set aside your grief for the moment in order to be a leader for your people. Can you do that, Roan?"

"Why she attack this . . . traitor?"

"He threatened to kill us if we didn't accede to the Sythians' demands. They demanded that we surrender and hand your people over to them so that the Gors could be punished for their rebellion. In exchange, they would agree to leave us in peace."

"And, what do you say?"

"I said that we don't make deals with Sythians. The traitor was not satisfied with that." Hoff turned to Leskin with a scowl. "That traitor was your very own Captain Ocheron. He killed himself, Tova, and at least one of my men."

Leskin looked up at Hoff and at last he spoke. "Ocheron was a fool, but he was not wrong to say we should give in to the Sythians' demands."

Roan rounded on Leskin, and again his voice boomed through the operations center. "I kill you for your treachery!"

"Hold on, Roan," Hoff said raising a hand to stop the alien from doing something rash and following in his mate's footsteps.

Leskin turned to glare at Roan as the alien subsided. "That's a good skull face. Remember who has who on the leash."

"That's enough!" Hoff roared.

"Yes, it is," Leskin said, rising to his feet. "Enough of this charade! Enough of this phony alliance! We've all seen the enemy fleet, Hoff, and we know what we're up against. You can't honestly expect us to believe that we can win. If we don't give into the Sythians' demands, it won't be just the Gors who are on their way to the netherworld, it will be all of us! If you want to take us down with you, we're not going to be a part of it."

Hoff held Leskin's gaze with a grim smile. "Who's this *we* you speak of, Commander?"

"Myself and all of those who agree with me."

"You're suggesting a coup."

"I'm suggesting we stop fooling ourselves."

"Very well," Hoff nodded. "You leave me no choice. Guards, arrest that man for treason."

Neither one of the sentinels standing at the door responded to his command. Hoff turned to them with a frown. "I said . . ." he trailed off suddenly as he realized his mistake. The sentinels had drawn their weapons and had them pointed at his chest, which could only mean one thing.

They were former outlaws and not true ISSF officers.

"So you're going to shoot me, and what? Take over the Imperium yourself?"

Leskin shrugged and pushed out his chair to leave. "If that's what it takes to make an intelligent decision around here, then yes."

But Hoff wasn't the only one who'd made a miscalculation. As soon as Leskin vacated his seat, Roan's arm shot out in a blur and grabbed him by the throat.

"Shoot, and I squeeze," Roan warbled at the guards.

Hoff nodded, smiling. "What do you say Leskin? Now we can both die. We can leave the Gor to command us. I dare say it will be an improvement."

Leskin struggled to speak despite the giant hand constricting his trachea. "Put your guns down," he croaked.

The guards reluctantly did so, and Hoff nodded to Roan. "Release him."

The alien turned to look at him. "You are sure?"

"Yes."

Roan released Leskin, and the man almost fell to the deck. He stood rubbing his throat and grimacing. Hoff shook his head in dismay. "I'm going to pretend that little incident didn't just happen. We'll blame it on a bad case of stim poisoning."

Leskin's glowing blue eyes narrowed.

"Outlaws aren't *ever* going to enjoy taking orders from me, and I can't get rid of all of you. We need each other, Commander. Especially now. So I have to convince you that my plan is the best one, and for that, I need you to listen."

Leskin seemed to consider that. "All right, if you don't plan to give in to the Sythians' demands, what do you propose?"

"I propose we call their bluff."

"What bluff?"

"Sit down—both of you—" Hoff said with a quick glance in Roan's direction. "—and I'll explain."

As soon as both were seated, Hoff began to invent a half fictitious story about how he had used a cloaked cruiser to slip out into the enemy formation and scan the Sythians' ships. He told them the scans revealed that the Sythians' fleet was all but empty, and the Sythians hadn't had time to enslave enough humans to properly crew their ships.

The truth was Hoff *had* sent out a cloaked venture-class while they'd made the Sythians wait for an audience, but the scans had come back with bad news, not good—the Sythian ships waiting at the edge of the nebula were teeming with human crews.

But neither Leskin nor Roan had seen those scans, at least not yet, and they both bought the lie completely.

"Then they don't have the force to beat us," Leskin said.

Hoff smiled and shook his head. "No."

"Sythians are without honor," Roan added. "To them lies taste sweet and the truth is bitter."

"So it would seem," Hoff said, feeling a stab of doubt. Roan was going to think the same of him when he found out that the Sythians' bluff wasn't a bluff at all. "With that in mind, our strategy is the same as it was. We stand together, and we hold our ground."

Leskin began nodding slowly, and Hoff turned to Roan, his lips curving downward in sympathy. "One more thing before you both go—Roan, you should know that the Sythians claim to have killed all of your people in retaliation for the Gors' rebellion. He said that they even killed your people on Noctune. We have no way of knowing if any of that is true, but..."

Roan abruptly rose from his chair. "I leave you now."

"Did you hear me, Roan?"

"I hear you, but you ask me to put my grief aside to lead my people, and that is what I do. I feel pain later, when it is safe to feel."

Hoff blinked, surprised by his answer. "Humanity could stand to learn something from your people, Roan." He turned to Leskin. "Do you have any questions?"

"No. If what you say is true, then your plan makes sense—for now."

"Good. Then we are in agreement." Hoff rose from the table and started for the doors. When he reached them he stopped to glare at the pair of sentinels who'd drawn their weapons on him, and then he turned to Leskin with a scowl. "Do me a favor and take your dogs with you when you leave."

Leskin returned his scowl with a thin smile. "Of course."

Hoff stood at the doors, waiting for them to leave. Roan came to stand beside him and watch the ex-cons go. Once Leskin and his goons were far enough away, Hoff turned to the alien and whispered, "I need to speak with you, Roan—in private."

The alien regarded him silently. "What do you wish to speak about?"

Hoff shook his head. "Meet me in my office in one hour."

"Human time."

"Yes. Make sure Leskin does not see you."

"No one sees me unless I wish them to."

"Good."

Roan turned to leave, and Hoff waited until he was out of hearing before reaching up to his ear to make a call to

Commander Leskin.

As soon as the outlaw answered, Hoff said, "Leskin, don't speak. Listen carefully. Make sure Roan sees you on your way to the hangar, but then find a way to come back to the operations center. Meet me as soon as you can, but leave your guards waiting at your ship. We need to talk in private. It's about the Gors. I'll be waiting."

"Of course . . ." Leskin purred on the other end of the comm.

With that, Hoff ended the call and went back to his chair at the head of the holo table.

It was time to put together the real battle plan.

* * *

Commander Leskin returned to the operations center and took his seat beside Hoff. "All right, I'm here. What did you want to discuss with me?" he asked, folding his hands on the table.

Hoff nodded. "I brought you here alone because I wanted to tell you the real plan, and the truth about the enemy. We *did* perform scans on the Sythian fleet, but the truth is we found their ships fully-crewed and ready for war. Their posturing at the edge of the nebula is no bluff, Commander. It's a reality we have to face."

Leskin sat back suddenly. "Then I was right. We have to surrender."

"Yes, but the Gors can't know we intend to give them up to the Sythians."

"I understand."

"When I give the word, your fleet and mine are going to fly away from them. At that point I will contact the Sythians and tell them to go get their slaves."

"What about us? Are we setting any terms for the surrender?"

"I'll try, but we're in no position to negotiate. We'll just have to trust that the Sythians keep their end of the deal and leave us in peace."

"And if they don't?"

Hoff shrugged. "Pray that you're still in a position to flee. I'm not sure why the Sythians would want to kill us at all, but they may choose to disarm us and take more direct control over our sector, perhaps using us as a resource base to begin colonizing the galaxy. Either way . . ."

"It's still better than extinction."

"Exactly," Hoff said.

"What will you tell the Gors?"

"I'll tell them we're going to give the appearance of betraying them in order to launch a surprise attack."

"Do you think they will buy it?"

Hoff shrugged. "With luck they'll believe it long enough for me to at least get all the Gors off this ship. Have your people ready for a surprise attack from the Gors, just in case."

Leskin nodded. "We'll be ready."

This time Hoff and Leskin left the operations center together. They parted ways at the lift tubes, with Hoff heading up to his office near the ruined bridge deck and Leskin heading down to the hangars.

A few minutes later, Hoff reached his office and opened

the door with a wave of his wrist over the controls. He walked inside and the door automatically swished shut behind him. On his way to his desk Hoff heard a rustle of movement behind him. A jolt of adrenaline set his heart pounding. He spun around to face whatever unseen assailant had managed to gain entry to his office—

And saw the air before the door shimmering, followed by the appearance of a hulking shadow. It warbled at him. "I am here. What is it you wish to talk about?"

"Roan," Hoff said, his shoulders sagging with relief. "Come, sit down. We have a lot to discuss." He rounded his desk and sat behind it. "How did you get in?"

Roan crept forward and eased himself into one of the too-small office chairs. Hoff heard a crack, followed by one of the wooden armrests of that chair hitting the deck with a hollow-sounding *thunk*.

He ignored Roan's clumsiness. The chairs hadn't been built for a 350 pound Gor.

"I walk in behind you," Roan explained.

Hoff nodded. "Well, I'm glad you're here so soon, because we don't have much time. The Sythians are not bluffing."

"What is *wuffing*?"

"Lying. Their ships are more than amply crewed with human slaves."

"Then you lie to me."

"I regret the deception, but it was necessary for Leskin to believe that he was being made part of our plans. Clearly we cannot trust him. I just met with the commander by himself, and I led him to believe that I've decided to turn my back on your people. I told him we are going to give you up to the Sythians."

"I kill you for this!" Roan said, rising from the chair and looming over Hoff's desk. Then he seemed to hesitate with his helmet mere inches from Hoff's face. "Why do you tell me, foolish human?"

"Because I'm not telling Leskin the truth. The truth is, we are only going to pretend to give in to the Sythians' demands. We are not going to abandon your people."

Roan sat back down. "I am listening."

"What we need right now is to buy time. Your mate, Tova, knew of a mission we sent to a lost sector of humanity for help. This group of humans is much more powerful than either us or the Sythians, and if they agree to send reinforcements to Dark Space, we'll never have to fear the Sythians again."

"Tova tells me this already."

Hoff frowned, for a second wondering if Tova were still among the living due to the strange lack of past and future tenses in the Gor language. "Then you understand why we must *appear* to give in to the Sythians' demands?"

"What do you ask of the Gors?"

"I am going to give orders for my fleet and Commander Leskin's ships to fly away from yours. Once we are at a safe distance I will comm the Sythians and tell them to go and get your people. As soon as you see the Sythians make a move toward you, your entire fleet must cloak and hide. You will stay in Dark Space and wait until reinforcements arrive, at which point your people will de-cloak and help them take our sector back from the Sythians."

Roan shook his head. "How long must we wait?"

"That depends how quickly reinforcements come. It could be a month. It could be two."

"We do not survive two months without deliveries of

food. When we serve the Sythians, their command ships supply our vessels."

Hoff nodded. "The Sythians have no way to detect a cloaked vessel, just as we have no way to detect one, correct?"

"That is correct."

"The way they keep track of their own fleet while cloaked is with beacon signals, and more recently, via your people's ability to telelocate one another."

"Yess."

"So we will use a cloaked cruiser to deliver supplies to your fleet. I have designated the *Baroness* for this task. We will need to crew it with at least a few Gors in order to coordinate with your vessels without giving ourselves away by using comms."

"You are to be aboard this ship," Roan said.

"I wish I could be, but the Sythians will expect to find me still in command when we surrender, and I don't want them to realize we're not really surrendering after all. I will stay with the *Valiant*, but I'll send my mate to oversee supply operations until such a time as I am able to openly fight the Sythians once more."

Roan hissed. "May the *Zarn* and the mighty *Kar* watch over you."

"There is one other matter that you should know about. I believe the Sythians are not after your people at all. They are here to find the location of the lost sector of humanity I told you about. They want to know where Avilon is, and I am the only human in Dark Space who knows its location."

"If the Sythians are trying to find this ... *Awilom*, then you must hide."

"No, they have to believe we are cooperating with them."

"Then they hurt you until you tell them where *Awilom* is."

"Yes, quite likely, but I don't have to tell them the truth."

"They can sense a lie even more easily than I."

"Yes, but a lie is impossible to detect if you believe it yourself. I will undergo a procedure to alter my memories. By the time the Sythians can get me to tell them where Avilon is, I won't even know that I'm telling them a lie, and we will have bought the time we need to survive this occupation."

"You risk much. The Sythians kill you if they find out. If these humans in *Awilom* are so mighty, perhaps they do not need your protection."

"Perhaps," Hoff conceded, "But they will not come to our aid if I have given them away to the enemy, and I cannot risk that the Sythians will eventually overwhelm their defenses, too."

"You are a man of much honor, Hoff. I do not see this before, but I see it now. You lie as easily as a Sythian, and you do not trust, but your honor is greater than the sum of these weaknesses."

"Thank you . . ." Hoff said with a thoughtful frown. "So your fleet will agree to remain in hiding until help arrives?"

"We hide until you or your mate tell us it is safe to reveal ourselves."

"Good. I'm sending your créche mates aboard the *Valiant* to board the *Baroness* and leave while they still can, but as for the rest of your people currently serving aboard our ships and throughout Dark Space, they'll have to cloak and hide until we can find some way to rescue them. Make sure they don't reveal themselves unless forced to do so. The Sythians will kill any Gors they find."

Roan bowed his head. "As you command, My Lord."

Hoff quirked an eyebrow at that, but decided not to question the honorific. If the Gors began to respect him as their leader, so much the better. "One last thing—I need at least one Gor you can trust to stay aboard the *Baroness* and facilitate human-Gor relations. Someone who can serve in an advisory role to my staff."

Roan nodded. "I send my créchling."

Hoff was surprised to hear that Roan had a child, but there was no time to inquire about it. "Good. Have him board the *Baroness* and wait. My wife and daughter will be aboard soon. They will depart the *Valiant* before we officially surrender."

"I tell him."

Hoff nodded and they left the operations center together.

By the time Hoff reached the auxiliary bridge, he found most of his crew already seated at the appropriate control stations. Here the viewports were simulated rather than real, but otherwise the auxiliary bridge was just a slightly smaller version of the real one. Hoff walked up to his XO, Deck Commander Akra, where she stood leaning over the captain's table. When he appeared beside her, she turned to him with a grim smile and gave a quick salute.

"Admiral," she said.

"Commander, you may take your seat at the helm. We're moving out."

"Yes, sir. Where to?"

"Set a waypoint as far from the Gors as we can possibly get within the next 20 minutes."

"Yes, sir," she said, already on her way down the stairs from the gangway and the captain's table. Hoff turned to his comm officer. "Lieutenant Hanz, contact the rest of our fleet with the coordinates the commander sets for us, and then get me an audience with the Sythians."

"Yes, sir . . ." Hanz let his voice trail off curiously. Hoff knew what Hanz had left unsaid. He wanted to know the plan to deal with the Sythian threat. All of Dark Space wanted to know that, but they would have to wait. Hoff could only imagine the scale of the riots which would erupt when the citizens of Dark Space realized that he had surrendered to the Sythians.

Just five minutes later Lieutenant Hanz turned to look up at Hoff and nodded. "Connection established with the Sythian command ship," he said. "Transmitting in three . . . two . . ."

The main viewport shimmered and then stars and space were replaced with the pale gray face of High Lord Shondar. The Sythian bared his sharp, glistening black teeth in an ugly imitation of a smile. "I see your fleet leaving the Gorz. Doesss this mean we have a deal?" Shondar hissed.

"It does," Hoff replied. Everyone on the bridge abruptly stopped what they were doing and turned to stare at their leader with looks ranging the gamut from astonishment to outrage. Deck Commander Akra rose to her feet and turned to glower at him, but to her credit she said nothing.

Shondar's ugly smile grew so wide that his sallow cheeks nearly disappeared. "You are wise, Admiral."

"I have terms. My people will not be harmed."

Shondar blinked his glowing white eyes. "We agree not to harm them. What else?"

"You will allow us to maintain our sovereignty."

Shondar made a sissing sound which was probably laughter. "Too much. No."

"Fine." Hoff had known that was a long shot. "It is enough if you agree not to harm us."

"I like a reasonable human."

"Go get your slaves. We will not stop you."

"Nor could you. We sssee you ssoon," Shondar hissed.

With that, the transmission ended, and Hoff turned from the viewscreen to answer his crew's collective outrage and fear. He couldn't tell them his real plan. In fact, he couldn't even allow himself to remember it, and soon he wouldn't be able to. It was not safe for them to know there was still hope, so Hoff chose to reinforce the appearance that there was none.

"How could you, sir?" Commander Akra demanded, her pale blue eyes searching his face with the stubborn hope that perhaps he had just lied to the Sythians.

Hoff met her searching gaze. "In war, it is not wise to give a superior foe an excuse to kill you. You beg him for mercy and hope you find some." Turning from her to address the rest of his crew, he said, "We are all at the Sythians' mercy, as we have been since they came to our galaxy. I understand if you hate me for this, but the chance of survival is always better than the certainty of defeat. Lieutenant Hanz, set condition green, and tell all of our forces to stand down."

"Yes—" The comm officer was interrupted before he could finish acknowledging the order. "Incoming transmission! It's from the Sythians."

"Sir!" The gravidar officer called out. "The Gors have just disappeared from our scopes. They've cloaked!"

Hoff had to suppress the urge to smile. "Put the Sythians back on screen, Lieutenant."

The main viewport shimmered once more, and Shondar was back. "What are you doing, human? You said we could have the Gors."

Hoff shook his head. "I said we wouldn't stop you from going to get them."

"Then why are they cloaking?"

"To hide from you, I would assume."

Shondar hissed. "You warned them!"

"Anyone with one iota of sense could see your intentions toward them—and ours for that matter, when we left them all alone. But I don't see what your problem is, Shondar. Why don't you just use your own Gors to locate them for you?"

Shondar's glowing white eyes narrowed. "We do not have Gors."

"Oh, yes ..." Hoff feigned a look of dismay. "It's unfortunate you decided to kill *all* of your slaves."

"Yesss," Shondar hissed. "Very unfortunate. Have your fleet arrest its momentum and prepare for boarding."

Hoff nodded and bowed his head. "Of course. It will be done, My Lord."

The transmission ended, and they saw stars and space once more. "Lieutenant Hanz," Hoff began in a worlds-weary voice. "Have our ships stop where they are and lower their shields." He turned and started from the bridge. "If anyone needs me, I'll be in my quarters."

"Yes, sir ..." Hanz replied in a small voice.

Deck Commander Akra caught up to him just as the doors of the auxiliary bridge swished open for him. She caught him by the arm and spun him to face her. He studied her usually kind honey-brown features, now twisted up in contempt, and met her accusing eyes with a defeated look. "Yes, Commander?"

"You are a fool and a coward," she spat.

Hoff nodded, pretending to accept that. Without offering so much as a word in his defense, he continued on his way, heading not for his quarters, but for the med bay where Doctor Elder was standing by with a mind probe to alter his memories. When he judged that he was out of earshot of the commander, Hoff placed a hand to his ear and put a comm call through to his wife.

She answered a moment later. "Hoff, what's going on? I heard we surrendered; please tell me that's not true...."

"Destra, I'll explain everything in a minute," Hoff whispered. "I need you to meet me in the med bay. Ask for Doctor Elder, and explain that I sent you. We don't have much time, so hurry."

"Okay ... what about Atta?"

"Bring her, Des. You're both leaving the *Valiant* before the Sythians get here."

"They're coming aboard?"

"They're already on their way."

"I hope you know what you've done, Hoff."

"So do I, Des. I'll see you soon."

Chapter 10

Destra Heston stood in the med bay, watching as her husband sat down in the probe chair. Her eyes burned with unshed tears. "There has to be another way. This is too dangerous."

Hoff shook his head. "There is no other way, Des."

"Mind probes kill people, Hoff."

"So do Sythians."

"Yes, but . . ." Destra turned to the doctor with a helpless look. "Tell him to stop this!"

The doctor didn't even turn from his probe control console. "What the admiral wants to do is quite safe, and he is right, ma'am. If the Sythians are after what's in his head, the only way to stop them from getting it is to erase what's there or alter it."

"And what happens when they find out you've sent them on a wild rictan hunt?" Destra demanded, rounding angrily on her husband. "They'll kill you."

Hoff shrugged. "I'm going to alter the location of Avilon to a point in the middle of the Devlins' Hand Nebula, halfway between our galaxy and theirs. By the time they get back to report that I gave them the wrong coordinates, help will have arrived from Avilon."

"And if not?"

"Then we are all dead anyway."

"What about Atton? You won't be able to send a rescue for him if something happens. You won't even know where he is anymore!"

"I won't even know about the mission. I'll have to erase any memory of my having sent it in order to prevent the Sythians from seeing through our surrender. But it won't matter whether or not I can send help. If Atton doesn't return, it will be because the immortals refused to let him leave, and that can only mean that they have decided not to help us. In that case, Atton will be the only mortal human in the galaxy who doesn't need helping."

"So let's all leave! Evacuate as many as possible and then run before the Sythians get tired of playing nice with us and finish what they started. From what you've told me, Avilon will be much safer than Dark Space."

"And what happens when we get to Avilon and the Avilonians decide that we're not good enough for them?"

Destra's eyes narrowed sharply. "What do you mean?"

"Immortals don't think like us, Des. If you are not perfect—if you don't fit their mould—then you are not worthy to live among them. If they refuse to send us back where we came from for fear that we could reveal their location to the Sythians, and they refuse to let us live among them, then what other option is there?"

"Are you saying they'll execute us?"

He shook his head. "I don't know. Do you really want to find out?"

Destra's hands began to shake and they balled into white-knuckled fists. "You sent Atton there, knowing that he could be in real danger!"

"Atton is in no danger. One of the reasons I sent *him*, rather than someone else, is because the boy is young and innocent enough to adapt to the Avilonians' rules if he has to. He will be fine. At worst he will make a new life for himself there, and I'm sure he will be happy for many thousands of years to come." Hoff reached into his pocket and pulled out a thumb-sized rectangular wafer, a holo card. "Put this somewhere only you can find it."

"What is it?"

"The real location of Avilon." Destra accepted the card with a frown, and Hoff went on, "After this procedure, you'll be the only one besides Atton who knows where it is."

Destra turned to stare at the back of Doctor Elder's head while he prepared the mind probe. "What about him?"

"Yes, and him. I've given Stevon another set of the coordinates, recorded on a micro dot in a suicide tooth. If he's captured before he has a chance to destroy the coordinates, he'll kill himself to keep them hidden."

"*Stevon*, huh? You and the doctor must go way back if you trust him enough to have a copy of Avilon's location."

"He is one of the few besides Donali who knew about me, so yes, I trust him. He will be the only one on board who knows what he did to me, and he'll be the only one who can help me find Avilon if I'm forced to flee. He'll be my lifeline after this procedure."

Destra gave a wry smile and raised her voice to address the doctor, "You won't be tempted to flee to Avilon, Doctor?"

He turned from his console with a smile on his deeply-lined face. Rare magenta eyes stared unblinkingly back at her as he shook his head. "No."

"He's an Etherian," Hoff explained. "That's why I chose him."

"A what?"

"It's an old religion. It means he believes in the Immortals, Etherus, Etheria, the Netherworld ... all of that, but he doesn't believe the Avilonians are the real Immortals. He believes Lifelink implants are a cheap imitation of the immortal soul."

"So ..." Destra shook her head, uncomprehending.

"The immortals in Avilon are strict atheists. They believe religion is a force for evil, not for good, so they would never allow the doctor to join them. To them, he is evil incarnate."

Doctor Elder snorted. "I dedicate my life to healing people and I'm evil incarnate."

Hoff shrugged. "Paradise is only as good as the people who live in it. One way of elevating society is by trimming away all of the low-hanging branches that weigh us down."

"That may be true, but how does religion weigh us down?"

"If you believe in an afterlife where you will live forever in paradise, why bother going to so much trouble to make a paradise here and live forever in it now? That's a lot of work for nothing."

"I suppose ..."

"Moreover, the whole argument behind immortality via implants and clones is that consciousness can be transferred without losing anything in the process. If we have a soul which is our real essence, don't we still lose that when we transfer from one body to another?"

Doctor Elder smiled. "Exactly."

"Then you know where I'm going with this. It's not so much that the Avilonians won't accept you or the other Etherians, Doctor, it's that they know you and others like you will never accept *them,* or their way of life. Even if you do for a time, eventually you will turn against them because of what you believe, and you may even try to destabilize their society in the process. It has happened in the past."

Doctor Elder smiled. "Correct me if I am wrong, but didn't you tell me on the way here that you were one of these immortal clones, and that that is how you know of Avilon?"

"That is correct."

Doctor Elder cocked his head suddenly to one side. "So doesn't it bother you that *you* do not have a soul?"

"It might bother me, if I believed that such a thing exists."

Destra looked on with a frown as they debated spiritual matters. She wasn't sure what she believed, but she was a lot more worried about what the doctor was saying than Hoff. It meant that her husband had long ago made a deal with the Devlin and traded his soul for immortality in this life. Now, she had convinced him to give even that up, to disable his Lifelink implant and become a mortal man once more. That meant that even if there was an afterlife, she wasn't going to see him in it.

"Enough philosophy," Destra said, getting uncomfortable with the conversation.

"Yes," Hoff agreed. "We're running out of time. You may proceed when ready, Doctor."

"Yes, sir."

"Don't do this, Hoff," Destra pleaded one last time, watching as Doctor Elder stood up from the probe console with a wicked looking needle—an implanter.

Hoff met her eyes as the probe was injected into the base of his neck. "Hurry, Des. Take Atta and go to the *Baroness*. They have orders to leave as soon as you're aboard. You'll be running food to the Gors' fleet, supporting them covertly until Atton comes back with reinforcements. I'm going to have the doctor erase my memory of what you are doing and where you are. All I'll know is that you are someplace safe."

Destra bit her lower lip and shook her head. "Aren't you going to say goodbye to Atta? She's in the waiting room outside."

Hoff shook his head. "There's no time, and I don't want her to worry. If she asks, tell her I'm going to get help so we can defeat the Sythians."

Destra hesitated, still chewing her lower lip.

"We're ready to begin, sir," Doctor Elder said, already on his way back to the probe console.

Hoff caught her eye. "Destra, go!"

She snapped into motion, leaning over the chair to drop a quick kiss on her husband's cheek. "I'll be with you in your dreams, Hoff," she whispered beside her ear.

"And I in yours," he replied.

With that, she turned and ran from the room. On her way through the waiting room, she grabbed Atta's hand and pulled her daughter along.

"Ouch!" Atta said, trying to wriggle free. "Where's Daddy?"

"He's busy, sweetheart."

Atta stopped suddenly, just before the double doors of the med bay, causing Destra's arm to snap painfully taut. "I want to see him!" she said.

Destra rounded on her daughter with flashing blue eyes. "We'll see him later. Right now, we have to run, Atta. We have to hurry! Come on."

"What's going on?" Atta asked.

"The Sythians are coming," Destra said without thinking, and promptly winced. She had hoped to spare her daughter from the ugly truth of what was happening.

But the truth worked better than any comforting lie—Atta shut right up, and she didn't try to stop or turn around again.

* * *

Destra watched from the bridge of the *Baroness* as swarms of Sythian shuttle craft poured between the Sythian fleet and the human defenders in Dark Space. Not a shot was fired from either side, making the surrender uncontested. As for the Gors, they were somewhere nearby, no doubt watching the same scene from afar.

"Surreal, isn't it?" Captain Covani said, coming up beside Destra.

She turned to him with a frown. Captain Ekram Covani was a man of forty-something, bald, with a skin as black as a Gor's armor. His piercing tangerine eyes made him look at times more alien than human—his eyes similar to a Gor's—

but Destra knew Covani was one of the few officers left in the fleet that Hoff would entrust his life to. Covani had been in Dark Space since the exodus, but he and Hoff had known each other long before the war had separated them.

Destra replied, "We've spent so long fighting them and now we're just going to give up. It feels like we're reliving the invasion. Like it's the end of everything, and this time there's no escape."

"We have to hold on to hope. The Gors are still out there, waiting for the right time to attack."

Destra nodded.

"Besides that, we have to hold on to the hope that reinforcements will come."

"Hoff told you about that?"

"About your son's mission? Yes, ma'am. He told me that he sent your son to get help from another group of survivors."

Destra's eyes narrowed suspiciously. "Why would he tell you about that?"

"The admiral knew that if he expected my crew and I to wait around, ferrying food and supplies to the Gors, then he had to give us hope. He had to give us a reason to stay. We have our orders. We'll wait here until we can't wait any longer, and if help doesn't come, I've been told we are to rescue as many as we can and flee."

"It won't come to that."

"Well, let's hope not. Our fate is in your son's hands, ma'am."

Destra nodded slowly and she turned back to watch the swarms of Sythian shuttle craft streaming into the *Valiant's* hangars. "Not just ours . . ." she whispered. "The fate of the entire galaxy is depending on him."

"I hope he's up to it."

Dark Space IV: Revenge

I just hope he stays safe, Destra thought.

* * *

Hoff blinked his eyes open and shook his head. Pain stabbed through his brain with the movement, and he winced. "Where . . ." He lifted his head off the pillow to look around. He was in the med bay, lying on a bed in one of the ward rooms. A doctor was sitting at a nearby desk taking notes. Presently, that man turned around, and Hoff found he recognized him. "Doctor Elder, what am I doing here?"

The doctor smiled, and his already bright magenta eyes grew a few shades warmer. "You passed out and hit your head, Admiral. Low blood sugar and a potassium deficiency, it seems. And perhaps, the shock of our surrender."

"Surrender?" Suddenly Hoff remembered, and his eyes flew wide. His memory was hazy, and it felt like he was trapped in a bad dream, but one thing was crystal clear: he had surrendered to the Sythians. "Why . . ." he shook his head again, and it began throbbing mercilessly. "I don't remember why we surrendered."

The Doctor's expression became grim. "Because we are badly outnumbered. We had no choice. The Sythians demanded we give them the Gors so they could bring their slaves to justice, and in exchange they offered to leave us in peace—if we would agree to join them."

Hoff's jaw dropped; he remembered now, but he still

didn't understand. It seemed like death would have been preferable to surrender. "How long have I been out?"

"Less than an hour. We have Sythians coming aboard now. You should be there to greet them if you're feeling up to it."

"Yes . . ." Hoff trailed off. "I probably should. What about the Gors? They're . . ."

"They cloaked. For all we know they're already long gone, fleeing to some other part of the galaxy."

Hoff began nodding slowly. "They must have seen the betrayal coming."

"Indeed," Doctor Elder replied. "Shall I send an escort to take you to the ventral hangar concourse or can you find your way there on your own?"

"Have an honor guard of sentinels meet me there, but make sure they're not armed. I don't want a firefight. It's too late to change our minds about surrendering now."

"Much too late," the doctor agreed.

Hoff swung his legs off the gurney and the doctor helped him down. "Did we set any terms for the surrender?" Hoff asked, now standing on the deck.

"No, sir. It was unconditional—apart from the condition that they agree not to harm us."

"Right." Hoff grimaced. "Why is my memory so poor? I can remember after you tell me the answers, but it's hard to summon those answers for myself."

"Amnesia is not uncommon after a head injury. The answers will come clearer in time."

"Well, thank you, Doctor. I'd better hurry."

"Immortals be with you, sir."

Hoff strode quickly to the entrance of the ward room. He passed his wrist over the scanner and then turned back to the doctor as something else occurred to him. "Do we know what the Sythians want?"

"They said they wanted the Gors, but the Gors left, so you'll have to ask them what else they're after."

"Very well." With that, Hoff hurried out the door and down the corridor to the waiting room. Five minutes later he reached the rail car tunnel that would take him down to the *Valiant's* ventral hangar bays, and ten minutes later he was standing in the hangar concourse, watching through the transpiranium walls as Sythian shuttles landed by the dozens in the port and starboard hangar bays. These were the venture-class hangars, and they were big enough to accommodate over a hundred shuttles each. Hoff found himself wondering at the absence of the *Intrepid* and the *Baroness*, the two venture-class cruisers which should have been docked inside those hangars. He decided that he must have forgotten he'd launched them to deal with the Sythian threat.

Hoff stepped closer to the starboard hangar and squinted out at the bustle of gleaming lavender-hued shuttles. Each one was at least twenty meters long and had the same teardrop shape as all of the larger Sythian vessels.

The stream of shuttles streaking in through the distant, fuzzy blue wall of static shields began to slow down, and they began opening up like mechanical flowers, their sides peeling away to form ramps in three different directions at once. Hordes of troops in glossy black armor with glowing red optics poured out onto the deck—Gors. Hoff's brow furrowed and a stab of adrenaline sent his heart pounding. The Gors had tricked them! They'd been on the Sythians' side all along! They were . . .

His thoughts trailed off as he saw a few squads of the

black-armored troops form up and march toward him. He realized as they drew near that they were far too small to be Gors. The troopers were all human-sized. Now that he thought about it, he remembered the scans they'd taken from the Sythian fleet, scans which had revealed human crews on board the Sythian warships. Somehow they had recycled thousands of Gor-sized suits of armor into new, human-sized suits in just over a month.

Hoff heard a nearby clatter of armor and the sound of heavy boots clanking toward him from the direction of the rail car he'd arrived on. He whirled around to see a full platoon of sentinels, sans plasma rifles, marching toward him in their matte gray armor—the honor guard he'd requested. All sixteen troopers stopped as one and the platoon leader stepped forward to offer a salute. "Sir," he said.

Hoff nodded and his eyes went to the man's upper arm to read his rank insignia. Four bronze chevrons and three bars emblazoned on the black shield of the sentinels marked him as a Master Sergeant. "Are you ready to greet our conquerors, Sergeant?" Hoff asked.

"Ready as we'll ever be, sir."

"Let's go." Hoff turned and led his men toward the broad double doors leading from the concourse to the port ventral hangar. "This is it," Hoff said, stepping to one side of the doors and raising his wrist to wave his imbedded identichip in front of the door scanner.

The doors swished open, revealing what seemed like an endless horde of troops wearing identical glossy black armor, their helmets glowing with countless pairs of blood red optics. Hoff heard a sharp hiss and his eyes were drawn to the front of the crowd to find the only being who stood out from the sea of identical black helmets—a human-sized creature in matching black armor, but with his helmet off and tucked under one arm. His breastplate was marked on one side with glowing bars and symbols which were the alien's rank insignia, but his features were what caught Hoff's attention. His skin was translucent but for a pattern of lavender-colored freckles on his gaunt cheeks. The sides of his neck were slashed with gills, and the top of his bald head was crowned with a bony cranial ridge. Large, wide eyes the color of dark sapphire found Hoff's face, and the creature's rubbery lips stretched in a facsimile of a human smile.

"High Lord Kaon," Hoff said. "You're back. I was beginning to worry you didn't make it to a new body."

Kaon warbled something in return, and Hoff waited to hear the translation. When it didn't come, he realized he wasn't wearing a translator. *Must have lost it when I passed out,* Hoff thought. He was about to turn and ask the platoon behind him if any of them had a translator he could borrow, but Kaon circumvented him by having one of his troopers step forward to translate.

"The Mighty Kaon ignores your sarcastic remark. He asks what you think of his new army," the trooper said in a distinctly human voice.

"Tell him it is impressive and ask him what he intends to do with it now that we have surrendered. It would seem he no longer needs an army."

"He understands you," the human replied, followed by more warbling from Kaon. "Our Lord Kaon says that he plans to use us to take control of his new fleet—your fleet. It is to be his recompense for the fleet you took from him."

"Yes . . ." Hoff frowned. "My apologies. I'm sure you can still find some fragments of your command ship out there somewhere. . . . enough for a souvenir at least."

Warble.

"You are smug," the human translator standing beside Kaon replied, followed by more warbling. "It is not fitting for slaves to speak to their masters that way, but in time your people learn."

Hoff's eyes narrowed sharply. "You agreed to leave us in peace, Kaon. You agreed not to harm us."

Kaon warbled something and his translator said, "That is correct, you are not to be harmed, but the lords said nothing about your people's freedom."

Hoff gritted his teeth and turned to yell at the human translator, "My people? You *are* my people, you frekking skriff!"

"I am, and we *are*, servants of the lords, no less and no more."

Warble.

The translator turned to look at his Sythian lord and passed on Kaon's next message. "Kaon asks if you remember how you tortured him."

Hoff felt a flutter of trepidation. "Why?"

Warble.

"He says now you are to know his pain. Justice is found in reciprocity."

"I believe that's revenge you're thinking of," Hoff replied.

Kaon smiled his rubbery smile once more and replied with more warbling. The translator passed on his message a moment later, "Revenge, yesss ... why do you think I return?"

WHERE THE DARKNESS FINDS US

Chapter 11

Four days later...

The door swished open to reveal Commander Lenon Donali; the glowing red iris of his artificial eye dimmed and then brightened again as he blinked. "You've made your decision?"

"I have," Atton replied slowly.

"Well, come on in." The commander left the door open and retreated to his desk. "Can I get you a drink?" he asked, his hands landing on a crystal decanter with a fiery red spirit inside.

Atton stepped into Donali's office and eyed the decanter,

wondering at its contents. *Some type of Aubrelian Brandy perhaps.* "No, sir. We're about to revert to real space, and I need to be alert and ready to launch."

"Ah, well, that is true ..." Commander Donali said, leaving the decanter where it was. By declining the drink, Atton had practically given Donali his answer already. "A glass of water instead?" the commander asked as he rounded his desk and took a seat behind it.

"I'm fine, sir. This won't take long."

"I see."

"I've given your offer a lot of thought." Atton stepped up to the pair of chairs in front of Commander Donali's desk, but made no move to sit in one of them. "In a lot of ways sending you to Avilon instead of me makes sense."

His senior officer raised an eyebrow. "But ..."

"But, Admiral Heston is the only one who has ever been to Avilon, and it occurs to me that although I am young and inexperienced, and I *am* a mortal, as opposed to you, a human with a Lifelink implant ..."

"Go on."

"In spite of that, it occurs to me that the admiral must have had a good reason for sending me. I cannot second-guess his orders or his decision without knowing his reasoning."

"I see," the commander said again. "That's your final decision, then?"

Atton nodded. "It is."

Donali said nothing, the seconds ticking by until the silence became uncomfortable.

"I'm sorry if you are disappointed by my decision, sir."

The commander gave a broad smile, but it never reached his eyes. "Not at all. I admire your conviction. Were I in your shoes, I would feel considerably less sure about my orders."

Atton frowned. "I'm *not* sure, but I have made my decision."

"So it would seem. Well, that will be all, Mr. Ortane. As you mentioned, we are about to revert to real space, and you had better be ready and waiting on the flight deck when we arrive."

"Yes, sir," Atton said, snapping to attention and offering a brisk salute. He left the commander's office with a furrowed brow. Donali definitely hadn't been pleased to hear his decision. Clearly he thought he was the better choice to send to Avilon, but they had their orders and they had to follow them. It was tantamount to treason if they didn't. Commander Donali would just have to be content with his role as head of the extraction team.

Atton switched his focus to the mission ahead. He'd been preparing for it during their week-long journey through SLS, and now it was almost time for him to leave the *Intrepid*—and his squadron—behind. That meant he wouldn't see either Ceyla or Gina again—at least not for a while, but perhaps never. If the Avilonians wouldn't let him leave, and Donali couldn't effect a rescue, Atton would be trapped there.

For that reason, Atton had kept to himself as much as possible over the last week. He wasn't very popular with his squadron, anyway. As for Gina and Ceyla, they had seemed hurt by his sudden withdrawal from all things social, but now they had formed something of a friendship with each other. He suspected their mutual dislike for him was what they had in common. For her part, Gina had hooked up with the resident smart mouth of the squadron, Horace "Hawkeye" Perkins. Atton was certain she'd done that just to slight him.

He sighed and shook his head as he stepped inside a lift

tube and rode it down to the flight deck. He needed to have his mind clear and free of distractions if he hoped to succeed in his mission. Humanity was depending on him; romance could wait. Atton smiled bitterly. That had been his philosophy for the last three years, ever since he'd agreed to take over from his adoptive father and impersonate the almost 100-year-old Supreme Overlord of the Imperium. Now, no longer wearing the holoskin which had made him old and unattractive to women, he had found a new reason not to get involved with anyone.

Convenient . . .

Atton scowled at the smug tone of that inner voice. It might be a convenient excuse, but it was also true. The lift tube opened and his comm piece buzzed. *Incoming call from Captain Caldin.* Atton reached up to answer it as he stepped out of the lift.

"Commander," Caldin said. "We're reverting to real space in five minutes. I see you're not in the briefing room. What are you doing?"

"I'm on my way to the hangar, Captain."

"Ahead of your squadron? Explain yourself."

"I was told that the admiral had informed you of my mission."

"Not the details of it, no."

"But you know that I'm supposed to depart the *Intrepid* at some point."

"Yes."

"That time has come, Captain."

"What about your squadron?"

"My XO is already in the ready room delivering the briefing that I was meant to give."

Captain Caldin sighed on her end of the comm. "All right

then. Immortals be with you, Commander Ortane."

Atton smiled at the irony. "May they be with us all."

* * *

Hoff hung from the torture rack, sweat dripping from his face and landing in a puddle at his feet. His chest was heaving, desperate for air. He felt simultaneously alive and dead, his head swimming, his nerve endings throbbing and stabbing with echoes of the pain the Sythians were inflicting. They'd rigged him up to a machine which could simulate any degree of pain in any or all parts of his body. Kaon told him he was lucky the pain was only simulated. He would be able to walk away from it without a scratch—no scars, no missing digits or limbs.

"I ask you again, Hoff," Kaon said, his warbles converted into human speech by the universal translator they'd stuck in his ear. "Where is Avilon?"

Hoff shook his head. Fat droplets of sweat broke free from where they clung on his eyebrows, chin, and the tip of his nose. He looked around to distract himself from the echoes of the pain Kaon had just inflicted. He was aboard a Sythian ship. The dim lighting and the glossy black walls and floor gave it away.

"You ignore me," Kaon said. "I see that you require more convincing." With that, he flicked a switch on the torture rack's control panel, and waves of searing, white-hot pain sparked through Hoff's legs. Simulated flames made him believe that they were actually on fire. He could even hear the flames crackling and smell the burnt meat. Hoff gritted his teeth and squinted his eyes shut. It wasn't real, just part of the simulation. Or perhaps the Sythians had grown tired of their simulator and resorted to inflicting real pain. Would it matter if they did? At least with real pain there was always the chance that the injuries inflicted could kill him.

Why had he surrendered? *Why*, if he'd known the Sythians were after the location of Avilon? How could he have been so stupid! He'd walked right into their trap!

"I offer my congratulations. Your endurance improves. Now you are able to handle a level five simulation. Perhaps you would like to try a level six?"

Kaon flicked another switch and Hoff's mouth opened in a soundless scream. Conscious thought evaporated. Now the flames were cooking his entire body at once. He couldn't see through the acrid smoke, or even breathe. His eyes felt like they were about to explode.

Then the pain eased somewhat and he could think again.

"Where is Avilon?" Kaon repeated.

Hoff's mouth was dry and he had an excruciating headache which made it difficult to think let alone speak, but he managed to get out a strangled whisper, "Go frek yourself."

"I am physically incapable of copulating with myself."

Hoff saw movement out of the corner of his eye which he thought might have been Kaon walking up next to him, but he didn't have the energy to lift his head and check. Then the alien warbled something close beside his ear. Hoff felt his head was about to explode. He irrationally wished it would and that the shrapnel would kill Kaon.

"You know, Hoff," Kaon went on. "Your stubborn resistance is ultimately futile. We know about the mission you sent to Avilon to get reinforcements."

The relentless pounding in Hoff's head intensified as he struggled to understand what he was hearing. "What mission?" he demanded.

"Feign ignorance, human, but you are too late. Your very own Commander Lenon Donali is on that mission, and despite your best efforts to prove he is on your side, he is in fact a loyal slave. Soon he finds Avilon and tells us where it is, whether you reveal the location to us or not."

"What mission?" Hoff screamed, pouring all of his residual agony into that question. The Sythians were messing with him. Donali wasn't a traitor. There was no mission to Avilon!

"Very well," Kaon replied. "The longer you deny it, the longer you must suffer."

Hoff heard Kaon walk away, back to the control panel of the torture rack. "It is time for you to try a level seven simulation."

Kaon flicked a switch, and the agony returned, but this time with blinding force. Hoff literally couldn't see through the pain. All he saw were streaks of light and color. His nose stopped registering smells, his ears picked up nothing but a high-pitched squeal of white noise. There was no room left in his consciousness for anything but the pain.

His heart beat so hard in his chest that it should have stopped, but it couldn't. The torture rack was designed to keep a subject alive. Hoff's heart had been supercharged with chemicals, nanites, and drugs, and the same went for his brain. No heart attack, stroke, or aneurism would end this torment, which meant the pain would go on forever.

Hoff began to scream curses at Kaon and all Sythians

everywhere. He couldn't hear what he said, but it was more to distract himself than anything else. When he tired of cursing the Sythians, he switched to railing against humanity and the universe in general. Nothing good existed in the universe. A place with so much pain could never be good. It was a cursed place. Nothing mattered. Nothing was important anymore! All that mattered was ending the pain. Hoff screamed something else, and this time the fabric of his universe was torn, and his torment eased. The eternal ringing in his ears quieted enough that he could hear what he was screaming—"Thstop! I'll thalk! Thstop it!"

Belatedly he realized that the pain had stopped, but he was still left shuddering with the residual effects. His wrists and ankles felt like they were on fire, and when he opened one bleary eye to look, he saw why. The metal manacles which bound him to the torture wrack had torn bloody furrows in his skin.

He tried to take a deep breath, but his lungs only filled halfway with air before coughing up blood. It splattered to the deck, landing in a puddle of his own filth which had accumulated at his feet. Hoff tasted the warm tang of blood welling up in his mouth, and he spat it out on the deck. That was when he noticed that his tongue was flopping about strangely in his mouth. He'd bitten straight through it in several different places, and the tip seemed to be missing altogether.

"I am listening, Hoff," Kaon said, sounding like he was a great distance away.

So Hoff told them. His shredded tongue didn't make it easy to get the coordinates right, but the Sythians let him down off the rack and handed him a stylus and a digital pad to write on. When he was done, he fell out of the chair where they'd seated him, and lay on the glossy black deck in a tangle of heavy limbs. It felt like every bone in his body had been broken. He tried to move, but his muscles were too weak. A fierce determination to rise to his feet bubbled up inside of him. He wanted to show the Sythians that they hadn't broken him. Miraculously, his determination overcame the pain and exhaustion, and he stumbled to his feet.

No sooner had he regained his footing than something cold and wet splashed across his face. He woke up with a gasp, his arms and legs flailing to fight some unseen assailant. That was when he realized that he hadn't risen to his feet after all—he'd passed out.

Warble.

"Get up, Hoff," the translator in his ear ordered.

Hoff saw Kaon standing over him, his translucent skin seeming to glow in the low light of the Sythian warship. The alien's wide blue eyes caught stray light from the room, reflecting the glossy black walls and floor, making them appear like twin pools of endless shadow.

Hoff tried to rise to his feet, but his torn and battered muscles refused to obey, just as they had in his dream. Then a pair of strong hands seized him, carrying him over to a coffin-sized chamber which was leaning at an angle against one wall. Hoff began to struggle and make blubbering noises with his swollen tongue.

Then a hateful warbling reached his ears, followed by the translation, "We are pleased that you choose to cooperate, but now we must verify what you tell us."

Hoff couldn't believe it. He'd been tortured for what felt like an eternity, and now after all of that, they were just going to use some kind of mind probe on him to find the location of Avilon for themselves anyway. "Ffwhy?" he spluttered, spraying blood into the coffin.

Kaon answered, "Why torture you? I tell you the answer already—I come here for revenge."

* * *

Captain Caldin watched the reversion timer on the captain's table until it reached ten seconds. "Here's hoping we didn't come all this way for nothing," Caldin said.

"Indeed," Master Commander Donali replied from beside her.

"Engineering, have you double-checked our cloaking shield?" Caldin asked, her eyes finding the back of Deck Commander Cobrale Delayn's head. His short gray hair and sickly-pale skin made him easy to pick out, even at a distance.

"Yes, ma'am," Delayn replied.

The reversion timer reached five seconds and the countdown became audible, booming out from the bridge speakers. Caldin's gaze turned to the fore to watch the bright star lines and streaks of SLS. "Three, two, one . . ."

The streaks of light vanished, abruptly replaced with stars and space. Dead ahead was Ikara, the planet where Hoff had once based his refugee enclave. The world was brown, streaked with bright blue and dotted with patches of muddy red. Due to a local species of algae the red patches were actually lakes and seas, while the blue was the planet's native vegetation. The world wasn't exactly hospitable, but it was temperate and the air was breathable, so there was a chance that some had survived the Sythian attack and fled into the Ikaran jungles. This was the alleged reason for their journey—to look for survivors—but Caldin knew the real reason was to give Commander Ortane a chance to do whatever it was the admiral had sent him out here to do. All she knew was that his mission was critical to humanity's fight against the Sythians. She didn't know why, or what that mission entailed, but she didn't have to. She had her orders, and Commander Ortane had his. She would simply have to trust that those orders were the right ones.

"Report!" Caldin called out.

"All systems green," Donali replied right beside her ear as he checked the captain's table. "Jump successful."

"Gravidar, what do we have out there?"

"Debris, ma'am. Lots of debris."

Caldin frowned. "Human or alien?"

"Both."

The captain turned to her temporary XO, Master Commander Donali, "Have your Gors checked the area for cloaked ships?"

"Give me a moment to contact them," Donali replied.

Caldin waited while Donali used his comm piece to make a call to the troop bay where his Gors were staying. A few minutes later he turned back to Caldin and shook his head. "All clear."

She nodded and turned to her comm officer. "Comms, have both Guardian and Renegade squadrons launch and start grid-searching the planet. Someone must have escaped."

"Yes, ma'am," the comm officer replied.

Caldin turned to watch the grid. Just moments after she'd given the command, she saw Nova Fighters streaming out the back of the *Intrepid,* roaring out the twin launch tubes in wing pairs. Peripherally, she noted another blip appear on gravidar besides those novas, but it flew out the side of the ship rather than the back. That blip was Commander Atton Ortane's transport, the *Emissary.*

"All our Novas are away, Captain," the comm officer said, "as well as one assault recon-class transport with priority clearance."

"Good," Caldin nodded. "Let's—"

"Contact! Bearing K-76-43-27 by T-55-01-16."

"Red alert!" Caldin called. The alarm sounded almost immediately, followed by the lights on the bridge dimming to a bloody red. "Recall our fighters. Helm come about and set course 180 degrees from enemy contact's heading. Throttle to 100%."

"Yes, ma'am."

Caldin whirled on Donali and jabbed a finger in his chest. "Didn't you say we were clear?"

"The Gors told me they cannot sense anyone out there."

"So what's that?" Caldin demanded, jerking a thumb toward the red mass of enemy blips which was appearing on the grid.

"A trap . . ." Donali replied slowly, his real eye widening suddenly.

"More contacts inbound!" Gravidar reported. "Decloaking at K-32-41-26; 10-6-14, and 41-2-89 . . . they're surrounding us, Captain."

"They don't even know where we are! How can they surround us?"

"They can see our fighters," Donali whispered.

Caldin turned back to the captain's table to see it for herself. Red enemy blips were swarming all over the grid at impossibly close range. It was almost as though the Sythians had known they were coming. She watched her Nova Fighters retreating from the enemy, leaving one green blip all alone to face the onslaught—the *Emissary*. *Frek!* Caldin cursed. She couldn't let Commander Ortane be killed. Getting him out here had been the whole purpose of the *Intrepid's* mission.

"Comms, belay those orders—send our fighters back out there. Have them cover that transport."

A scattering of acknowledgements came back from her crew. Donali appeared in her field of view, leaning over the captain's table and staring at the grid. He caught her eye with his real one and gave her a knowing look. "The admiral told you," he whispered.

Caldin sent him a thin smile. "Told me what? I'm just looking after my own, Commander."

"Of course."

"Engineering—on my mark, get ready to de-cloak."

"Yes, ma'am."

"Mark! Engage pulse and beam shields."

The *Intrepid's* icon brightened on the grid, and a few dozen blips began changing their headings in response to the cruiser's appearance.

"Helm, reset our course. Follow the *Emissary* until she jumps to SLS. Weapons—lay down covering fire as soon as they get in range."

"You're going to fight?" Donali asked, looking and sounding astonished. "There are at least 20 battleships out there."

"Yes," Caldin nodded. "I believe there are."

"If just one of them gets in range of us, we're dead."

"Then let's make our deaths count for something. Ruh-kah, Commander."

Donali gave her a blank, disbelieving stare. After a moment he began to nod. "Ruh-kah," he said softly.

Chapter 12

Atton sat behind the *Emissary's* controls, his features awash in the blue glow of the transport's holo displays. Twin engines rumbled through the deck underfoot with a comforting hum. Countless stars sparkled beyond the cockpit canopy. Atton flexed his gloved hands on the flight yoke and began slewing his ship to port by applying a bit of pressure to the left rudder pedal. He felt nothing from the maneuver, so he dialed the inertial management system down to 98%. Now the transport's acceleration pushed him gently against the back of the pilot's chair. Dead ahead, a blue ring appeared on his HUD, which was his SLS entry waypoint.

Soon—a matter of another two days' journey through SLS—Atton would reach Avilon. It was hard to imagine what the sector would look like. If there were trillions of humans hiding out there as the admiral had said, then it would be teeming with life. Atton tried to picture an immortal city, but it was hard enough to picture a mortal one. The only populous cities in Dark Space were on Karpathia, and even those were ramshackle by comparison with the ones that had existed before the invasion. Back then, Atton had been just seven years old, and he hadn't yet had a chance to see the galaxy.

A sharp tone sounded from the cockpit speakers, pulling Atton rudely from his thoughts, then came a red alert siren, and Atton sat suddenly straighter in his chair.

"What the frek?" he muttered, his eyes flicking over the glowing blue grid rising out of his main holo display. There were dozens of red contacts appearing all around him— Sythian analogs. They'd just run into an enemy fleet. Soon those capital-class warships would begin pouring Shell Fighters into the void, and Atton wasn't stupid enough to think they would ignore him.

He pushed the slider up past the stops and into the red. His afterburners would run out of fuel in a few minutes, but hopefully he'd get up enough speed before then that the Sythians wouldn't be able to keep up. Atton tuned his comm system to listen in on the Guardians' channel. He immediately heard a stream of chatter begin pouring in.

"I've got incoming!"

"Bogeys at five, eight, and two o-clock."

Atton picked out Gina's voice next, "Orders are to return to the *Intrepid*, Guardians."

"We'll never get back to her before they reach us! We're already up to speed."

"Orders are orders, Six. The Captain's planning to run, not fight. Look at those odds."

The chatter quieted as the Guardians took in the seriousness of their situation.

"Roger that, Lead," someone said.

Atton turned down the volume on the comms and studied the grid once more. No Shell Fighters had appeared yet, but he suspected they were cloaked and would remain so until they reached firing range with their targets. Then he saw the *Intrepid* de-cloak in response to the Sythian fleet, and he frowned. Why would the captain de-cloak her ship? The only reason he could think of was that she intended to stay and fight, but the *Intrepid* didn't stand a chance by herself against such superior numbers.

A crackle of static caught Atton's attention, followed by: " . . . new orders. We are to . . ." He turned up the volume and heard, " . . . the *Emissary* at all costs. Repeat, protect the *Emissary* at all costs."

Atton frowned and shook his head. That was him. And that was why the *Intrepid* was sticking around to fight. The captain was risking everything to give him a chance to get to Avilon. He was about to key his comms to tell mission control that he didn't need an escort, when another series of sharp tones sounded from the cockpit speakers, drawing his attention back to the glowing blue grid on the main holo display. A few dozen blips had appeared between him and his SLS entry point. Shell Fighter analogs.

"Frek me," Atton whispered. "I guess I do need an escort." He targeted the nearest enemy fighter and checked his time to target. The nav calculated eight minutes until he reached that fighter, ten until he should reach his SLS entry waypoint. Atton adjusted his trajectory by a few degrees to keep the Sythians guessing, and then he set his throttle to full reverse. He had to start slowing down now if he were going to reach the SLS-safe entry speed limit in time for his jump. If he wasn't flying at 999 m/s or less when he entered SLS, his ship would be torn apart by the gravitational forces.

In the next instant his comm buzzed with a direct message from Guardian One.

"Iceman, what the frek? My sensors show you slowing down."

"I have a jump plotted at ten klicks out, Tuner," Atton said, using Gina's call sign.

"That's lovely. I don't suppose you noticed the red cloud of krak headed your way?"

"I see it."

"So you thought you'd slow to a crawl and make it easier for them to tag you?"

"The jump is our priority. Once I'm away, you can bug out, too. Until then, we're all stuck. Follow your orders and I'll follow mine."

Gina clicked her comm to acknowledge that, and Atton went back to focusing on the task at hand. She was right. It made no sense for him to slow down, but keeping his speed up would only delay his jump, and time was critical. If he delayed the *Intrepid* unnecessarily, the cruiser would be obliterated by those enemy battleships. She couldn't jump away until he did. So somehow he had to stick it out, dodging Sythian missiles and lasers until he could jump to SLS. *No problem*, Atton thought, eyeing the approaching wall of enemy fighters, now only six klicks away.

He thumbed over to Hailfire missiles and began lining up

the nearest Shell in his targeting reticle. Suddenly a loud roar thundered through his SISS (sound in space simulator). He turned to look out the side of his canopy just in time to see a pair of Nova Fighters go rocketing past him to greet the enemy fighter wave. That pair was followed by another, and then another, and then nine more wing pairs, until both squadrons of Novas were flying out ahead of him, their triple thruster banks lighting up the space ahead of him like a string of blue festive lights.

As Atton watched, missiles began streaking out from those Novas, followed by stuttering red lines of lasers. Explosions flashed in the distance as Shell Fighters flew apart, and then Sythian Pirakla missiles streaked out from the enemy fighters—dozens of spinning purple stars tracking toward the approaching line of Novas. The Novas held their course for just a second before they broke formation, jinking and juking in a dozen different directions to get away from the enemy missiles.

A pair of purple stars collided with Nova Fighters, and space lit up with blinding starbursts of light as their dymium reactors went critical.

Now Atton was alone, flying at the enemy fighter wave. Streams of bright purple pulse lasers flickered out toward him, scoring a few hits on his shields and provoking sharp hissing noises from the SISS.

Atton passed his targeting reticle over the nearest enemy fighter, waiting until the *beeping* tones of an acquiring target lock became a solid tone and the reticle flickered red. He pulled the trigger twice in quick succession and two Hailfire missiles roared out on hot orange contrails. Then the Sythians replied with six warheads of their own. Missile lock alarms screamed in Atton's ears. He used his command control implant to turn down the volume with a thought. As he watched the approaching missiles, he noted that these missiles didn't look like spinning purple stars, they looked like glowing blue orbs. *Some new weapons tech?* He wondered. He hoped the strategy for dealing with them was still the same. Holding the flight yoke steady, he hovered his feet over the rudder pedals, waiting until the last minute to juke away. The missiles reached 500 meters, and Atton depressed the right rudder pedal fully and rolled to the left. Three of the six missiles sailed by overhead, only narrowly missing him.

The next three slammed into the topside of his ship. The *Emissary* shuddered with the impacts. Deafening booms sounded across the SISS, followed by a warning from his ship's computer: "Shields depleted."

Frek! Atton thought.

Then the threat detection system screamed a warning and out of nowhere a pair of glowing blue orbs appeared on his six. Atton tried to evade but the controls felt sluggish, as if the maneuvering jets and thrust control nozzles had jammed. This time all of the missiles stayed on target. They arced straight in toward him. . . .

Atton winced and then came a deafening roar from the SISS. Abruptly that sound ceased as all the lights and displays in the cockpit flickered out, leaving him in utter darkness. He tried moving the stick, but nothing happened. He tried flicking the ignition switch to re-initiate the transport's reactor, but still nothing.

The *Emissary* was derelict. He should have been dead. His shields had been depleted and then they'd hit him with yet another wave of missiles, but instead of his ship being atomized, it had simply lost power. Atton frowned and shook his head. It must have something to do with the new weapons they'd fired at him. Somehow those missiles had disabled his ship without causing severe damage. But why? And why had no one ever seen that technology before?

Then, suddenly, he had the answer. The Sythians were trying to capture him, not kill him. No one had ever seen such technology from the Sythians before because they'd never been interested in capturing humans—until now. *Until they began making slaves of us for their fleets.* Atton shuddered at the thought. They'd come all this way just to suffer the same fate as the refugees in the Enclave.

No one was going to get to Avilon now.

* * *

Why isn't he moving? Caldin wondered, her heart beating frenetically in her chest. The *Emissary* had stopped cold, which of course was relative, because the ship's momentum remained the same. The difference was, the ship wasn't maneuvering, nor was it accelerating or decelerating, and its icon had gone dark on the grid.

"Gravidar! Get me a pulse scan on the *Emissary*. I want to know what's wrong with it."

"Already ahead of you, ma'am. She's drifting without power."

"Not even emergency backups?"

"Not even that."

"The frek . . . ?" Caldin wondered aloud.

"We registered a strange spike from her reactor just before she shut down, ma'am. If I had to guess it must have had something to do with those new weapons we saw."

New tech was the last thing anyone wanted to see from the Sythians. "Okay, so they disabled it. Why?"

Master Commander Donali shrugged and offered a suggestion. "Perhaps because the Sythians are now using human slaves to crew their ships?"

A few gasps rose from the crew, and Caldin turned to her XO with a frown. "That's not common knowledge, Donali, and I'd appreciate if you kept it to yourself."

"Yes, ma'am. What I meant to say is that they must be trying to capture more of us to turn into crew for their fleets."

"Again, classified information, but . . ." Caldin considered that for a moment; then her eyes narrowed and she shook her head. "No, that's not it. They've killed three Nova pilots so far," she said, pointing to the grid where the *Intrepid's* Nova squadrons were embroiled in a dogfight with at least twice as many Shell Fighters.

"Then I don't know."

"I'll tell you what I know," Caldin said. "They want the *Emissary* alive and to the netherworld with the rest of us. Whatever the reason for that, we can't let them have what they want. Helm, set course for that transport; bring us alongside. Comms—tell the hangar bay operators to stand by for a grav lock on her."

"Yes, ma'am," they chorused.

"What's our ETA to the *Emissary*?"

"Two minutes, ma'am."

"Good. Start spooling for a jump."

"Coordinates?"

"Dead ahead, two light years. That should give us a good lead on any pursuit."

"Dead ahead, ma'am? We don't know what's out there."

"No, we don't, but we can't stay here, and we don't have time to turn around and head for known space, so we stay the course and hope we don't run into anything."

"Yes, ma'am . . ."

"Gravidar! How close are those battleships?"

"We've got three angling for a flank attack, port and starboard. The nearest will be in firing range in three and a half minutes."

"And the other two?"

"Approximately five and six minutes, ma'am."

Caldin grimaced. By her estimation they would have to survive a barrage from at least one Sythian battleship for two full minutes—and that was just the time it would take for their SLS drives to spool. "Comms, have our Novas get back on board, ASAP. Renegades first, then Guardians. They have until the *Emissary* is on board. If they don't make it in that time, we can't wait."

"Yes, Captain."

Her XO sent her a worried glance from the captain's table. "Those battleships are much stronger than us. We should leave the *Emissary* and get out now while we still can."

Caldin's eyes narrowed thoughtfully. "And let the Sythians have what they want?"

He shrugged. "It seems the better option."

"How much did the admiral tell you about Commander Ortane's mission?"

"Enough to know it is important."

"Critical to our survival as a species, is what he told me,"

Caldin replied. "Knowing that, how can we forfeit that which is critical to our survival in order to survive? The logic runs back on itself."

"Ma'am..."

"I've made my decision, Commander. Let's hope that if they're so desperate to have the *Emissary* intact, then they won't risk firing on us with live weapons when we're right alongside her."

"Yes, ma'am."

Chapter 13

Cold and still—trapped in the dark—Atton's transport drifted on without power, direction or purpose. The infinite sprawl of stars shone like a million tiny flecks of quartz glinting in the sun against a blacktop as dark as death. Atton tried to make sense of the patterns woven by those pinpricks of light, just as a more distant part of his brain tried to make sense of what was happening.

Sythians had been waiting for them at the reversion point, meaning that either they were extraordinarily lucky, or they'd known the *Intrepid* was coming. The latter possibility made the most sense given the vastness of space, but even if there was some type of Sythian agent in their midst, when would he or she have had the chance to send a message to the Sythians? And how?

Human comms were limited to the speed of light unless there was a jump gate with an open wormhole nearby. The Gors they had on board couldn't have sent the message telepathically, since even they couldn't send a message when a ship was travelling through SLS, and the *Intrepid* had been travelling through SLS for the past week.

Except . . .

About three hours ago the *Intrepid* had stopped to navigate around a pulsar. At the time, however, they had still been more than 10 light years away from their reversion point, and it was widely known that the Gors' telepathy had a limited range of just under 10 light years. That meant their spy wasn't a Gor.

Just then a pair of Novas raced by Atton's cockpit, their triple thrusters burning up the void with bright blue tongues of fire as they chased a quartet of Shell Fighters. The Novas spat blinding streams of red dymium lasers at one of the Shells, scoring a few dozen hits in quick succession. Then a sudden flash of light ripped the enemy fighter apart.

Atton's hands flexed into fists on the transport's lifeless flight yoke. He was itching to join his squadron in the battle, but powerless to do so. The stars winked at him, dragging slowly by his cockpit with maddening serenity. Frustrated, he flicked the transport's ignition switch back and forth a few times, just in case the *Emissary* still had a spark of life in her.

Nothing.

"Frek it!" Atton released the flight yoke and pounded it with a fist.

Unable to do anything useful, he returned to wondering who was responsible for this mess. If they had a traitor on board, and that traitor wasn't a Gor, then who was it?

Sythians also possessed faster than light, near-instantaneous telepathy, and for whatever reason, theirs was not limited to the 10-light-year radius of the Gors'. That meant their traitor could be a Sythian, but the *Intrepid* was fitted with displacement sensors that would have detected a cloaked Sythian onboard by now, so he would have to be hiding in plain sight.

A human agent . . . Atton realized, his green eyes widening to twice their normal aperture.

Suddenly, something jerked the *Emissary* violently to starboard. The seat restraints dug into his shoulders and chest, making it hard for him to breathe. Atton gritted his teeth, waiting for the sensation to pass, but if anything the inertial pressure increased. With all the *Emissary's* systems offline, even the inertial management system and artificial gravity wasn't functioning.

What the frek is going on . . . ? Atton wondered. Had he been hit by something? *No,* he decided. If he'd been hit by something, the inertial tug would have eased after the initial impact. The fact that it hadn't meant something was accelerating the *Emissary* with a constant force. His mind supplied a likely reason for that: a grav gun must have seized his ship. The Sythians had come to claim their prize and turn him into another mindless soldier for their fleet.

But there was something in that explanation which didn't make sense. Why disable him and not the squadrons of Novas that had rallied out? Atton had watched two Novas blown to pieces with live warheads before the enemy had fired so much as a shot against him. Why pick on his transport?

The obvious answer was that they knew something about his mission, but that was impossible. No one knew about his mission besides the admiral.

And Donali.

Atton's eyes narrowed to slits. He remembered the commander's insistence that he take Atton's place and his eyes flew wide. "You motherfrekker . . ." He gritted out against the g-force. No wonder Donali had wanted to take over his mission. *Well, you got what you wanted,* he thought. Soon the Sythians would be able to interrogate him for the location of Avilon.

With a monumental effort, Atton managed to turn his head against the naked g-force of the grav beam that had seized his ship. He stared out the starboard side of the cockpit . . .

And hope surged in his chest. Rather than see a Sythian warship or fighter pulling him along behind it, he saw the rugged lines of the *Intrepid* and the welcoming blue glow of her hangar bay growing steadily closer as she guided him in.

Atton would have grinned in triumph were it not for the *Intrepid's* troubled state. Shell Fighters swarmed her from all sides, firing Pirakla missiles. Those bright purple warheads were slamming into the top and port sides of the ship in a continuous stream, peppering her hull with explosions. The *Intrepid* fired back with red dymium pulse lasers, ripper cannons, and Hailfire missiles, nailing Shells by the dozen and lighting space on fire with their explosions, but it wasn't good enough. Dozens more were streaming in to take their place, and the few Novas he could pick out of the chaos were stretched mighty thin.

At this rate, the *Intrepid* would be torn apart before they could even get the *Emissary* on board, and the Sythians would simply pluck him out of the wreckage.

Atton gritted his teeth and silently cursed Donali for his treachery. If only his comms were working, he could at least warn the *Intrepid* about the traitor in their midst, but with all his systems mysteriously disabled he couldn't even initiate a self-destruct sequence to keep the Sythians from getting to him.

Atton decided that if it came to it, he'd shoot himself before they captured him. Better that than to doom the last safe refuge humanity had to yet another Sythian invasion.

* * *

"Augment our port shield arrays!" Caldin screamed over the hiss and roar of Sythian missiles exploding against their hull. "And turn down the volume on the SISS!"

Immediately the roar of explosions faded into the background.

"Ma'am, we're venting atmosphere on decks fourteen, six, and eight!" engineering reported.

"Seal them off!"

"We still have crew in those areas."

"They know the drill. We'll get them out later, but if they're not already suited up, there's nothing we can do for them."

"Yes, ma'am."

"Helm, how long until our drives are spooled?"

"Three more minutes, ma'am."

Caldin shook her head. "Another one and a half minutes until those battleships are in range." She turned to watch on the captain's table as the *Emissary* sped toward them. The pair of numbers beside the *Emissary's* gravidar icon put her range at just over three klicks and her time to reach the *Intrepid* at 20 seconds, but that time was wrong. The hangar bay controllers would have to start slowing the *Emissary's* approach if they expected to get Commander Ortane back alive.

"Comms, please remind our grav gun operators that the *Emissary* has no power, which means her IMS is not functioning. They'll have to keep acceleration and deceleration vectors below 10 g's if we want to get our pilot back in one piece."

"Yes, ma'am. I'll warn them."

The deck shuddered underfoot and damage alarms sounded. "Engineering! What was that?"

"I don't know ... give me a second to calibrate damage sensors ..."

"It's one of the battleships," Donali replied, pointing to the grid. "They're in range already."

"Frek," Caldin hissed, watching as warheads ten and twenty times the size and explosive power of those which Shell Fighters carried spiraled toward the *Intrepid* from the nearest Sythian battleship.

"One minute till we're spooled for SLS," the helm reported.

Another explosion rumbled underfoot.

"Are all of our Novas on board?" Caldin yelled.

"No, ma'am! The Renegades are, but the Guardians are

just coming about now."

"Tell them to hurry! Comms—can I get an estimate of how much longer before the *Emissary* is on board?"

"Checking . . . our grav gun operators estimate another three minutes, ma'am."

"So we're stuck until then."

"We could punch out now," Donali suggested, pointing to the missiles vectoring in on them. "At least we'll live to fight another day."

Another missile reached them, and the lights on the bridge dimmed as their shield arrays drew extra energy to buffer the impact.

"Hull breaches on decks five and six!"

"Seal 'em off!" Caldin roared. She whirled on Donali, her dark blue eyes wild, her short blonde hair sticking up at odd angles. "What's the point in living, Commander, if you can't live well? And if you can't live well, then by the Immortals you should at least die well!" Caldin rounded on her crew, her gaze finding the weapons officer. "Return fire on that battleship! All batteries! Ruh-kah!"

"Ruh-kah!" the crew roared back, and now the deck was shuddering with their own weapons' fire.

"You can't hope to destroy them. They're five times our size," Donali whispered close beside her ear, like the pessimistic devlin who sometimes sat there.

She ignored him.

Another two missiles from the battleship hit them, and Caldin watched through the viewports as a brief gush of flames blew out a chunk from the top side of the *Intrepid*.

"Shields equalizing at 25%," Delayn reported from engineering.

"Ten seconds until we can jump," the helm said.

"Engage our cloaking shield!" Caldin replied, eyeing the stream of missiles still streaking toward them.

"We have to disengage our energy shields first," Delayn warned. "We won't last long like that."

"We won't last long like this, either! At least if they can't see us, they can't target us!"

"I thought you wanted to die well?" Donali asked.

"I do, which is exactly why we've got to live a little longer."

"Cloaking shield engaged."

"Helm, go evasive! Shake those warheads off our tail."

"We'll end up jumping somewhere else if I don't maintain this heading!"

"Either way we're jumping blind, Lieutenant. Now go evasive before another missile hits us!"

Their view of space began to spin and whirl, and Caldin watched the stream of warheads heading toward them go streaking by with a narrow margin to spare. Her shoulders sagged with relief and she felt a brief wash of light-headedness as the adrenaline pumping through her veins began to wane.

The Sythian battleship stopped firing.

"Good work everyone," Caldin said, leaning on the captain's table for support.

"Captain! The Guardians are asking how they're supposed to get on board if we're cloaked. I can't reply without giving away our location."

"Use a tight beam comm signal; tell them to match approach vectors to the *Emissary*."

"Yes, ma'am."

"The Sythians are going to use the same method to find us," Donali said a moment later.

"I'm sure they will," Caldin replied, "but without accurate target readings, their missiles won't lock on to us. They'll be forced to resort to pulse lasers, and we all know how short-ranged those are. We've just bought ourselves another sixty seconds, which is all we needed."

"Indeed," Donali replied, nodding slowly.

Caldin watched him curiously out of the corner of her eye while studying the grid rising out of the captain's table. There was something about Donali's attitude that she didn't like, but she didn't have time to focus on it. She watched the *Emissary* and the Guardians roaring toward the *Intrepid's* port hangar bay. In less than a minute their gravidar icons converged, and she heard the comm officer announce: "The *Emissary* is on board!"

"Guardians?" Caldin asked.

"All but one."

"Where is he?"

"Three klicks out, inbound."

"Without the *Emissary* to guide him in, he's going in blind. He's not going to make it." Caldin grimaced, feeling a sudden weight settle on her shoulders. "Helm, punch it."

After a brief hesitation, the stars elongated to bright lines and then whirling streaks of light joined those star lines as they jumped to SLS. Caldin turned to look around the bridge at her crew. The looks on their faces and their solemn silence mirrored what she was feeling. They'd escaped what should have been certain death for all of them, but they'd left a man behind and lost dozens more in the course of their escape. This was not victory, but a near miss with an ignominious end. Death had come capriciously for some, leaving the rest to drown in a sea of guilt.

Caldin's comm piece buzzed in her ear—*incoming call from*

Commander Ortane. She walked to one side of the gangway to answer it and listened intently to what he had to say. When he finished explaining, she thanked him and turned around.

Commander Donali was standing right behind her.

She nearly jumped with fright.

"Good job, Captain," Donali said.

"Yes..." she replied, frowning. "We did it."

"A successful retreat."

Caldin nodded. "It wouldn't have been if you'd had your way. We would have left the *Emissary* behind for the Sythians. Would you care to explain that?"

Donali appeared to freeze in place, as if he'd abruptly stopped breathing. "I didn't think we had enough time to effect a rescue," he replied, sounding calm but looking otherwise. "I didn't think we could do it."

"I don't think anyone thought we could, but here we are."

"Indeed we are, ma'am," Donali replied, the glowing red optics of his artificial eye dimming and then brightening again as he blinked.

"I am curious about one thing, however..." Caldin replied, her head canting to one side. "How did they know we were coming?"

"I don't know that they did."

"No? Then why were they already surrounding us when we dropped out of SLS? Space is too vast to allow for that type of coincidence."

Donali smiled thinly at her. "What are you suggesting, Captain? That we have a Sythian agent on board?"

"Yes," she replied, holding Donali's gaze. "And I'm suggesting that agent is you."

Every head on the bridge abruptly turned their way.

"That's ridiculous!" Donali spat. "I'm the Admiral's XO,

his most trusted advisor!"

"Yes, but even though you are his most trusted advisor, the Admiral chose to send his stepson on a top secret mission instead of you. That wasn't part of the plan, was it Donali? You were supposed to be the one he sent. So you tried to convince Commander Ortane to let you go instead of him."

"How did you know I spoke to Ortane?"

"He just called to let me know."

Donali held her gaze without blinking. "I'm the better choice for the mission. That *doesn't* mean I'm a Sythian agent!"

"No?" Caldin shrugged. "I had my doubts about you when we rescued you, Donali, and now I've got enough circumstantial evidence to do something about it. You're going to ride out the rest of this trip in stasis."

"You can't do that."

"Well, I *could* always put you through a mind probe to find out for sure whose side you're on."

Donali's real eye widened to a panicky aperture. "That could kill me."

"Then I suppose you should be grateful for stasis technology which enables us to delay that fate. Guards! Stun him." Caldin roared.

Donali opened his mouth to object, but two stun bolts hit him before he could get out another word. He collapsed to the deck in a pile of twitching and jittering limbs. Caldin stepped up to him and kicked him hard in the ribs to make sure he really was unconscious. When he didn't so much as stir, she withdrew and watched as the pair of sentinels she'd summoned bent down to bind Donali's hands and feet with stun cord.

"Take him to the med bay and put him in stasis. The admiral can decide what to do with him when we get back."

"Yes, ma'am," the nearest sentinel replied as he levitated Donali off the deck with his grav gun and carried him away.

Caldin heaved a deep sigh and shook her head. How were any of them supposed to sleep at night with the threat of Sythian agents lurking in their midst? For all her crew knew *she* was a Sythian agent, and for all she knew, all of them were. She turned to pass a critical eye over her crew. They watched her with expressions ranging the gamut from shock to horror.

"Eyes on your stations!" she barked. "We revert to real space in less than half an hour, and we need to be ready for another jump if we're going to elude pursuit." Sythian SLS drives were slower than human ones, but they weren't so slow that Caldin felt they could afford to delay.

Her crew grudgingly went back to their stations. She turned and headed for the bridge doors just as the sentinels carried Donali out. "Delayn! You're the CO until I get back, and you're reinstated as my XO."

"Yes, ma'am."

Caldin toyed with the idea of following those sentinels to the med bay and actually submitting Donali to a mind probe, but on the off chance that she was wrong about him she didn't want to be responsible for his death. At least this way, no one could blame her for anything.

"Comms, have Commander Ortane meet me in the operations center in five."

"Yes, ma'am."

Time to find out why Commander Ortane's mission is so damned interesting to the Sythians.

Chapter 14

Ethan sat opposite his bride at an expensive restaurant in the Vermillion Palace, now into day seven of their honeymoon. It should have been one of the most relaxing, enjoyable times of his life, but rather than staring across the table into his wife's startling violet eyes, his head was turned at an awkward angle to watch the holoscreen mounted above the restaurant's bar. Alara's gaze was similarly fixed upon that screen. Karpathia's news channel was playing with nonstop updates from the Sythian occupation. There were scenes of troopers marching down city streets in the glossy black armor with glowing red optics which had been the Gors' hallmark, a symbol of the horrors visited upon humanity during the initial invasion. Those scenes were made more horrifying still by the knowledge that those troopers weren't Gors at all, but rather *human* slaves wearing recycled Gor armor. Unlike the original invasion, there were no images of mass destruction and slaughter. A few suicidal citizens ran at the advancing armies only to be shot dead before they could reach them, but apart from those incidents the Sythians didn't appear intent on killing anyone. Instead, their armies walked the streets in orderly formations, ignoring innocent bystanders and local security forces alike.

It was confusing to watch, but the obvious reason for their ambivalence was that this time the Sythians hadn't come to kill and destroy; they'd come to occupy. Ethan frowned, wondering what the Sythians could possibly hope to get from Dark Space. Leaning in close to Alara, he whispered, "We should go."

"Where?" she whispered back. "They have the planet blockaded! No one's getting on or off unless they say so."

Ethan turned to her. "We have to try. You think we can afford to stay here with that?" he gestured to the holoscreen and the marching armies depicted there. He gave her a grim look. "We're witnessing another invasion, Kiddie. Just because they haven't started slaughtering us yet, doesn't mean they won't."

Alara stared back at him, her lips trembling, her eyes wide and terrified. Abruptly he saw her gaze brighten with a sheen of moisture. Reflected there he saw visions of a cottage by a lake and two little children racing around it with their father chasing them; then she blinked and fresh tears welled up to wash away those dreams.

"It's the only way," he said.

"What do they want from us?"

Ethan shook his head, not knowing what to say, but the holoscreen answered what he couldn't, and suddenly a loud, alien warbling filled the restaurant. Ethan's head snapped back to the screen and he watched with slack-jawed astonishment as the face of a real Sythian appeared. That alien—with his translucent skin, lavender-colored freckles, and the gills slashing the sides of his neck—looked disturbingly like the one Ethan had seen before, the one and only Sythian humanity had ever captured and interrogated—High Lord Kaon. Except Kaon had died with his ship, meaning that this could only be his clone.

Kaon's warbling was muted, and a translation began to stream out in the neutral tones of a universal translator. "Humans, I am High Lord Kaon," the alien said, confirming Ethan's suspicions. He went on, "Your rulers surrender to us, and you are now subjects of the Sythian Coalition. You surely require proof to convince you, and so . . ." The alien turned and gestured to one side of the podium where he stood. The camera panned away from Kaon's face to show none other than Admiral Hoff Heston—at least, Ethan thought it was him. It was hard tell from his outward appearance—greasy, matted gray hair; days' old stubble on his face; dirty, tear-stained cheeks; haunted gray eyes, and rounded shoulders. His usually pristine white Supreme Overlord's uniform looked like it had been soaked in blood, sweat, and tears. If defeat had a face, it was his.

Had his eyes been any other color, Ethan would have said it was an imposter. He had known the admiral as a daunting personality, a man who tolerated little and asked much, a man with supreme confidence in his abilities. Now that man with his impeccably high standards and arrogant strength was broken. He looked like a homeless *grub*.

Ethan gave an involuntary shiver, and the camera panned back to High Lord Kaon's face. His rubbery lips stretched into an unconvincing smile. "Welcome to the Coalition," Kaon said. "Your people make a wise decision by joining us. Our rules for humanity are simple and easy to follow. Rule number one—your people are to provide us with food and whatever other supplies we should require for our fleets. Two—you must cease your pointless infighting. Those found disrupting the peace or resisting the new order are to be enslaved. Three—every mated pair must produce a minimum of four offspring. Life mates with extra offspring are to be rewarded. If you have no mate, you must find one. If you and your mate cannot provide for your offspring, those you cannot feed are to be taken as slaves until death finds them. And finally, at the age of 16, which I am told is the age humans become adults, all must serve in the Coalition Fleet for a minimum of five standard Sythian years—that is six years to your kind.

"If you obey these rules, your race is to be left in peace. Any humans found attempting to flee are to be killed. There is no dissonance, we are one. We are Sythiansss."

Abruptly, the alien's face faded, replaced by a local news reporter's frightened visage. "That ... we ..." the reporter stumbled over his tongue and then turned to look down at his notes. For a long moment he didn't look up, and then the screen faded to show footage of more Sythian cruisers setting down on the plains outside Karpathia City. Those alien warships caught the fading light of the setting sun on their highly reflective hulls and began shining like suns in their own right—dozens of them.

Ethan turned back to Alara. "We have to go, Kiddie," he repeated. To his astonishment, she shook her head. "Kiddie . . ."

"Ethan, you heard what that skull face said. If we try to run, they'll shoot us down."

"What's the alternative? *Stay?*"

Alara's eyes drifted out of focus and she began nodding slowly. "It might not be so bad. They're actually encouraging us to have children. We already have one on the way."

"You're glossing over the reason they want us to have kids. They need more soldiers and crew for their ships."

"The war is over, Ethan! And we lost. Their terms are not ideal, but they're the only ones we've got. We're lucky we're still useful enough that they want to keep us alive."

"Alara, snap out of it! Our children will have to serve in the Sythian fleet! They might not even live through that. And we're being forced to have four. Everyone is. The ones we can't support will become Sythian slaves! To top it all off, our overburdened economy will have to supply their war machine!"

Finally Alara's eyes focused on his face, and Ethan felt a spark of hope that perhaps she hadn't completely lost it. That spark died with what she said next.

"If the Sythians are no longer at war with us, who are they going to fight? There will *be* no war machine to support. Our children will serve for six years without ever having to fire a shot at anyone, and then they'll come home to live a normal life."

"And supposing we don't have the resources to provide for all four of our *mandatory* offspring?"

"*That's* what we should be concerned about, and it just proves my father's point. We need to sell our ship, Ethan.

After that we'll have more than enough to support a family of any size."

Ethan gaped at his wife, unable to continue the argument any further. He shut his gaping mouth and began nodding slowly, as if he'd conceded to her wisdom. He would have to plan their escape without her. "All right, fine. You want to stay, we'll stay, but we're not selling the ship yet. I'm still going to try to make it as a freelancer first."

Alara's eyes narrowed, and an unhappy frown graced her lips. "Ethan . . ."

He held up a hand to forestall her. "We had a deal, remember? Six months." *We'll be out of here long before then,* he thought.

"Fine," Alara agreed. "Six months, but you're not getting any extensions on that."

Ethan smiled grimly. "Don't worry, I won't need them." He turned to find their waiter, but of course the man was standing frozen in the middle of the restaurant, staring up at the holoscreen as footage of the Sythian occupation played in a loop. "When do you think our food is going to arrive?" Ethan asked absently, as if he hadn't just permanently lost his appetite.

His return to the mundane seemed to fool Alara, and she replied. "I'm not sure. I think we'll be waiting a while with all of these developments. Maybe we should go back to our room for a while until things settle down?"

"Yes," Ethan said, rising from the table and holding out his hand to help Alara up. "Let's do that."

* * *

"I want to know what's so damned important about your mission, Commander."

"It's classified," Atton replied with a frown.

Captain Caldin shook her head. "Not good enough. I just risked my ship and all of our lives to make sure you don't fall into Sythian hands. Commander Donali is in the med bay in stasis right now because you suspect him of being a traitor. I need some explanations."

"He wouldn't be in stasis if you didn't suspect him as well," Atton pointed out.

"I can't take the risk you're right."

"Look, Captain . . ."

"Can I be frank with you, Ortane?"

Atton hesitated. "I suppose."

"I'm not here to expose your mission, or to put it in any danger. I need to know what you're trying to accomplish out here so that I can help you. Your transport is damaged beyond immediate repair. Whatever the Sythians did to it, the reactor is completely slagged."

"What? When did you find that out?"

"While I was waiting for you to get here, I checked in with the chief greaser on deck. He ran a diagnostic and passed the good news on to me. Now I'm sharing it with you. What do you think that means for your mission, Commander?"

Atton grimaced. "How long will it take to fix?"

"A few days at least—assuming we can rebuild it with parts we have on hand. If not, that bird will be grounded until we get back. Now, I'm going to take a guess here, but since your transport is a long-range assault recon-class, that means whatever you need to do, it's quite a bit farther out than we are right now. With that assumption in place, you should know that we don't have another ship like yours on board. So, either you keep your mission details to yourself and hope your ship gets repaired before long, or you tell me now, and we use the *Intrepid* to get you to wherever you're going on schedule. Bearing in mind of course that the admiral told me your mission is unspeakably urgent."

Atton let out a long breath and shook his head. "Captain, I appreciate what you're trying to do, but there's a reason I'm being sent alone rather than with a fleet to accompany me."

"And what reason is that, Commander?"

"I can't say." Caldin sighed, but Atton held his ground. "I'm sorry, Captain."

"Very well, you're entitled to your—"

Suddenly the ship lurched and shuddered. The lights flickered overhead, and Atton heard a muffled screech of duranium rending, followed by an ominous groan. His eyes flew wide.

Caldin looked just as shocked, her face pale and her knuckles turning white where she had suddenly gripped the armrests of her chair. She reached up to her ear to answer an incoming comm call. "What in the netherworld was that, Delayn...?"

Atton waited while the ship's chief engineer replied, and watched as concern flashed across the captain's face. "I'll be right there. Do *not* disengage our cloak!" she said, already rising from her seat at the head of the holo table.

"What's wrong?" Atton asked, rising with her.

"We've been pulled out of SLS ten minutes ahead of schedule."

"By what?" Atton asked, his mind racing to fill in the blanks. As far as anyone knew, Sythians didn't have SLS disruptor tech. Then again, as far as anyone had known, they didn't have disabler tech either and yet somehow they'd turned the *Emissary's* reactor to slag.

"We're not sure." Caldin replied, hurrying to leave the operations center.

Atton followed her out with a frown. They reached the lift tubes in the corridor outside and rode one of them straight up to the bridge. Caldin stepped up to the bridge doors and opened them with a swish of her wrist across the scanner. As soon as the doors parted, Atton saw not stars and space as he was expecting, but a pure, unadulterated black. Space was so dark that the only way Atton could see the *Intrepid's* bow, which the bridge overlooked, was by the faint light shining out from her external viewports. Yet even that light threatened to disappear in the void, obscured by a shadowy black mist.

"What the . . ." Atton shook his head, unable to decide what he was looking at.

Caldin strode down the gangway. "Report!" she called out.

Atton snapped out of it and hurried to catch up with her.

"We are approximately one and a quarter light years out from our SLS entry point, and point eight four light years short of our designated exit," the gravidar officer announced.

"Do we know what pulled us out of SLS?" Caldin

demanded as they reached the captain's table.

"Hard to say, the strength of the gravitational field that pulled us out of SLS suggests there's a super massive object nearby."

"A black hole?" Caldin asked.

"Maybe, but electromagnetic radiation isn't consistent with what we should find for that to be the case," gravidar replied.

"But the field *is* naturally occurring?"

"It must be. No artificial gravity field could span such a large area of space, ma'am."

Deck Commander Delayn rose from the engineering control station and hurried up the stairs to join them. "Captain," he said, offering a quick salute.

"Would you care to explain what's going on here, Commander?" Caldin asked.

"The short explanation is that we're stuck."

"Stuck?" Atton asked.

"I'm afraid I don't understand either," Caldin replied. "Why can't we jump out?"

Delayn regarded them for a moment with his startlingly pale blue Worani eyes. "I can't explain it."

"Try," Caldin demanded.

"SLS drives are built with fail-safes to avoid getting too close to gravitational forces which can tear spaceships apart while travelling in superluminal."

"I know the mechanics of SLS drives, Delayn. I want to know why we're stuck here." Caldin gestured out the viewports to the murky black nebula they had landed in.

"That's just it. We shouldn't *be* stuck. The fail-safes should have prevented us from getting this close."

"But..."

"The fail-safes didn't work, and we've been pulled out of SLS in the middle of a strong gravitational field."

"That's not possible. We would have been ripped apart, as you just pointed out."

"I can't explain how we survived, or why the emergency fail-safes didn't work." Delayn sighed and ran a hand through his short gray hair. "At least they pulled us out of SLS before we could go any further."

"But not before we ended up stuck smack in the middle of the deepest, darkest corner of the galaxy," Caldin replied.

"This doesn't make any sense," Atton insisted. "We made it this far, so why can't we jump back out?"

"That's like saying we survived jumping off a cliff so we should jump again," Caldin replied. "If the fail-safes hadn't pulled us out when they did, right now we'd just be another layer of interstellar krak floating through this filthy quagmire."

Delayn added, "Gravitational force is maximal upon entry and exit from SLS. Our hull suffered stress fractures in a dozen different places when the fail-safes finally kicked in. If we deactivate them and try to jump out, we'll be ripped apart."

"How far do we have to go to get to a safe jump point?"

"By our calculations we are point six light years from the center of the field and point five light years from the closest point where we could safely jump out."

Caldin's eyes flew wide. "Half a light year?!" She pounded the captain's table with a fist, and the star map projected above the table shuddered. She stood staring at the map for a long, silent moment.

"Ma'am . . ." Delayn began in a quiet voice, "What are your orders?"

Caldin shook her head. "We go back in real space."

"Sythians could be following us."

"Then we pick a slightly different trajectory!" she said, rounding on him. "If they manage to follow us this far in, then they'll be just as frekked as we are." Caldin turned to look out at the dark nebula where they'd ended up stranded. It was a dense cloud of interstellar dust far from any light source bright enough to pierce it, hence the classification—dark nebula.

Atton turned back to Delayn. "How long before we can get out of here?"

"There's a lot to calculate, but if I had to guess . . . well, it would depend on the speed we can get up to. I'd say we can probably make one tenth the speed of light—but we're going to drain a lot of fuel to keep our shields up under the barrage from all that dust."

"Half a light year at one tenth the speed of light . . ." Atton ran the math quickly in his head. "We're going to be stuck in this nebula for five *years?*"

"Keep your voice down," Caldin growled.

"It will probably be less . . ." Delayn replied. "The nebula should begin to thin out the further we get from the gravitational force. At some point we'll be able to speed up."

Atton wasn't ready to give up yet. "So, best case scenario, we make it out in four years." He turned to the gravidar officer who'd reported the situation when they'd arrived on deck. "Gravidar—you said sensors show a strong gravitational field, but not the radiation we'd expect from a black hole."

"That's correct, sir."

"So what if this really is an SLS disruption field?"

"No field generator ever constructed has a range of

several light years, Commander," Captain Caldin replied quietly.

"The captain is right," gravidar replied. "It would take the energy of an entire sun to create a field that large."

"And then some," Caldin said. "No," she began, turning away from the viewports to address her bridge crew, "we only have ourselves to blame for this. We're here because of an equipment malfunction, because someone on this ship didn't do their job properly. I'm going to conduct a formal inquiry into the matter. Whoever is to blame for the faulty fail-safes will be punished accordingly. Unfortunately, we're all going to suffer for that person's mistake. As of this moment, emergency rationing is in full effect. Crews will begin rotating in and out of stasis in order to preserve what supplies we have. This ship was equipped for extended range; we're going to stretch the definition of the term. Helm—plot a course back the way we came with a positive five degree deviation with respect to the x-axis."

"Yes, ma'am."

"Better get comfortable, people," Caldin went on. "We have a long, dark trip ahead of us." Atton watched her turn to him. "Seems like you'll have the time you need to repair your ship, Commander."

Atton frowned. "Too much time."

"Why don't you go spend some of it with your squadron. They'll need cooler heads around them when I give everyone a sitrep. This is going to be a bitter lesson for all of us."

"Yes, ma'am." Atton gave a swift salute and then turned on his heel and left the bridge. It took all his energy just to focus on putting one foot in front of the other and not collapse in the corridor along the way. He couldn't believe it. *Five frekking years!*

The captain was no stranger to long-range missions. A few years ago she'd made the year-long round trip from the Adventa Galaxy to the neighboring Getties Cluster in order to gather Intel on the Sythians and the Gors. But this mission was five times as long as that. The *Intrepid* could probably make it with emergency rations and rotating crews, and if anyone could get them home, Caldin would, but Atton wasn't sure there would be a home to go back to. Dark Space wasn't going to get the reinforcements they needed, and something told him the Sythians weren't going to wait five years to make a move.

As he waited outside the bridge for one of the lift tubes to arrive, Atton turned to look out a nearby viewport at the vile, inky blackness which had snared them.

Looks like the darkness finally found us . . . he thought, *and it's not letting go.*

Chapter 15

By the time Atton entered the *Spacer's Rest*, the officer's lounge on deck 17, he was still in a daze, so shocked by what had happened that he was completely oblivious to his surroundings. He stumbled up to the bar counter and signaled to Kerk for a drink. The bartender nodded and headed his way. "Maverick," he croaked.

"Sure."

"Hoi, motherfrekker, over here!" Gina called to him from the other end of the bar.

Atton turned and shook his head. *Not now Gina*, he thought, and looked away. He wasn't in the mood to deal with her. Not taking the hint, she made her way over to him and arrived just as Kerk sent a black maverick sailing down the counter into his open hand.

"You hear me?" Gina asked, tapping him roughly on the shoulder while taking an indecorous gulp from her own mug of beer.

"Put it on my tab," Atton said to the bartender, determined to ignore his XO. She reeked of beer, which was no small feat, since she couldn't have been in the lounge for more than twenty minutes. In that time only a third of the other pilots had made their way to the lounge. The others were likely catching up on sleep or grieving the dead in a less social way. Atton hadn't even had a chance to check their casualties. He was afraid to look and find someone he'd actually started to like missing from the Guardians' roster. *At least Gina's still around. But does she have to make that so painfully obvious?*

Atton turned and left the bar, heading for the most isolated part of the lounge so he could be alone.

Gina didn't let him get that far. She grabbed him by his shoulder and spun him to face her, forcing him to notice the fire burning in her amber eyes. He saw something else there, too, but he didn't immediately recognize it. Then some of the fire in her eyes spilled to her cheeks, and he realized what it was.

"Frek you, Atton!" she spat, swiping angrily at her tears with the back of one hand. "You know a thank you would be nice."

Atton shook his head, uncomprehending. "For what?"

Gina's eyes flashed and she gave him a sudden shove which made him stumble backward a few steps. "For *what?*" she echoed.

Atton's own ire began to build. He recovered his balance with a scowl and loomed suddenly close to her face. "Watch yourself, Lieutenant. Would you care to explain that outburst?"

"Sure," she shrugged. "Why the frek not? You want to sit down for this, or take it standing up?"

"Just make it quick. I'm short on patience right now."

Gina's mouth curved in a bitter smile. "All right, let me summarize it for you. We're halfway to the *Intrepid* when we get ordered back out there to cover your ass. We're facing five to one odds, increasing by the second. Guardians lose Shafer and Tails on the first pass, but we manage to keep them off you. We give you your chance to get away so you can do whatever the frek it is you were doing out there. Then you go and get your ship disabled, and we're ordered to keep those fighters off your six until the *Intrepid* can grav you back in.

"Ordinarily no one pilot would be worth that kind of risk, but I guess being the admiral's stepson really does making you frekkin' special, because we're kept out there until the last frekking minute!"

"Gina, I . . ."

"I'm not done, Iceman! Not long after that, the *Intrepid* cloaks. They're still gravving you in so you'll be fine, but what about us? We can't even see the hangar! Orders come through to follow you in. I pick up three Shells along the way, and my wingmate gets the bright idea to peel off and distract them. He pulls off the impossible and sends all three to the netherworld with a pair of Hailfires. Just as he's coming back around to join the tail-end of our formation, hangar bay controllers pull the last Nova inside, leaving not even a trail of debris for him to follow. Then the Captain gives the order and we jump out, leaving him behind. Another few minutes and we would have been able to get him on board, too."

Atton felt like someone had dumped a bucket of ice over his head and now he was left shivering from the cold. He shook his head. "Saving one pilot wouldn't be worth the risk of sticking around."

"No? So why was saving your ass worth that risk? That man died for *you*. Because of *you*," she said, stabbing his chest with a finger.

"I..."

"Gettin' all choked up, are we, Iceman? No, your eyes are bone dry, aren't they? Bet you don't even have tear ducts."

Atton swallowed. "Who was it?"

"Perkins," she said with a brittle smile. A few more tears spilled to her cheeks and she shook her head. "It would just frekkin' figure that the one man who's actually better than he seems goes and gets himself killed for having such a big damn heart."

It wasn't lost on Atton that Gina and "Hawkeye" Perkins had been hooking up over the last week and that now Gina felt doubly bad—bad because he had meant something to her and now he was gone, and worse because of the mountain of guilt she felt over the fact that he'd saved her life only to be left for dead.

There was an even bigger mountain resting on Atton's shoulders. Three pilots in Guardian Squadron alone had lost their lives to rescue him. And who knew how many other officers had died while the *Intrepid* had slugged it out with Sythian warships, waiting for him to be pulled back on board. He'd already noticed several decks grayed out on lift tube control panels.

"Gina ... I'm sorry," Atton managed in a thready whisper.

"You killed him."

"Tuner!"

Atton saw Ceyla Corbin come up behind Gina. "Leave him alone," she said.

"Why?" Gina asked, rounding on her. "Huh? What's he to you?" She gave Ceyla a shove, followed by another one, and—

Atton stepped between them and pushed them apart before Gina could find an excuse to start throwing punches.

Ceyla made an irritated noise in the back of her throat. "He's my commanding officer, and yours, too—or have you forgotten that?"

"A good commander should die for his men!" Gina spat, trying to get around Atton. "Not sit by and watch them all die for *him*!"

"It wasn't his fault. Captain's orders, remember? He couldn't even send comms, and he wasn't in charge of the squadron—*you* were."

"You frekkin' little sclut . . . !"

Atton had to work hard to keep her away from Ceyla. "Hoi!" he yelled. "Cut it out Tuner! Frek it, Gina, I'm sorry, okay?" Atton said again, and he meant it. For some reason his eyes weren't supporting his apology with tears. He wasn't much of a crier, but that didn't mean he was as cold-hearted as Gina seemed to think.

"Frek you, Iceman!" Gina replied. "Couldn't have picked a better call sign for you if I'd asked your own mother to come up with it!"

Atton ignored her insults. "Look, if there's anything I can do . . . when's the memorial for . . . the people we lost?"

"You don't even remember their names, do you?"

Atton was ashamed to admit that was true. He did know

his squad mates by name, but right now he couldn't remember which ones Gina had told him they'd lost. He'd had too many shocks in the last half hour to take it all in.

Gina took his silence for her answer. "That's what I thought!" she said, nodding slowly. "You know what, that's it! You want to make up for it? Let's see you put your own ass on the line. I'll be waiting in the ring, just in case you figure out what those ornaments dangling between your legs are for."

Atton watched, slack-jawed and wide-eyed as Gina turned and stalked away, heading for the ring on the other side of the bar. There in the distance, lay a square with high walls of red flexi-bars. Two miniature assault mechs stood awaiting activation in opposite corners of the ring, each of them almost as tall as a man, green status lights blinking on their chests in readiness. Those mechs were the avatars which officers typically used to settle their quarrels, but Gina had no intention of letting him hide behind a bot.

"She's just hurting, Commander," Ceyla said slowly. "Don't let it get to . . ." Atton strode by her, hot on Gina's heels.

"Hoi! Where are you going? Commander!" She caught up to him a second later. "Don't tell me you're actually going to fight her."

"That's exactly what I'm going to do," Atton replied.

"No offense, but she went through flight school and basic. She's trained in hand-to-hand combat. You didn't go through either basic or regular flight school, and you're *not* trained for this."

Atton turned to her with his eyebrows raised. "Since when is my training or lack thereof public knowledge?"

Ceyla grimaced. "Since Lieutenant Giord spent the last

fifteen minutes telling everyone how unqualified you are to lead the squadron."

Atton sighed.

"I'm sorry, sir," Ceyla said. "I could be a witness if you want to file a report about her behavior."

"That's all right, Corbin."

"Don't fight her, sir. She's looking for someone to take it out on. You're not going to teach her to respect you by getting yourself beat within an inch of your life."

"I'm not going to teach *her* a lesson, Corbin. I'm going to teach myself one."

"What?! You feel guilty because some good men died following their orders to save you, and now you're going to punish yourself?"

They reached the ring right behind Gina. She turned to see Atton standing there and smirked. "Maybe they're not ornaments after all, hoi Commander?" With that, she turned to address everyone on deck, calling out, "Listen up! Commander Ortane's about to have his ass handed to him by myself and my two friends—" She held up both fists and waved them around. "—'black,' and 'eye.' You don't want to miss this!"

Within seconds a crowd had gathered. Everyone in the lounge in fact—some fifteen men and women. Kerk the barman was nominated referee. He stepped up to Atton and handed him a pair of padded black gloves.

"Thanks," Atton said, accepting the gloves and undoing the straps to put them on.

Brawls weren't exactly against regulations. That was up to the captain of the ship, and most captains found that giving their crew a controlled way to hurt each other prevented more uncontrolled outbursts at less opportune times. Gina climbed through the padded flexi-bars surrounding the ring and clapped her fists together with a meaty smack. "Next one's for you, Iceman!" she said, lisping around a black mouth guard.

Kerk came up to Atton and patted him on the cheek to get his attention. "You know the rules?"

Atton shook his head. He'd never actually been in one of these fights, and he hadn't bothered to waste his sols betting on them.

"No eye gouging, no cheap shots, nothing below the belt, no elbows, and no kicks. Everything else is fair game. You want out, you tap the mat three times or say 'yield.' If no one yields, the winner is whoever can pin the other down for ten seconds or knock them out." Kerk handed him a blue mouth guard, and Atton popped it in. "You ready?"

He nodded.

"Atton . . ." Ceyla whispered, using his first name to get his attention. He turned to her and stared into her bright blue eyes for a long moment. "Don't do this," she pleaded.

"Sorry," he said, and with that, he ducked into the ring and went to stand in the corner opposite Gina.

"Frek him up!" someone yelled.

"Any bets?" Kerk asked, turning in a quick circle.

Atton saw a few hands shoot up. After that, Ceyla's hand went up, too, and Atton frowned. When he saw the bets go up on the holoscreen above the bar he noticed that Ceyla was betting on him to win. She'd put down 500 sols—half a month's pay at ten to one odds. He wanted to tell her not to be a skriff. She was the only one covering all the bets against him, meaning the winners would get to share out her paycheck—not that paychecks meant a whole lot now that they were going to spend the next four to five years stranded a thousand light years from Dark Space.

"All right! On the count of three," Kerk said. His count reached zero and Atton saw Gina come at him, stalking lithely with a sudden grace he'd somehow never noticed from her before.

He took a few steps forward to face off with her and brought his hands up in what he imagined to be a proper guard position to cover his face.

"Come on, Commander!" Ceyla called. She was all but drowned out by a dozen others rooting for Gina to beat the krak out of him.

"Hoi there, Iceman," Gina said as she took another step toward him.

Atton tightened up his guard.

Her right arm shot out in a blur and hit him in the gut, knocking the wind out of him. Atton grunted and took a step back. Cheers erupted from the audience. He brought up his guard again, this time with his left arm hanging slightly lower than his right to protect himself from any more blows aimed at his midsection. Gina came at him again, and she deliberately aimed for his left arm with hers, knocking it out of position so she could sneak in with a right cross to his face.

Smack.

That blow connected with the left side of his head, and he stumbled into the flexi-bars along the side of the ring. More cheering made it through the ringing in his ear. He just barely managed to duck another blow that was aimed for the back of his head. He ran away to face Gina from the opposite side of the ring. She grinned, revealing her shiny black mouth guard instead of teeth. "Come on!" she said. "Fight back!"

Atton took a quick step toward her as she approached. He ducked down to take a stab at her midsection, but she sidestepped the attack and hammered him on the back with both fists. He fell over and hit the springy floor with a *thud*. He wondered for a moment if Kerk had decided to stop refereeing, because the explosive ache he felt in his upper back felt like she'd hit him with her elbows rather than padded fists.

He tried to get up, only to have her land on top of him a second later. She got him in a choke hold and flipped him onto his back. His eyes began to bulge and his face turned red. He tried to pry her arm away, but part of him was resigned to it. Another few seconds and he could tap out. He began to count backward from ten inside his head.

"You know somethin' Ortane?" Gina interrupted. "I'm glad you turned me down. You're the last man on the planet I'd *ever* want to be with."

That hit a nerve. Atton gave a sudden shove, and Gina's arm came away from his throat. He twisted it with brute strength until she shrieked and let him go. He stumbled to his feet and turned to see her clutching her right arm to her body like a broken wing.

Seeing that he felt a sudden flash of regret, and he noticed Kerk walk up to Gina's side of the ring. "You okay to continue, Lieutenant?"

"I'm fine," she spat.

Atton was just about to yield when Gina let out a roar and ran at him. Unsure what to do, he just stood there, biding his time until she came within arm's reach so he could sidestep her momentum.

Somehow, she anticipated him and leapt to the same side he did, knocking him to the floor. His knees hit with a painful *thud*, and then Gina began pummeling his face with her fists. He tried to curl up into a fetal position to protect his head, but she actually pulled him to his feet and began hammering him in the stomach instead. He had the sense to double over and protect that area, but then the blows found his face again, and pretty soon her fists were the only thing he could either see or hear. He ended up backed against the flexi-bars at the edge of the ring feebly trying to fend off alternating blows to his stomach and face.

"Gina, I'm sorry!" he croaked. He wasn't sure she heard him through all her grunting, but it didn't matter. Even if she forgave him, he wouldn't forgive himself. An untold number of officers had died to save him, and for what? The greater good? He wouldn't even have a chance to complete the mission they'd fought and died to help him accomplish. It was all for nothing. They'd died for nothing!

"That's enough!"

Atton heard that scream only dimly through the ringing in his ears. Through one badly swollen eye he saw Gina being lifted away from him, kicking and screaming. Then she was thrown to one side where she hit the floor with a *bang* and a roar of outrage. A blurry Ceyla Corbin turned to address the not-so-innocent bystanders. "You should be ashamed of yourselves! This isn't an honorable match! It's an excuse to beat up your commanding officer!"

"I'm going to kill you," Gina mumbled around her mouth guard. She bounced to her feet and started advancing on Ceyla, who for her part, took up a professional fighting stance and turned to face off with her commanding officer barehanded. They were almost within striking range before Kerk magically appeared between the two women.

"Stand down, Tuner!" Kerk said, giving Gina a shove to emphasize his point. "Stand *down*! Corbin isn't part of this match."

For a moment, Gina looked like she was about to hit Kerk

instead, but then she lowered her fists and stalked away. The barman was an old navy sentinel, forty plus, with a pair of artificial legs that had left him tending bar aboard the *Intrepid* during his rehab. He was a giant of a man with sledgehammers for fists. Atton saw Kerk stalking toward him with both of those hammers ready to go to work on him, and he irrationally assumed that's what the barman was going to use them for. He began struggling against the flexi-bars where he was still slumped, trying to regain his footing and get away.

When Kerk reached him, he winced in anticipation of the blow, but it never came. One of those giant hands opened up to land on his shoulder. "You all right there, Commander?"

"Awul eee wime," he slurred.

"How many fingers?" Kerk asked, holding up one hand with a dozen fingers.

"Fifteen?" Atton suggested.

Kerk shook his head and bent down to drape one of Atton's arms over his shoulders. He stood up, forcing Atton to his feet. "I'm calling it," he said, turning to address the crowd in a booming voice. "Tuner wins, but Green V's right—this was no match."

A few subdued cheers reached Atton's ears.

"Hoi!" Ceyla said. "That's it—pat yourselves on the back for kicking a man when he's down!"

After an indeterminate amount of time spent stumbling through the ring with Kerk, Atton noticed Ceyla Corbin appear on the other side of him. She draped his other arm over her shoulders and asked, "Is he going to be okay?"

"Doc will have to answer that. I'm no expert, but I'd say he's lightly concussed."

"What the frek were you thinking, Commander?" she

asked. "You have a death wish or something? Why didn't you tap out?"

Atton smiled. He'd never heard Ceyla curse before. He tried to summon the energy for a reply but gave up when he realized how nauseated he was. When they carried him out through the bars on the other side of the ring he almost threw up on the deck.

"I'm fine," he finally managed as they half carried, half dragged him to the lift tubes at the far end of the lounge.

"No, you're not," Ceyla hissed.

And then the intercom buzzed and Atton heard Captain Caldin's voice begin echoing through the room to give everyone the bad news. After that, no one was fine. Kerk began cursing, and Ceyla abruptly lost her hold on his arm. Atton hit the deck and a spark of pain erupted in his coccyx; then he fell back and lay staring up at a blurry ceiling. He watched the room spin around his head a few times before his open eye drifted shut. The darkness found him, and he wondered for a moment if this was what it would look like if he stepped out an airlock into the dark nebula where the *Intrepid* was stranded. He was tempted to ask Ceyla to join him in the nebula, but before he could, his thoughts sailed away in a parade of nonsense.

* * *

One day later...

Ethan sat on the overlarge bed in the honeymoon suite of the Vermillion Palace, his back propped up with a pair of thick pillows while he watched Karpathia One, the holonews station with the most up-to-date coverage of events. So far the Sythians hadn't shut down any of the news channels. Based on the news being reported, Ethan suspected he understood why. Right now the live news feed showed a few dozen meteors lighting up the night sky and raining fire down all over Karpathia City. Ethan's jaw hung open and his expression was frozen in horror as those meteors hit occupied buildings and expensive suburbs with explosive force, leveling them in seconds and leaving nothing but rising clouds of smoke, dust, and bright, flickering flames. When it was over, the camera panned to show columns of smoke rising into the night to punctuate the sky, and then it cut back to the reporter on scene, standing high above the city on a nearby escarpment.

"This marks the tenth group of runaways to be shot down since the occupation began. The Sythians' message is clear—if you run, we *will* catch you. As a fellow citizen of the former Imperium and a fellow human being, this reporter urges you, do *not* resist, and do *not* run. We—"

Ethan heard the bedroom door open and he waved his hand to turn off the holoscreen just seconds before Alara breezed in with a wan smile on her face. "Did you have a nice nap, darling?" she asked. Then her smile faded to a frown as she noticed his expression. "What's wrong?"

Ethan shook his head and forced a smile of his own. "Nothing, sweetheart."

Alara had spent the past day basking in denial. Humanity had lost its freedom and the war, and she appeared to be welcoming their Sythian masters with open arms. Ethan wasn't sure when she was going to snap out of it, but he couldn't sit around waiting for that to happen. He had to act before it was too late.

Until just five minutes ago, he'd been planning to lure Alara aboard their corvette and then lock her in a storeroom while he attempted to run through the Sythian blockade, but that plan was looking more and more hopeless as time went by. In the last day there had already been almost a hundred ships that had tried to flee, and not one of them had actually escaped. Ethan considered himself a good pilot—far better than the average with his 5A rating—but no one was good enough to run through an entire Sythian fleet all by themselves. Enemy ships could be cloaked and hiding anywhere in orbit, or even in the atmosphere. Anyone blasting off from the surface without a cloaking shield would be spotted and intercepted by Sythian forces immediately.

Alara held Ethan's gaze for a long moment before turning to look at the holoscreen sitting opposite the bed. Then she turned back to him with one eyebrow raised. "You've been watching the newscasts."

"Yes," he admitted.

"I thought we agreed not to watch them anymore. We agreed we were going to lie low up here and try to enjoy our honeymoon, because there's nothing we can do about anything that's going on."

"I agreed *we* would stop watching the news. I said nothing about watching it on my own."

Alara's violet eyes narrowed. "Fine. Any new developments you'd like to share?"

Ethan shook his head. "Just more of the same. Nothing you need to worry about."

She held his gaze a moment longer before her expression softened and she turned away with a shrug. "All right."

Ethan watched her walk into the bathroom and shut the door behind her. How could she be so blasé about everything that was happening? She should have been glued to the holoscreen, just like him. A moment later he heard the shower running, and he waved the holoscreen back on. Images swirled out of the screen. Karpathia One was still showing live footage of the burning capital. Then it switched to an earlier recording of a transport fleeing for orbit only to get struck down seconds after liftoff by a squadron of Shell Fighters which came swooping down out of the clouds. Those Shells flew past the holocam with a stuttering blast of *sonic booms* that rattled through the suite's sound system. Ethan raised his hand and snapped it shut, imitating a mouth closing with his hand. The volume of the newscast dropped swiftly, and he turned to eye the bathroom door, expecting Alara to burst out and see what the noise was about, but the shower stayed on, and the door stayed closed.

Oblivious, he thought, shaking his head. Alara's attitude was infuriating, but in some ways she was right. He'd just finished watching what happened to people like him—people who refused to give up. Those people got sent straight to the netherworld.

Ethan got up from the bed and walked over to the wall of windows on the far side of the suite. He stopped there and stood beside the suite's whirlpool tub to peer down through the breaks in the clouds to the town of Ostin far below. The city lights were dim and bleached of color by the thick blanket of smoke which hung over the town. Here and there, bright patches of orange peeked through the smoke. Ostin was on fire. Ethan knew from watching the news that most of the damage was from looters and rioters rather than crashed starships. The Sythians had a zero tolerance for disorderly conduct, but that didn't stop people from panicking and running away with whatever supplies they could find or steal.

People kept running, and the Sythians kept chasing. Planet- and space-bound runaways alike were all greeted with the same ruthless efficiency, and the same inevitable result.

A cold weight of despair settled in Ethan's gut, and suddenly he felt far older than his 46 years. He watched the fires of Ostin burn between dark puffs of cloud. From where he stood, high above the town at the top of White Cap Mountain, those fires looked like candles, flickering feebly against the night. As he watched, a new candle flared to life, marking some other patch of resistance. Ethan shook his head, thinking about all the trillions of lives lost in the original invasion. He thought about the last few million humans in Dark Space, now throwing their lives away again in a stubborn bid for independence that they could never win. From up here it all seemed so pointless, and so futile. His thoughts turned to his son, Atton, and Ethan hoped that he'd had the sense to stand down when the order to surrender had come. He hoped that Atton was somewhere safe, biding his time until the resistance died down and everyone accepted the new status quo. And with those thoughts, Ethan realized that even he had given up. There was nothing any of them could do. Even if a lucky few made it as far as the entrance of Dark Space, they would just encounter more Sythians there and be intercepted before they could jump out.

Alara's right, Ethan thought, his eyes widening with the realization. His wife wasn't deluding herself the way he thought. She wasn't in denial, and she hadn't lost her mind. He was the one who'd been in denial—denying that the war was over, denying that the Sythians had won. *Alara's not happy about any of this; she's just smart enough not to fight a battle that can't be won ... smart enough to make the best of a bad situation.* It wasn't as though the Sythians were promising death to everyone. They wanted loyal, trained soldiers and crews for their fleets. Humanity was going to give them that, just like the Gors once had. The Sythians would have their endless supply of officers. Humanity would give them their children until the end of time, because anyone who refused to serve them would be killed, and when faced with death, a life of servitude didn't look so bad.

Except that it was.

What's life without freedom? Ethan wondered. *Is that what we've come to? Living life for the sake of living it just one more day? Better to die fighting to be free than to live life in a cage.* Ethan had learned all about cages during his stay on the prison world of Etaris. The planet had no prison cells. It was run by criminals and populated by criminals. Certain trade restrictions applied, and no one was allowed to leave, but otherwise the prisoners there were free. During his sentence there, Ethan had learned that sometimes the strongest cages are the ones people build for themselves.

The strongest of those was despair.

Ethan began nodding slowly, his eyes narrowing on the smoke-clouded pinpricks of firelight raging through the town of Ostin below. *You want to clip my wings? You'll have to cut them off.* His jaw muscles bunched as he ground his teeth together. *Come and get me, Skull Faces.*

Chapter 16

Atton blinked his eyes open and stared up at a shiny white ceiling. Med bay. He tried to sit up, but his head began pounding mercilessly, like someone was practicing on a battery of drums inside his head. What was he doing in med bay? Then he remembered the fight with Gina. *That explains the drums.*

A minute later, the ship's doctor came striding in and greeted him with a tight smile. "You're awake," he said, stopping beside Atton's bed with a holo pad and stylus at the ready. "How do you feel?"

Atton frowned, trying to remember the man's name.

Belerus. Fontane. Bell for short. "Feel like I'm still asleep . . ." Atton replied slowly. "How long have I been out?"

"A day and a half."

"What?" Atton sat up suddenly, and immediately regretted it as the pounding in his head found a faster tempo.

"Relax," Doctor Bell soothed. "You took some hard hits to the head. You're lucky you woke up so soon. Besides, if you've heard the news, you know there's no rush. Now that you're awake it won't be long before you're cycled off into stasis for a different type of sleep."

Atton's brow furrowed as he tried to remember what the doctor was talking about. Then he recalled—the *Intrepid* was on a four to five year journey through real space to escape the gravity well which had plucked it out of SLS. *Frek*, Atton thought as the bad news hit him for the second time. "Right. Well, thanks, Doc," he said, swinging his legs over the side of the bed.

"Hold on—" Doctor Bell laid a hand on Atton's shoulder to stop him. "—I still have to run a few tests before I discharge you. Lie down please."

Atton subsided with a frown. The tests were routine—brain scan, memory test, coordination test. He passed them all without a hitch. Less than an hour later he was riding the nearest lift tube down to the flight deck. Once there, he made his way down a deserted corridor and around the corner to the pilots' quarters. He waved his wrist over the door scanner and walked down another deserted corridor, this one lined with doors on both sides. He walked past those doors with a frown. Was everyone in stasis already?

He passed Ceyla's room and then Gina's. Finally he came to his quarters and hurried inside. As the Squadron Commander, his room wasn't shared with anyone else, and it had some extra space along the far wall. There, beneath a simulated viewport sat his desk, comm suite, and a holo projector. Atton headed there, his gaze fixed upon the starless void beyond the viewport. *Four years of this . . .* he thought, wondering how he was going to keep sane.

There were stories, from the old colonial days of the Imperium, of explorers travelling for years to chart the galaxy, and then getting lost between the stars and going mad. Many years later, those ships were found, drifting and full of holes, as if some unknown enemy had found them. Then the ship's logbox would be read to find out what had happened. The story was always the same; the crewmen ended up killing each other in a fight for limited supplies. The last man standing usually ended up killing himself.

Would that be the *Intrepid's* fate?

Atton took a seat behind his desk and waved the holo projector to life. Using his command control implant he mentally called up a star map to see where the *Intrepid* was in relation to the rest of the known galaxy. Zooming out, he found they were little more than a light year from the Enclave and Ikara, where a Sythian fleet had recently ambushed them.

Zooming out again, this time by several orders of magnitude, Atton found that in relation to the rest of the Adventa Galaxy they were near the end of the spiral arm closest to the Sythians and the neighboring Getties Cluster. That put the *Intrepid* nearly a thousand light years from Dark Space, and more than two thousand light years from the heart of the old Imperium. The civilized galaxy had once spanned over 25,000 light years, but most of that hadn't been colonized, with the farthest-flung settlements being little more than outposts for research. Now the human race was down to just two sectors—Dark Space, which was blockaded by

Sythians, and Avilon, made up of immortal humans who were as insular as they were numerous.

Atton swallowed thickly. He knew that even if the *Intrepid* returned with reinforcements, they would be too late to save anyone in Dark Space. Trying not to think about what that meant for his family he switched his focus to the problem at hand. If they couldn't go back to Dark Space, then the *Intrepid* would have to go to Avilon.

But how would the Avilonians react to the intrusion of over a hundred refugees? The admiral had said they wouldn't kill him when he arrived, and he remembered that the Avilonians had been sending aid to the Enclave before the Sythians had found it and enslaved everyone there. Based on those facts, Atton hoped the Avilonians would be sympathetic enough to take them in.

On a whim, he decided to check how far they were from Avilon. Thinking about the coordinates he'd been given brought them out of memory in his command control implant, and a sequence of numbers and letters flashed into his mind's eye.

Calling up a holographic control panel, he began typing in the coordinates. As soon as he'd finished, a green diamond appeared hovering inside the star map. Atton was shocked to find it right on top of the glowing blue icon which represented the *Intrepid's* current location. *It can't be* . . .

Hope soared in his chest, and he zoomed in until the scale of the map was just a few light years across.

His hopes died there. The *Intrepid* and the green diamond which represented Avilon's forward base were now sitting at opposite sides of the map, over two and a half light years apart—close on a galactic scale, but still very far away as long as they were stuck travelling through real space at one tenth the speed of light.

Atton slumped back in his chair and stared into the glowing blue star map until the grid lines became blurry and his eyes burned with the need to blink. A few minutes later his comm piece trilled, interrupting his despondent stupor— *incoming call from Captain Caldin.* Atton touched his ear to answer the call.

"I hear you're awake."

"I suppose I am."

"Good. You're just in time to go to sleep with the rest of the crew."

"The rest of the crew? How many of us are you putting in stasis?"

"All but six."

Atton shook his head. "That seems . . ."

"Extreme? It's not. I don't think we want to find out what happens when 116 officers are forced to compete for food, space, and other supplies over the course of the next four years."

"Standard stasis rotation for long journeys leaves a skeleton crew, ma'am. In this case we should have at least 25 officers awake at all times.

"We should, but these aren't standard circumstances. We have no hope for rescue and nowhere to go even after we get free of this gravity trap. Whatever happens in the next four to five years, whether the citizens in Dark Space evacuate or get slaughtered by Sythians, there's no point in us going back there. Our homes are gone forever, Commander. That puts added mental and emotional stress on our crew which makes them a threat to themselves and the well-being of my ship. Besides, if we are ever going to find a planet far enough from the Sythians and habitable enough for humanity to start over, we're going to need all the supplies we can possibly save."

"And what about you? How are you going to deal with the stress?"

"The six I've picked to stay awake are those who have the best psych evaluations and a proven track record for dealing with this type of situation—all survivors of the original invasion."

"Even the most stable person in the world will go skriffy after spending a few years in isolation, Captain."

"We won't be isolated. We'll each have our partners for support. Three couples. And we have another three to relieve us when we need a break."

"Sounds like you have everything figured out," Atton said. In a way he was relieved not to have to spend any part of the journey awake and slowly succumbing to madness, but there was something he had to tell the captain before she put him to sleep with the rest of the crew. "There is one thing you haven't factored in, however, ma'am."

"What's that?"

"We do have somewhere to go."

"Oh? And where is that?"

"It would be easier to discuss this in person."

"Very well. Meet me in the Operations Center as soon as you can get there. Don't keep me waiting."

Atton heard a *click* which was the captain ending the call from her end. He waved the holo projector on his desk off and then headed for the door to his quarters.

Five minutes later he was sitting in the operations center for a private audience with the captain. She regarded him quietly, her indigo eyes boring into his green. "Well?" she demanded. "If this is some trick to avoid stasis, it's not going to buy you much time."

"It's no trick. Let me explain." And so he did. He explained all about his mission, about Avilon, and about the immortal humans who had been hiding out there for eons.

"That's quite a story," Caldin said.

"It is. I'm afraid I don't have much proof except for the fact that the admiral sent us out here for a reason. He thought we might be able to save Dark Space if we could get reinforcements from the Avilonians. With their superior technology, we might be able to wipe out the Sythians for good."

"If that's the case, why didn't they help us sooner?"

Atton shook his head. "Most likely because they didn't know what was going on, or they didn't think it was their fight."

"You're assuming that's the case. They might also be on the run from the Sythians, staying hidden because they know they would lose if it came to a straight fight."

"Maybe," Atton conceded.

"And there's something else about all of this that doesn't make sense." Caldin turned to gaze into the star map which Atton had pulled up from the holo table where they sat. He'd highlighted the coordinates the admiral had given him. Now the captain jabbed a finger at the green diamond which represented those coordinates. "These Avilonians, as you call them, are not far from what used to be civilized space. At least, their forward base isn't. You don't have the coordinates for their actual location?"

Atton shook his head. "The admiral felt it best to reveal as few of the Avilonians' secrets as he could. He thought my knowing their actual location could anger them and make them unwilling to cooperate with us."

"All right. Let's assume their actual location is close to

their forward base. But even if it isn't, their forward base is in the middle of known and charted space ... why, in all the millennia that the Imperium flourished in this quadrant of the galaxy, did no one ever find these Avilonians and document their civilization? Why has no one ever heard of them?"

"But we have. The Immortals are—"

"Stories we tell to children, Commander. I'm talking about a real documented case of an encounter with Avilonians, not myths and legends about the lost world where humanity evolved."

Atton shrugged. "According to the Sythians, that world isn't in our galaxy at all. They call it Sythia, and it's located in the Getties Cluster. Sythians were humans once. They were the mortals who won the war for Origin that ultimately drove us to the Adventa Galaxy long before the Imperium was even founded."

The captain regarded him for a long moment with her eyebrows skeptically raised. "Really? Explain to me why they're aliens, then."

"Apparently, many years after the war, they began manipulating their genes, selecting them for longevity. Eventually they became something that wasn't even human anymore. When that wasn't good enough, they went back to cloning themselves and transferring their consciousness to those clones before they died, making their system for immortality an improvement on the old human method."

"And how exactly do you know about all of this?"

"The admiral told me. He was once an Avilonian—before he was exiled here."

"So he knew about our mutual history with the Sythians, about our past, and he didn't think to warn anyone that there was a serious threat lurking beyond our galaxy? He was an admiral of the fleet."

"Apparently he didn't know. That knowledge was lost over the eons. The admiral rediscovered the truth about our past when he went aboard the Sythians' command ship."

"And I suppose he heard that convoluted story from the Sythians themselves."

"Yes."

"What if they lied?"

"What would they have to gain by lying to us?"

The captain spread her hands. "That story of theirs *literally* humanizes them. From there they can build a foundation of trust which might earn them some level of cooperation from us."

"But to what end? Why would they need us to cooperate?"

Captain Caldin shook her head. "I don't know, and I'm not sure that they were lying, but we shouldn't just take their word for it. Until we find Origin or Sythia, as you call it, we shouldn't believe a word they've said. As for the rest of what you've told me . . . it's a very unlikely story, Commander—you *do* know that?"

"Yes, ma'am."

"The only reason I haven't thrown you out of here for lying to my face is that we have the technology to do what these Avilonians are supposedly doing. We *could* clone ourselves and transfer the contents of our minds to those clones, but to what end? Why bother?"

"To live forever."

"I could make ten of me, Commander; we'd all look and sound the same, but only one of them would actually *be* me, and that's the original."

Atton shrugged. "That is one theory."

"It's backed up by the facts."

"I'm not arguing the existential philosophy with you, Captain. I agree, it does seem like a naive way to achieve immortality, but I saw it with my own eyes. Admiral Heston cloned himself in the last battle with the Sythians. There were two of him alive at the same time. One of those clones died on the Sythian command ship. The other is now ruling Dark Space."

"Suppose I were to believe all of this—why would we want to go to Avilon and join the Avilonians in their mad existence? It sounds to me like they have a lot in common with the Sythians."

"Some things, yes, but the admiral told me the Avilonians are nothing if not civilized. They won't greet us with violence, and I suspect that means they won't turn us away when we have nowhere else to go."

"You *suspect*. Did the admiral say why he was exiled?"

"No, he just said not to tell the Avilonians *he* sent me. Commander Donali was the one who told me that the admiral was exiled because he believed that people should be allowed to choose a mortal life if they wished."

The captain let out a long breath. "Said the suspected traitor. Donali might have told you that just to gain your confidence. It could be pure krak, meaning we don't know why the admiral was exiled."

"Avilon is not far from our present location, ma'am. When we do get out of here, before we go running to the farthest corner of the galaxy to find a world where we can rebuild, we should at least send an envoy to Avilon and see if it's worth going there instead."

"Agreed."

Atton was taken aback. "So you believe me?"

"I'm not sure why you would lie, but no I don't. I'll believe all of this when I have some proof. For now, I'm willing to keep it in mind and give you the benefit of the doubt, at least enough to further investigate."

"I understand. You won't regret that decision."

"We'll see about that," Caldin replied. "Meanwhile, there is one other thing we should do."

Atton cocked his head. "What's that?"

"Call for help."

"Call who?"

Caldin smiled. "The Avilonians of course."

"Without a jump gate and an open wormhole our comms will be limited to the speed of light. They'll arrive in—"

"Two and a half years," she said, pointing to the glowing green diamond on the star map once more.

"And then what? I'm not sure the Avilonians will care enough to send a rescue, but even if they did, it wouldn't get us out of here any faster."

"Maybe, maybe not. If they are as technologically advanced as you say, they might have a way to travel through a gravity field at superluminal speed."

"That's a big if, ma'am."

"At this point everything is a big if, Commander."

"What if Sythians intercept our comm signal? We have reason to believe they are looking for Avilon in order to wipe out humanity there, too."

"Really? Well, that does sound like them. Either way, our message won't contain any coordinates except for our own, and I'll be sure to keep it generic enough that it doesn't give the skull faces anything to go on. The worst that can happen is some Sythians come jumping into this gravity well and they end up stuck right along with us. If that happens, good riddance, but chances are *their* fail-safes will work and they won't even be able to get close to us."

"Well, then I guess it can't hurt."

"No," Caldin said with a tight smile. "Now, you had better get to the stasis rooms with everyone else. I'll handle this. If we get lucky and if everything you said is true, then we'll be waking you up a year or two earlier than expected. Dismissed, Commander."

"Yes, ma'am," he said, rising to his feet. He left the operations center and made his way back to the med bay where he'd woken up all of an hour ago. On his way there, Atton considered the implications of what he and the captain had just discussed. It was quite possible that the Avilonians would welcome them as refugees, but what that would mean for them and their futures was anybody's guess. Even the admiral couldn't say how Avilon had changed since he'd been there. He hadn't been back in tens of thousands of years. When Atton thought about how much the Imperium had changed in that time, he realized that anything was possible. The future was uncertain, but one thing was certain—once they arrived in Avilon they wouldn't be allowed to leave. If the Avilonians were in the habit of letting people come and go as they pleased, then someone somewhere would have found their sector a long time ago.

That meant he would never find out what had happened to his family.

Atton felt a rising ache in his chest, which became a painful lump in his throat. It was hard to accept that he would never see his mother, father, half-sister, or stepfather again. By the time he woke from stasis they would all be dead.

It was that depressing thought which Atton took with him to the stasis rooms, and when the transpiranium cover of stasis tube number 97 sealed him in with a hiss of pressurizing air, it was that thought which he carried with him into the cold, dream-filled world of near-perfect metabolic suspension. In there, time lost all meaning, and a dream could last for days or years. Atton's dreams were nightmares filled with haunting images of all the people he loved most—people he would never see again.

* * *

High Lord Kaon stood on the auxiliary bridge of the *Valiant*, the lights and heat turned down low to his liking. He turned in a slow circle to watch his crew of human slaves work. They already knew how to operate the warship. They were, after all, the very same humans who had been controlling the ship before, except now the Mind Web had turned them into obedient slaves.

The Mind Web could implant any knowledge, skill, or memory; it could sculpt the mind until the person became whatever the sculptor wished them to be. Humans turned out to be much more susceptible to the Mind Web than Gors, and the structure of their brains was better understood, so rather than wipe out the rest of humanity as they had originally intended, the Sythians had come to occupy Dark Space and conscript its people to serve in their fleet. That way they could replace the rebellious Gors.

Kaon's gaze wandered out the forward viewport to the

stars. Silhouetted against a nearby ice planet were the ruins of his command ship, the *Sharal*. That was what he had to show for the Gors' treachery. As if it weren't bad enough that they'd subsequently stolen his entire fleet, now they were interfering with the occupation in Dark Space.

Initially, everything had gone smoothly, but now there were hidden cells of Gors cropping up here there and everywhere to disturb the peace. In the last twenty four hours alone Gors had killed over a thousand human slaves, and almost all of those were on Karpathia. The Sythians were being forced to conscript greater and greater numbers of humans in order to make up for losses.

Kaon hissed with displeasure. Something would have to be done about it, but for now he had other concerns. Kaon stalked up to the *Valiant's* command control station. Humans called it the *captain's table*. He stared at it for a long moment, his big blue eyes watering and itching with frustration. He'd forgotten how to turn the thing on. He understood Imperial Versal well enough, so the language barrier wasn't the problem, but human control systems were less intuitive than Sythian ones. In a Sythian ship one merely had to think a command and the ship would answer. Anything the ship knew, it would display, and anything the ship could do, it would perform. Human ships on the other hand required hands-on manipulation of control systems. Endless gestures and linguistic queries were required just to get at a specific bit of information.

Kaon refused to submit to the Mind Web in order to learn how to operate human control systems. He'd done it once before to learn their language, but it was not an experience he wished to repeat. No, for now, he had *The Pet* to help him. Kaon turned from the captain's table to see The Pet standing behind him, his wrists bound with a few lengths of human stun cord. The Pet's shoulders were rounded, his eyes and expression haunted. Flanking him were a pair of fully-armored human slave soldiers, standing ready to kill him if he did anything wrong. Not that he *could* do anything wrong.

"Come here Pet," Kaon warbled. The Pet took a few steps toward him as soon as those words were translated by the device it wore in its ear. Ten years had passed since the original invasion of the Adventa Galaxy, and in all that time humans hadn't bothered to learn Sythian. No wonder they had lost the war. Their ignorance was astounding. "Show me what is around our ship. I want to see the fleet," he instructed.

The Pet stepped up to the captain's table and began waving his hands, bound as they were, through the air. A holographic map flickered to life, rising out of the table with a blue glow. Kaon gave an eager hiss and peered into the open cube of space which had appeared. He realized that he still had much to learn about human systems of measurement and annotation. He could see miniature representations of each major ship on the display. Whole squadrons and wings of fighters were shown with small Shell Fighter icons. They were the only fighters on the map, since the humans' Novas were all grounded until loyal slaves could be trained to pilot them. A few of The Pet's best pilots were already hooked up to a Mind Web so that their skills and knowledge of piloting could be isolated, downloaded, and then transferred to obedient slaves.

As for The Pet himself, he was also a slave, but a different kind of slave. He had been implanted with a device which forced him to obey, but rather than alter his brain to make him a *willing* slave, instead it made him a prisoner in his own mind and body, a victim of suggestion and authority. He couldn't resist any orders, even though his mind was surely screaming for him to do so. It gave Kaon no small amount of satisfaction to see the former admiral who had destroyed his mighty *Sharal* now a desiccated husk of his former self, locked in an endless struggle against himself.

"Are you watching, Pet?" Kaon pointed to the map, his armored finger tracing a line around a group of Sythian ships which was now splitting off from the rest. "Those ships go to Avilon. They go as the first wave of the next invasion."

"The Avilonians are very strong. Those ships won't be enough to defeat them," The Pet said in a toneless voice. The implant in his brain forced him to speak his mind even if he didn't want to. That added layer of transparency helped Kaon gain insight into his enemies.

"Do not worry. We have many more ships to fight this new enemy," Kaon replied. "We are already culling your population of its troublemakers to fill these fleets with fresh slaves. Any and all who resist are forced to join the forces they fight against. The irony is delicious," Kaon said, licking his rubbery lips.

"I think it's despicable," The Pet replied.

"I know you think this, but even you must admit that it is an efficient way to subdue your people."

"Yes, it is," The Pet replied, his face scrunching up in dismay.

Kaon's eyes greedily tracked the ships leaving Dark Space. High Lord Quaris had elected to go, since the Second Fleet, which he commanded, was the smallest of the Sythians' remaining fleets. Thanks to the Gors and their terrorism, the Sythians couldn't afford to leave Dark Space undefended, so Kaon and Shondar would stay behind and wait to hear back from Quaris. He had orders to run with his command ship before losing the entire fleet, but even if he did, the data collected from that battle would be worth it. Armed with advance knowledge of their enemy's weaknesses and strengths, they would defeat Avilon just as easily as they had defeated the rest of humanity. None could stand against the might of the Sythian Coalition, and soon their mission in the Adventa Galaxy would be complete.

Kaon felt a pleasant warmth rise in his chest as his twin hearts began beating faster at the thought. He basked in that warmth for a moment before turning his thoughts back to the matter at hand.

He and High Lord Shondar were going to stay behind to continue the work of re-crewing their ships with human slaves. They needed to hurry, especially now that they were sending a fleet to poke their sleeping enemy in the belly. Within a week, High Lords Worval, Rossk, Thorian, and Lady Kala would all arrive with their behemoth command cruisers. Docked inside those massive ships would be over a thousand starships—empty and waiting for their new slave crews. Even at the rate they were going, conscripting over a hundred thousand slaves per week, it would take several months to completely crew those ships.

Kaon considered that a few million slaves was probably more than they could justify by claiming those citizens were resisting the occupation, but Sythians didn't have to explain themselves to their slaves. Any justifications they gave were just a courtesy to make their slaves feel like their lives actually mattered. *A happy slave is a productive slave.*

The Pet interrupted Kaon's thoughts by asking, "How will you fill all of your ships with humans if you only take the ones who offer resistance?"

Kaon turned to The Pet, the gills in the sides of his neck

flaring with surprise. Had The Pet read his mind?

"Our population is small," The Pet went on. "You will destroy our economy if you take too many of us."

"Your people have their orders to breed. They are to replenish what we take."

"They will not obey."

"Then those who do not are to become slavesss," Kaon hissed. "Either way, you give us what we desire."

"Why don't you just clone us?"

"Cloning takes time and resources. Taking from an existing population is much faster. It puts the burden on your people and keeps your population under control. Humans are never to become strong enough to challenge us again."

"I hate you," The Pet said, his private thoughts making themselves known once more.

Kaon turned to offer him a rubbery smile. "I know."

Chapter 17

Beep beep, beep beep, beep beep . . .

Doctor Stevon Elder reached into his outer lab coat pocket and fumbled with his holo pad to turn off his alarm. As soon as the incessant beeping stopped, he subsided with a sigh and began shivering violently where he lay. He realized he couldn't feel his toes, and he could barely see his hands in front of his face. The cold and darkness were a reminder that he was no longer living among his own kind. The Sythians had come, and even though they now used human slaves—as opposed to Gors whose native environment was dark and frigid—somehow these humans weren't bothered by either the darkness or the cold the way they should have been. Perhaps it was a question of mind over matter. *Thank the Immortals they haven't messed with* my *mind yet.*

Stevon turned his head and felt a sharp stab of pain in his neck. He reached around to find a molten chunk of transpiranium poking him there. He threw it to one side, and it landed a few feet away with a *thunk*. All around him were debris, shattered equipment and twisted girders. It was hard to believe he was still aboard the *Valiant*. He'd found this abandoned alcove by accident a few weeks ago. An old med lab, hiding almost at the bottom of an abandoned lift tube. Based on the amount of destruction it had seen, there had been some kind of explosive accident.

Whatever had befallen the lab, Stevon was grateful for it. He had known the Sythians would do one of two things when they came aboard—execute the fleet's officers en masse, or turn them into slaves the way they had with the refugees they'd found in the Enclave. The skull faces had opted for the latter option, which was far worse than the former in Stevon's opinion. Better to die and go to Etheria than to live and be forced against one's will to serve a heartless, soulless enemy.

Then again, the Sythians likely wouldn't let him live once they found out what he knew. If they had the chance to turn him into a slave, his newfound loyalty to them would make him tell all, and one of the first things he would tell them was what he had done to hide the location of Avilon. After that, his life and Admiral Heston's would be forfeit, but not before both of them were thoroughly tortured to find out what they knew. Stevon would use the suicide tooth the admiral had given him long before it came to that, but it occurred to him that there was a better option than sitting around in the ruined med lab, waiting to be discovered. The admiral had given him the coordinates to get to Avilon, recorded on a micro dot inside his suicide tooth.

Perhaps the Avilonians wouldn't welcome him—an

Etherian—or perhaps the sector had become more open-minded since Hoff had been there all those millennia ago. Either way, Stevon knew the Avilonians were the key to humanity's survival. Even if they killed him upon arrival, at least he might have a chance to warn them about the Sythians and what they were doing in Dark Space. When Atton had left to get help, the invaders had been at a standoff with humanity. Now, things were much more serious.

Stevon stood up and brushed a fine layer of white dust from his clothes which had accumulated while he slept. Clearly the air filters weren't working in the ruined med lab. Taking a deep breath to steel himself, Stevon turned toward the far wall and the out-of-service lift shaft which he'd climbed down to get here. It was now or never. He'd set his alarm for the middle of the night cycle in the hope that he'd run into fewer of the Sythians' slave soldiers. He had to try to get to the hangar and steal a ship. If he failed and had to use his suicide pill, or got shot to pieces while trying to escape, then he would suffer the same fate as if he stayed here, only swifter.

Even rationing himself and sleeping as much as possible, it had taken him less than a week to exhaust the 100 pound grav bag of supplies he'd brought with him. Now he had just two options—stay and die a slow, painful death from dehydration, or make a run for it and go down fighting.

Stevon started toward the broken lift tube shaft. Bits of transpiranium and duranium crunched underfoot. There was a hollow ache in his belly, and he was swaying on his feet as he walked. He reached the shaft and looked up. It looked as daunting as a mountain, but he reminded himself he only had to climb up three floors to get out. After that . . .

He wasn't sure what he would do.

One step at a time, Stevon, he told himself. *Immortals help me . . .*

He found his first handhold and almost lost his grip while trying to pull himself up onto a fallen girder. But, step by awkward step, handhold by handhold, somehow he made it. Panting and sweating from the exertion, he reached the doors on the third level up from the ruined lab. He pried them open with shaking hands and slithered out into the corridor. Exhausted, all he could do was lay there on his belly and catch his breath. Thankfully, the corridor was deserted, but he knew better than to rely on that. The *Valiant* had holocorders everywhere, and someone, somewhere would be watching. His heart pounding, Stevon pushed himself off the cold deck and hurried down the corridor. As he ran, he struggled to remember which way he had to go to get to the nearest hangar. But the ship was too vast, and he barely knew where he was. His best bet would be to get to the nearest rail car tunnel. Once there he could search the ship's directory for its hangar bays. He hurried on, his booted-feet pounding down the corridor.

Then something caught his eye.

Up ahead, gleaming in the low, lavender-hued light, which the Sythians had set the ship's glow panels to produce, Stevon saw a suspicious-looking black dome hanging down from the ceiling—a holocorder. His legs shaking, he ran faster as he passed beneath the camera, irrationally hoping that if he ran fast enough it wouldn't see him.

Come on, Stevon . . . pull yourself together. . . .

* * *

"My Lord, there's a security alert on level 15," the *Valiant's* security officer said.

Kaon turned away from the Captain's table with a hiss. "What is it?" he warbled.

"A man, Doctor Stevon Elder, according to visual analysis. He appears to be in a great hurry to get somewhere. The security system flagged his behavior as suspicious. He is not one of us."

Kaon walked up behind the officer in charge of security and studied the hologram projected above his station. It showed footage of the doctor in question, running as fast as he could down one corridor after another. "What is the reason for his haste?"

"I do not know. Perhaps he is trying to get off the *Valiant* before we find him and make him join us."

"We already find him."

"He must be desperate to believe we wouldn't catch him."

"I like to know what he intends to do," Kaon replied.

"Should I seal off the section where he is and send in a squad to capture him?"

Kaon considered that. "No. Seal off sections around him so that he is to take the path we choose." Kaon turned to find The Pet standing behind him, the man's gray eyes glued to the hologram. "You—Pet—you are to go meet this doctor.

You are to pretend to be escaping, too. Gain his trust; find out what he is doing, and then incapacitate him and bring him to me."

The Pet hesitated only slightly before turning away from the screen and bowing his head. "As you will, My Lord."

Kaon turned to the pair of guards standing watch over his Pet and then pointed to the former admiral's bound wrists. "Cut him loose and give him a weapon."

"A weapon, My Lord?"

"He cannot disobey me or betray us. To do that would take more strength than he has left. I have broken him, and he is mine. My *Pet*. Are you not?" Kaon reached out to stroke the human's cheek with the back of one armored hand.

The Pet stared back at him with haunted eyes. Abruptly Kaon hissed and gave him a vicious backhanded slap. The Pet stumbled away, shock written all over his face. Kaon advanced quickly and hit him again, this time breaking his nose with a spray of blood. The human cried out and collapsed to the deck, trying to staunch the blood streaming from his shattered nose. "You tell the doctor you escape, and that you sustain these injuries during that escape."

Turning back to his guards, Kaon gave them a deadly look. "Set him free and give him a weapon!"

This time neither of the guardsmen hesitated to obey.

* * *

Doctor Elder reached a junction in the corridor and tried the doors at the end, waving his wrist over the identichip scanner. It beeped and flashed red.

Locked.

Stevon whirled in a quick circle to see another two sets of doors to either side of him. He tried the pair on his left. They swished open and he ran through.

That was the second set of doors he had encountered which refused to open when he tried them. It wasn't unusual for certain sections of a ship to be restricted access, but it *was* unusual to find whole corridors blocked off. That only ever happened when they were exposed to space, and the *Valiant* hadn't seen any action recently, so what were the Sythians doing?

Stevon hoped he could still make it to one of the hangars. Up ahead he saw a glowing sign hanging down from the roof which read *Rail System* with an arrow pointing to the right. Hope swelled in his chest. He might actually make it!

So far he hadn't run into any Sythians or their slaves, but that wasn't surprising. The *Valiant* had been running on a skeleton crew when the Sythians took it, and during the night cycle, there'd be even fewer people to walk the ship's 150 plus decks. The ship's size was working in Stevon's favor now.

He came to another set of doors and raised a trembling hand to the scanner, hoping the doors would open for him.

Swish.

Stevon ran through into a much broader corridor. Along one side lay a set of rail car tracks, separated from him by a wall of transpiranium doors. Right now there wasn't a rail car waiting in the station, so Stevon stepped up to a nearby directory and brought up a map of the ship. He found the nearest hangar bay—port ventral—and punched that in as his destination. While he waited, he shot a quick look over his shoulder to make sure no one was watching.

Then he spotted the roving black eye of another holocorder hanging down from the ceiling, and he looked away before the eye could turn to see his face. The fact that squads of armored troops hadn't descended on him yet was encouraging, but Stevon didn't want to push his luck.

A rising whistle heralded the approach of a rail car; it screeched to a halt in front of the station, and eight sets of transpiranium doors swished open in perfect synchrony. Just as Stevon started through the pair of doors in front of him, a thought occurred to him: what if there was someone waiting on the rail car?

Stevon's right hand fumbled past his lab coat to find the butt of the sidearm strapped to his waist. He drew the plasma pistol and clicked off the safety before peering around the corner of the rail car doors.

To the left—no one. To the right—

A man slumped against the far wall, wearing a tattered and blood-stained white uniform. For a second Stevon didn't recognize that uniform, but then he caught a glimpse of the insignia. Six golden stars surrounding a clenched fist. The symbol of the Imperium and the Supreme Overlord.

"Admiral?" Stevon asked, unable to believe his eyes.

The admiral raised his head to offer a weak smile. "If you think I'm going to surrender peacefully, you're wrong," he said.

Stevon heard a subtle click followed by a screech of energy being released. The shot went wide and hit the wall behind him. "Hoi!" Stevon said, raising his hands. "Admiral! It's me! Doctor Elder."

"You're not . . . one of them?"

"Not yet. How did you escape?" Stevon's gaze flicked over the admiral from head to toe, taking in his disheveled, unshaven appearance. Between his facial hair, the accumulated grime, and the layer of dried blood caked over his nose and upper lip, it was obvious he hadn't been treated well.

The rail car began moving again, and Stevon walked slowly toward the admiral. The man's breathing was slow and labored, his eyes narrowed to slits, as if he barely had the energy to keep them open. "It's a . . . long story," Admiral Heston managed. "We don't have time for it right now. We have to get out of here."

"Yes . . . in hindsight, surrender was not our best option."

"Perhaps not, but at least we are alive."

"For now," Stevon replied, taking a seat beside the admiral.

"Tell me you have an escape plan."

"I was going to ask you the same thing."

"I'm just surprised I managed to escape. Haven't had time to figure out the rest."

Stevon frowned. "Well, I did. I'm going to steal a ship and head for Avilon."

The admiral turned to regard him with one eyebrow raised. "Even if you escape, and even if the Avilonians accept you, the Sythians already know where Avilon is." The admiral's expression twisted miserably and his voice filled with self-loathing as he explained, "I told them."

Stevon gave a wry smile. "No, you didn't. Avilon is still safe. Before you surrendered, you had me alter the coordinates in your memory. That's why you were suffering amnesia when you woke up in med bay a week ago."

The admiral's eyes widened. "Is that why I can't

remember where my wife and daughter are?"

"They're with the Gors, stirring up krak for the Sythians."

"And Atton?"

"You sent him to Avilon to get reinforcements."

Relief shone in the admiral's eyes, but then something dark and ugly rose up to steal that light away. Abruptly all the muscles in his neck began standing out. His jaw muscles bunched and his eyelids began fluttering. "I . . . I need to tell you . . ." He began in a strained voice. His expression became a rictus and veins began standing out on his forehead.

"What's wrong?" Stevon asked quickly. "Admiral? Are you okay?"

"I . . ."

"Admiral!" Stevon began to worry that the admiral was suffering a stroke. His face did appear to be drooping, and he was definitely having difficulty speaking. Then, abruptly, the symptoms passed, and his features smoothed into a more orderly smile.

"I'm fine," he said. "Sorry. It's just a bad headache. Came out of nowhere."

"I see . . . and what is it you needed to tell me?"

"I need to tell you that if it comes to it, we can't let them take us alive."

Stevon accepted that with a frown. "Yes, I know. You're the one who gave me a suicide pill, but let's hope it doesn't come to that. As soon as this car arrives we need to make a run for it. Do you think you'll be able to make it, or should I grav you to the nearest ship?"

"No, you'll need my help if we run into trouble. I'll be fine. Just tell me you have the real coordinates for Avilon."

"It's on a micro dot in a fake tooth right alongside the suicide pill. . . . You really don't remember any of that, do you? I did a better job erasing your memory than I thought."

"You must have," the admiral replied.

The rail car began slowing down, and Stevon looked up. "We're almost there." He watched out the nearest window as they pulled into the rail car station next to the ventral hangar bays. Light flickered through the rail car from passing glow panels. He scanned the station platform, looking for any waiting Sythians or human slaves, but it was deserted. "Looks like we're clear. You ready?" Stevon asked, turning back to the admiral.

"Are you?" he countered.

That was when Stevon noticed the sidearm Admiral Heston was aiming at his belly. "Frek!" He fell out of his seat in his hurry to get away, but he wasn't fast enough. Hoff pulled the trigger with a screech, and this time he didn't miss. A powerful jolt went through Stevon's body, leaving him twitching on the floor. His eyes drifted shut, and then the darkness took him and he knew no more.

Chapter 18

Kaon listened to The Pet explain what the human doctor had been doing. The Pet explained all about his clever ruse to keep Avilon hidden by altering his own memories. Kaon tried to contain his building rage as The Pet handed him the fake human tooth which supposedly contained the real coordinates for the lost human sector.

"If this is the real location of Avilon, then where is it that you make me send Lord Quaris?" Kaon asked, tucking the tooth into a compartment on his belt for later study.

"I don't know," The Pet replied. "Perhaps into a black hole."

Kaon hissed and lunged at the human, knocking him to the deck. He pinned his Pet there and delivered a wicked blow to his already broken nose. Blood spurted once more, and the human screamed. Kaon aimed his second blow for The Pet's mouth, knocking out the man's front teeth and silencing his screams. "You think me to be a fool, Pet? You delay us, but you do not stopped usss," he hissed.

The Pet tried to say something, but all he could do was gurgle on his own blood. "Guards!" Kaon warbled, leaping off the admiral before he completely lost his temper and killed the fragile human. "Lock him away until I decide what to do with him!"

"Yes, My Lord," one of the guards said, stepping forward to haul the human to his feet and bind his hands with stun cords once more.

"And take the doctor to the Mind Web. I want to know what else he is hiding," Kaon said, pointing to the unconscious form of Doctor Stevon Elder, still lying motionless on the deck where the admiral had deposited him.

"Yes, My Lord," his other guard said.

Kaon watched as The Pet and Doctor Elder were carried off the auxiliary bridge deck. His thoughts raced in angry circles. The humans would pay for this treachery. Kaon had just sent over 50 warships into the middle of who knew where. *Lord Quaris and the Second Fleet may never be heard from again!*

Kaon retrieved the fake tooth from his utility belt and studied it in his hand, wondering how to access the data supposedly stored there. He supposed one of his slaves would know—assuming the data were really there. There was no way to be sure that Doctor Elder had told the admiral the truth, but soon the Mind Web would reveal all.

Meanwhile, Kaon had to find a new fleet to send to Avilon. He turned to his communications officer and called down to the human. "Contact High Lord Shondar of the Fourth Fleet. I must speak with him."

"Yes, My Lord."

Now, Shondar would have to go to Avilon, leaving Kaon alone to deal with the Gors' petty disturbances and humanity's feeble attempts to resist their fate. Perhaps that temporary vulnerability would drive the Gors out of hiding just in time to be crushed when the other lords arrived with their fleets. If not, then eventually starvation would force them to reveal themselves.

Yesss . . . revenge is mine, Kaon thought.

* * *

Captain Loba Caldin and her partner, Corpsman Terl, stood side by side, up to their elbows in wires in a claustrophobic access corridor on the port side of the *Intrepid's* SLS drives. Standing further down the corridor with a diagnostic tool was her chief engineer and XO, Deck Commander Cobrale Delayn. Although he didn't have a romantic partner, she had paired him with her gravidar officer, Lieutenant Esayla Carvon, based on their mutual consent and the fact that they had a good working relationship. Neither one of them seemed interested in the other, but that could easily change over the next four to five years while the *Intrepid* snailed along at one tenth light.

As for herself and Terl, they were busy investigating the equipment malfunction which had landed them in their present mess. Delayn had them sifting through bunches of colored fiber optic cables to find the ones marked *F-S* while he ran various tests on the fail-safes which should have pulled them out of SLS at the *edge* of the gravity field where they were stranded, rather than the middle of it where they were now.

"I don't get it," Delayn said, shaking his head.

"What?" Caldin asked, rubbing the sweat out of her eyes with her sleeve.

"They're working perfectly."

"What do you mean they're working *perfectly*? Did someone fix them before we put the crew in stasis?"

"No, I had that work slated for last. Our engineering teams were too busy making repairs after the last engagement. I thought we could do the low-priority repairs ourselves, but . . . in the case of the fail-safes, there's nothing to fix."

"Double check that, Commander."

"I've already *triple* checked," Delayn replied. "The only thing wrong with this equipment is it's a little dusty."

Caldin made an irritated noise in the back of her throat as she stuffed the bundles of wiring back into their compartments. "Let's get out of here."

"Right behind you, ma'am," Terl replied.

When they were all standing outside the access corridor, Caldin turned to Delayn with a scowl and planted her hands on her hips. "If the fail-safes are working fine, then why didn't they pull us out of SLS?"

Delayn shook his head. "I don't know. Perhaps some type

of interference prevented them from detecting the gravity field until it was too late?"

"Or?"

"Or . . . the gravity field wasn't there until we'd already landed in it."

"That makes no sense, Delayn."

He shook his head. "None of this makes any sense. I'll stay here to run some more tests, just in case there's something I missed."

"You do that. Let me know if you find anything."

"Yes, ma'am."

* * *

Admiral Hoff Heston sat in his cell, his mouth throbbing and aching, his nose itching from all the dried blood. He was barely conscious, and he knew there was no way out. The Sythians had made him a slave without making him a slave. They'd made him a tormented wretch. He tried to say one thing, but ended up saying another. He tried to hide his thoughts from the Sythians, but whenever he was around them he couldn't help but say everything that was on his mind. At least right now he couldn't speak—not clearly anyway. Kaon had knocked out his teeth and broken his jaw, leaving him a blubbering mess.

Hoff couldn't tell how long he had been sitting in his cell. He suspected quite a while, but he wasn't certain that he had been conscious the entire time, and the guards had confiscated his holo pad when he'd arrived, so he had no idea what time it was. Adding to his disorientation, he kept nodding off to sleep.

After another indeterminate period of time passed, Hoff felt his stomach grumbling, and then a plate of food came sliding under the door. He eyed it bitterly. He wasn't sure how he could eat it in his condition. They would have to fix his jaw first, and something told him the Sythians weren't that good to their prisoners.

Hoff's head lolled to one side and he subsided into a troubled sleep. Some time later he was roughly awoken to find himself face to face with the glowing red optics of a Gor's helmet. For a moment he was confused—hadn't the Sythians stopped using Gor slaves?

Then he heard a human voice tell him to get up, following by someone lifting him to his feet, and he remembered that the Sythians had recycled Gor armor for their human slaves.

"Warr ooo aking ee?" *Where are you taking me.*

Somehow the slave soldier understood his slurred speech and replied, "To see your ancestors."

As they passed through the cell door, and the soldiers carried him off the brig, Hoff tried to remember who his ancestors were. If he still had any, they would be in Avilon, and he hadn't seen them for many thousands of years. Perhaps the Sythians were taking him to Avilon?

Then a far more likely thought occurred to him, and Hoff began to struggle against the guards carrying him. Weak from pain and hunger, his efforts were wasted. His suspicions were confirmed when they reached the nearest airlock and Hoff saw Kaon waiting with a squad of armored soldiers and a civilian holonews crew. The crew looked nervous, and when the reporter's eyes found Hoff, he thought she was going to cry. The guards carrying him stopped in front of Kaon.

"Hello, Pet," the Sythian said. "Have you any final words before you die?"

"Go fwek youswef," Hoff replied as he was forced to his knees. The implants the Sythians had injected into his brain still allowed him some degree of autonomy, enough to speak his mind, but not enough to actively resist.

Kaon gave a rubbery smile. "You and I are not so different, human. We are both immortal, and we are both warriors. I wonder where you are to be resurrected now? Are you to come back to life in Avilon, or aboard this very ship? Be certain of this, human, wherever you return, I will find you and kill you—*again.*"

Hoff realized that Kaon didn't know he had deactivated his Lifelink implant, and before he could stop himself, he told the Sythian all about it.

"Then this will be a real death. Good." Kaon turned to the news crew who were recording the entire scene with wide eyes. The reporter hadn't said a word yet. She was speechless. Hoff realized she didn't even know what they were talking about. Avilon and the Immortals were a well-kept secret. Kaon inclined his head to the reporter, "Humans are beasts to be tamed, nothing more. This one has proven too difficult to tame, and he must be put down. Perhaps this will teach you humans the cost of resistance." With that, he turned to the guards who held Hoff between them and said, "Open the airlock and leave him inside."

They yanked him to his feet and carried him to the doors. The airlock opened with a groaning and grinding of gears. The guards carried him to the middle of the chamber and then they dropped him and withdrew. Hoff sat on the cold deck, hunched over and barely able to lift his head. Somehow he managed to look up just as the doors began to close. He found himself staring directly into the black lens of the news crew's holocorder. He tried to rearrange his face in a smile for the sake of all the millions of people across Dark Space who would be forced to watch the recording later.

He knew he was going to die. If he hadn't let his wife convince him to give up his immortal life, not long from now he would have been resurrected in a cloning tank somewhere aboard the *Valiant,* the state of his brain saved and transferred to a new body just before he died. As it was, however, he was finally about to see whether or not he still had a soul, and whether or not such a thing even existed.

The airlock doors shut with an ominous *boom*, and the news crew went on recording through the transpiranium panels in the tops of the doors. Red emergency lights began to flash, and a warning siren wailed, indicating that the airlock was about to be opened without depressurizing it first. Hoff knew he had only seconds left. In that time, he managed one last gesture for the camera and the citizens of Dark Space who would soon be looking on in horror.

He gave a salute.

With that, the doors behind him burst open and he was sucked out into space.

* * *

Hundreds of klicks from Karpathia City, Destra Ortane stood on the bridge of the *Baroness,* studying a map of the city with Captain Covani and a hulking Gor—Roan's son, Torv. This would be the most daring raid they had planned yet. Until now they had just been sending out teams of cloaked Gors to cause mayhem and hunt the Sythians' new slave soldiers, but the Sythians had merely responded by increasing the rate at which they were taking civilians and turning them into slaves for their fleet. As soon as they had realized that, both Destra and Covani had been forced to admit their strategy was counter-productive. They were killing the very people they sought to protect.

A week had passed since the occupation began, and it was beginning to look like the best form of resistance would be to do nothing. They needed to keep the Gor fleet hiding in Dark Space supplied and ready for when Atton returned with reinforcements from Avilon.

If he comes back, Destra thought grimly. Hoff had told her at the last possible minute that there was a chance the Avilonians wouldn't let him leave Avilon once he arrived. If that happened, Destra would go find Atton herself. Hoff had left her with the coordinates to get there, and she had every intention of using them if it came to that.

"We'll have to make a low pass over the warehouse after our teams on the ground open it up with detlor charges," Captain Covani said, interrupting her thoughts. "Soon as those supplies are exposed, we can get a lock on them with our grav guns and haul them in."

"What type of supplies are we looking at?" Destra asked.

"Foodstuffs, but that's what we need most anyway. A fleet flies on its stomach—especially a Gor fleet," Covani added, sending Torv a wry look.

Torv missed the remark. He was staring out the forward viewports. With his helmet on, it was impossible to see the alien's expression, but Destra imagined a faraway look in the Gor's eyes. "Torv," she said quietly. "Do you think you could have your people on the ground get to that warehouse and set the charges for us?"

Torv's giant head slowly turned, and he stared at her with the big, glowing red optics in his helmet. "They are leaving."

"What? Who is?"

"The Sythianss," Torv hissed. "My créche lord tells me that they leave the entrance of Dark Space."

Captain Covani turned to stare at Torv. "All of them?"

Destra blinked. "If that's true, then we need to make our move now."

"Wait . . ." Torv replied. A moment later, he went on, "Not all of them leave . . . a cluster—one fleet."

"How many fleets do they have?"

"Your human fleet, which is now in their hands, and half of another cluster with no command ship."

Covani frowned. "Can they fight without a command ship?"

"That depends," Torv replied.

"On what?"

"Whether their masters let them."

"So, if they trust their crews to fight, then they will, and we'll still be outnumbered." Covani shook his head.

"But they'll be vulnerable," Destra said. "Perhaps more vulnerable than they ever will be again."

"And what happens when the rest of them come here? They could be here tomorrow, or in just a few hours. They have to be on their way. If you think the Sythians are vulnerable, just think how vulnerable *we'll* be after we've exhausted ourselves fighting their rear guard. If we try to face them head-on now, the resistance will be over before it has even begun. We need to wait for reinforcements. When they arrive we'll be in a much better position to take back the sector."

"Fine, but we should at least send a team of Gors to get the admiral out. You saw what they're doing to him."

Covani shook his head. "We've already discussed this, Madam Councilor. If we use Gors to get the admiral, the Sythians will know the surrender was a ruse and that the Gors are still on our side. I can't risk that the Sythians will take that out on the people of Dark Space. Besides, if the rescue fails, which it almost certainly will, then the Sythians will do more than just torture the Admiral. They'll *kill* him."

"What if they kill him anyway? He's your commanding officer!"

"And he's your husband. I can appreciate that you're having difficulty putting your personal feelings aside, ma'am, but my *commanding officer* wouldn't want me to rescue him at the expense of the very people he's trying to protect. The admiral planned for it to be this way. We have to have faith that his plan will buy enough time for reinforcements to arrive. If it doesn't, then we'll try to arrange a rescue for the

Admiral before we abandon Dark Space. Until then, I have my orders, and you have your husband's wishes to respect."

"I'll be sure to tell the admiral you said that when he gets back," Destra replied with a thin smile. Turning to Torv, she asked, "Where are the Sythians going?"

"I do not know this," he replied.

"Begging your pardons, Mrs. Heston and Captain Covani—" Destra turned to see the comms officer staring up at them with wide eyes and a pale face.

"What is it, Lieutenant?" Covani snapped.

"The Sythians just released another one of their ... motivational holocasts."

"Put it on the main holoscreen."

"Yes, sir... sorry, ma'am," he said, glancing at Destra before punching a key on his control station. She had only a moment to wonder about that apology before she understood. The main viewport turned opaque and then a scene appeared and she found herself staring at a familiar man—or at least she thought he was familiar. It was hard to tell if it was him through the mess of dirt, blood, and stubble which had turned his face a ruddy brown. The blood-stained white uniform gave him away, but the look of abject horror on his face made him look like an entirely different person. Destra gasped and shook her head. She remembered the first time she'd seen her husband after the Sythians had gotten hold of him. They'd pointed to him as a symbol of humanity's defeat. And now ... Hoff looked worse than ever. What possible point could they be trying to prove?

Kaon began to speak, and subtitles appeared at the bottom of the projection. Destra shook her head, horrified by what she was seeing and hearing. They were going to kill him. Then she heard Hoff explain that his Lifelink implant was deactivated and her eyes blurred with tears. If she hadn't made him do that, then he might still have lived through this. As it was, however, he was about to meet a very definite end.

Kaon turned away from the camera to look at the guards who held Hoff between them, the subtitles on the screen ordering them to *open the airlock and leave him inside.*

"No!" Destra cried.

But by now Hoff was already dead. With the time it took for data to travel from one end of Dark Space to the other, this newscast was at least several hours old. Destra saw her husband look up and smile at the camera revealing a row of bloody, crooked teeth. Red emergency lights began flashing all around him, and an alarm began to sound. He raised his arm slowly, deliberately, and gave a sloppy salute to the camera.

Then the airlock doors opened behind him and he was ripped off the deck and sucked out into space.

Destra watched, horrified, as the dwindling speck that was her husband vanished against the stars, and then the outer airlock slid shut and he was gone. The transmission ended there, but for Destra it would never end. It was already playing on an endless loop inside her head. She felt strong hands on her shoulders.

"I'm sorry you had to see that," Captain Covani said quietly.

Destra turned and collapsed into his arms, sobbing.

"I hate them!" she screamed with a sudden, explosive force which surprised even her. Destra pushed away from the captain and shook her head, sending tears pinwheeling from her eyelashes to the deck. "Frekking skull faces! They've taken everything from me! They took everything from all of us!" she said, turning in a slow circle to address the bridge crew. "When will enough be enough? When will we finally get our revenge for what they've done?" Crew looked up from their stations, their expressions blank and full of horror.

"We're lucky that we're still alive and free," Covani whispered. "Revenge will have to wait."

Destra shook her head and made her way wordlessly from the bridge. On her way, she shot an acid look at the lieutenant manning the comms station. "Make sure my daughter doesn't get a chance to see that. No news feeds in the mess or any of the common areas."

"Yes, ma'am."

The bridge doors swished open and then shut behind her. Her body was physically trembling with rage. She would have her revenge. Sooner or later she would find a way to make the Sythians pay. *Just a few more weeks*, she tried to tell herself. *A few more weeks and reinforcements will be here.* Then she would hunt Kaon down and throw *him* out an airlock.

Chapter 19

Two weeks later . . .

Two more days, Ethan thought, admiring the view from one of the Vermillion Palace's balconies. Far below, the bright turquoise of the Argyle Sea sparkled in the sun. Semi-tropical islands dotted that expanse, overgrown with vegetation that was all the colors of the rainbow. Fluffy white clouds sailed by close below their cliffside vantage point. Two more days and they'd be back to reality. Thanks to the Sythian occupation, it was an even harsher reality than they'd had to endure in the past.

Hoff had been executed for all the sector to see. Citizens were being taken by the thousands every day. They were taken from their beds at night, or taken off the streets in broad daylight. People were being enslaved left and right to serve in the Sythian fleet, without warning or explanation. Initially those reports had been seen on the news nets, warning people not to trust the Sythians. The invaders had promised to leave Dark Space in peace, but they were leaving it in *pieces*. No one was safe. After the first such report had aired, no further outcries had been heard from the press. They were feeling the weight of the Sythians' rule, just the same as everyone else. The only truly free press humanity had left was the one which could be heard whispered from one ear to another.

Ethan tightened his grip on his wife's shoulders and shot her a wan smile. "Did you enjoy your honeymoon?" he asked, trying to lighten the mood.

It was the wrong question to ask.

Alara raised her eyebrows and shot him a bland look. That was her *don't be stupid* look. The Vermillion palace had its own water, power, and food supply—enough to last for months without replenishment, so they hadn't suffered any of the worst effects of the Sythian occupation, but being stranded for a month in a luxurious hotel whilst they knew the rest of humanity was suffering one of the worst times in human history had been more than enough to ruin their honeymoon.

The blockade had been lifted, for what that was worth, but where could they possibly hope to go? Ethan wasn't sure. Without a cloaking device and a hold full of red dymium fuel, they wouldn't get far. As far as he knew cloaking devices had never been adapted to ships as small as his *Trinity*, and red dymium fuel was still restricted to the fleet, which was now controlled by Sythians, so they were just as stuck as anyone else in Dark Space.

"What if they take *us* next, Ethan? What's going to happen to our baby?"

"Let's hope the drafting stops soon. They only have so many ships, and if they expect us to be a renewable source of crew for the future then they'll have to leave the majority of our population alone."

"The majority. How many do you think they'll take before they have enough?"

Ethan thought back to the initial invasion and how many Gors had been in the Sythians' fleet. "Assuming they haven't brought any new fleets to our galaxy . . . they'll need to take at least a few million of us to replace the Gors."

"A few *million*? Our entire population *is* a few million!"

"Just over ten," Ethan corrected.

Alara shook her head. "This is a nightmare. Maybe we *should* leave."

"No, you were right," Ethan said. "There's no way out and nowhere for us to go. We have to lie low. We can find a safe place to hide somewhere out in deep space until they're done abducting people."

"I'm tired," Alara said suddenly. "I want to go back to our room now."

"Okay," Ethan replied, turning away from the view and walking back inside the palace.

When they got back to their room, Ethan waved his wrist over the identichip scanner and held the door open for Alara. He walked in behind her and turned to shut the door behind them, but as he moved to do so, there came a *thunk* and it bounced back into him, as if something had been wedged between the hinges. "What the frek ..." Ethan muttered, trying to push the door closed once more. This time it bounced more violently back into him, and he heard a familiar hiss. Ethan's hand automatically dropped to his gun belt, but he wasn't wearing one.

Then the air before him shimmered and a hulking shadow appeared. Fear struck Ethan like a hot knife. He backpedaled into the room, and the shadow advanced. Then Ethan realized the shadow was too big to be human. The glowing red eyes and glossy black armor were Sythian construction, but the dimensions were all Gor, and the Gors were allies now.

"Who are you?" Ethan asked, stopping to stand his ground before the alien.

It warbled something at him which he didn't understand. He wasn't wearing a translator.

"Ethan, what's going on?" Alara called. Then Ethan heard her scream right beside his ear as she came to see for herself. He turned to see her stumbling away from the Gor who had barged into their room.

"Stay back, Kiddie—what do you want?" Ethan demanded of the alien.

"It's not what he wants," a familiar voice answered. Ethan noticed the door swing shut behind the Gor, but not what had shut the door. "It's what I want," the voice went on. Then the owner of that voice stepped out from behind the hulking alien and Ethan found himself staring into a familiar pair of blue eyes. His ex-wife's eyes.

Ethan's eyebrows shot up. "Destra? What are you doing here?"

"Hello, Ethan—Alara," she said, nodding to each of them in turn. "We need to talk."

* * *

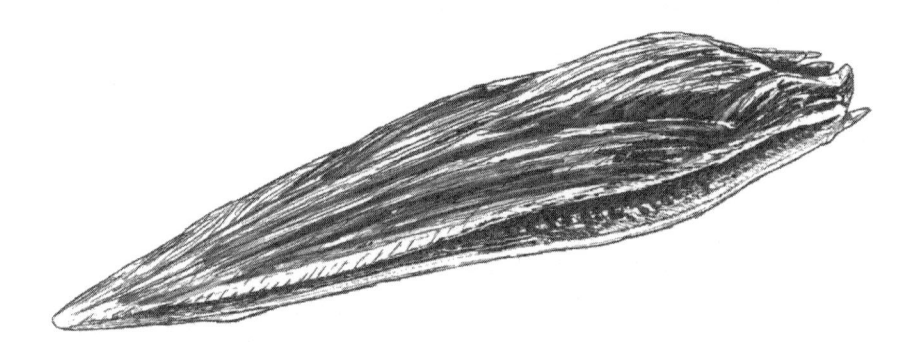

High Lord Shondar watched the timer hovering in front of his command chair. Soon his ship, the *Gasha* would arrive at the coordinates for Avilon. The real coordinates. As of two weeks ago when Shondar had left Lord Kaon and Dark Space behind, Lord Quaris and the 2nd Fleet had *still* been missing. Perhaps they would never be heard from again. That was unfortunate for Quaris, but it gave Shondar a chance to steal the glory. Now *he* would be the one to discover the lost human sector of Avilon. He would be the one everyone praised when he returned to the Getties, and he would be the one they *rewarded*. Never more would he be forced to live on harsh, inhospitable worlds like Etica, Caas, or Ramad.

Before the invasion the Sythians had been left with but one option—expand or die from sheer scarcity. Like Lord Kaon, Shondar came from a harsh world. Kaon's world was dark, watery, and cold, while Shondar's was dark, *rocky*, and cold. Both were equally bleak and pitiless in Shondar's opinion. The ultimate honor was to live on Sythia in Shangrila. There the word scarcity didn't even exist. There was no pain or suffering. Not even death could touch the chosen, because they had ways to extend their lives even beyond the average thousand years of life which most Sythians would see. No more cloning. No more mind transfers. No more niggling doubts as to whether or not they really died when they were reborn. He hadn't been engineered to live on Sythia. None of them had. They had been born to live on cold, inhospitable worlds where none of the chosen would dare to go, but in Shangrila, even that could be changed. There were ways of altering the body without touching the mind—expensive ways.

Those nettlesome details would all be taken care of when Shondar returned from war. All of that and more had been promised to him—to all of them—as payment for risking their lives in service to the Coalition. Few who were immortal would risk an untimely death—or for that matter the chance to be killed permanently if one died too far from the nearest command ship. The behemoth-class cruisers were the only places in the Adventa Galaxy which could receive their brain scan data and use it to resurrect them in a new body. Transmission time for such data was near-instantaneous, but limited in range to just over a thousand light years, depending on interstellar interference. Shondar knew he was pushing those limits by flying so far from Dark Space and the other fleets, but the prestige he stood to earn by being the first to engage the Avilonians was too tempting to pass up.

Ultimately, Shondar had decided to take almost half of his fleet—105 warships and a skeleton crew of slaves. His mission wasn't to take planets or to somehow conquer the Avilonians. They had been forewarned—the Avilonians were too strong for that. Thus, he would gather intelligence data that would later be used by the other lords to conquer Avilon. Shondar would come back with them when the time for that honor came.

Turning his gaze away from the timer counting down to the *Gasha's* reversion to real space, Shondar studied each of his crew in turn. Here were the twelve Sythian *operators* who tirelessly kept watch over the *Gasha's* automated systems and helped give orders to the *drivers,* each of whom was the commander of one slave ship. They kept in constant contact with the slave captain and his crew, but from a distance, safely ensconced aboard the command ship, which would stay cloaked behind enemy lines. Still, if something horrible befell the command ship—as had happened recently with Kaon's *Sharal*—then immortal or not, all 270 Sythians on board would go down with their ship, either to be reborn aboard the nearest command ship, or to be lost forever. In this case most of the drivers had stayed behind in Dark Space with their ships, so the *Gasha* only stood to lose the 105 drivers who were needed, plus its 12 operators—*and one high lord,* Shondar thought.

He felt a horrible heat creeping down his spine. He couldn't recall clearly what it was like to die, but he knew what it was like to be reborn. Even after more than five hundred orbits had passed, he could still remember the awful rush of heat coursing through his brain, the violent spasm as all of his muscles twitched in the same moment, and the identity-stealing reminder that his previous body had just died. That triggered the suspicion that perhaps he wasn't really alive anymore, but merely a clever copy of his old self which had in turn merely been a copy of the iteration that had preceded him. That chain of doubt went so far back it boggled the mind. Shondar remembered being overwhelmed with a strong urge to kill himself just to stop the madness.

But of course, that wouldn't end it. It would just start a new iteration of life.

Thankfully those first few moments of self-doubt and existential questioning never lasted long. The initial confusion and horror passed. Shondar had been told that everyone dealt with resurrection in their own way, and that not everyone suffered the same ill effects from the birthing process. Sadly, Shondar was not one of those lucky individuals.

A raucous noise erupted, tearing into Shondar's thoughts and drawing his attention back to the fore. It was the ship's reversion alarm. But it was too soon for them to have arrived. Then the deck shuddered and lurched underfoot. The swirling streaks of light which accompanied superluminal travel abruptly vanished from the simulated star dome that covered the *Gasha's* bridge. Yet instead of seeing stars and space as Shondar had expected, now all he could see was a pure, unadulterated black.

"What happens?" Shondar demanded. "Where does the display go?"

"The star dome is functioning perfectly, My Lord," the *operator* in charge of engineering reported.

"Sensors show we are pulled out of the light stream inside of a dark nebula," the sensor operator added. "We cannot see any suns because their light is blocked by the particles of the nebula."

"Where are we?" Shondar was already pulling up a star map at his command control station so he could see for himself. A glowing hologram of the *Gasha's* surroundings appeared floating in the air before him. He saw their destination marked on the map, still over three light years distant, and he hissed angrily. "What causes this delay on the path to glory? Chart a course around the obstacle!"

"I . . . cannot, My Lord," the operator at the helm replied. "We are in the middle of the gravity field which does pluck us from the light stream. We cannot re-enter it until we move beyond the field."

Shondar couldn't believe what he was hearing. He had to take a moment to calm himself. "Why do our sensors not detect this field and drop us out of the light stream before we land in the *middle* of it?"

The operator at the engineering station gave a strangled whimper which Shondar recognized as shame. He had no excuse.

"Are the sensors operating effectively?"

"I go to find out, My Lord," engineering replied.

"Do so. Navigation, make us to leave this field as quickly as possible that we may continue on our way. When your path is ready, tell me how long this ... *unfortunate incident* will take to correct."

"I already calculate this, My Lord," navigation replied.

"Then? How long? I must report our progress to Lord Kaon."

The navigation operator took a suspiciously long time to reply, and Shondar was about to yell at him again. Just as he was taking a breath to do so, the operator replied, "The shortest path out of the field is to take us ... five to six orbits, My Lord," the operator said in a quiet voice.

Shondar thought perhaps he was asleep and dreaming. Something this terrible could only happen in a nightmare. If it would take that long to leave the gravity field, then Shondar and his crew would not only *not* be the ones to have the honor of discovering Avilon, but they would not have the honor of conquering it either.

The war would be long over by the time they escaped the snare which had interrupted their journey.

* * *

"We should go sit down," Destra said.

Ethan's gaze flicked from her to Torv and back before he nodded. "Right. Follow me." He turned to find Alara standing behind him, her eyes wide, her jaw slack and hanging open.

"What's going on?" she whispered as he took her hand and led her further into the suite.

Ethan shook his head. "I think we're about to find out."

They reached the living area of the honeymoon suite—an enclosed balcony overlooking the Vermillion's worlds-class view. Ethan led them to the love seat and sat down with Alara. Destra came and sat opposite them in an armchair, while Torv remained standing by the front door.

"I'm sorry to surprise you like this, but there was no other way to contact you without risking that the Sythians find out."

"Find out about what?" Alara asked.

Destra spent a moment studying them each in turn, and Ethan studied her back. She looked terrible. There were dark circles and puffy bags under her eyes as well as a skein of wrinkles he'd never seen before. This was no-frills Destra, with no makeup, no skin treatments, and no age defying tricks at work. Like that she looked much older than her 45 years of age.

"I need your help," she explained. "As you probably already know, the Sythians executed Hoff."

Ethan winced. With the shock of seeing Torv and then Destra pop up out of nowhere, he'd forgotten all about Hoff. That explained Destra's neglected appearance. "I'm sorry, Des," he said. "I can only imagine what you're going through."

Alara leaned forward and reached across the small table between them to touch Destra's hand. "We're both sorry. I can't imagine losing Ethan."

Destra offered her a wan smile. "No, it's not easy, but Hoff isn't the first husband I've lost," she said, her gaze finding Ethan once more.

Ethan's eyes narrowed suspiciously. "Hoi, Des, if that's why you're here . . ."

"No, I haven't come to intrude upon your newly-wedded bliss by telling you I want you back. Even if that were true, this isn't about me. We have far greater concerns than my own personal burden of grief. Every day, thousands of people are going through exactly what I went through as their fathers, husbands, mothers, wives, and even children are taken without warning or excuse and turned into obedient slaves for the Sythians' fleet. Not only will our loved ones not come back to us, but they are no longer even the same people that we once loved. For all intents and purposes those slaves are as dead as Hoff right now. Humanity is at its end, Ethan. There is no coming back from this unless we defeat the Sythians soon. I've been working with the Gors to destabilize the Sythian occupation and slow them down, but it's not working nearly as well as we had hoped."

Ethan's eyebrows shot up. "So you're behind the Gor raids?"

Destra brushed a lock of dark hair out of her eyes and turned to study the view from the indoor balcony. Ethan followed her gaze. It was a relatively overcast day, so what they saw from the balcony was a carpet of white clouds stretching out beneath a bright blue sky. "One human cruiser escaped," Destra explained, "as well as all of the Gors. They are now our only hope to defeat the Sythians."

"Ironic," Ethan said.

"Yes, the same aliens who defeated us and slaughtered us by the trillions are now going to be our saviors."

"I suppose it's one way for them to make amends. So that's why you're here . . . to ask us to join your rebellion?"

"No. We're not actively recruiting. We have enough trouble supporting our numbers as it is. I'm here because of Atton."

Ethan felt a cold spark of dread in his chest. His heart began to pound. "What do you mean? Is he okay?"

"I don't know."

"What do you mean you don't know?!" Ethan said, rising from the couch.

Destra raised a hand to stop him. "Let me explain. Before Hoff surrendered to the Sythians, he sent Atton on a mission to get help."

Alara looked puzzled. "From who? I thought we were the only survivors."

Ethan already knew what she was talking about. "From Avilon."

"Yes," Destra replied. "The Avilonians are the only other surviving humans we know of, and although even Hoff hasn't—hadn't—been back to Avilon for countless centuries, he did get them to help his refugees in the Enclave by providing much-needed supplies. Avilon itself is rumored to have a population in the trillions, with a fleet every bit as strong as the Imperium once had. Their technology is more advanced than either ours or the Sythians', so if anyone can help us, it's them."

"Then why didn't they?" Alara asked.

"Why they didn't help us before is a mystery, but it's too late for recriminations. Regardless of their reasons for staying out of the war, our need has never been greater, so we had to take the risk. The worst they could say is no."

"Yea, and then kill Atton for invading their precious privacy," Ethan put in.

"Hoff assured me they are not like that, but he did warn that Atton might not be allowed to leave. That's why I'm here. Atton should have been here weeks ago. I need you to go look for him and while you're there, make one last attempt to convince the Avilonians to help us. They should know that the Sythians are looking for them, and that by leaving us at the Sythians' mercy they are only making them stronger. Our invaders now have a free source of slaves, food, fuel, munitions—even shipyards which can build more ships for their fleet."

"I doubt they can produce Sythian warships...."

"No, but they can build human ones, and our ships are no weaker than theirs."

Ethan turned to his wife. She was busy chewing her lower lip. "What do you think, Kiddie?"

"I'm *pregnant,* Ethan."

"You're what?" Destra said. "When did you find out?"

Alara shot her a quick smile. "Just before the wedding."

"Well . . . congratulations."

"Thank you ..." Alara turned back to Ethan with a pleading look. "What if they don't let *us* leave? Where will we live? What will we do for a living? We don't even know what life is like there!"

"It can't be any worse than life is here," Destra replied. "Freedom is worth a whole lot of hardship."

"There's just one thing I don't understand—why are you coming to *me*? You said a human cruiser escaped. That means you have at least 24 Nova pilots you could call on for a mission like this."

"Yes, and then I would have to clear it with the captain of the ship. He's getting restless, Ethan. Hoff told him support the Gors for just a few weeks, until reinforcements arrived. In the case that those reinforcements never came, he was told to rescue as many people as he could and leave. If the captain finds out about Avilon, he won't just send another envoy to look for Atton and appeal to the Avilonians for help—he'll take all of us there."

"Is that such a bad thing?"

"I'm not sure we would *all* be welcome—particularly the Gors—and I'm not willing to abandon either them or Dark Space yet. We might not be able to stop the Sythians, but we can make their lives more difficult. If you don't return within a few months, however, we may have no choice but to follow you to Avilon."

Ethan took a deep breath and let it out slowly. "This is a lot to think about." He turned to look at Alara once more. "I need to know what you think about this."

She shook her head. "I don't know what to think about anything anymore, Ethan."

"Neither do I, but I'm not sure we have a choice."

"We could stay," Alara suggested.

"Yes, we could, but we'll have to live under the constant threat that either one of us could be taken. Even if we aren't, we'll have to raise our children knowing that as soon they turn sixteen they'll be drafted into the Sythian fleet for the next five years. I'm not even sure the kids who return will be the same ones who left, and who knows if the Sythians change their minds and decide to keep our children indefinitely?"

Alara bit her lip and shook her head. "How will we get there? We can't leave Dark Space without a cloaking device, and even then, our ship isn't loaded with high grade fuel. It won't get us very far."

"There's a Gor cruiser waiting to carry you out. The Sythians won't see you while you're under the cover of the Gors' cloaking shield. As for the fuel problem, before you go, we'll load your ship with red dymium fuel as well as any other supplies you might need."

Ethan tried to contain the surge of hope now swelling in his chest, waiting to see Alara's reaction. She eyed him for a long moment, uncertainty warring on her face.

"What do you say, Kiddie? One more adventure before we settle down?"

She hesitated a moment longer before, but at last she nodded. "All right."

Ethan grinned. Turning back to Destra, he asked, "When do we leave?"

Destra returned his grin with a wan smile. "Right now."

AVILON
ASCENDANCY

Chapter 20

One week later . . .

Captain Loba Caldin paced up and down the bridge of the *Intrepid*, passing back and forth in front of the crew stations and the bridge viewports. Every now and then one of her officers would look up from what they were doing and cast her a worried glance. She could read their minds. They were wondering if their captain had gone space sick already.

But she wasn't skriffy from spending too much time cooped up in space. She was worrying endlessly over a question which had no obvious answer. How had they ended up stranded in a gravity field if their SLS fail-safes were working flawlessly? There were only two possible answers to that question, but neither one of them made any sense. Either the fail-safes had stopped working temporarily at precisely the wrong moment, or else the gravity field hadn't existed until they'd already flown into it. With respect to the space-time continuum, the latter option was impossible, and the former was just stupid. No one was that unlucky.

So what had happened?

Caldin's thoughts were interrupted by a hand landing on her shoulder. "Ma'am . . ."

She turned to find her friend and lover, Corpsman Terl, standing behind her, regarding her with a worried frown. "Not now, corpsman," she said to forestall his concerns.

"Ma'am, with respect, you need a break. You've been on your feet all day. You even skipped lunch. The crew is worried about you—*I'm* worried about you," he added in a gentler voice.

Caldin's eyes skipped from Terl's handsome face down to his broad chest and chiseled arms. She could think of one thing worth leaving the bridge for, and it wasn't a bad idea for dealing with her stress and frustration, either. She was just about to concede to his suggestion that she take some down time when Lieutenant Esayla Carvon's voice cut into her musings—

"I don't believe this . . . contact!"

"What are we looking at?" Caldin asked as she ran to the gravidar station.

"Target de-cloaking at K-35-12-72—just 357 klicks out!"

"*De-cloaking?*" Caldin shook her head. "Double check that scan, Lieutenant!"

They'd been followed. Caldin wasn't sure how that was possible, but she didn't have time to worry about *how* it had happened—only what she was going to do about it.

"The scan is accurate, ma'am! Contact confirmed."

"Sythians! Red alert!"

Ambient lighting dimmed to a bloody red, and the red alert siren blared a few times to emphasize the point.

"I don't think they're Sythians," Esayla said slowly.

"Why not?"

"The sensor profile is not suggestive of known Sythian hull types. It has too many sharp angles."

"Yet it has a cloaking device, and we only developed that tech recently. Are you trying to tell me the admiral sent another mission out here and they ended up stuck in exactly the same place as us?"

Esayla shook her head. "No, ma'am; that would be highly improbable."

"The only way anyone could have found us here is if they were around to see us jump. That means they had to have come from Ikara with us. Get me a visual," Caldin demanded.

"The nebula is blocking our optics, but I can have the computer generate a model from sensor readings."

"Do it." Caldin frowned, her head spinning. No ship could drop out of superluminal space at speed, so the mysterious contact had to have been following them for quite some time without their knowledge.

A hologram of the ship in question appeared projected over the main viewport. Caldin's eyes tracked over the shaded model of the warship from stem to stern. As Esayla had said, the ship looked more human than anything else—made up of hard angles and geometric shapes rather the organic lines and curves which Sythians preferred. The broad, flat deck on top of the ship looked like it might serve as some type of landing field in atmosphere for "hot" landings and non-vertical take-offs. That led Caldin to believe that the warship had been designed with planetary defense in mind. A quick look at the scale markings around the rendering revealed that the ship wasn't much larger than the *Intrepid,* at just 302 meters long and approximately 21 decks high.

"What class of ship is that?" Caldin asked.

"I don't know. It's not in our databanks," Esayla replied. "Maybe some type of cruiser?"

"Corpsman—" Caldin began, looking away from the hologram to find Terl, whom she had employed as her comm officer.

"Yes, Captain?" he replied. He was already seated at his control console.

"Hail them for us. I want to know who they are and why they followed us."

"Yes, ma'am."

Caldin waited impatiently for Terl to reply, but before he could, the bridge speakers let out a sharp squeal of protest. Then came a deep, gravelly voice, which said, "Cancel your ship's momentum and lower your shields. We are coming aboard."

Caldin did a double take. "Who is this?" she demanded.

"I haven't established a connection yet. They can't hear you...." Terl said from the comms station, sounding bewildered.

"Then how are they communicating with us?"

"I don't know! They're overriding our gateways."

The gravelly voice returned. "You have 30 seconds to comply."

This time Caldin noted the strange accent which accompanied the voice. The deliberate way the man spoke told her that either he was slow-witted or Versal was not his first language. She guessed the latter, but he would have to be from one of the outlier worlds in the old Imperium for that to be the case, and that raised the question of how it was that they had a cloaking device. Cloaking tech had only recently been developed by humanity, and then only because of their alliance with the Gors.

"Helm—full speed ahead; let's outrun them if we can."

"I don't think that's going to be possible," Esayla said.

"Why not?" Caldin asked, hurrying down to the gravidar station.

Esayla pointed to the grid rising out of the left side of her control station. She had toggled a red vector to indicate the enemy ship's heading, velocity, and acceleration, as well as a green one to indicate their own. The two heading vectors were running parallel to one another, and the enemy ship was just above and behind theirs on the grid. Running below each vector line were two numbers. The first was velocity as a fraction of the speed of light, while the second number was acceleration in KAPS. The enemy ship's acceleration was what really caught Caldin's eye. It was accelerating at 150 KAPS— approximately 150 meters per second squared. No human capital-class ship in existence had acceleration like that.

"Are you sure those readings are accurate?" Caldin asked, her gaze now turning to look at the *Intrepid's* speed and acceleration so she could calculate the difference. The enemy was gaining on them by one klick every second, with that rate increasing by 75 meters per second.

"Sensors are working fine, ma'am," Esayla replied.

"How is that possible?"

Esayla shook her head.

A cold chill crept down Captain Caldin's spine and she called out to her engineer, "Delayn, I want our crew out of stasis—now!"

"Yes, ma'am," he replied.

The bridge speakers crackled and the gravelly voice was back. "You are out of time. I am disappointed in you."

"What do they think they're going to do? We're travelling through a nebula at one tenth the speed of light. Energy weapons will refract and dissipate at anything but point-blank range, and there's no warhead in existence with shields strong enough to survive the frictional force at these speeds."

"Maybe they're going to wait until they can get up to point-blank range?" Esayla suggested.

"Maybe," Caldin conceded, eyeing the enemy contact on the grid. They were still 185 kilometers out, but gaining fast. "Delayn, is our crew awake yet?"

"They will be in just a few more minutes."

"We don't have a few more minutes!"

Suddenly, the *Intrepid* shuddered and the sound in space simulator (SISS) produced a sharp hiss as whatever it was hit their shields.

"Aft shields at 85%—equalizing," Delayn reported.

"What the frek was that?" Caldin demanded.

The ship shuddered again and another hiss came from their shields. "Seventy percent!"

"Fire back!"

"With what?" the weapons chief asked. "They're too far out of range!"

"Then how are they shooting us?"

The deck shuddered again.

"Shields at 64%!"

Caldin turned away from the gravidar station and sprinted for the set of stairs leading up to the gangway and the captain's table. By the time she reached the top of the stairs, the deck shuddered twice more in quick succession, and this time the lights dimmed, followed by a sudden, sickening sense of weightlessness. Caldin made a grab for the grav gun on her belt just as artificial gravity failed and her momentum carried her free of the deck. She aimed the gun between her feet and fired, grappling back down.

"Shields critical!" Delayn said from engineering.

Gravity returned in a slow gradient as the inertial management system (IMS) stabilized. Caldin turned off her grav gun just before her knees could buckle.

"Frek it! What kind of weapons are they using?" Whatever was hitting them, it was strong—at least as strong as the *Intrepid's* main beam cannon.

"Computer analysis suggests that something is exploding in front of us and we're running into the explosions," Delayn replied.

"I thought it's impossible for warheads to travel at this speed inside a nebula?"

"It is. They would need shield generators almost as strong as ours in order to survive it."

"Then?"

"We're not detecting any warheads firing from the enemy ship," Esayla added as another violent tremor shook the deck, followed by a loud roaring noise which wasn't simulated at all.

"Forward shields at 15%! Nebular dust is bleeding through our shields," Delayn explained. "If they fail, the nebula will rip us apart in seconds!"

Caldin saw her life flash before her eyes as she waited impotently for the next mysterious explosion to take out their shields entirely, and with them, the *Intrepid* herself.

Then the ship's sound system squealed once more. "This

is your final warning, *Intrepid*. Cancel your momentum and lower your shields. You have five seconds to respond."

"Respond?" Caldin screeched. "How are we supposed to respond if they won't let us establish a connection!" Then, a split second later, she understood what the speaker meant, and she felt stupid. "Helm—reverse thrust one hundred percent! Let's show these kakards that we're complying with their demands."

"Yes, ma'am," the helm replied.

A few seconds later the sound system screeched once more and back was the same deep, gravelly voice, now speaking in a much more pleasant tone: "You are wise to heed us. We will be aboard as soon as you are able to drop your shields."

Captain Caldin wanted to tell that man, whoever he was, that it would take them several days to slow down enough to drop their shields without taking serious damage, but the voice returned saying, "Do not deviate from your present heading. You can expect to see us in . . . approximately 112 of your people's hours—four and a half of your standard galactic days."

Caldin's brow furrowed. "*Your people's hours*—what is he, a Sythian?"

"He sounds human to me," Terl replied.

"Then either he's a skriff, or he's been cut off from the Imperium since before the establishment of standard galactic time."

"That was almost thirty millennia ago . . ." Delayn put in from engineering.

Caldin couldn't think of anyone who had been cut off from the rest of the galaxy for that long, except for . . . *Avilonians*.

Caldin felt hope and terror rise up simultaneously—hope because the Avilonians were real and they could rescue the *Intrepid* and her crew, possibly even Dark Space, and terror because the Avilonians did not appear to be friendly.

Captain Caldin turned to the comms station. "Cancel the red alert and set condition green. Tell our crew to make their way to their postings in a leisurely fashion. For now, they don't need to know what's happening."

"Yes, ma'am," Terl replied.

Caldin turned back to the captain's table and gazed down on the enemy contact. *What are you doing here?* she wondered. The fact that Avilonians had followed them into the gravity field raised more questions than it answered. Reaching up to her ear, she activated her comm piece to make a call. The only one aboard who knew anything about Avilon was Commander Ortane. They still had a few days to prepare before the Avilonians came aboard, and Caldin was determined to prepare for their arrival as much as possible before then.

* * *

Atton awoke, cold and naked in the dark. He found himself standing up inside a coffin-sized chamber with a transpiranium barrier mere inches away from his face. Visible just beyond that barrier was another coffin like the one in which he was standing, filled with another person, a familiar-looking woman ... Ceyla Corbin. By the expression on her face, her horror and shock was no less than his own. Then Atton remembered where he was and why. The whole crew had been locked in stasis tubes until the *Intrepid* escaped the gravity field which had snared it.

They'd been scheduled to come out of stasis after four years. To Atton, those four years seemed to have passed in the blink of an eye. It felt like just yesterday that they'd put him in stasis. By now plenty of things would have changed, not the least of which being that Dark Space was no more. Perhaps a lucky few had managed to escape, but Atton doubted those survivors would include his family. His mother and father had been lucky enough to escape the first invasion, but that kind of luck didn't come around twice. As for Hoff and Atta ... their chances were just as abysmal.

No, now the crew of the *Intrepid* were, for all anyone knew, the last surviving members of the human race—besides the immortal Avilonians. That thought struck Atton with dull force as he stumbled out of his stasis tube. Was that where they were headed now? Had Captain Caldin made contact with Avilon already?

People were stumbling out of their own tubes all around him. This stasis room had space for 30 people, all of whom were busy waking up in various states of confusion and shock. Atton waved to Ceyla just as guide lights came on in the deck of the stasis room and cast a wan green glow into the dark, airy room. Rather than wave back, Ceyla turned away. The fact that she was naked had no doubt provoked her sense of modesty. It wasn't possible to see very much of her now that she had stepped out of her stasis tube's internal light, and he'd been too distracted to really look before that, but he did see her turn to follow the guide strips to the lockers on the other side of the room.

He was about to follow her when something cold seized him in a painfully tight grip just below his waist. He let out a sharp gasp, and a familiar voice said, "I should break it off."

"Gina . . . for frek's sake, we have bigger problems than our personal issues right now."

"Yes, I suppose you're right—*sir*," she said, releasing him. He turned to watch her stalk away, a fuzzy shadow which revealed only a hint of her naked backside. He caught himself staring and looked away with a scowl. Gina was the last person he wanted to be thinking that way about. She would probably stab him in his sleep.

Atton followed the guide lights to the lockers. Once there, he passed his wrist over his locker's identichip scanner. It popped open and he retrieved his things. As soon as he was dressed, he began following the guide lights out of the stasis room. On his way out, a hand slid into his and he turned to see Ceyla walking along beside him, now fully clothed. "Hoi there, Commander. Did you have a good sleep?" she asked.

Atton nodded mechanically, taking a moment to feel the electricity passing between his hand and hers. "Well enough," he said. "How about you?" The question sounded lame to his ears, but any pretense of small talk was bound to sound lame. What he really wanted to know was what the *frek* had happened in the last four years.

"I had nightmares," Ceyla replied. "What do you think we're going to do now?" she asked as they filed out through the double doors of the stasis room and into the blindingly bright corridor beyond.

"I'm not sure," Atton lied as his eyes began tearing from

the brightness. He noticed that the ship's P.A. system was playing a pre-recorded message on a loop.

"Please proceed to your duty stations in an orderly fashion and await further orders. Thank you.... Please proceed to your duty stations in an orderly..."

Atton tuned out the message. His eyes finally stopped tearing from the light, and he found himself staring into Ceyla's deep blue irises and her startlingly beautiful face.

"I guess we're the only ones left," she said. Atton didn't have to ask what she meant. "Maybe we're going to start over somewhere new?" she suggested while tucking a lock of blonde hair behind one ear. Ceyla didn't know about Avilon. She had been asleep already with the rest of the crew when Atton had explained his mission to the captain, so she obviously thought that the 100 plus crew aboard the *Intrepid* were the only humans left in the galaxy and that now they had to begin the work of repopulating the species.

Atton guessed that was the motive behind her holding his hand. She'd decided that if she had to breed with someone, she wanted it to be him. Atton tried not to be flattered by that. After all, there were probably only 50-70 other eligible men on board, and most of them would be too old for her. Atton decided to put her out of her misery. People were bumping into them on all sides on their way out of the stasis room, so he pulled her to one side of the doors.

"What is it?" Ceyla asked.

Atton waited a few moments, until everyone was out of earshot, and then he said, "Look, this is going to come as a shock... but we're not the only ones left."

"How do you know that?" Ceyla asked, her eyes widening with hope.

"The whole reason we came out here was to get

reinforcements, not to look for survivors at Ikara."

"Reinforcements from who?"

"From Avilon."

Ceyla shook her head. "I don't—"

Atton placed a finger to her lips. "Shh, just listen."

"Okay . . ."

He launched into a long explanation about the immortals and Avilon, about their history with the Sythians and the once-thought-to-be mythical world of Origin where it all began. That world was actually Sythia—the Sythians' home world, found in the heart of the Getties Cluster.

"I don't believe you," Ceyla said, shaking her head quickly. Now she jerked her hand out of his and shot him an angry look. "The Immortals are in Etheria."

Atton offered an apologetic smile. "I'm sorry, but they're not. They're in Avilon."

"No," Ceyla said, still shaking her head. She obviously didn't want to believe that her religion had sprung up out of legends about people who had attained eternal life through technological rather than spiritual means.

"Look, just because your religion speaks about the Immortals, doesn't mean they are the same immortals as the ones living in Avilon. The Immortals you believe in, which are immortal souls that have died and gone to Etheria, are not threatened by the existence of immortal humans living in a lost sector of our galaxy."

The angry lines in Ceyla's expression faded somewhat and Atton reached for her hand once more. "I'm sorry. I'm not trying to invalidate your beliefs. I'm just telling you what I know."

"I . . . it's a lot to take in, Atton. Why doesn't anyone know about this? Why am I only hearing about it now?"

"Admiral Heston was one of them before he left—or was forced to leave. That was a long time ago, but he's a witness to their existence, and he told me. He's the one who sent me out here to find them and convince them to help Dark Space. It's too late for them, but it isn't too late for us. We're going to Avilon, Ceyla. That's the plan."

"I don't want to live forever," she said, looking defensive again.

Atton felt a headache building like a volcano inside his head. "Then why do you believe in Etheria?"

"Because . . ." Ceyla withdrew her hand again. "First of all, I don't believe in Etheria because I want to be immortal. I believe in it because the physical world doesn't explain everything. It doesn't explain where we come from, for one thing, or where we go when we die."

How about the ground, Atton wanted to say, but he bit his tongue. Besides, the truth was he couldn't answer the first question, and that was the reason behind all religions in the history of the human race; they all existed to explain that one damnable question—*where did we come from?*

Science could explain how the universe had inflated from a microscopic speck to an unimaginable vastness; it could predict what would eventually happen to everything; it could even suggest how humanity and everything else may have evolved without any need for a creative agent, but it couldn't explain where the universe had ultimately come from, or what, if anything, had unleashed everything from that infinitesimally small point all those billions of years ago. So, Atton had no choice but to concede Ceyla's point.

"Okay," he said, "but wouldn't you trade the theoretical immortality in your religion for a real and plausible immortality via technological means?"

Ceyla crossed her arms over her chest. "What I believe isn't theoretical."

"So you're saying it's a fact? Show me the proof then."

"It's not a fact either. It's not something you can prove or disprove, and my certainty comes from my heart, not from my head."

Atton gave up. "Okay, well, I'm sure the Avilonians will let you die if you really want to." He couldn't keep the sarcasm from his voice as he said that; Ceyla accepted his remark with narrowed eyes and a frown. Before she could respond, however, Atton's comm piece buzzed—*Incoming call from Captain Loba Caldin.* He excused himself and took a few steps away from Ceyla to answer the call.

"Captain, I was just about to—"

"Commander, I need to see you in the operations center *right now.* There have been some important developments while you've been in stasis."

"Yes, ma'am. I'll be there in two minutes."

"Make that one minute, Ortane."

Before Atton could reply, the captain ended the comm, leaving him feeling bewildered once more. He'd just spent the last four years in stasis and now all of a sudden the captain was in a rush to see him?

"I have to go," Atton said, turning to find Ceyla.

But she was already gone.

He looked the other way to find her walking down the corridor ahead of him, obviously too annoyed with him to stick around any longer. Atton hurried after her with a frown. *You dumb skriff, Atton. The first girl in forever who shows any real interest in you, and you drive her off by making fun of her beliefs. Nice work.*

Chapter 21

The first thing Atton noticed when the doors of the operations center opened was that the room was already full. The second thing he noticed was how serious everyone looked.

"Take a seat, Commander," the captain said.

Atton nodded and moved to take the only available seat on the near side of the table. He had in mind a million questions to ask the captain, but he waited for her to speak first.

"I've called you all here for one reason," Caldin began, while Atton looked around the table to see who else was seated there with him. There was Lieutenant Esayla Carvon,

Deck Commander Cobrale Delayn, Corpsman Markom Terl, and Captain Loba Caldin. "We need to discuss the arrival of the Avilonians."

"The arrival of the who?" Delayn asked.

Caldin turned to him. "We'll get to that in a moment."

Atton fixed the captain with a wide-eyed gaze. "They're here? Where is here—anyway? I'm guessing we've made it out of the gravity field or I wouldn't be awake."

"You'd be guessing wrong, Commander. The rest of the crew is probably finding out now as they check their holo pads. You've only been asleep for three weeks, not four years."

Atton blinked, shock coursing through him as that revelation sunk in. "Then Dark Space is . . ."

"We don't know," Caldin replied. "The fact is, we are still stuck here, but the Avilonians clearly are not, or else they wouldn't have been stupid enough to follow us."

"Begging your pardon, ma'am," Delayn said, "but I think we're all lost. Who are these Avilonians? You know who's chasing us?"

"I *think* I know, yes," Caldin replied. "Commander Ortane, would you please explain to everyone here who the Avilonians are, and the real reason for the *Intrepid*'s mission?"

Taking a moment to recover from his shock, Atton explained everything for what felt like the umpteenth time. When he was done, the silence was ringing. Everyone was speechless.

The first one to recover from his shock was the XO and chief engineer, Cobrale Delayn. "So, humanity isn't really defeated after all. There's still trillions of us out there somewhere."

"It would seem we've been saving our best for last," the

captain replied. "Commander Ortane tells me the Avilonians' technology is far more advanced than our own, and after our brief encounter with them, I'm forced to agree with that assessment. They took us down before we could even fire a shot."

"If they're so numerous and their technology is so advanced then why didn't they intervene during the invasion?" Esayla asked.

"I think everyone wants to know the same thing, but we're not going to know the answer to that until we ask them ourselves. For now, we need to study the battle data from our brief engagement, and based on that data, form some likely hypotheses about our visitors. Commander Ortane, if you've been holding out on me, now's the time to tell me what else you know about these people."

Atton shook his head. "I've already told you everything that the admiral told me."

"Very well—play back the battle for us, Lieutenant Carvon," Caldin said.

A star map appeared hovering above the center of the table with a three dimensional representation of each ship, as well as vector lines to indicate their headings, speeds, and accelerations. Then a translucent blue bubble swelled around the *Intrepid*, showing her shields at 100% on all sides. Finally, a recording of what was obviously a commcast from the Avilonians' captain crackled through the room. Atton listened carefully, fascinated by the speaker's strange accent.

When the *Intrepid* didn't reply within the 30 seconds which the Avilonians gave for them to surrender, Atton watched mysterious explosions begin appearing in front of the cruiser as it flew through the nebula. After just a few minutes, the explosions stopped, and the *Intrepid's* forward shields were left glowing in the red at just 14%. Then the Avilonian captain spoke once more, and this time the *Intrepid* stopped her futile attempts to flee and put her engines in full reverse. It was then that Atton noticed the enemy cruiser's acceleration was well outside the usual norms for a ship of its size. The battle had lasted only a few minutes before it was over, which told Atton that the enemy ship was much more powerful than the *Intrepid,* even though it was a similar size. So far the Avilonians had demonstrated superior weaponry and superior drive systems. Atton had a feeling that was just the beginning.

"Discuss," Caldin said.

"I have something to say," Atton replied. "Has anyone considered the implications of this?"

Caldin regarded him quietly. "What do you mean?"

"I mean, they're here, so either they followed us from Ikara or they somehow *detected* us here, and if they detected us . . . then I'm not sure anyone knows just how advanced the Avilonians really are."

Delayn began nodding. "Gravidar with that kind of range . . . it's hard to imagine. A venture-class cruiser like ours has a sensor range of just over half a trillion klicks, or point oh five light years. That's one tenth of the range someone would need to see us from beyond the SLS-safe threshold of the gravity field where we are now. And of course, our sensor range is much, much more limited in a dense nebular cloud like this one, so the real comparison becomes something like 10,000 times the sensor range we have."

Caldin shook her head. "I think we can all agree that the computing power it would take to scan such a massive volume of space with conventional gravidar is beyond anything we can imagine. Either they've spent the last three weeks sweeping the gravity field with sensors because they somehow knew that we were here, or else they followed us from Ikara. That said, we can't rule anything out, and how they found us isn't the only mystery we're looking at. There's also the question of how they got here. In order to jump this far into a strong gravity field they must have superluminal drives which are far more advanced than ours or which work on a different principle."

"Or else they disabled their SLS safeties to follow us in," Delayn said.

"Which means they're stranded here, too," Caldin pointed out.

"There's another question we need to ask," Atton added. "Why attack us? Why not simply talk with us, or just leave us in here? We're no threat to anyone as long as we're stranded in real space for the next four years."

"Right," Delayn replied.

Atton looked around the table to see if anyone had an answer to that, but no one ventured a theory, so he took a stab at answering his own question: "Their weapons are invisible, long-ranged, and obviously very deadly. If they'd wanted to kill us they clearly could have. The fact that they gave us not one but two chances to surrender means they don't want us dead. They want something we have. Whether that's our ship, us, or some type of information they think we have, I don't know, but they definitely want something and they think we can give it to them."

"That would be my analysis as well, Commander," Caldin replied, "and without knowing exactly what it is they're looking for, we need to take some precautions. There's a team of eight Gors on board. I put them into stasis with everyone else, but I haven't given the order for them to be woken up yet. I think now it's time to do that. The Gors are our insurance policy. Sensors can't see through a cloaking shield, and when the Avilonians come aboard, they'll be expecting to deal with a vanquished *human* foe. They won't be expecting cloaked Gors to pop out and rip their heads off."

"There's just eight of them," Atton said.

"Gors are particularly deadly when they are cloaked and have the element of surprise. Using that advantage to its fullest it only took a few million of them to mop up on the ground after the Sythians' fleets were done with us. So, no matter how many Avilonians come aboard, or how advanced their technology is, I'm confident we still stand a chance with the Gors on our side. If nothing else, should things go bad, we'll take the Avilonians down with us. As a secondary precaution, I want every pilot we have ready to scramble on a moment's notice. If the Avilonians try anything, at least we'll be ready for it."

Heads bobbed around the table—all except for Atton's.

"Avilonians are immortals," he said. "If they die, they'll just be reborn someplace else. I'm assuming from that and the fact that they're willing to come aboard a potentially hostile warship that they don't fear death. If that's true, then we can kill them and threaten to kill them as much as we like—it won't change our circumstances. Any attempt to answer their force with our force is a waste of time. If this goes badly, it could be a blood bath, and with their superior technology, I'm not sure there'll even be very much Avilonian blood in the mix."

"What would you rather we do, Commander?" Captain Caldin asked.

"We need their help. If we're going to have any chance of getting the Avilonians to send reinforcements to Dark Space, then we need to be willing to give them whatever they ask. We need to beg and wait on bended knee if that's what it takes. We need to cooperate as much as possible—not hide Gors behind our backs so they can pop out and kill the Avilonians when they're not looking."

"I'm sorry, Commander," Caldin replied, shaking her head. "But right now these Avilonians of yours are acting like common space pirates. For all we know that's exactly what they are, and we don't *bow and wait on bended knee* for pirates. No amount of help is worth selling our souls to get it."

Atton accepted that with a shallow nod. "Yes, ma'am."

"You all understand the plan," Caldin went on, her gaze finding each of them in turn. "I'm going to issue a statement to the crew as soon as we're done here so that everyone is up to date. It's time we all knew what's at stake and what's going on. I do agree with you, Commander Ortane," Caldin said as her gaze settled on him. "We need to do everything we can to win the Avilonians' sympathy and their support, but we also need to prepare for the eventuality that they are either unwilling or unable to help us. Keep in mind that they have already shown significant hostility toward us. Add that to the fact that they didn't send so much as a single ship to help us fight off the Sythians when they first came to our galaxy, and you'll understand my caution."

Caldin looked up and her gaze passed over each of the officers present before she continued. "If you are honest with yourselves you'll come to the same conclusion that I have—things are going to go to the netherworld when the Avilonians come aboard. The only question is, what are we going to do about it? Are we going to roll over and play dead, or are we going to fight back?" A murmur of agreement swept through the room, and Caldin gave a decisive nod.

"Then *fight!* Ruh-kah!"

Death and Glory, Atton translated silently as the others sitting around him repeated the old Rokan battle cry.

Officers began rising from the table, and Atton stood up with them. There was so much more he wanted to say, but it was clear that no one was going to listen. *Hopefully the captain has the sense to keep the Gors as a last resort. If not . . . perhaps the Avilonians will accept* my *surrender.*

* * *

On the second stage of its journey, the *Trinity* departed the Gor cruiser which had carried it out of Dark Space right under the Sythians' noses. From there, Ethan and Alara spent the subsequent week travelling through SLS in order to reach the Avilonians' forward base. In that time Ethan had grown thoroughly bored, while his wife had grown increasingly anxious about what was to come. Now almost three months pregnant, she spent her days worrying about the future. Where would their child grow up? Would the kid get a good education? Would there be food on the table? A roof over their heads? Would they be safe?

When Alara finally tired of asking those questions, she withdrew from the real world and its problems, adopting a vacant, glassy-eyed stare. Whenever Ethan saw her like that he tried to snap her out of it, but he rarely succeeded. Yesterday, her morning sickness had begun, arriving later than usual, and Ethan realized that they didn't have any medication on board to treat it. At that, Alara had adopted another vacant look, saying in a quiet voice that it was just *a sign of things to come.* Ethan tried to reassure her that the Avilonians probably had even better medical care than what they were used to, but she'd countered that by asking how they were going to pay for it. . . .

"We could sell the Trinity," he suggested, even though it felt like he was suggesting they sell his right arm.

She smiled bitterly and shook her head. "If the Avilonians are so technologically advanced, then what use will they have for our ship? You'll have to sell it for scrap, and something tells me that won't give us enough to buy a mansion on a lake, or a spacious habitat on some space station. We're frekked, Ethan! We should have stayed!"

"You agreed we should go!"

"You convinced me!"

"Well it's too late now."

"What do you mean?"

"We don't have enough fuel for a return trip."

"What?!"

"We're not going back, anyway. We can't. There's nothing to go back to."

"What if Avilon sends reinforcements to Dark Space?"

"Even then. Where would you rather raise our child, Kiddie— in a warzone with the scarcity, the criminals, and the Gors, or in Avilon, where all of that will be just a distant memory?"

"They'll have their own problems."

"Yea, like whether to eat seafood or steak for dinner. They'll probably also have a lot of trouble picking which vintage of wine to drink. From what I've heard the place is a paradise, but even if it isn't—it has to be better than where we're coming from. So no, we're not going back. Besides, remember what Destra told us. They probably won't even let us leave."

"Exactly! Doesn't that sound like a trap to you?"

"You think they want a bunch of skriffs like us to go looking for them? If that's the case, then they wouldn't have been hiding all this time. No, Avilon is a well-kept secret, because if everyone knew about it, then they'd all want to live there, and my bet is they have enough people living there already.

"Make people immortal and what's the next thing that happens? The next thing that happens, Kiddie, is their population growth explodes. If no one ever dies and everyone keeps having kids, that growth curve becomes exponential and pretty soon the entire galaxy is overrun with people. That's exactly what happened with the Sythians, and it's why they're here now."

"So why don't we see Avilonians everywhere?" Alara asked. "Why didn't they take over our galaxy instead of the Sythians?"

"Maybe they have a way of keeping their population under control. Maybe they don't even have kids anymore."

"And I'm pregnant," Alara snorted. "You still think it'll be a good place to raise a child?"

"Alara, we don't have a choice, so just try to be positive, okay?"

She was quiet for a long while, contemplating that. Then he felt a soft tug on his arm as she pulled one of his hands away from the controls. He turned to see her wide violet eyes full of unshed tears. "Just promise me we're going to be okay, Ethan. That's all I ask."

Ethan shot her an unconvincing smile. "We're going to be okay, Kiddie." With that, he leaned across the space between the pilot's and copilot's chairs and gave her a kiss.

"Are you sure?" she asked, withdrawing slowly to look him in the eye.

He'd nodded and squeezed her hand. "I'm positive."

Ethan snapped out of his reverie and shook his head. He wasn't positive at all, but he couldn't afford to sit around paralyzed with fear. He had to focus on the solution, and right now that solution was for them to find Avilon.

Ethan glanced at the *Trinity's* SLS timer. They were just five minutes from reversion to real space, and this time, they wouldn't be reverting at some intermediary nav point along the way. They were about to reach the actual coordinates which Destra had given them. Ethan's heart began to pound and his palms grew slick with sweat. He tried but failed to contain his excitement. He considered calling Alara to come up to the cockpit, but she was resting in their quarters, and the last time he'd checked in on her she wasn't in the best of moods, so he decided to let her sleep.

Ethan watched the timer slowly tick down to zero. He didn't even bother to look up as the streaking swirls of superluminal space disappeared with a flash of light. His eyes remained glued to the grid, searching for any blips on gravidar. After a few seconds, when the grid was still devoid of contacts, Ethan frowned and shook his head. He tried expanding the *Trinity's* sensor range from the default one hundredth of a light year to a full one tenth of a light year. At that range it would take over 15 minutes rather than one second for his ship's computer to completely scan the accompanying volume of space and update his gravidar with any new contacts, but when it did, he was sure to find *something*.

While he waited, Ethan found the nearest planet and set course for it. A mottled blue sphere came into view. He magnified that view and queried his ship's sensors for details on the planet. It was a water world with 1.25 times standard gravity, a breathable atmosphere, and approximately 2% of its surface dotted with small islands. The equatorial temperature was 317 degrees Kelvin, making it on the hot side of balmy, and although it was listed on his star charts, the world didn't even have a name, just a designation—*GK-465*. That was a good indication that it was worthless. Even barren rocks had names.

Ethan felt a crushing weight of despair. He worked hard to calm his racing heart as a sweaty surge of anxiety pulsed through him. If this was the Avilonians' forward base, then where were they?

They must be hiding. If they'd gone to so much trouble to hide themselves from the rest of the galaxy, then of course they wouldn't just suddenly change their minds about it now. Ethan keyed his comm to broadcast on an open channel and then he said, "This is Ethan Ortane, Captain of the *Trinity*, hailing from what remains of the Imperium of Star Systems. If anyone can hear this message, please respond; we are in urgent need of assistance."

He waited a full minute with the comms open, listening for a reply. When none came, he tried repeating the message, but again, there was no response. Ethan accepted that with a frown. *You want to hide? All right, I'll play that game.*

Fifteen minutes later, his ship finished updating the grid, now to a range of one tenth of a light year, but besides a few more planets and some outlying asteroid belts, there was *still* nothing out there. Cold dread began trickling through Ethan's gut.

Now the planet was all he could see out the forward viewport. It lay close beneath his ship. A moment later, the *Trinity* began to shudder and shake around him as it hit the upper atmosphere. "Frek . . ." he hissed, fumbling with the dial to set the IMS from 98% to 100%. The shuddering stopped. He hoped he'd adjusted the controls in time to keep from waking Alara, but he supposed he'd know the answer to that soon.

A carpet of angry storm clouds appeared below him, racing up to greet his ship. The *Trinity* sliced into them and everything turned a dark, purplish blue. Raindrops began pelting the forward viewports, and then a blinding flash of lightning lit up the clouds from within, followed by a crack of thunder which rumbled through the cockpit. Ethan grimaced at that. Alara had to be awake by now. Decreasing the ship's angle of descent, he began configuring the autopilot for a grid search of the planet. He couldn't assume that the Avilonians were hiding on one of the planet's islands; they were just as likely to be found hovering above the surface, or floating beneath it in some type of underwater facility.

While he was still configuring the autopilot, Ethan heard the cockpit door *swish* open behind him, followed by Alara's voice: "What's going on?"

He turned to her with a smile. "Hello, Darling."

"Darling, hoi? Why didn't you tell me we'd arrived?"

"I thought you could use the sleep."

"Thanks, I guess. Have you made contact yet?" Alara asked as she slid into the copilot's station.

Ethan cleared his throat. "I'm working on it."

"What's that supposed to mean?"

"It means I haven't found them yet."

"Well haven't they found you?"

"Not that I know of."

"Did you try the comms?"

"Yes—no reply."

"Are you sure we're at the right coordinates?"

Ethan sighed. "Look, I've checked everything, and tried

everything—my guess is they don't want to reveal themselves until they have no other choice."

"Either that or your ex-wife sent us on a one-way trip into the middle of frekking nowhere."

The clouds parted and an angry black sea appeared below them. Even from several kilometers up, the waves were marked wrinkles on the face of the water. Lightning flashed overhead and another rumble of thunder roared through the cockpit.

"Why would she do that?" Ethan asked.

"Maybe she's jealous. You saw the way she was looking at us—like we have everything she wants."

"That's ridiculous."

"Is it?"

"Our son is *missing*. Dark Space is overrun. Hoff is dead. Even if she is jealous, she has bigger issues to deal with. Whatever else Destra may be, she's not that petty. The Avilonians are here. We just have to find them. Think about it, if you were trying to hide from the rest of the galaxy, why would you leave your forward base out in the open where everyone could find it? You'd find a way to hide it from nosey passersby."

"Yea, well there aren't exactly a lot of passersby left in the galaxy, so what are they hiding from now?"

"Maybe they're hiding from the same thing we were—" Ethan suggested. "—Sythians."

"Maybe," Alara replied. A frown graced her smooth, pearly white skin, and she bent over her control station. "Or maybe you're just not asking nicely enough. Let me try the comms."

Ethan watched with one eyebrow skeptically raised as Alara set the comms to broadcast on all channels and then spoke into the audio pickups. "This is Alara Ortane of the *Trinity*, we know you're out there, you motherfrekkers!"

"Hoi!" Ethan slapped the mute button. "What are doing?"

"What?"

"We want to find them so we can talk, not so they can blow us out of the sky!"

All the same, Ethan found himself listening to the crackle and hiss of the comms, hoping to hear a reply.

None came.

"Look," Ethan said. "We'll grid search the planet. I'll put it on auto and set an alert to notify us when something comes up on the scopes. A few days from now when we've scanned every square meter of this planet, we're bound to have something to go on."

Alara shook her head slowly and turned to him with wide, frightened eyes. "What if we don't?"

Ethan noticed that she had one arm wrapped around her belly as if to protect their unborn child from some unseen threat. He reached for her other hand and gave it a reassuring squeeze. "We will. Everything is going to be all right, Alara. I promise." Ethan forced a smile for her sake and then leaned over to kiss her. His lips brushed hers, softly at first, but she returned his kiss with unexpected force. Ethan let himself be carried away by the moment until they broke apart, panting and gasping for air. "Why don't you go back to our quarters," he said. "I'll finish setting up the autopilot and then meet you there."

Alara nodded and shot him a wan smile. "Don't be late . . ."

Her hand trailed lightly up his thigh as she left, and he turned to watch her leave. The tight black leggings she wore clung to her in a way which left nothing to the imagination.

Ethan let out his frustration in a long, slow breath. Alara opened the cockpit and turned from the open doorway with a sly grin. "See you soon, handsome."

He nodded and returned that grin. If nothing else, at least they could distract themselves from the fact that their future, which had looked so bright a month ago, now teetered on a knife's edge above an uncertain abyss.

Chapter 22

112 standard galactic hours since last contact with unknown vessel . . .

Captain Caldin stared at the grid, her eyes fixed on the enemy warship. They were still trailing behind the *Intrepid* by more than a hundred klicks, safely out of range. Now that they'd slowed down, torpedoes were no longer out of the question, but Caldin didn't think a volley of torpedoes would get past whatever passed for the Avilonians' AMS (anti-missile system). No, they were defenseless and at the Avilonians' mercy. The *Intrepid* had spent the last four and a half days decelerating from over one tenth the speed of light to their present velocity of just over one kilometer per second.

"Stand by to lower our shields," Caldin said.

"Standing by ..." Delayn replied from the engineering station.

"Lower them."

"Shields disabled."

Caldin waited, chewing her lower lip and tapping her foot. A full minute passed like that. She looked up from the star map to find her comms officer. Now that the crew was awake, Corpsman Terl was back in med bay with the other medical staff, and her regular comms officer was sitting in his place.

"What are they waiting for?" Caldin asked.

"Maybe they haven't noticed yet?" Delayn suggested.

"I'd hail them to let them know, but they're either unwilling or unable to receive comms from us. Are the Gors standing by at the hangar?"

"Yes, ma'am," the comms officer replied.

"Good, and our Novas?"

"Ready and waiting to launch."

"Then I suppose all we can do is wait for the krak to hit the turbines."

"Or us," Delayn added.

"Mind your station, Commander."

Another minute later the bridge speakers squealed in protest and the gravelly voice from four days ago returned. "We are coming aboard now ..." it said.

"This is it, people!" Caldin called out, starting from the captain's table at a run. "I'm going to the hangar bay to greet them. Let me know the instant anything changes."

"Yes, ma'am," the comm officer replied.

But Caldin never made it off the bridge. The air in front of the doors began to shimmer, and she skidded to a stop a dozen meters from them. A sound like rushing water filled the air, and then she was slapped in the face by a strong gust of wind. That gust almost knocked her off her feet, and the shock of what she saw next left her gaping in silence.

Three men in dazzling suits of armor had just appeared out of nowhere.

Caldin's brain hurried to fill in the blanks. They must have sent a cloaked ship to board the *Intrepid* and then somehow snuck aboard and made their way to the bridge using cloaking armor.

Their armor was highly reflective and it glowed a brilliant blue-white, dazzling her eyes. They wore matching helmets with even more brilliantly glowing visors. The taller man, who stood in the middle of the three, wore a shimmering blue cape that cascaded down from his shoulders, and a strange emblem was etched into his breastplate. The emblem glowed a deep blue, the same color as his cape, and was comprised of the letter *A—A for Avilon?* Caldin wondered. In the center was a spiral suggestive of a spiral galaxy with brilliant white points of light that resembled stars, and in the center of that was a pattern which looked disturbingly like an eye.

The man whose armor bore that emblem stepped forward, and the same deep gravelly voice which they had heard only a few minutes ago now echoed out across the bridge. "In the name of the Ascendancy and the almighty Omnius, I accept your surrender. You stand in breach of ancient covenants. Not only have you trespassed, but you have told others to do the same. Have you anything to say in your defense?"

Caldin shut her gaping mouth and shook her head. "Who are you?" she asked.

"That is irrelevant to these proceedings."

"No, it's not. You are accusing us of crimes we know nothing about. We have a right to know who our judge is."

"I am not your judge. Your judge is the same as ours—he is Omnius."

"And who is this Omnius?"

Suddenly the room flashed with a blinding light, Caldin winced and looked away. When she looked back again, she saw that the center of the symbol on the taller Avilonian's breast plate was now glowing as bright as a sun, and the entire bridge was awash with the light.

"I am," a new voice boomed. The voice was so loud and resonant that it sounded like rolling thunder.

"You are what?" Caldin asked in a small voice.

One of the other Avilonians took a sudden step forward and raised glowing palms toward her. Before Caldin could wonder what he was doing, she heard a *whoosh* of air; her stomach lurched, and she saw the ceiling rushing up to greet her. She hit with a *crunch,* and a sharp spike of pain erupted in her shoulder. Caldin began falling back to the deck, but an invisible hand seized her just before she could land on her knees and shatter them, too. The hand released her and she was left kneeling on all fours. Afraid to move and aggravate her throbbing shoulder, Caldin stayed down, panting heavily and working hard to suppress the pain. Her shoulder was almost certainly broken. *What the frek was that?* she wondered. *Some type of grav gun?*

"That is better," the deep, gravelly voice said. "Now you are showing the proper respect. Do not speak again unless Omnius asks you a direct question."

Caldin shook her head and gritted her teeth. She heard murmurs of discontent rumbling across the bridge as crew members took umbrage at the way their captain was being treated. It was tough to see through the blinding light, but Caldin thought she saw a few officers getting up from their control stations to kneel on the deck along with her. Seeing that only infuriated her more. Under the guise of checking her injured shoulder, she raised a hand to her ear to activate her comm piece. They needed the Gors up here ASAP. Things were already going to the netherworld.

"You do not know me," the voice like thunder began as Caldin whispered orders into her comm piece, "but I know all of you. I know all of you as if you were my own children. Yet you are not my children, because my children know me."

Caldin was tempted to say she was happy not to be one of those *children*. Of all the things she had expected from the Avilonians when they came aboard, this was the last thing she had imagined. Clearly the glowing *eye* in the center of the Avilonian leader's chest was a symbol of this Omnius they spoke of. Now he, or *it* . . . whatever it was, was somehow communicating with them remotely.

Caldin finished whispering orders into her comm piece. While she waited for the Gors to arrive, her mind turned to wondering about the eye, but she was at a loss to understand who or what was speaking to them. Whatever it was, the Avilonians were treating it like a deity.

"You have come to my kingdom uninvited," the thunderous voice said. "And your Sythians came with you."

"Sythians are here?" Caldin couldn't help from blurting out.

"Do not speak!" the gravelly voice of the taller Avilonian warned once more.

Thunder rolled again, "No, let her defend herself. She does not yet understand our customs, so she cannot be held accountable for her disrespect."

Caldin took that as her excuse to say everything else that was on her mind. "I don't know who or what you are, and I don't know what you want with us, but I do know that you are mistaken," she said. At that, Caldin heard the Avilonians gasp.

The thunder was quiet for a long moment. When it returned, it was much softer than before, "Go on."

Caldin tried to look up into the blinding light, but her eyes began tearing almost immediately, and she was forced to look away. "We have not brought any Sythians with us. None that we are aware of, at least. We *were* sent to find Avilon, but until recently only one of us knew that. Allegedly, we were sent out here to look for survivors, but our mission was cut short when we ran into Sythians. We made a blind jump and accidentally ran into this gravity field. We've been stranded here for the past three weeks."

"You are telling the truth, but one of your people *is* responsible for the Sythians' presence here."

Caldin shook her head. "Who?"

"He is not aboard this ship."

"If you knew that, then why did you accuse us?"

"I didn't. I told you the Sythians came with you. You assumed I was accusing you of bringing them here. As for why you are stranded, it is because I determined that you should be. No one shall enter the light without being first invited, and I would know had I invited you."

Caldin shook her head. "*You* trapped us here?"

"There are twelve overlapping gravity fields surrounding my kingdom. When an intruder is detected, the nearest field turns on and they are forced to turn around. I then decide whether or not to meet with them. In the past I would do so to make them forget what they had discovered here. Now with so few of your people left, it is rare that anyone happens upon us by accident, so I meet with everyone. So far, the only trespassers have been refugees. In my mercy I allow them a chance to prove that they are worthy to become children of the light."

Caldin felt shock coursing through her. She opened her mouth to say something, but the words got stuck in her throat, leaving her mouth agape. The Avilonians' technology was astounding—artificial gravity fields several light years across, sensors that could passively detect a ship moving through SLS . . . Caldin shut her gaping mouth in an effort to contain her awe. She didn't want to give this *Omnius* any more justification for arrogance than it already had.

"What makes a person *worthy?*" she asked, trying but failing to suppress her scorn. It bled clearly into her tone of voice.

"I can see that you do not like me," the thunder said. "I also know that you have called for help and that the ones you called are standing outside right now, about to burst in and kill my three servants here."

Caldin's heart seemed to freeze in her chest. How could Omnius possibly know that? Had he overheard her speaking into her comm piece?

"Tell your . . . *Gors* to surrender before they get hurt."

Caldin forced herself to look up at the blinding light just as the doors behind the three Avilonians swished open. She smiled. "Too late, Omni-frek. Tell your men to stand down before *they* get hurt. They're trespassing on my ship."

Suddenly the blinding light diminished as the three Avilonians turned away from her. Nothing appeared to have come in, and the bridge doors swished shut almost as soon as they had opened, but Caldin knew better than to let that fool her. The Gors were all cloaked.

The caped Avilonian crossed his forearms in front of him and a shimmering bubble of light expanded out from where he stood to surround all three of them. The air seemed to buzz and crackle with energy. Then the two flanking Avilonians raised their arms with palms outward, just as Caldin had seen one of them do before she'd been thrown against the ceiling.

Suddenly the mysterious bubble of light flashed and Caldin saw something glossy and black hit the floor with a *thud*. She gaped at it in horror. It was a Gor's arm, sliced off cleanly at the elbow. A loud hissing noise filled the air—the Gor who'd lost his arm screaming in pain, or more likely, outrage.

The Avilonians began gesturing wildly in the air. Then came a raucous series of booming *thuds* as if someone were beating the bulkheads with sledgehammers. Caldin's eyes were drawn toward each *thud* as it sounded—to the bulkheads, the deck, the ceiling, and finally to the bridge doors. A deep dent appeared in the doors, revealing a slice of the corridor beyond. It looked as if they'd been hit with a battering ram. The battering ram in question appeared a moment later, a glossy black shadow lying on the deck, hissing and writhing in pain.

Back was the thunderous voice of Omnius. "Do not let them suffer," it said. The glowing bubble of energy vanished, and then the Avilonians unleashed screeching beams of blinding white light from their palms. One Gor at a time, the hissing stopped, and fallen Gors appeared all around them, their armor smoking and glowing with a faint orange light. Caldin was left staring in horror at the scene.

"How did you see them?" Caldin asked, unable to believe

what she'd just witnessed. The Gors had been cloaked!

The taller Avilonian turned back to her and the glowing *eye* in the center of his chest swelled to a blinding brightness once more. "I see everything!" Omnius replied. "Did you really think you could hide them from me?"

"You didn't have to kill them! They were already incapacitated."

"Not all are worthy of redemption," the thunder said. "Now, explain to me why you came."

"We came to get help! The last of us are holed up and hiding in an isolated corner of the galaxy called Dark Space. A few weeks ago the Sythians arrived there with a fleet. We need your help to fight them off before they can finish what they started when they came to this galaxy. If you won't help us for our sake, consider this—they're coming for you next. We know they've been looking for Avilon for some time now. It won't be long before they discover you."

"They have already discovered us," Omnius replied. "And it is too late for us to help you. Your people have lost the fight. Your leaders surrendered, and the Sythians now have complete control of Dark Space. They are busy enslaving your people to replace the Gors as crew for their fleets."

"*What?*" Caldin couldn't believe it. "How can you possibly know that?"

"I know many things."

"I don't believe you," Caldin replied. "We would never surrender to Sythians."

"No? Look. . . . and you shall see." With that, the blinding light diminished and Caldin risked looking up. The air before the Avilonians shimmered briefly and then a hologram appeared, projected from the *eye* of Omnius. A familiar Sythian with translucent skin, pale lavender freckles, and gills in the sides of his neck appeared. Caldin watched the alien's lips move and listened to the translation which followed.

"Humans, I am High Lord Kaon. Your rulers surrender to us, and you are now subjects of the Sythian Coalition. You surely require proof to convince you, and so . . ." The camera panned to show Admiral Hoff Heston standing to one side of Kaon. His hands were bound, his gray hair dirty and matted with sweat. Stubble covered his dirty, tear-stained cheeks, and blood stains marred the once pristine white of his now torn and tattered uniform. The holo froze there, and then it faded and the blinding light returned. Caldin winced and looked away.

"Now that you know the fate of your people, we must get back to deciding the fate of you and your crew. "What do you know about us?"

"Nothing," Caldin lied.

"If you wish to live, you won't lie to me again. What do you know about us?"

Caldin wondered how Omnius knew that she'd lied, but she decided it didn't matter. She told the truth this time, explaining what Atton had told her about the immortals and the Sythians. She told them how humanity had evolved in the Getties Cluster on a mythical world called *Origin*, which was really Sythia. She recounted how humanity discovered a way to live forever by cloning themselves and transferring their consciousness to those clones at or before death via Lifelink implants. Then she explained about the Great War which had erupted between mortals and immortals, eventually driving the latter to flee the Getties Cluster. She told them how the mortals who won the war and stayed behind in the Getties had turned to manipulating their genome in order to live longer lives. When that failed to make them immortal, they went back to doing the very thing they had fought to stop—cloning themselves to live forever. By this point all their genetic tampering and unconstrained evolution made them into an entirely new species—the Sythians. As their population grew out of control, the Sythians continued their genetic tampering in order to create bodies for themselves which were uniquely suited to the worlds where they were forced to live, thus the Sythians became a collection of similar, but different species. Once their population grew too large for their galaxy to support, they turned to the Adventa Galaxy to continue expanding, but the Adventa Galaxy was already populated with humans, so they set about to annihilate humanity in order to make room for themselves.

Despite the blinding light radiating from Omnius, Caldin noticed the Avilonians exchanging wide-eyed looks, as if they were hearing all of this for the first time.

"How do you know all of this?" Omnius boomed, sounding as though he were surprised, too.

"It was told to me by one of my commanders—the one we sent to find you and ask for help. He was in turn told by his stepfather, Admiral Hoff Heston—the man from the hologram. The Admiral found out about these things from the Sythians. I am told that he was once one of your people—an Avilonian himself."

"An exile. Yes, I know this man. He came to us for help not long ago. He needed food for his refugees."

"Why was he exiled?"

"That was before my time, just after the Great War between mortals and immortals. . . . If what you are saying about these Sythians is true, then that war, which we all still remember, was not the first war which we have fought over immortality."

"It would appear that history has repeated itself at least once," Caldin agreed.

"That explains why your admiral's offense was so grievous to the royal council."

"What did he do?"

"He advocated mortality as a choice. He said that people should have the freedom to live a natural life and to have at least one child per person as a reward for that choice. He argued that the Great War and the rebellion all started because breeding was strictly regulated, and because not everyone wanted to live forever. He believed that giving the rebels what they wanted would prevent another war, but the council did not agree about the causes for the war, and his proposal was rejected. He was stripped of all rank and privilege for daring to propose such a thing. Rather than leave it at that, he appealed directly to the citizens, hoping to gain popular support and force the council to admit that he was right. He was caught and exiled for treason."

"If what the admiral did was so despicable, why did you agree to help feed his Enclave?"

"Why should innocent people suffer for his mistake?"

"That's a noble sentiment." For some reason Caldin didn't buy Omnius's concern for *innocent people* but she let it go. There was something else that didn't add up. "Why didn't Hoff mention you?"

"Me?"

"You—what are you? I've never heard of any *Omnius*."

"Yes you have, but you don't know it, and neither does your admiral. He went to our outpost, and I did not meet with him personally. I do not reveal myself to everyone."

"So what makes us so special?"

"You are trespassing in Ascendancy space, so I am forced

to cast a judgment. If I decide to let you leave, you will not leave here with any memory of this encounter."

"And if you don't let us leave?"

"Then it will be because I have decided to let you join my kingdom."

Caldin shook her head. "What *are* you?"

"Your legends speak of me, and of my chosen people—you call them Immortals, and you call me—"

"Etherus . . ." Caldin breathed.

"Yes," Omnius replied.

Caldin's jaw dropped and she forced herself to look up into the blinding light. "Etherus is a god."

"I *am* a god," Omnius boomed. "The only god you will ever meet."

Caldin's eyes began to burn and tear. "Are you saying that you created us?"

"No, you created me."

"Then whatever you are . . . you aren't really our god, are you?" Tears streamed down her cheeks, but she refused to look away from the light, determined to show this Omnius that she was not subservient to it. "We are *your* gods," she added with a sardonic smile.

"Blasphemy!" one of the Avilonians screamed. There came another *whoosh* of air, and Caldin felt herself ripped off the deck once more. This time when she hit the ceiling, she hit her head, and the infernal light of Omnius disappeared as she plunged into a hazy darkness.

* * *

Captain Caldin awoke with a tickling sensation in the back of her head; then her eyes popped open and she saw one of the Avilonians standing over her with a glowing wand. She watched him pass the wand over her shoulder and the tickling sensation moved to there. When the sensation passed, the nauseating ache in her shoulder went with it.

"What are you doing to me?" she asked.

The Avilonian gave no reply. She sat up, and he withdrew, walking back toward the blinding light which was *still* suffusing the bridge. Based on that, she assumed that she hadn't been unconscious for long.

"What now?" she demanded of the light. "If you won't send reinforcements to Dark Space, what are you going to do with me and my crew?"

"I did not say I wouldn't send reinforcements. I merely told you that it is too late to save your people. Nevertheless, the time has come for the Sythians to meet their end."

Caldin shook her head in bewilderment. "That's it? Just like that you decide that they should be stopped? Why now? Why didn't you stop them ten years ago when they came to our galaxy?"

The blinding light seemed to swell and then diminish to half its former brightness. "We were not aware of the threat until it was too late to stop it."

"You have sensors that can detect ships travelling at superluminal speeds while they're still *light years* away, and you expect me to believe that you didn't know we were being slaughtered by the trillions?"

"No, we became aware of the Sythians long before your people did. We have been preparing for their arrival ever since."

"What? You *knew* and you didn't think to warn us?"

"If I have been unable to adequately prepare in the last half a century, then what makes you think you could have? They are the threat of all threats, a species so ruthless and so numerous that we could not have stopped them even if all of humanity had found a way to stand together. The only way to survive the invasion was to hide from it, and we are very good at hiding."

"Coward," Caldin spat.

"Great One, I beg your permission to kill her," the taller Avilonian said, sounding as though he spoke through gritted teeth.

"No, she will learn. As for why now—the answer is that your Sythians have finally found us, and it is pointless for us to go on pretending that we do not exist. Now it is time for us to put our preparations to the test."

"I get it. So when your asses are on the line you do something, but when it's ours, you can just leave us to die."

"You may not believe this, but I and my children have gone to a great deal of trouble to save your people."

"Like *what*? I'd never even heard of Avilon until recently, so explain to me how the *frek* you've been trying to save us?"

Omnius gave no reply for a long moment. The light shining from the "eye" in the center of the taller Avilonian's chest swelled once more and then disappeared entirely.

Caldin's eyes narrowed angrily. "Come back here! You can't answer me, can you?"

The three Avilonians began speaking quickly amongst themselves in a language that Caldin didn't understand. They gestured wildly and then turned in a quick circle to look around the bridge.

She was peripherally aware of someone crouching down beside her. It was her XO, Cobrale Delayn. "What do you think's going on?" he asked.

Caldin shook her head. "I don't know."

"They don't look too happy," Delayn replied, pointing at the trio of Avilonians who were still talking at high speed and gesturing frenetically.

A loud banging interrupted Caldin's thoughts, drawing everyone's attention toward the source of the noise—the bridge doors. Even the Avilonians were distracted by the sound. Caldin heard muffled shouting beyond the doors. Some of the other crew had obviously come looking for them. A few seconds later the crackling hiss of a cutting beam started up, and the Avilonian with the cape turned away from the doors to stare at her. The glowing ellipse which was his faceplate remained fixed on her for a long moment. Then he seemed to come to a decision and he began stalking toward her.

"You—" the Avilonian said as he approached, "—you are the captain of this vessel, are you not?"

Caldin nodded as Delayn helped her to her feet. "I am."

"I'm commandeering this vessel for the Ascendancy. Your crew and your ship will fight for me. You will relay my orders to them. If they do not obey, they will die, is this understood?"

Caldin shook her head, bewildered by those demands. "Our technology is far less advanced than yours. What possible use could we be to you?"

"This vessel is the only one I now have to call upon."

"What? What happened to yours?"

"It has been remotely deactivated, along with every other vessel and weapon that we possess. Omnius is not responding, and the gravity fields where you and your Sythians were stranded have all now been deactivated."

Delayn whistled quietly. "Someone frekked things up good. You have centralized control for everything, don't you?"

"Yes, how do you know this?"

"Just a wild guess," Delayn said. "Here's another one for you. That little flashlight of yours—Omnius—he's the one who controls everything."

The Avilonian standing before them loomed close to Delayn and shook an armored fist in his face. "If you wish to live, you will show more respect."

"You need me. I don't need you."

"For now . . ." the Avilonian growled. He turned back to Caldin. "We must go. I fear something terrible has happened."

Caldin nodded slowly. "Comms!" she bellowed, spinning around to find the officer at the comms station. "Tell our crew outside the bridge not to be alarmed; everything is under control, but do have them finish cutting through the doors—just in case we might like to leave the bridge some day. Make sure they understand the Avilonians are on our side, and that they're going to be joining us for a while."

"Yes, ma'am!"

"All right," Caldin said, turning back to the Avilonian

with the cape. "What now, your lordship?"

"I am not a lord. In your language you would call me a Strategian—a Captain, I believe."

"Do you have a name, Mr. Strategian?"

"I am Master Galan Rovik."

"Master?"

"It is a title."

"I see . . ."

"We are wasting time. No more questions. We must go—*now*."

"All right, Master Strategian . . . where are we going?"

"To Avilon."

"All right, but I have one question before we go," Caldin said. "Who is Omnius?"

Galan regarded her silently, but it was Delayn who replied, "He is an AI. Obviously far more advanced than any of our own artificial intelligences."

"Yes," Galan replied, "but he is much more than that. He is our ruler, a benevolent intelligence so vast that we cannot even begin to comprehend him; for countless millennia Omnius has selflessly devoted his life to rule our people with fairness and wisdom—he is a god. He is our god, but now I fear something terrible has happened to him."

"If he's a god," Caldin said, "then why does he need our help?"

"I do not know. All I can say is that nothing like this has ever happened before. Omnius does not simply stop *being*; he does not lose control for even an instant. He is constantly in contact with us and us with him. For that to have changed, and for all of our vessels to suddenly be deactivated . . . Omnius must have been shut down."

"Some god you have there, Galan. He's the first deity I've

ever heard of that has an on/off switch."

"Silence! Take us to Avilon or I will kill you for your blasphemy."

Caldin snorted and shook her head, turning to stalk down the gangway to the captain's table. "Well, you'd better give me the coordinates!" she called out. Then the bridge doors opened with a *boom* as two freshly cut pieces of duranium fell out of place and crashed to the deck. Caldin turned to see Commander Ortane standing in the opening with a handful of pilots and sentinels. They had their rifles and sidearms drawn. "What the frek?" someone called out.

"Stand down!" Caldin said just as the pair of Avilonians still standing by the doors crossed their forearms in front of them and produced another shimmering blue shield like the one which had sliced a Gor's arm off. One of the sentinels called out in alarm and opened fire on the expanding bubble of energy. The laser bolt bounced straight back at him and hit the bulkhead beside his head.

Caldin's gritted her teeth. "I said stand down! They're on our side! All of you—back to your stations!"

The Avilonians' shield disappeared as quickly as it had appeared, and the men standing gawking in the entrance of the bridge began to withdraw. Caldin shook her head and turned back to the captain's table just as Galan Rovik came up beside her.

"Your people lack discipline."

"Yes," she agreed. Gone were the days of strict military discipline. Now the ISSF had to take what it could get, and these days, what it could get were the dregs.

"It will not go well for them in Avilon."

"What do you mean by that?"

"Never mind. Time is short."

"No, I want to know—if we're going to help you, I'll be frekked if I'm going to let you turn around and throw us to the rictans when it's all over."

Galan regarded her patiently. "I will vouch for you to Omnius, but we must hurry, or all of us may soon be beyond helping."

"Fine," Caldin replied. "Give me the coordinates."

Galan shook his head. "You will not understand them. Show me your navigation system and I will do my best to find Avilon."

Caldin pointed to the star map already rising out of the captain's table. "There you go."

Galan frowned at the map for long seconds before turning to her. "We need a common reference point. The speed of light for distance, and one of your standard orbits for time."

Caldin arched an eyebrow at him. "You mean a year?"

Galan took a moment to reply. "Yes . . . a *year*."

"How is it that you can speak our language but you don't know our systems of measurement or time?"

"Because I use your language, but I do not use either your time or your measurements."

Caldin shrugged and turned back to the map. She played with the controls until the map zoomed out to a scale of several light years. Then she pointed to the glowing green icon in the center of the map, which was the *Intrepid*. "We are here." Then she pointed to the red icon which appeared to be right beside them. "You're in the same place for all intents and purposes." The red icon had a line trailing from it to the exact same point where the *Intrepid* was in the 3D map. At the scale she'd set, the spatial distance between their ships was so slight that it was impossible to see, so the icons had to be artificially separated.

Galan pointed to their two ships. "How many orbits would it take for light to travel between our ships?"

"You want me to tell you that in light years? We're less than two hundred klicks away from each other."

"It will be a very small number, but the distance between our ships was known to us before we lost power. Our forward velocities are matched unless you have begun accelerating; therefore, it is another common reference point which we can use to translate between the two systems of scale."

"How long is this going to take?" Caldin asked.

"I am not sure. Once we know how to translate our distances to yours, we will have to translate your coordinate system to our own, but that part should not take long. Is there someone who can help explain your coordinate system and put it in terms of the distance light travels in one of your standard orbits?"

Caldin sighed. "Delayn!"

"Right here, ma'am," he said, appearing on the other side of her.

"Help Master Rovik translate our coordinate system. We can't leave here until we know where we have to go."

"Yes, ma'am."

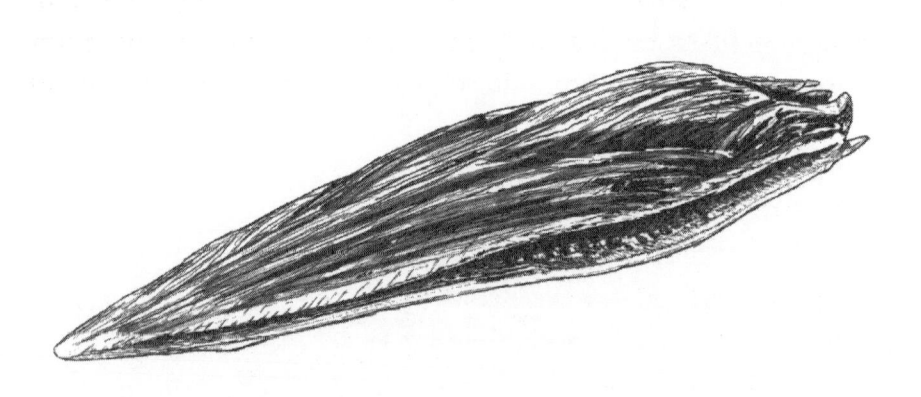

* * *

"My Lord . . ."

The telepathic intrusion jolted Shondar out of his dream.

"*What isss it? I am resting.*" Shondar was not resting; he was drowning his sorrows in the *Gasha's* dream room. He lifted the helmet from his head, forcing himself back to cruel reality. Not even the endless enjoyment which he could derive from immersing himself in his waking dreams was enough to diminish the depressing truth. They were doomed to spend five or six *orbits* travelling through real space just to get back to a point where they could jump to SLS once more. Even for one with a life as long as his, it was almost too much to bear. In five orbits' time he was supposed to have been on Sythia basking in the fame and glory of his conquests. Now, he would be returning in shame.

"*There is a new development. We are no longer trapped here. Our superluminal drives work once more.*"

"What?" Shondar's heart began to pound and his pallid gray skin flushed a darker shade of gray with his excitement. "*You lie.*"

"*It is the truth, My Lord.*"

"*Then why do we wait? Get us out of here!*"

"*Where do we go?*"

Shondar hesitated only a moment. "*To Avilon,*" he said, baring his black teeth and hissing eagerly. How quickly things changed. The glory of Avilon's discovery and subsequent conquest would be his after all.

Chapter 23

On GK-465 the nights were dark and terrifying. No stars or moon were visible, and endless storms raged through the swollen sky. Ethan watched out the viewport as a fork of lightning split the horizon all the way down to the black, raging ocean below. The sky turned purple, as if bruised by its own violence. Then the light was gone, plunging the world into darkness once more. The roar of thunder never came, because the *Trinity* was travelling many times the speed of sound.

A few minutes passed in the dark. Deprived of sight, Ethan's ears took over, magnifying the sound of the ship's air cyclers and Alara's steady breathing where she lay on the bed beside him. Then the world beyond the viewport grew light once more, and a red glow appeared on the horizon. Ethan frowned, wondering what it might be. Hope abruptly swelled in his chest and he sat up in bed to watch that light more carefully. Could it be the Avilonians? Was that the light of a starship hovering high above the surface of the world?

Then the angry red eye of the moon poked through a rare hole in the planet's stormy sky, and Ethan's hopes were dashed. He stared at that red iris for long seconds. The moon stared back, seeming to follow their ship with malevolent scorn. They were out of place. What were they doing on GK-465? No man-made object had any right to be here in a place of such emptiness. There was nothing to see and nothing to do. The planet's barrenness mocked them, warning them away and telling them to go home. But they had no home, and no fuel to go back to it.

Then the moon was gone, retreating into a thick black veil of clouds. Darkness reigned once more, and Ethan held back a sigh. He turned to study the walls of his and Alara's quarters aboard the *Trinity*. Lacquered wood paneling gleamed in the faint light of the room's glow panels. Having once belonged to the decadent crime lord, Alec Brondi, the *Trinity* still bore the mark of his excesses. It was an old military corvette, converted to become a rich mobster's yacht, then converted once more to be a freelancer's trade ship—*Ethan's* trade ship. The *Trinity* had seen a much longer life than was ever intended for her. Were the Imperium still alive and well, she would have been decommissioned long ago, replaced by a more modern model. Now humanity scarcely had the resources to maintain the ships it had, let alone build new ones, but with the Sythian occupation, none of that mattered anymore. Millions were being enslaved. By Ethan's calculations, one in every five people would disappear, never to be seen or heard from again. He'd thought he and Alara would be escaping that fate by accepting this mission, but he'd been wrong. They'd come all this way just to find an uninhabited world which, if it came to it, wouldn't even be hospitable enough to support the two of them. They weren't going to be seen or heard from again either.

Ethan was beginning to wonder if Alara had been right. She'd suggested that maybe his ex-wife, Destra, had sent them out here to die. Ethan wasn't sure if Destra were capable of such outright evil, but he hadn't thought her capable of remarrying so soon after losing him, and yet she'd done that, too.

Shaking his head, his thoughts turned back to the problem at hand. The week leading up to their arrival at GK-465 had been accompanied by anxiety over how the Avilonians would react to the *Trinity's* unexpected appearance at their forward base. That heart-pounding anticipation had long since faded. Now the focus of their anxiety had switched to wondering where the Avilonians were. The *Trinity* had spent the last four days on autopilot, grid-searching the surface of GK-465 with sensors actively scanning, and an alarm set to sound through the ship at even the faintest sign of life. So far, no alarms had sounded, and gravidar logs corroborated that. No electromagnetic radiation had been detected, and no man-made objects had been found either floating above the raging black waters, or lurking in their warm depths. The planet's smattering of islands had been ruled out almost instantly. They were barren rocks, washed clean by frequent tidal waves. Even if some type of base were clinging to one of those rocky outcroppings, it would be immediately visible to both the naked eye and scanners.

If the Avilonians had ever used this world as a forward base, clearly it had long since been abandoned, and whatever signs they had left of their stay had been washed into the deep.

Beside him, Alara stirred. Ethan turned to look at her—her porcelain face was smooth, the worry lines which had accumulated there with the stress of the past few weeks had been swept into the unknowing bliss of sleep. Afraid to wake her with his restless tossing and turning, Ethan climbed carefully out of bed, and padded up to the doors.

Waving his hand across the door scanner, he stepped out into the corridor and walked down past the ship's combined living area and mess hall. The luxurious appointments of the living space no longer seemed inviting to him—his gaze skipped over the opulent white sofas and matching arm chair, and he scarcely noticed the stain-resistant blue carpets or the recessed gold glow panels which came on automatically as he approached and faded as he left. Elaborate moldings at the tops of the shiny white bulkheads were just more ambient noise. No matter how luxurious the coffin, it was still a coffin.

Ethan reached the cockpit and sat down in the pilot's chair. Glowing displays, readouts, and status lights filled the cockpit with a dim, blue-green light. Beyond the forward viewport lay nothing but impenetrable black; the night was absolute. Ethan checked over the gravidar logs, just in case something actually had been detected and somehow failed to trigger the alarm. . . . But there was no sign of even the faintest blip. No indication that anyone had ever even set foot on GK-465.

Ethan tried not to dwell on the crushing weight of despair

which was threatening to suffocate him. Instead he brought up his ship's gravidar configuration on the main holo display and began playing with the settings. He doubled the range and depth and waited half a minute for the ship's computer to finish a new scan.

Lightning split the sky once more, momentarily drawing Ethan's gaze away from the grid.

Then the impossible happened—the alarm he'd set sounded, indicating a possible contact. The lightning vanished and his gaze was back on the grid. Neutral yellow icons were appearing en-masse, in a high orbit above the *Trinity* and GK-465.

How the frek? Ethan's heart pounded with excitement. The contacts were the right size and shape to be starships, but they hadn't been there a second ago, so where had they come from? After so much time spent searching, it almost didn't matter how the *Trinity* had detected them. Ethan aborted his grid search of the planet and pulled up at almost a 90 degree angle in order to make orbit as fast as possible.

Ethan opened the comms. He was just about to hail the ships when he noticed something else. His brow furrowed and his hand drifted away from the comms. *What the . . . ?* Some fifteen capital-class vessels had appeared on the *Trinity's* scopes, but they were all dark on the grid. They weren't radiating anything on the electromagnetic spectrum— no engines running, no comms or sensors active, no weapons or shields—they were all derelict.

It was a ghost fleet.

The cockpit door *swished* open and Ethan turned, his eyes wide and his mouth agape.

"I heard the alert," Alara said, an almost forgotten hope lurking in her voice.

"We found them . . ." Ethan said slowly.

"What?" Alara's eyes flew wide and she broke into a broad grin. "That's amazing! We've got to . . ." She trailed off as she realized that Ethan's expression didn't match her enthusiasm. "What is it?"

Ethan shook his head. "I don't know. They're all dark. There's no sign of life in any of the ships we detected."

"Maybe that's why they were so hard to detect?"

"I doubt it. They just appeared out of nowhere."

"Are you saying they have cloaking shields?" Alara asked as she sat in the copilot's station beside him.

"No, well . . . I don't know."

"Have you tried hailing them?"

"I was about to when I realized that they probably won't hear us if they're drifting without power."

"You won't know until you try."

"Go ahead. I'm going to bring us in for a closer look."

"Don't get too close . . ." Alara warned. "I don't like this."

"Neither do I, but I don't see how they're a danger to us. How are they going to shoot us? Stick their heads out the airlocks and throw rocks?"

Alara smiled and warmth bled into her violet eyes as she turned to speak into the comm. "This is Alara Ortane of the *Trinity*. We are low on fuel and require immediate assistance. Please respond if you receive this message."

The comms crackled and popped with static as the *Trinity* roared through the planet's upper atmosphere. Clouds and stormy skies yielded to the diamond sparkle of stars. Ethan set visual auto-scaling to 500% and suddenly the Avilonian fleet appeared in the distance. Their ships were oblong and rectangular, white and glowing with reflected light from the system's sun, which was just now peeking over the horizon of the planet below.

"There's no response," Alara said, turning to him with wide violet eyes. "What should we do?"

"I'm going to get us closer to one of those ships."

"What for?"

"We're going to board them."

"I don't see any open hangars . . ."

"So we make one."

"That's a nice way to ask for help—*we tried knocking on your door, but you didn't answer, so we decided to break it down.*"

"Maybe they need *our* help?" he suggested. Alara looked dubious, and he shrugged. "Either way, we don't have a choice. I don't see any other starships around here that might hail from the Avilonian Empire."

"You're right, but we're not going unarmed."

"You're not going at all," Ethan replied.

"Excuse me?"

"You're going to be in the cockpit with the thrusters hot and ready for a getaway. If I don't come back, or if you suddenly lose contact with me, you take off and get as far from here as you can. Look for a habitable world."

"I'm not leaving you behind, Ethan, and you're not going alone."

But half an hour later, when Ethan had finished cutting a hole in the nearest derelict vessel's hull, Alara wasn't standing beside him in the airlock. She was waiting at the pilot's station, staying in touch with him via comms.

"You better come back here in one piece, Ethan Ortane, or I'm going to rip you apart myself."

"I love you, too, sweetheart."

"Don't you sweetheart me."

Ethan grinned behind the faceplate of his vac suit and

began playing with the settings on his grav gun. He set the gun for a heavy load, and then targeted the glowing, red-hot circle he'd cut in the outer hull of the Avilonian ship. Holding down the trigger, he heard a metallic groan, followed by a hiss of molten metal dripping down to the hermetic seal which had extended from the *Trinity's* main airlock. Ethan hoped those molten beads of duranium or whatever other alloy the ship's hull was made of didn't burn a hole through that seal and into space. He was wearing a vac suit, but that didn't mean he'd survive sudden depressurization of the airlock.

"Everything all right down there?" Alara asked.

"Just fine . . ." Ethan replied as the glowing hot circle of alloy popped free and began drifting toward him. He set it down on the floor. That done, he turned to peer into the shadowy hole he'd cut. Unable to see anything clearly, he drew his sidearm and snapped on the scope light. A regular ship's deck appeared *below*. The Avilonian ship was oriented so that its deck lay dead ahead, rather than *down* as it should have been.

"I'm going in."

"Are you sure? Is it safe?"

"I'll find out soon enough."

"Ethan!"

He jumped down into the ship and bounced back off the deck before he could turn on the grav field emitter on his belt. The ship's artificial gravity was obviously offline along with everything else.

"I'm going to see if I can find the crew . . ." Ethan said as his feet touched the deck once more. Walking within his own personal bubble of gravity, he made his way slowly through the dark, abandoned corridor where he now found himself.

"What do you see in there?"

Ethan panned his scope light over the walls and ceiling. "Nothing unusual so far," he said, noting shiny white walls, gray ceiling, and the silvery deck under his feet.

"Does it look like one of our ships?"

"Hoi, Kiddie, hold on . . . I'm looking."

"So you found us at last," came an unidentified voice.

Ethan whirled around. Turning on his helmet's external speakers, he called out, "Who said that?"

"Ethan?!" Alara interjected in a panicky voice. "What's going on?"

"I did." This time the voice was right beside Ethan's ear.

Startled, he spun toward the sound, his finger already twitching on the trigger of his pistol. He glimpsed something bright and glowing which came swelling out of thin air. Then came a *whoosh* and something heavy hit him in the chest, throwing him backward. Ethan hit the opposite wall of the corridor with a *bang* and slid to the floor with a groan.

"Your timing could not have been better," the voice said. Ethan looked up to see a man in a suit of glowing blue-white armor stepping toward him. The man's face was hidden by a shiny helmet and glowing visor.

"Who are you?" Ethan asked.

"I am an acolyte of Omnius and a templar of His peacekeepers."

"Omni-what?"

"You will help us."

Ethan was tempted to laugh, but somehow he held it in. "We came here looking for *your* help. If you need us to help *you*, then I'm pretty sure we're all frekked."

"Can your ship fly?"

"Yes, but it doesn't have much fuel."

"We do not have far to go."

"Look . . ." Ethan said, picking himself off the deck and shaking his head. He felt like he'd run into a wall. "I don't know what all of this is about, or what you think we can do to help you, but you sure do know how to ask. What did you do, hit me with a grav truck?"

"You were startled and aiming a weapon at my face. I had to ensure that you did not kill yourself before I could talk with you."

"Kill myself—" Ethan broke off, chuckling. "I'm not sure you know how weapons work."

"My armor is shielded. It will reflect whatever you shoot at me. We must hurry. There is no time to waste."

"Hurry where?"

"To Avilon."

Ethan's eyes lit up behind his helmet. "Now we're getting somewhere. Why the frek didn't you say so earlier? Let's go."

Chapter 24

It took nearly half an hour to translate the Avilonians' coordinates to ones which the *Intrepid* could use. Now they were about to revert to real space and arrive in Avilon—or the Ascendancy, as the Avilonians called it. There was still no sign of Omnius, and the Avilonians on board were growing increasingly restless.

Caldin watched the reversion timer on the captain's table, trying not to pay attention to the trio of glowing men impatiently crowding around the table with her.

"How much longer?" Galan Rovik asked.

"You asked me the same question five minutes ago," she said.

"Because it is hard to believe. How can your ships take so long to travel such a short distance?"

Caldin accepted that criticism with a thin smile. Avilon—the real location rather than the location of their forward base—was straight through the gravity field and just 1.75 light years away. The *Intrepid* could make roughly five light years per hour with red dymium fuel and an extended range SLS drive such as they had on board. Thus, their total travel time was just over twenty minutes. Caldin didn't think much of that, especially not after being forced to consider a four year journey through real space, but the Avilonians were appalled by how slow the *Intrepid* was, leaving her to marvel yet again at how advanced their technology must be.

"How do your SLS drives work?" she asked to distract the Avilonians from their growing impatience.

She wasn't expecting an answer, but to her surprise, Galan replied, "They transport us directly from one point in space to another. Much the same way we came aboard your ship."

Caldin's eyes flew wide. "You mean you can ... *teleport* from one place to another?"

"It takes time to calculate a jump and time to energize the transporter field. The further the jump, the longer calculations take. Omnius can make such calculations almost instantly, but he rarely has the attention to spare for that."

She accepted, nodding absently. It occurred to her that Omnius seemed to have a lot of limitations for a *god*, but by now she knew better than to offend the Avilonians' delicate sensibilities by saying that aloud.

The reversion timer reached ten minutes, and Caldin turned to find the comm officer. "Sound a red alert, and send a message to the ready rooms on the flight deck. Make sure our pilots are ready to launch as soon as we revert to real space."

"Yes, Captain."

"Engineering, is our cloaking shield engaged?"

"As of five minutes ago, ma'am."

"Good. Whatever is happening in Avilon, we don't want to go blundering into it."

"*On* Avilon," Galan said quietly.

"I'm sorry?" Caldin turned to find Galan regarding her silently.

"Avilon is a planet."

"All right, *on Avilon*. What is it you call the star system, then?"

"Domus Licus. In your language this would be, Home of Light."

"That explains all the glowing motifs...." she said, eyeing Galan's shining faceplate. "I don't even know what you look like behind that thing. For all I know you're really a skull face."

"A skull...?"

"Sythian."

"I do not sound like a Sythian."

"It was a joke," Caldin replied.

Suddenly the man's glowing white visor disappeared, and in its place Caldin saw the face of a handsome young man—twenty years old at best. His eyes were bright blue and subtly glowing—*of course his eyes glow*, Caldin thought with a wry smile. She assumed the effect was cosmetic.

"Is that better?" Galan asked.

"You're just a boy," Caldin said.

"I am older than you."

"You don't look it."

"What something appears to be is rarely representative of what it actually is. I am over eight thousand years old."

"Eight . . . how many times have you been cloned?"

"Five."

Caldin shook her head, marveling at that. "How long since you last . . ."

"Resurrected? Over six thousand years. At my rank I am rarely sent into dangerous situations anymore. Not all are as fortunate as I."

Caldin shook her head. "You don't look more than twenty! How is that possible?"

"Our bodies do not age, and they do not die," Galan replied.

"I was told that you live forever because you transfer yourselves to clones before you die."

"That was the original idea, yes, but it has been a long time since we've had to do that. Now we only clone ourselves in the event that we should suffer an accidental death."

Caldin's mind balked at the possibilities once more. Galan's words echoed softly inside her head. *Our bodies do not age, and they do not die . . .* That made the business of cloning oneself and transferring to clones seem like a cheap imitation of eternal life. What Galan was describing went far beyond that. "Then your people are truly immortal."

"Most of us, yes. Not everyone wants to live forever."

"Why wouldn't they?"

"You ask many questions, *martalis*."

"Martalis?"

"A child. A mortal. These words are synonymous to us."

Caldin felt her ire rise at being called a child by a man who looked to be many years her junior, but she kept herself in check and changed the topic. "If you don't age, why risk your life by coming aboard my ship?"

"It was not a great risk. It would be hard to kill me. But regardless, I am a Peacekeeper, and it is my job to risk my life so that others don't have to."

"But why? Why not do something else?"

"To serve one's god and fellow man is the highest calling there is."

Caldin turned back to the captain's table with a frown. Reversion to real space would occur in just two and a half minutes. She was about to drop the conversation when something else occurred to her. "How did you die? Avilon has been hidden for millennia, and you didn't fight the Sythians with us, so who *are* you fighting?"

"The real fight is the same one which has been going on since the dawn of time," Galan replied. "It is within *us*. Good and evil war daily for control of our actions and our thoughts."

Caldin tried hard to understand what she was hearing. "So you died fighting yourself . . . ?"

"No, I died trying to save others from themselves. Omnius is our first and best defense against the evil in our hearts, but there are some who have rejected him. They are a danger to themselves and others. They are the Nulls."

"Nulls, huh. Let's cut through the krak, Galan. You're saying that this Omnius of yours controls everyone else. That's why they're not dangerous."

"No. He guides us."

"I see . . ." Caldin replied, but she really didn't see. She couldn't understand what Galan was talking about. Clearly he was some type of law enforcement officer, but if life were so perfect in Avilon, why would these Nulls want to stir up trouble? And if Omnius were such a benevolent *god* then why would anyone reject him? Clearly Avilonian society wasn't perfect for everyone.

"Reversion to real space in 30 seconds!" the officer at the helm called out.

An audible countdown began at ten, and Caldin looked up from the captain's table to watch out the forward viewports as the *Intrepid* reverted to real space. The streaks and swirls of light which accompanied SLS vanished in a flash of light, and then there were stars everywhere. Dead ahead lay a dark planet whorled with radiating, geometric patterns of light. Those patterns stretched from the north pole to the south, spanning the entire visible hemisphere of Avilon. Caldin understood from those lights that she was looking at some type of world-spanning city—an ecumenopolis.

"What are these?" Galan asked, pointing to a cluster of gravidar contacts on the star map which rose above the captain's table.

Caldin turned to look and saw a dense knot of contacts which were only now appearing in front of the *Intrepid*. They looked like starships. Based on the scale markings beside those contacts, some of them were truly massive—many times the size of the *Valiant*.

"My guess is that's your fleet," she said. "Do you know how to make contact with them?"

"I already have," Galan replied. Caldin wondered how she'd missed that. "They do not know what is going on or what happened to Omnius. They are busy working to override the protocols which disabled their ships, but without Omnius to help them, it will take some time."

"Why would you give Omnius control over everything in the first place?" Caldin asked.

"Because our human natures cannot be trusted," Galan

replied.

"And Omnius can? Look, he shut you all down! Isn't that the last thing he should do when there's a threat to your security?"

"Threats to our security come from within. The best way to prevent a rebellion is to disarm it."

"Seems like this Omnius has everything figured out; there's just one problem. He opened the sector up to an attack. Didn't you say that Sythians were stranded in the gravity field with us? That field was disabled right along with your ships, so where do you think the Sythians are now?"

Galan's glowing eyes grew big and frightened. "Scan for them!" he ordered.

"We can't detect cloaked ships," Caldin replied.

Galan did a double take, and then his upper lip curled in disgust. "*Spackt!*" he spat. "Head for the planet. We must get to the Zenith Tower as quickly as possible."

"Helm, you heard the man. Full speed ahead!" To Galan, she said, "What is the Zenith Tower?"

"It is where Omnius resides. His temple. It is the tallest tower on the planet. You cannot miss it." He pointed out the forward viewport to a particularly bright and dense pattern of lights shining into space from the dark side of Avilon. "There. How long will it take for us to reach it?" Galan asked.

Caldin selected the planet on the star map and then queried the ship's computer. "Half an hour before we hit the upper atmosphere. I'll launch our fighters while we wait. They'll reach the planet ahead of us."

"Is there no way you can get us there faster?"

Caldin turned to him with a speculative look. "I suppose I could send you and some of your men aboard an assault transport."

"Do so."

"Comms—tell the Guardians and Renegades to launch. Guardians will go ahead of us to recon the planet and report the situation on the ground. Have the Renegades hang back to escort our transports to the surface—and get our sentinels on those transports! I want three squads of Zephyr assault mechs to support the Avilonians when they get dirt side."

"I did not give your people permission to set foot on Avilon," Galan said quietly.

"Do you want our help or not?"

He held her gaze for a long moment before looking away, back out the forward viewports. "They will not fire their weapons unless ordered by one of us to do so, and they will obey us at all times, or they will die. The use of weapons above the Celestial Wall is strictly prohibited."

"Of course . . ." Caldin replied, wondering what Galan was talking about. "I'm sure Omnius will make an exception to save himself."

Galan shot her a dark look. "Your scornful attitude will not serve you well here. I suggest you adjust it."

Caldin gave no reply. If the Avilonians were so strict and so utterly subservient to an artificial intelligence, she wasn't sure that Avilon would be such a paradise after all. It all depended on just how benevolent their AI really was, and Caldin wasn't sure she liked the idea of trusting an intelligence which was so vast as to be incomprehensible. *The smarter you are, the easier it is to take advantage of others. So the question is, how are you taking advantage, Omnius? And if you're so good, why would anyone want to shut you down?*

The obvious answer was that some people in Avilon weren't happy with the way Omnius was running things. So were *they* the problem, or was Omnius?

That question was infinitely harder to answer.

* * *

"All right, Guardians! It's go time! We have no idea what's waiting for us out there. It's our job to find out. Do not engage anything until mission control gives us clearance. This is strictly a recon mission. Is that understood?" Atton scanned the myriad faces in the briefing room with him. There were just seven of them, including Atton himself. They were down a few pilots from the last engagement. So was Renegade Squadron. Right now the Renegades would be sitting in a matching briefing room on the other side of the hangar bay, receiving a different briefing with a different set of mission parameters. "Are there any questions?"

Gina Giord's hand shot up. "We're nine pilots. That leaves one of us flying solo."

"Seven will be joining Five and Six as a trio."

Gina frowned. "Or you could pair Seven with you and I could fly solo."

Atton scowled at her. "Are you, or are you not the XO of this squadron, Lieutenant?"

"You tell me, sir," she said.

With a frown, Atton recalled her insubordinate behavior and her challenge for him to meet her in the ring, which had ultimately landed him in med bay, but he decided not to hold any of that against her. "We all have our personal differences, Lieutenant, but as soon as we climb into those cockpits it's not personal anymore. We're fighting for the survival of the human race, so all those petty differences mean krak—and they're the krak that will get you killed. We don't need any more ghosts in this squadron. Is that understood?"

"Yes, sir," Gina replied.

"No one is flying solo out there. Are there any other questions, something related to the mission perha—"

The P.A. system crackled to life, interrupting him before he could finish. "Guardians, you are cleared to launch. Proceed to the hangar bay with all possible speed."

Atton clapped his hands together. "You heard 'em. Ruh-kah!" With that, he turned and ran down the corridor leading away from the briefing room. He heard booted feet pounding down the corridor after him. As soon as he reached the double doors at the end, he waved his wrist over the scanner, and they parted with a *swish*. Beyond the doors, Nova Fighters sat in gleaming rows on the hangar deck. Atton ran down those rows, heading for the fighter nearest to the pair of glowing red launch tubes at the far end of the hangar. To his right lay the yawning opening of the hangar bay—stars and space tinted liquid blue by the *Intrepid's* static shields.

As soon as Atton reached his Nova, he leapt up onto the wing and swiped his wrist over the control panel beside the cockpit. The transpiranium canopy rose with a hiss of pneumatics, and he slipped inside. He slapped the button to close the canopy before it had even finished opening, and then he hit the fighter's ignition switch. The Nova's reactor whirred to life and the ship began to hum and vibrate all around him. Glowing holo displays and buttons came to life and his fighter's AI greeted him—"Welcome back, Commander."

"Sara, run a quick preflight and set IMS to 95%," Atton said as he reached behind his flight chair for his helmet. He pulled it on and sealed the clasps at his neck. A green icon on the helmet's HUD appeared in his periphery, indicating a good seal, although his suit would only pressurize in the event that the cockpit depressurized.

"All systems green," Sara said.

"Good." Atton touched a key on his comm board and selected the channel reserved for his wing pair. "Ready, Tuner?" he asked, using Gina's call sign.

"Punch it."

Atton nodded. Speaking to his AI, he said, "Initiate the launch sequence."

"Initiating . . ."

The Nova rose swiftly off the deck and swiveled in place. As soon as it turned to face the pair of glowing red portals in the back of the hangar, the fighter's thrusters roared, and Atton was pinned to his seat. The launch tubes grew rapidly larger, still somehow seeming too small for his fighter. Atton winced as the Nova rocketed inside the rightmost of the two. Bright rings of light raced by the cockpit, faster and faster until just a split second later he was catapulted into the starry blackness of space.

A quick look at the grid showed Gina roaring out right behind him. The Guardians came out in a steady stream, one after another, and then the Renegades began streaming out the launch tube beside theirs.

Atton stomped on the left rudder pedal to bring his fighter around in a tight arc which would set him on the same path as the *Intrepid*. The blinding orange glow of the cruiser's engines hove into view, and Atton grinned. It was good to be back in the cockpit. He was curious to find out what had the Avilonians so scared, but so far the details were need to know. All Atton and the other pilots really *needed* to know was that the Avilonian fleet had been remotely disabled, and now they were heading into a potentially hostile environment with an unknown threat. The threat was described as *probably local* but Atton wasn't convinced. Maybe the Sythians had found Avilon already?

That wasn't a happy thought.

"Form up, Guardians," Atton said as soon as everyone had launched. "It's time to see what has these people so spooked."

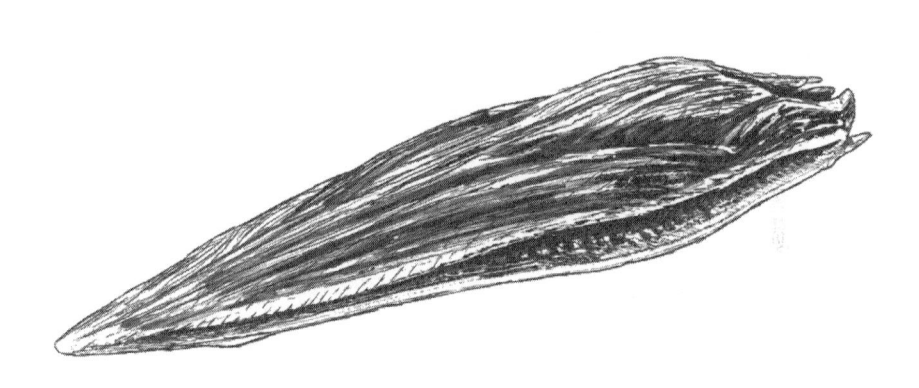

* * *

High Lord Shondar gawked at the pitiful number of ships defending the Avilonians' world. "That is it?" he warbled aloud. "This is no fleet." There were at most fifty capital ships in the immediate area, and although many of them were giant warships, Shondar's own fleet of over 100 capital-class vessels was arguably much stronger. "Have the *drivers* launch our warships," he commanded. "They are to remain cloaked until they surround the enemy fleet. Once they are in position they are to await my orders."

"Yes, My Lord."

Meanwhile, Shondar sent a telepathic update to Lord Kaon in Dark Space. The last time Kaon had heard from him there had been bad news. The *Gasha* and her hundred plus warships had been mysteriously stranded in the middle of a strong gravity field. Now Shondar's news was all good. They were free, and they had reached Avilon. Even better still—the Avilonians did not appear to be as strong as initially reported. Kaon responded to that news with eagerness and relief. He also gave Shondar an update. The rest of the lords had arrived in Dark Space, and now their ships were brimming with human slaves. It would not be long before Kaon came to join Shondar in the glory of their final conquest.

Shondar finished speaking with Kaon and settled back in his command chair to watch the battle unfold. He called up live footage from the bridge decks of the cruisers which were closest to the enemy fleet, and then he magnified that view so he could see the enemy ships with his own eyes. Unlike most human warships that Shondar had seen, which were radiant with bright lights, these were dark. Not even a single viewport shone with light. Absent even were the glowing blue maws of hangar bays. If these ships had hangars, they didn't shield the openings.

Shondar bared his teeth and his brow wrinkled in confusion. *Is the enemy already dead?* he wondered. "What do sensors say of our enemy?"

"No radiation of any kind. They are dark, My Lord."

"Without power?"

"Or shielded with a cloak to prevent us detecting them."

"Then why not shield themselves from the visible spectrum? No, that is not it."

"My Lord! There is movement . . ."

"I see it," Shondar replied, watching the map as a stream of small contacts appeared.

"These are a known type—Nova Fighters. They are not Avilonian..."

"No, they are not."

"Then...? Are we in the wrong place?"

"The other ship types are not known to us, therefore, it is likely that these other humans are visiting," the operator at the sensor control station replied.

"Interesting. Have a wing of our fighters intercept this new enemy."

"Yes, My Lord."

Shondar watched his fleet surround the Avilonians, washing over them like a tidal wave. The Avilonian ships made no move to escape, nor did they show any signs of life. Shondar didn't expect them to react—his fleet was cloaked and undetectable. When the enemy was completely surrounded, and all 1468 Shell Fighters had deployed in vast, buzzing clouds, Shondar bared his teeth once more. "De-cloak and engage the enemy. Let us kill as many of these *shakars* as we can!"

Chapter 25

"Let's do a fly by on our way to the planet," Atton said as he guided his fighter toward the densest cluster of disabled Avilonian ships. "Line Abreast formation. We're going to fly over top."

"Roger that," Guardian Three commed back.

Click. Click, came the affirmative responses from two other pilots.

"I've got just 57 warships on the grid ..." Guardian Five—*Razor*—said. "Anyone else confirm that? Seems like too few for a sector supposedly populated by trillions."

"The rest might be out of sensor range," Atton replied, "But even if that's the extent of their home fleet, some of those cruisers are over ten klicks long. I'd say what they lack in numbers they make up in other ways."

"Lead ... are you suggesting that size matters?" Gina replied.

Snickering followed that remark and Atton frowned. "Cut the chatter, Guardians." Shaking his head, he touched a point on the grid which was above the enemy fleet and more or less in the center of their formation. A green diamond appeared on the grid. That would be the nav point for their fly by. It was 1,199 klicks out. Atton's velocity was just over 2.5 klicks per second, but with an acceleration of 145 KAPS that speed was rising fast. A number below the icon he'd place on the grid gave an ETA in minutes and seconds—1:52.

They'd have to slow down to do a proper fly by, but Atton figured a quick glance would be good enough. Their orders were to recon the planet, not the mysteriously derelict fleet.

The comms crackled with more chatter—this time from Guardian Six, otherwise known as Ogles. "So, if these people are the Immortals, I guess that solves the old debate," he said.

Atton frowned and keyed his own comm system. "What debate is that, Six?"

"The religious one—you know, all that existential krak. The Immortals aren't real, so that means no Etheria and no Etherus—no gods and no God. We ended up being our own gods. Funny that—always knew I was almighty."

"You're an ignorant skriff, Ogles," Ceyla replied.

"Hoi, stow that, Four!" Atton said. "No personal attacks, you copy?"

Click.

Atton couldn't blame Ceyla for getting upset. Ogles was belittling and attacking her faith, which must have felt like a personal attack. Seeing an opportunity to redeem himself for his own prior comments about her beliefs, Atton added, "And, Og?"

"Sup, SC?"

"You might want to brush up on logic when we get back on deck. The fact that there are human immortals living here in Avilon does not mean that they are the same ones Etherians believe in. Maybe the Avilonians fixated on the idea of eternal life *because* of their belief in souls. Then, once they found a way to attain immortality in this existence, they outgrew the need to believe in life after death. Regardless, none of that has any bearing on whether or not there actually is an afterlife."

"Well maybe it don't disprove it, SC, but I don't see why anyone would want to find out whether there's a life after death if they didn't have to. Give me the choice between living forever in this life and living forever in some other one that might not even exist, and I'll take this one thank you very much. Immortals forgive me!" he wailed in mock repentance. "I just got too much to live for down here."

"Like what?" Gina challenged. "Admiring your collection of holo girls? I might believe you if you had a life, Ogles."

"Hoi, I don't make fun of your hobbies."

"That's because my hobbies aren't stupid."

"All right, that's enough!" Atton said, eyeing the ETA to the nav point—15 seconds. "We have a mission to perform. I don't want to hear any more personal comments on this channel."

"Copy that," Ogles said.

Click, Ceyla added.

"We're coming up on the Avilonian fleet . . . make sure you swivel your holocorders to get a good look as we fly past."

"I doubt we'll see anything at this speed," Guardian

Three put in.

"Doesn't matter. Vidcorders will catch it all the same. Control can always magnify and slow down the footage for analysis."

"SC . . . my scopes are picking up some—*skrissrssss* . . ."

Ogles' reply cut off suddenly, and a bright flash of light blossomed off Atton's port side, followed by the distant *boom* of a simulated explosion. His head jerked toward the light in time to see the tail end of an explosion. And like that, Ogles was off to settle the debate himself and find out firsthand about all that *existential krak*.

"What the frek—" Gina said. She was interrupted by another explosion which blossomed off to starboard, taking Guardian Three this time.

"Evasive action!" Atton yelled, already yanking up on his fight stick. Another explosion boomed right beneath him and his nova rocked violently, his shields hissing with shrapnel.

"Mines!" someone screamed.

"I've got nothing on sensors . . ." Ceyla added.

Then a stream of familiar lavender-hued lasers began stuttering by Atton's cockpit, and the enemy contact siren screeched out a warning as Sythians suddenly appeared all over the grid.

"Skull faces!" Gina roared.

"Frek it," Atton muttered, his eyes on the grid as hundreds of red enemy blips began appearing all around them.

"There's a whole fleet of them!" Gina went on.

"I've got one on me!" Ceyla screamed over the comms.

"Keep your acceleration up and set shields to double aft," Atton said. "We'll pass out of range in a minute. We're going too fast for them to catch up."

Click.

Atton kept up a random set of maneuvers to confuse the aim of the pair of Shell Fighters on his own six o'clock. Most of their shots went wide. "Sara," Atton began, speaking to his AI. "Set comms to the command channel and establish a connection."

"Connection established . . ." the AI replied a moment later.

The lasers flashing by his cockpit ceased, and a quick look at the grid showed the pursuing enemy fighters had dropped out of range. Even though they had no hope of catching up, they made no move to break off their pursuit. "Control," Atton began, "this is Guardian Leader. We have encountered a Sythian Fleet and we've picked up pursuit from enemy fighters. They're following us to the planet. Please advise."

The comm crackled with a reply. "We see them, Guardians. Do not engage. Your orders remain the same. Once you drop below the cloud layer, head for the Zenith Tower, which is marked on your navs, and report on the situation there. We're sending ground units to that location. As soon as they arrive, you will provide air support and keep them safe."

"Roger that," Atton replied, wondering why he hadn't heard about the *Zenith Tower* earlier. He decided that mission control must be bogged down with all the recent developments. Atton eyed the Avilonian fleet as he flew over top of it. Rolling his Nova to put that fleet 'above' rather than 'below' him, he set visual auto scaling to 400% in order to watch the Avilonian fleet in greater detail as he streaked by. The first thing he noticed at that level of zoom was that there were no lights shining out from those ships' viewports.

As he flew by one of the larger cruisers, space erupted

with dozens of dazzling points of bright purple light—Sythian Pirakla Missiles. They swarmed out the side of a distant Sythian cruiser and crashed into the Avilonian fleet with explosive force, hitting two different ships at once and cutting ragged black holes in their hulls. The Avilonians didn't even try to evade, but Atton knew that was because they couldn't.

Suddenly, his nav screamed out with a collision warning, and Atton noticed the Avilonian cruiser rushing toward him. He pulled up at the last second, roaring out close over the hull of that ship. Then a volley of Pirakla missiles hit right in front of him. Debris burst into his flight path, followed by brief jets of flame which billowed out into space, fed by escaping air from the cruiser. One of those jets engulfed Atton's Nova and the debris pelted his shields with an angry *hiss*. Then something heavy hit his fighter with a *thunk* and sent him spinning away.

"Shields critical," the AI warned.

"Frek!" Atton screamed as he battled with his flight stick to get back on his previous heading. "Heads-up, Guardians! Those cruisers are flying apart! Keep your distance."

"Roger that . . ." Gina said, her voice soft with horror.

"They're being slaughtered," Ceyla added.

Dead ahead there were more than a dozen Avilonian ships, all of them taking heavy fire and throwing off molten debris. Sythian warships were swarming them from all sides, firing glittering purple sheets of Pirakla missiles into their listless foe. Atton watched the cruiser to his port side take two full broadsides at once from a pair of passing Sythian battleships. The Avilonian ship was at least twice their size, but with no shields and no weapons to defend itself, it was already full of gaping holes. As Atton looked on, another volley hit that warship, and it cracked into three pieces which began drifting slowly apart. At that, the pair of Sythian warships stopped firing and began turning away, already on the prowl for their next victim.

"I don't know *what* the Avilonians problem is," Atton said, "but if they don't fire back soon, we're all frekked."

* * *

There was barely room to breathe aboard the *Trinity*. Everywhere Ethan went and everywhere he looked he found Avilonians in their glowing blue-white armor. He had yet to see one of these mysterious people in the flesh, and there was no way for him to tell them apart. The only way he could even tell who was in charge was by the fact that the one who periodically broke his stoic silence to bark out orders wore a shimmering blue cape and had a strange symbol etched into the breastplate of his radiant armor.

Ethan turned to that one now and said, "We're almost there."

The mysterious man nodded without speaking, and Ethan turned back to his controls. He shot Alara a sideways glance, which she returned with a wary look. Neither of them felt comfortable with so many strangers on board. Making matters worse, the Avilonians refused to explain what was going on, and apparently they had neither seen nor heard from Atton. Either they were lying about that or Atton had been intercepted en route. Ethan wasn't sure which scenario would be worse. His brow dropped a dark shadow over his eyes as his thoughts took an even darker turn. How many times could a father lose his son?

He winced and pushed those thoughts from his mind. *Focus. One crisis at a time.* As for the immediate one, the only thing the Avilonians would say about it was that the leader of their people, someone named Omnius, was in trouble. Somehow this Omnius had disabled all of their ships and weapons in order to protect Avilon against the threat of an armed rebellion.

Ethan didn't understand why they didn't just call Omnius up and say—*Hoi, we're trying to help you; could you reactivate our ships, please?* At least that way they wouldn't have to use *his* ship. He supposed he should be grateful that he'd found the Avilonians at all, and that they were taking him to Avilon. He *should* be, but he wasn't. When he'd needed their help, they'd ignored him and refused to even show themselves for four *days*. Then, suddenly, when they needed *his* help, they were everywhere, and impatient as frek to get what *they* wanted from *him*. He felt used, and more than a little suspicious of the Avilonians traipsing through his ship.

"You will take us straight to the planet when we arrive," blue cape said.

"Well, I wasn't planning to take you to the moon—unless of course you want to go to the moon. I live to serve, after all. Does this planet of yours have a moon?"

"Ethan . . ." Alara began, sending him a warning look.

She obviously thought he shouldn't be adopting a sarcastic tone with them, and she was probably right, but he couldn't help it. *Dumb freks,* he thought with a glance in blue cape's direction.

"Reversion in ten," he said a second before the ship's computer began an audible countdown. When it reached zero, there came a flash of light as the bright streaks and star lines of SLS were replaced by stars and a mottled green and blue planet. On one side, the planet was illuminated by a red sun. Daylight painted the surface of the world in blue, green, and gray—the colors of water, vegetation, and rock. But that natural appearance on the day side was somehow deceptive, because on the night side the planet was lit up with complex patterns of light. Glowing circles, lines, and squares crisscrossed each other to form intricate patterns of light. Ethan whistled softly. "That is one *big* city!" It had been a long time since he'd seen a world so overrun with people that it shone like a glow lamp in the dark. "Where to now, boss?" Ethan asked, turning to blue cape.

"What do your sensors detect?"

Ethan took a quick look at the grid. He wasn't sure what he'd expected to find there, but what he actually saw was the last thing he ever would have imagined. "They're here!" he said, his eyes widening suddenly with the realization.

"Who is here?" blue cape demanded.

Ethan gaped at the grid, unable to believe what he was seeing. "The ISSF." A quick look at the grid confirmed it—there were over a dozen Nova Fighters out there, and that meant his son likely was, too. No sign of the *Intrepid,* but Ethan supposed it could be cloaked. *They're here,* he thought, relief flooding through him like a sudden rain in a desert.

"Your people?" blue cape asked.

"My people . . . your people . . . *Sythians!* Frek!" Ethan exclaimed, only now noticing all the other contacts on the grid. "There's a war raging out there!" Now Ethan hoped Atton wasn't piloting one of those Novas. The grid was teeming with neutral yellow and red enemy contacts, but only a hint of green, which were ISSF forces. As he watched, a pair of yellow contacts succumbed to enemy fire and winked off the grid.

"It's not going well for your people...." Ethan assumed the neutral yellow contacts were Avilonian ships, since none of them were firing back.

"Because we are defenseless! Get us to the planet immediately! We must get Omnius to restore control of our defenses in time to stop this sacrilege."

Under any other circumstances, Ethan might have taken offense to the commanding tone, but he was inclined to agree—if the Avilonians didn't get their fleet back online soon, there wouldn't be a fleet left to activate....

And there wouldn't be an Avilon either.

* * *

"They're decimating the Avilonian fleet, Captain!"

Caldin turned to Strategian Galan Rovik. "You still want me to get you to the surface?"

It took a moment for Galan to reply. His gaze was fixed upon the star map and the glowing yellow icons which represented his fleet. As he watched, a pair of cruisers winked off the grid, and he turned to her, his deceptively young features slack with shock and horror. "Unless you can defeat these invaders yourself, it is the only way. We must bring Omnius back online as quickly as possible. Whoever has done this was surely not aware that your Sythians were coming. If they are not stopped, there will be no Avilon left to fight over."

Caldin nodded and turned to the pair of guards flanking the broken entrance of the bridge. While en-route to Avilon, she'd called them up to help clear the dead Gors off the deck. Caldin waved them over. As soon as they were near, she said, "Sergeant, escort Master Rovik to the hangar and have him board the fastest shuttle to the surface."

"Yes, ma'am."

Galan and the other two Avilonians nodded once to her in parting, and Caldin turned to watch them leave. Her distraction only lasted for a second, however, before she turned back to the captain's table and began snapping orders at her crew. "Helm, get us closer to the engagement! Weapons, stand by. Engineering, get ready to switch from cloaking shields to beam and pulse. Let's show these skull faces our teeth!"

* * *

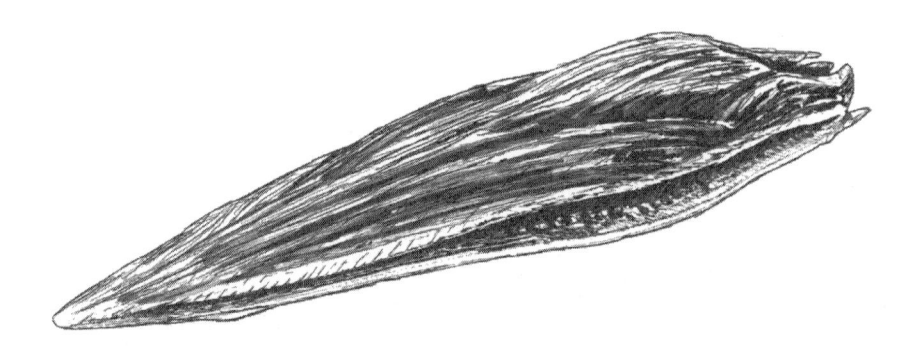

"Why do they not open fire?" Shondar asked aloud. His ships fired, and the enemy fleet responded not with weapons fire, but by belching flames, debris, and tumbling bodies out into space. It was a massacre.

Shondar bared his black teeth in a rictus of glee.

"The enemy does not appear able to respond to us. They are helpless, My Lord," one of the twelve operators on the bridge of the *Gasha* replied.

"Yesss," Shondar hissed. "This is an unexpected thing, but a good thing. We are to have all the glory of this last conquest to ourselves! Let us be done with this fleet quickly that we can proceed to purge the planet. When we leave here this day, we are to leave not a planet, but a smoldering husk! Not a man, woman, or child is to be left alive. This day, we kill them *all!* For glory!" Shondar roared.

"For glory!" his crew chorused.

Chapter 26

"How much longer?"

"Hoi, don't get your cape in a knot, I'm flying as fast as I can," Ethan retorted. Avilon had swollen to fill the entire forward viewport. They would reach the upper atmosphere in just a couple more minutes.

Blue cape began pacing around the bridge. "Hac enom at ipsa morientar!" he roared.

"What are you babbling about?" Ethan asked while diverting more power to shields for what was going to be a very *hot* atmospheric entry.

"They will die for this!" blue cape spat, whirling to face

Ethan.

"Good for you. I've never been a fan of the skull faces. Kill a few for me, too, would you?"

Blue cape turned back to look out at Avilon, and he began mumbling in that strange language of his again.

"Why do you have to antagonize them?" Alara whispered.

"Maybe because they antagonized me first. They're on my ship giving *me* orders, forcing us to help them when they clearly had no intention of helping us! They're lucky a bit of sarcasm is the only thing I've thrown their way."

"You will be rewarded for your service, *martalis*," blue cape said quietly.

"Name's Ethan, not Martalis, your skriffiness."

"Martalis, means mortal, and do not presume to insult my intelligence. I am far more knowledgeable than you on every and any topic you have ever studied."

"Then you must know a lot about arrogance, too," Ethan muttered.

"My ears are as keen as my mind, *martalis*. Declaring a fact about oneself is only arrogant when it is not wholly true. Now focus on getting us to the Zenith Tower, while I try to make contact with my people on the ground." With that, blue cape fell silent.

The *Trinity* hit the upper atmosphere of Avilon and almost immediately their view of the planet became shrouded in a bright blue glow, which was their shields dissipating friction with the air. Ethan yanked the throttle all the way back into full reverse, and then dialed up the shields some more, shunting energy away from weapons in order to do so. The surface of Avilon rushed up to greet them in a dizzyingly-bright pattern of lights. Now that they were just a few dozen kilometers up, Ethan could pick out other details—between the lights of the world-spanning city below, lay a diffuse blue color. Was it water? Perhaps the Avilonians were so short on space that they'd begun building hovering cities above their oceans.

Clouds began streaking by in puffy white wisps. The lights below resolved into the shapes of elaborate skyscrapers which soared above the ground, breaking up the night into jagged shadows and radiant mountains of light. Ethan's gaze wandered back to the blue spaces between the lights, and this time he saw a pattern emerge. The blue was broken up into shimmering hexagonal sections, like a vast honeycomb. "What the . . . what *is* that?" Ethan pointed out the forward viewport.

Alara shook her head. "I don't—"

"It is the Celestial Wall," blue cape said. "It is what separates us from the chosen—the *Celestials*."

"So, you're not one of those chosen Celestials?"

"No," blue cape replied, a note of sadness bleeding into his voice. "I have not ascended that far yet. Many of us will never get there."

"Don't worry, I'm sure you'll make it," Ethan replied with an accompanying eye roll. He felt a chill creeping down his spine, and shook his head to clear it. He had a bad feeling he'd stumbled upon some ages old religious cult. Who was this Omnius they spoke of so reverently? Alara cast Ethan a wide-eyed look, and he replied with a shrug. He was beginning to wonder at the wisdom of coming to Avilon after all, but it wasn't as though they'd had a lot of other options. Religious cult or not, Avilon was humanity's last hope for survival, and if they couldn't get the planet's defenses back online, even that hope would soon be lost.

"There!" blue cape pointed.

Ethan looked up from his controls to see a monolithic tower appear in the distance. That tower shone gold in the night.

Seeing the ground rushing up too fast, Ethan pulled up, leveling out at just one and a half kilometers from the apparent surface of the planet.

Skyscrapers rushed by underneath them, some rising high enough that their spires stared back at eye level, while others rose even higher than the *Trinity* flew. Whatever the pressure had been to build taller and taller buildings, the tallest of them were few and far between with most of the city lying close to the shimmering blue of the *Celestial Wall*.

Ethan studied that diaphanous membrane, trying to imagine what lay beneath it. He thought he caught a glimmer of city lights shining below. Curious, he descended to 500 meters and aimed the *Trinity* for a particularly vast expanse of blue. As they flew over it, he was sure he could see thousands of tiny lights shining up through that barrier—lights and . . . shadowy lines. Those lines came together in recognizable patterns, and then the lights adhered to those patterns, giving Ethan a complete picture of what he was looking at. His mouth dropped open and he guided the *Trinity* down for an even closer look.

"What are you doing?" Alara whispered.

"Hang on, there's something down there we need to see."

* * *

Dark Space IV: Revenge

Clouds whipped by Atton's cockpit like gauzy white curtains. His gaze remained fixed on the city below. He'd never seen a world so populous in all his life.

Someone gave a long, slow whistle over the comms. "So, there's trillions of 'em after all," Guardian Five said.

"What's all that blue krak between the buildings?" Gina asked.

"Water?" Guardian Seven suggested.

Atton shook his head. "Not sure. Let's get a closer look."

The jagged spires of kilometers-high skyscrapers rushed up to greet them and then raced by in a blur of shining lights. The buildings themselves were luminous, as if they were vast light sculptures crafted by some divine artisan.

"This is amazing . . ." Guardian Four, Ceyla Corbin, put in.

Atton's eyes skipped past the buildings to study the shimmering blue rivers flowing around their foundations. Then he noticed a hexagonal pattern on the surface of the blue, and he saw that it was both casting light and reflecting it from the buildings above.

"Hoi, looks like we've got some type of shield down there. That pattern is the emitter frame."

"Why would they shield the ground?" Ceyla asked.

"They wouldn't," Atton realized. With that, he dropped down to 300 meters, and leveled out above one of the larger rivers of energy for a closer look. He flipped his Nova upside down so he could get a better look out the top of the canopy. What he saw next forced him to adjust his impression of Avilon so far. He'd seen the scattering of kilometers-high buildings and all the shorter ones in between. Putting that together with the radiating patterns of light he'd seen from orbit, Atton had assumed the surface of Avilon must be covered by one massive city. Now he realized it wasn't just big—it was incomprehensibly vast.

Barely visible below the blue rivers of energy running between the buildings were the shadowy outlines of the very same buildings—their real foundations disappearing endlessly below the shield. Millions of tiny blue-tinted lights shone up from the depths of bottomless man-made chasms.

Someone called out, "There's a whole other city down there!"

Atton nodded slowly. He ran a quick surface-penetrating scan to confirm it and found that the real surface of the planet was buried under another kilometer of city, meaning that there were in effect *two* cities covering the surface of Avilon—one which soared high above the shield, and the other which lay below and served as a foundation for the first. The sheer scale of urban development was unimaginable. If the whole planet was like this, then there had to be countless trillions of people living on Avilon. It was mind-boggling. Atton rolled his Nova back over and saw monolithic skyscrapers racing by to either side of him, glittering mountains of light rising kilometers into the sky. Despite the massive scale of those buildings, the majority of the upper city was built just a few dozen stories above the shield, making the under city arguably the larger of the two.

The flat rooftops of the shorter buildings below were carpeted with a dark, leafy green. Descending to 200 meters

Atton picked out trees, grass, and flowers. Illuminated fountains bubbled up in the middle of man-made streams which flowed from one building to the next in thundering waterfalls. Descending still further, Atton rocketed over the top of one such waterfall. Brightly-lit synthstone paths wound through the gardens, and dozens of white-robed pedestrians populated those paths, out for a midnight stroll. As the Guardians roared by overhead, those pedestrians looked up and pointed at the sky.

It was hard to believe that there was a battle raging in orbit, and that all of this man-made and cultivated beauty was now in jeopardy. Atton tried to imagine what it would look like in the light of day. He realized that with prevalence of parks, and the vast, architectural beauty of the tallest buildings, the upper city would be an urban utopia. As for the lower city . . . he couldn't say without having seen it, but he couldn't conceive of anyone, or for that matter any green growing thing, that would want to live so far below the reach of natural light. Between the shadows cast by the buildings of the upper city and the light-filtering shield layer, the lower city streets would be dark and dingy. The contrast that struck in Atton's mind's eye gave him the impression of a vast rich-poor gap.

"This place is krakkin' . . ." Guardian Nine said.

"No krak," Gina added.

"All right, enough gawking, Guardians," Atton said, his eyes searching the grid for their nav point. The Zenith Tower was coming up at just under one hundred klicks away, but at this low altitude he couldn't see it for all the skyscrapers between him and there. "Let's gain some altitude and get to our objective," he said, already pulling up and away from the lush rooftop gardens and the shimmering blue of the shield that segregated the upper city from the lower.

Atton switched his comms to the Renegades' channel and listened to their chatter for a moment before interjecting with his own. "Renegades, this is Guardian Leader, we are about to reach nav point Epsilon. What's your status?"

"Renegade One here. Good to hear from you, Guardians. Anything we should know about down there?"

"Your eyes are going to bug when you see this place, but all's peace and quiet. Follow our flight path just in case. Transmitting now . . ."

"Got it. Thanks for that, Guardians."

"No problem. What's it look like up there?"

"Not good. Heavy losses. The *Intrepid's* dancing around the edges of the main engagement trying to distract them, but she's one against a hundred. She'll be lucky to make it out herself. Last I checked they were coming to join us planet side."

"They're abandoning the Avilonian Fleet?"

"Not sure they have much choice. Best we can do is stall the skull faces until these motherfrekkers get their defenses online. I'm assuming they have ground batteries. Maybe a few wings of fighters in reserve."

"They'd better have something," Atton replied.

"Roger that. See you at Epsilon, Commander."

"See you there."

It was worse than Atton had thought. The Avilonian fleet was already forfeit, which meant the Sythians were going to come for the planet next. Atton tried to imagine those majestic towers falling in fiery ruins to the parkland below, or telescoping down on top of the vast lower city.

The devastation would be beyond imagining.

* * *

"Set down over there," blue cape said, pointing to a broad, grassy square at the base of the Zenith Tower. The tower was fine to all outward appearances—no sign of turmoil or conflict—but there were crowds of people in the square, most of them wearing flowing white robes.

Ethan set the *Trinity* down gently to one side of the square. "Now what?"

Blue cape turned and stalked toward the entrance of the bridge. "Now, you wait here while we resolve this crisis."

"Hoi, I didn't bring you all this way just to sit on the sidelines and wait," Ethan said.

"You cannot enter the tower. Only Celestials are allowed in, and even then, only those who have the proper clearance. I will have enough trouble getting in myself without you there to make matters worse. Stay here and wait for us to return."

"You said all of your weapons have been deactivated," Ethan said, not ready to give up just yet. "*Ours* haven't. If there's some kind of revolution going on, then don't you think it would help for your men to be armed?"

Blue cape stopped in mid stride and turned back to look at him.

Ethan stared into the man's blindingly bright visor for a moment before going on, "I could arm your men and teach them to use our weapons. Take me along as a weapons tech. Maybe you need to blow open a door or cut through a wall. I can do that just like I cut open your cruiser and found you sitting in a corner picking your nose."

Ethan felt Alara grab his arm in a suddenly tight grip. She obviously thought he should show more respect, but as far as Ethan was concerned, they had to earn his respect just the same as anyone else.

Blue cape said nothing for a long moment, and the other Avilonians gathered round, as if waiting to pounce.

"As you wish, *martalis*. Take care that you do not get yourself killed."

Ethan unbuckled from the pilot's station and stood up with a wry grin. "Your people have no weapons. What are they going to do, beat me to death?"

"With an attitude like yours, that seems a fitting end," blue cape said. "Lead on, *martalis*."

Alara squeezed his arm even more insistently, her nails biting into his skin even through the tough weave of his flight suit. "Hoi, Kiddie, take it easy," he said. "I'll be back as soon as I can."

"What about me?"

Ethan briefly considered the danger in leaving her behind to face the Sythians versus the danger in taking her with him. Turning back to the Avilonian in charge, he said, "One more thing—my wife comes, too."

"Very well, but *hurry*."

Ethan raced from the bridge, dragging Alara through the living area and past the crew cabins. Upon reaching the ship's lift tubes, he keyed in the lowermost of the ship's five decks. That was where the storage and utility rooms lay. Avilonian soldiers crowded in around them and then the lift tube dropped swiftly through the ship. As soon as it arrived, they rushed out into the corridor beyond. This one was painted a utilitarian gray with conduits, pipes, and wires exposed. Unlike the lavish living area, this part of the ship had been left untouched since the vessel's service with the Imperial Fleet.

Ethan led the way down the corridor to a pair of doors marked with hazard symbols and warning signs. A glowing plate on the first door read *Sentinels' Armory*. Ethan waved the door open with his wrist and stepped into a broad corridor. The walls were lined with recessed panels. For each panel there was a glowing red identichip scanner and keypad. Ethan stopped by the first scanner and waved his wrist over it. The wall panel slid away soundlessly to reveal a rack of plasma rifles. He began handing them down the line of Avilonians who had crowded into the armory with him. When the next panel opened, it revealed belts and bandoliers of plasma grenades and timed explosives. Ethan took one of the latter for himself before passing on to the next compartment. This one revealed sidearms. Selecting a pair of stun pistols, he explained that they wouldn't kill like the rifles, but they would knock an enemy unconscious.

Blue cape responded to that with a shake of his head. "It will take much to penetrate our armor. Stun weapons will not."

"Take them anyway," Ethan said. "You never know if we need to subdue a few civilians."

"We?" Blue cape echoed, an incredulous note creeping into his voice. "I agreed to let you come with us. I did not agree to let you come armed."

Ethan's eyes narrowed swiftly. "Hold it right there you incandescent tin man."

"Do you wish to join us or not?"

"Ethan ..." Alara began, shaking her head. "We'll be safer with them than flying around in the middle of a war zone."

Ethan hesitated. He thought about taking the *Trinity* and running as far and as fast as they could until the battle for Avilon was over, but the chances of their being tracked and followed by cloaked Sythian fighters were very high. At this point, nothing was going to blast off from the surface of Avilon without catching the Sythians' attention—particularly not when the Avilonians' own outbound ships numbered exactly zero. "All right, let's go," Ethan said.

Chapter 27

Atton saw the Zenith Tower rising on the horizon, a glittering mountain of transpiranium and reinforced castcrete, or whatever passed for those materials in Avilon.

"My scopes are clear out to the tower. So far so good," Guardian Eight said.

"They could be cloaked," Atton replied. "We have to assume they're right behind us, or worse—already waiting for us at Epsilon."

"What's so important about that building?" Guardian Five put in.

"Need to know, Razor," Gina replied. "We don't need, so we don't know."

"I'm picking up a big crowd at the base of that building

..." Ceyla said. "Upwards of ten thousand. That's a lot of innocents. If we end up dog fighting over their heads, someone's going to get hurt."

"Frek it," Atton muttered. He keyed his comms for the command channel and then said, "Control, this is Guardian Leader; be advised Epsilon is overrun with civilians. The Avilonians would do well to get their people under cover before the Sythians get here."

"Acknowledged, Guardian Leader; we'll pass on your message. Orders are to defend Epsilon at all costs. We're going to lead them away and hold them off as long as we can."

"Roger that, control."

Atton passed along the news to his squadron just as they reached the Zenith Tower and began circling the vertiginous spire in a holding pattern. Atton couldn't help but admire the building; it was massive, over three kilometers high, not counting any foundations hiding below the shield layer. The skyscraper sprawled out in all directions, luminous from within, and glowing gold. It lit up the night for kilometers in all directions, a city within a city.

"Hoi, my scopes just went skriffy . . . is it just me or is there some massive interference around here?" Razor said.

"Likewise," Gina added. "I'm down to a radius of just 25 klicks. We're practically blind."

Atton eyed his sensors with a frown. His gravidar was the same, having auto-limited itself to scanning the immediate area.

"What do you think it is?" Ceyla asked.

"Frekked if I know," Gina replied. "Where are those blasted Renegades? Did anyone have eyes on them before we reached Epsilon?"

"I did," Atton replied. "They were right behind us. I sent them our flight path so they could follow us in."

"They should be here any minute then," Gina said.

"There's still a lot of activity on the ground," Ceyla put in. "Both soldiers and civvies, but I don't see any kind of conflict."

Atton pulled up a view from his Nova's nose cam and magnified the footage for a better look. Ceyla was right. No one was shooting down there; they were just milling around the base of the tower as if there to admire its grandeur. Platoons of armored soldiers were busy trying to clear a path to the entrance. A moment later, Atton saw why. A small hole had opened up in the hexagonal shield layer and a stream of assault mechs were marching out into the square. Clearly the Avilonians were regaining control of at least some of their weaponry. Swiveling his nose cam for a better look, Atton zoomed in again, and then he realized his mistake. Those weren't assault mechs. They were load lifters and constructors, not built for war at all.

"What are they planning to do with those?" Guardian Eight asked.

Atton watched them heading straight for the base of the Zenith Tower, and he had an idea about their intentions. "I think they're trying to break into their own building."

"What, someone locked them out?" Gina asked.

"Guess so," Eight replied.

"Why don't they just blow a hole?"

"Maybe they can't," Atton replied.

"What are they going to do, beat the doors down?"

"Hoi, incoming!" Guardian Nine interrupted.

Atton's gaze snapped back to the grid, but the only *incoming* he saw was the Renegades and a trio of assault transports which they'd escorted down to the surface. The Renegades raced into the square at the base of the Zenith tower and then peeled away and pulled up to join the Guardians in their holding pattern overhead.

Atton watched on his magnified view of the ground as the assault transports settled down in the grassy square below. That was when he noticed that another ship had already landed there. Off to one side of the square sat an old imperial seraphim-class corvette.

"Did the *Intrepid* send a corvette down here?" Atton asked.

"What?" Gina said. "How would we do that? We didn't have any corvettes on board."

"Well, we have one on the ground. Check it out." Atton swiveled his nose cam to follow the ship and get some close-up footage. It was painted white and blue—ISSF colors, but not in ISSF style. There were too many stripes and blue accents, and that blue was the wrong color—too bright. The ship was almost certainly civilian.

"It's not one of ours," Gina confirmed.

"So we're not the first ones here," Razor said. "So much for Avilon being a closely-guarded secret, hoi?"

"Right . . ." Atton said, keeping half an eye on that corvette as a growing suspicion formed in his gut. The ship was powered down and not broadcasting any SID codes which would confirm his suspicions, but he was almost sure he knew whose vessel it was. His father owned a corvette like that. It had been a gift from the admiral. It seemed like too much to hope for, but how many other civilians owned old navy corvettes? And how many of those civilians would ever have a chance to find out where Avilon was? Only Ethan might be let in on a secret like that, and only because he already knew that Avilon existed.

Atton let out a long, slow breath, feeling somehow relieved to know that Ethan was here with him. The big question was, what was his father doing in Avilon?

"Hoi! I've got Shell Fighters incoming!" Gina called out, and suddenly Atton had bigger problems than idle curiosity. "They're cloaked, but they're lighting the atmosphere on fire with their approach."

"Mark your targets, Guardians!" Atton replied. "I don't think they know we can see them, so let's catch 'em with their shields down. Switch to lasers, set to single fire for rapid cycling. On my mark we break and shoot!"

Click. Click. Click-click, came the affirmative responses from his squadron.

"Roger that!" someone else commed.

"Targets set?"

Atton listened to the handful of affirmative clicks which came over the comms once more, and then he called out, "Mark! Break and fire! Break and fire!" Atton lined up his target, visible only by the crescent of superheated air which preceded it. A dozen matching crescents were flying in formation with that one, revealing the phenomenon for what it was to anyone watching. Atton pulled the trigger and held it down. A brilliant red stream of laser fire stuttered out. Half a dozen matching streams of fire crossed his, drawing dazzling X's in the sky. The lasers kissed their targets, and three separate fireballs bloomed out of thin air, sounding in quick succession with a muffled *b-b-boom!*

"Three down!" Ceyla crowed.

"Ruh-kah!" Razor added.

"They're on to us," Atton said, watching on the grid as the enemy disengaged their cloaks and activated their energy shields, already veering off from their flight paths to greet the Guardians head-on. When Atton noticed how much red had suddenly appeared on his scopes, his mouth went suddenly dry.

"Oh ... frek me ..." Gina said, obviously noticing the same thing. "There's hundreds of them!"

"Stow that, Tuner!" Atton replied. "Stick to your wingmates, Guardians. We're faster than they are, and we have better aerodynamics, so we can fly circles around them down here. We don't have to take them all down; we just have to hold them off until the planetary defenses come back online."

"What if they don't come back online?" Ceyla asked in a small voice.

"They will," Atton insisted. *They have to.*

* * *

Simulated thunder rumbled through the bridge speakers, and then real thunder boomed below decks and the lights flickered. Captain Caldin saw on the grid that the cruiser they were using to shield their keel had just been eliminated, and part of the next volley had broken through to hit them instead.

"Find me another derelict to cover our flanks!" she

roared.

Another muffled *boom* rumbled underfoot and Delayn called out, "Hull breach on deck one! Ventral shields are critical."

"Equalize! Helm get us out of here! Head for the planet."

"Yes ma'am!"

"Comms update our transports on the situation up here. Make sure the Avilonians know the battle is over. We're going to try to draw the Sythians away from the Zenith, but whatever they're trying to do down there, tell them they'd better hurry it up!"

"Understood, Captain."

Caldin looked up from the captain's table to watch with her own eyes as the remainder of the Avilonian fleet was torn apart. Sythian missiles spiraled out in bright purple streaks, exploding against their targets with brief, intense bursts of light. Vast clouds of debris now floated wraithlike in the dark void between them and the glowing night side of the planet.

"How many of us are you going to kill?" she whispered. "When will it finally be enough? You already have the galaxy to yourselves, you kakards!" she roared. "Leave us the frek alone!"

Crew looked up from their stations to check on their captain. Then the deck shuddered as another stream of enemy fire found them, exploding against their shields and provoking a steady *roar* from the SISS. The *Intrepid's* beams, lasers, and ripper cannons flashed out in response, plowing glowing orange furrows in the nearest enemy cruiser's hull.

"Port shields critical," her XO reported from engineering as the deck shook once more.

Caldin was tempted to tell him to switch to cloaking shields and hide, but the enemy had more than enough ships to sound them out along their last known trajectory—see where their missiles detonated and then fire again at the same point in space. The only way they were going to escape this was to head for the planet and buy themselves some time while the Sythians mopped up what remained of the Avilonian fleet.

"This Omnius has a lot to answer for!" Caldin said. "He's abandoned his people in their hour of need."

"I don't think he's aware of what's going on," Delayn replied. "If he is, then he's suicidal, because he's compromising defenses that he'll need to ward off attacks on *himself*."

"Sythians are breaking off to follow us!" Lieutenant Esayla Carvon reported from gravidar.

"Good! Let them come. We've got to buy the Avilonians more time."

* * *

Ethan and Alara followed the Avilonians down the *Trinity's* boarding ramp and into the square. It was milling with people, but they were all remarkably calm. The civilians all wore the same matching white robes which seemed to shimmer softly with their own internal light. Those pedestrians were scanning the sky, looking up at the impossibly high Zenith Tower, walking this way and that as if they were all just tourists come to see the tallest building in the galaxy. No one was running around screaming. Ethan frowned. He overheard people talking to one another in measured tones in a language he couldn't understand. Some turned to point and whisper at Ethan and Alara as they walked by, but no one seemed particularly alarmed.

"Aren't they scared?" Alara asked as they walked by an elaborate fountain, the water lit up in all the colors of the rainbow.

Ethan shook his head. "I don't know. If they are, it must be part of their culture not to show it."

"Either that or they don't know what's happening in orbit."

A noise like thunder rent the air, and everyone turned skyward to see fireworks exploding high above the city. Except these weren't fireworks. Then hundreds of glowing orange points of light emerged from the clouds, raining down like a meteor shower, but it wasn't a meteor shower; it was the Sythians. Dark specks raced up to greet the meteors and bloody red streaks of light raced across the sky.

Still, nobody screamed, but now a booming voice cut through the square. Ethan didn't understand a word of what was said, but the tone was urgent, and he assumed it was telling the crowds to disperse and take shelter. Suddenly white-robed people began crowding them from all sides.

Alara was the first to notice the way people were looking at them—with narrowed eyes and urgent whispers. *Estum martales, estum martales!* they said.

Ethan pulled Alara deeper into the knot of armored soldiers they'd brought with them from GK-465. Blue cape led the way across the square toward a group of familiar-looking starships which Ethan somehow hadn't noticed sitting there before. As they approached, he saw the emblem of a clenched fist surrounded by six stars emblazoned on the side of those transports—the emblem of the Imperium. Those starships were ISSF.

Suddenly, Ethan remembered his son, Atton, and he began pushing his way through the group of Avilonians.

"What are you doing?" Alara asked, struggling to follow him through a sea of armored elbows and shoulders. When he reached the front of the group he tapped blue cape on the shoulder.

"What is it, *martalis*?" the Avilonian leader asked, not bothering to turn and see who it was. Ethan wondered how blue cape knew it was him, but he supposed the man's own men likely wouldn't tap him on the shoulder to get his attention.

"What are those ships doing here?" he asked.

"They brought Strategian Rovik to the Zenith, as well as—I am told—some of your soldiers."

"I need to speak with the pilots of those ships."

"We cannot wait for you."

"That's fine. I'll only be a moment." Ethan took Alara's hand in his and ran ahead of the Avilonians to the nearest transport. Once there, he jogged past the back of the transport where a squad of Zephyr light assault mechs were busy disembarking, and ran up to the cockpit. Climbing up the short ladder to the side of the cockpit, Ethan rapped his knuckles on the transpiranium window. Two helmeted heads turned. Pilot and copilot stared wordlessly at him before the copilot got up to open the side hatch.

"What is it?"

"I'm an Imperial," Ethan said.

"Why aren't you in uniform?"

"I'm not ISSF, but I'm here for the same reason as you—to get help. I'm also here to find my son—the late admiral's stepson."

"The *late* admiral?"

Ethan realized the copilot didn't know about any of what had happened in Dark Space since he'd left. "The Sythians executed Admiral Heston. They're occupying Dark Space and enslaving our people as we speak."

"What?"

"It's a long story, but right now I need a favor from you. Commander Ortane—Guardian Leader—is he alive?"

The copilot began shaking his head and Ethan felt something heavy and cold settle in his chest, but then the officer pointed up and said, "He's flying right over your head. They're holding off the Sythians while we get things sorted out down here."

As if to corroborate that, Ethan heard the not-so-distant *boom* of an explosion and caught a flash of light in his periphery. Then came the sound of people screaming. Ethan nodded his thanks before jumping down from the ladder and turning to see what had caused all the commotion.

Alara stood stock still, staring out over a rushing river of white robed civilians running away from the Zenith Tower. They were finally scared enough to panic. Ethan followed his wife's gaze to see a pillar of flames rising from the ground not far from where they stood. "What was that?"

A scream of engines answered before she could and Ethan looked up to see a Sythian Shell Fighter go streaking by low overhead. Hot on its tail was an Imperial Nova, its ternary blue thrusters roaring. Red lasers *screeched* out from the Nova in a steady stream. They hit home, provoking a plume of black smoke and then a jet of white hot flames from the Shell Fighter's glowing orange thruster pods. Then the Shell exploded with a wicked *ka-boom!* and a hot rush of air slapped them in the face. Flaming debris roared out of the sky and landed in the square with explosive force. The crowd screamed again, and the river of white robes flowed in a new direction, arcing away from the debris.

"We need to get inside the tower, and *fast!*" Ethan said, spinning in a quick circle to find blue cape and his cadre of identical crewmen. Two men in matching blue capes were conferring with one another near the boarding ramp at the back of a neighboring assault transport. One of them held a plasma rifle, courtesy of Ethan's armory, while the other was empty-handed. Three full squads of Zephyr assault mechs stood clustered there with them, forearm mounted ripper cannons tracking warily across the sky.

Ethan and Alara ran up to the two caped Avilonians, pressing as close to them as they could get. They were speaking in their language, so Ethan couldn't understand what they were saying, but abruptly they seemed to come to a decision and they turned to the sentinels standing beside them. Ethan heard one of them call out in a deep, gravelly voice. "You will accompany us to the gates of the Zenith. The building is in a state of emergency lockdown, and we cannot get in. You will make a hole for us to enter by."

"Yes, sir," the nearest sentinel replied in an amplified voice which echoed out across the square. "Lead the way, sir."

The Avilonians set out at a run, and the sentinels followed. Ethan and Alara brought up the rear of the group. The Zenith Tower turned out to be farther away than it looked. They ran for several minutes straight, all the while the sky flashed and boomed with explosions. Ethan winced every time he heard them. Atton was up there, and sooner or later, one of those explosions could be him.

They reached a sprawling set of stairs which led to the entrance of the Zenith Tower. They ran up the stairs, gasping for air. The Avilonians and sentinels reached the entrance first. By the time Ethan crested the stairs with Alara by his side, the Zephyrs were already setting detlor charges at the base of two massive doors.

Ethan led Alara over to a nearby column which was almost as thick around as the *Trinity*. She collapsed on the ground beside it and Ethan knelt down beside her, sweat trickling from his brow as he tried to catch his breath. The night air was cool, but he was still wearing his flight suit, and he was sweltering beneath the dense fabric.

Turning to look down on the square from the top of the stairs, Ethan caught sight of an incredible view. From their vantage point, now several stories up, they could see out over the grassy square to a vast garden populated with colorful trees, flowering hedges, and brightly lit walkways. A gentle breeze blew in from that direction bringing with it the sweet smell of spring—blossoms and ripening fruit. That smell and the gentle caress of the air struck a fierce contrast with the battle raging overhead and the still-burning ruins of two Shell Fighters which had crashed in the square below. Ethan heard Alara's breathing quieten, and he turned back to her. She was looking up at him with wide, frightened eyes.

"It feels like they're invading all over again," she said.

"They are, but this time it's someone else's homes they're taking."

"That doesn't make it any better! We don't even have a home! You told me *this* would be our home, and now look—it's going up in smoke, too!"

"Hoi, calm down, Kiddie. It'll be okay," Ethan said. He took her hand in his and squeezed, sending her a determined smile. But she was looking past him, her violet eyes darting, her chest heaving once more, her palm sweating against his. She looked to be in the throes of a panic attack. "Hoi, shhh . . . it's going to be okay," he said, opening his arms to enfold her in a hug. Those reassurances tasted like lies.

"How the *frek* can you say that?" Alara demanded, pushing him away. "This is the end, Ethan! They wiped out the Imperium, then they found and took Dark Space, and now they've come here—to wipe out another Imperium that's more developed and more beautiful than ours ever was! It's not going to end until we're all dead. It'll *never* end, Ethan! Let's just go while we still can! Let's get out of here!"

Alara was spiraling out of control. Ethan's grim smile vanished and he adopted a more serious look. He took both of her shoulders in a firm grip and shook her until her teeth rattled. "Cut it out, Alara! We're not running anymore. These people haven't given up yet, so neither should we! Where are we going to go?"

Alara's eyes glazed over, and she shook her head slowly. "I don't . . ."

Ethan turned back to the entrance of the Zenith Tower just in time to see sentinels running away from the doors to take cover by the columns and the stairs.

"Come on," Ethan said, dragging her to her feet and leading her around the back of the column beside them.

"Take cover!" one of the sentinels called out in a booming voice. That warning was repeated a second later by one of the blue capes, saying the same thing but in the Avilonians' language.

Ethan held his breath. A few seconds later there came a

deafening *boom!* Dust and debris blew past them and superheated air whipped around the column to scorch Ethan's face. He held Alara close to shield her from it.

"That got it!" one of the sentinels called out. "Blew her wide open! Let's go!"

"Come on," Ethan whispered, pulling Alara to her feet once more. "We'll be safer inside the tower."

Just then came more screaming from the crowds in the square below. Ethan turned to see a flaming Nova Fighter, spiraling out of control toward the top of the next nearest skyscraper. It hit with a blinding flash of light, followed a split second later by the deafening sound of the blast. Red-hot and flaming debris rained out of the sky, trickling down the side of the building like lava. Then came a secondary explosion as either the reactor fuel or the warheads on board the Nova detonated. The sound of the explosion was muffled, but the sight was terrifying. The top of the tower swelled like a balloon and then burst into flames, peeling down the middle into two separate pieces which slowly tumbled to the ground. The ground shook as though from an earthquake when the debris hit, and the sound of it was like a shatter bomb going off.

"I don't think we're going to be safe anywhere . . ." Alara said slowly.

Ethan wanted to disagree, but he was still frozen in place, unable to tear his eyes away from the fiery ruin at the top of the monolithic tower. Dozens of floors had been knocked off the top of that building, no doubt taking hundreds of lives with them, but all Ethan could think about was whether or not the pilot of that Nova had managed to eject before crashing into the tower. . . .

And whether or not that pilot was his son, Atton.

Chapter 28

"I've picked up three more on my six!" Ceyla called out over the comms.

"I'll be right there..." Razor said.

"I can't hold them! Shields are going!"

"I'm on it," Atton replied, banking hard to port and gaining altitude to follow Ceyla's pursuit. He had a pair of Shells chasing him, too, but they couldn't follow him through such a sharp turn. They went roaring by in front of him, shaken loose for the moment. Atton brought the nearest of the three chasing Ceyla under his sights and began peppering it with laser fire. The Shell immediately broke off and dove away. Not bothering to follow it down, Atton targeted the next one in line and did the same thing. By the time he got to the third, Ceyla was already thanking him for the save. "Stick with me, Corbin," he said. "No more wandering off on your own."

"Roger that," she said.

"Hoi! Iceman! Where the frek are you?" Gina called out. "I've picked up a whole squadron."

"I'll be right there, Tuner," Atton said, diving back down the way he'd come. A group of Shell Fighters roared up to meet him. His enemy missile lock alarm began to sound, and then half a dozen Pirakla missiles flashed out toward him and Ceyla. "Heads up, Four!" he warned.

"I see it!" she commed back.

Atton waited until the last minute and then threw his Nova into a downward spiral. The missiles went wide, but a stuttering rain of lavender pulse lasers followed him down. Impacts began hissing off his shields.

"Aft shields critical," his AI warned.

"Iceman!" Gina hissed. "I'm flattered you think I'm good enough to handle a twelve on one, but it would be nice to have a little help from my wingman!"

"I'll be right there!" Atton rolled out of his dive, pulling up hard to shake off the Shells on his tail. Looking for Gina on the grid, he found her a few dozen klicks away, *literally* being chased by an entire squadron of Shell Fighters. *Frek . . .* He'd thought she was exaggerating. He pushed his throttle past the stops into overdrive.

"I'm in trouble!" someone screamed. It was Ceyla again.

"Keep them busy, Corbin!" Atton replied.

"There're too many of them!"

"Someone go help, Green V!"

"Negative, Lead; I'm cornered," Nine replied.

"Likewise," Razor put in.

"Frek it—help yourself, Green!" Eight yelled. "We're all

engaged! Just jink hard to throw off any missiles, and then get on their tails. You're more maneuverable than they are!"

"I'm not!" Ceyla snapped, sounding stressed. "They clipped one of my engines and half my starboard wing is missing!"

"Lead..." Gina came back. "Where are you..."

Atton could hear the angry hiss of lasers hitting shields in the background of Gina's commcast. She was his wingmate. His responsibility was to help her first.

"They just sliced off my other wing!" Ceyla cried.

"I'll be right there, Corbin," Atton commed.

"Lead!" Gina screamed.

"Just hold on, Tuner! I'm going to help Green on my way to you." Corbin was in the opposite direction. "I'll be there in a few seconds!" He wouldn't.

"I'm going to kill you, Ortane!"

Ignoring her protests, he thumbed over to Hailfire missiles and rolled to starboard, banking toward Ceyla. He found her pursuers—all six of them—firing mercilessly on her. Bright purple beams streaked across the night sky, occasionally hitting Ceyla's Nova with a shower of sparks. She was flying in a relatively straight line—whether because she couldn't maneuver, or because she was afraid to bleed off any more air speed, Atton wasn't sure.

Hovering his targeting reticle over the nearest of the six, Atton listened to the *beep-beep-beeping* of a missile lock. As soon as the targeting reticle turned a solid red and the beeping became a steady tone, he pulled the trigger and two Hailfire missiles roared out on bright orange contrails. The Shell Fighter realized his peril and broke away just a second too late. The Hailfires split apart and eight shards spiraled off in separate directions, four of them angling for the original target. All four hit and the Shell Fighter flew apart. A chunk of debris clipped one of the others, causing him to wobble into the path of another shard with a sudden *boom*. The explosion set the enemy fighter on fire and sent it banking toward the ground.

Two down. Atton thumbed over to lasers and began lighting up the other four Shells chasing Ceyla. He traced his crosshairs back and forth over all four of them, hoping to scare them off, but they ignored his scattered fire and stayed intent upon their target.

The Sythians' pulse lasers began scoring consecutive hits on Ceyla's fighter, and a thick jet of flames erupted from one of her thrusters. Her engines sputtering, she began bleeding airspeed and altitude. She was going down. There was nothing more he or anyone else could do to help her.

"Punch out, Corbin!"

A second later, her canopy blew away and Atton saw her flight chair rocket out above her doomed fighter. Atton was already rolling back the other way to help Gina.

"Hang in there, Tuner! I'm on my way!" Atton said.

"Too late, you motherfrek—*kkksrrr*ss." Her comm died in static. Atton came about just in time to see her Nova spiral out of control into the distant spire of an adjacent skyscraper. Her fighter exploded with a blinding flash of light. Seconds later another explosion burst open the top of the building she'd crashed into, and it cracked away, falling in two giant flaming chunks to the city below.

"Gina . . ." Atton breathed. "Did anyone see her punch out?" he called over the comms.

"Negative."

"Frek you, Iceman," Razor replied.

"No," Eight put in.

Atton kept the comm open for a moment, as if he had a reply ready, but the words never came. If he hadn't gone chasing after Ceyla, he might have been able to save Gina. Ceyla had had to punch out anyway. He hadn't helped her either.

Instead of guilt, a cold emptiness filled him. There was no painful ache in his throat, or pulse-pounding burst of rage, just clean, cold numbness.

You really are the Iceman . . . Atton thought.

* * *

Ethan wasn't sure what he'd been expecting to see inside the Zenith Tower. Perhaps a vast entrance hall lined with thick columns and expensive artwork. Lavish displays of wealth and opulent furnishings seemed a given. He'd expected a palace or a fortress—something which befitted the government headquarters for a planet with many trillions of people. What he actually saw behind the 10-story-high doors was a vast, well-tended garden.

Lush, vibrant green sprawled out as far as the eye could see. Blossoming trees and flowering bushes splashed the scene with color. The distant walls of the building seemed to be made of luminous crystal, rising some twenty or more stories, curving up to a bright blue dome of sky overhead.

Faint, but visible within the clear blue of that sky was a glowing spiral pattern with bright points of light like stars. In the center of that pattern was an artificial sun with the same eye-shape as the center of the glowing emblem in blue cape's chest. Now that Ethan thought about it, the entire sky bore the pattern of that emblem, only without the circumscribed *A*.

Climbing plants and flowers grew up the luminous walls, in some cases all the way up to the sky, their fronds and blossoms turned inward and upward toward the eye-shaped sun. The air was fragrant and honeyed with the nectar of a million flowers. A warm breeze blew; the air was neither hot nor cold, but perfectly temperate. Waterfalls cascaded from dizzying heights, pouring from broad apertures in the walls. Small avian creatures flitted through the air, chirping as they went. It was as if someone had copied it all straight out of a children's storybook about the ages-old garden of Etheria.

Ethan watched the Avilonians lead the way through the garden. The sentinels in their Zephyr assault mechs stomped clumsily along behind them, their backs arching as they stared up at the sky. The pathway leading from the doors glittered brightly underfoot as though it were made of diamond dust.

"What is this place?" Alara whispered.

"I guess this Omnius of theirs likes open spaces," Ethan replied.

"Do not touch anything! Keep to the middle of the road," a gravelly voice bellowed from the front of the group. Ethan recognized that voice as belonging to the other blue caped soldier, the one whose presence he had not been forced to endure on his ship. "You are on sacred ground," he explained.

Ethan ignored their warnings, straying to the edge of the walkway to stare down into the silvery depths of a shining river running crosswise to the path. Fat blue and scarlet fish followed the current downstream. Ethan turned from looking down to looking up at the distant walls of the tower. They were at least several kilometers away. From that he estimated that the garden had to be a thousand or more acres in size. As they walked further into the leafy green depths, white-robed civilians began to appear along the sides of the path, their eyes narrowed and accusing. A few called out in Avilonian, sounding just as unwelcoming as they looked. Some of the soldiers replied, their tones more polite, but the white-robed civilians remained unimpressed.

"What's going on?" Ethan asked, walking up beside the nearest soldier.

The man ignored him, but Ethan insisted until the man's glowing faceplate turned to regard him. "They warn us that we are not allowed to be here. Only Omnius's disciples are allowed into the temple after the doors have shut, and we are not even Celestials, let alone disciples."

"The temple?"

"What you see around you. This is the dwelling place of Omnius. He lives here among his most faithful servants. During the day, the garden is open to all his chosen people, but at night the doors are shut and his disciples are free to commune with him without the impatient press of pilgrims come to bask in His glory."

"You speak of this Omnius like he's a god," Ethan replied.

"He is that and more."

"Right . . . so this is where he lives? Where is he?"

"He is not a person or an entity that you can point to and say—*there he is!*—he's all around us, ever present, always watching, all-knowing, and all-powerful."

Ethan frowned. "I don't feel him."

"Neither do I ..." the Avilonian replied in a shaky whisper. "I fear he has left us all to die."

"Nice god you have."

"Do not speak ill of him! He would not abandon us unless we deserved it."

"This ... invisible god of yours. He's in control of all your defenses? Every weapon on this planet?"

"That is correct."

"So no one fires a shot without his permission."

"No, ordinarily he trusts us as his Peacekeepers to do what we must, but someone must have threatened him terribly for him to deactivate everything."

"I don't see anyone here to threaten him."

"Omnius resides here, but his essence is spread out across our world. The threat could be somewhere else."

"Then why are we here?"

"This is the coming together of all that he is. Here the disciples come to know Omnius better and tend to him. Here the beauty of his mind is laid bare for all to see, that we might stand in awe of him. If there is something wrong with Omnius, we will find it here."

Ethan looked around the garden and struggled to wrap his head around what the Avilonian was saying to him. "So ... what exactly is he? A tree?"

"You make fun of things you know nothing about."

"It was an honest question."

"Leave me."

"All right, I apologize. If he's not a tree, then what is he?"

"Your people would call him an artificial intelligence."

"Oh," Ethan said, taken aback. "Well, we have that, too; we just don't worship ours."

"No, Omnius is different, he is self-aware."

"So are ours."

"You mean so they appear to be. True artificial intelligence evolves quickly, learns endlessly, and grows ever more potent with time. Your equivalents remain stagnant and do only what they are designed to do. They are slaves of humanity, while we are slaves of Omnius."

"I think I like our version better."

"Do not blaspheme to me, *martalis*. Omnius is benevolent and good. We are slaves to him because his goodness compels us to serve him, and because his wishes and demands are only for our best. Without him we would have long ago succumbed to our inner darkness and destroyed ourselves."

Alara grabbed Ethan's arm and pulled him away from the soldier. "Ethan!" she hissed. "Don't make fun of them—or *it*," she said, her eyes scanning the sky warily.

He decided not to press the point. Alara was right; they couldn't afford to make enemies here. He turned his attention to the path they were walking on. A muffled boom of thunder rumbled subtly through the air, and Ethan recalled the battle raging outside the tower. It occurred to him then that they should be running through this thousand acre garden rather than walking as though they had all the time in the world. Ethan suspected the only reason they weren't was because of the white-robed *disciples* who stood on the sidelines watching their every step. Perhaps they thought the intruding soldiers were part of the rebel army which was to blame for Omnius's sudden disappearance. Ethan eyed the *disciples* right back, wondering if *they* were to blame—after all, they were the only ones here.

The pathway came to a building which looked like a giant overturned bowl. That bowl was golden, smooth and reflective like a mirror. As they approached it, Ethan saw his blue cape holding one of the white-robed disciples at gunpoint, using the plasma rifle Ethan had given him to threaten the civilian's life. A sudden suspicion formed in Ethan's gut, and he wondered if they weren't in fact helping a rebel army to instigate a coup.

Hurrying to the front of the group, Ethan found the pair of blue-caped men yelling at the man in the white robe until at last that man held up his hands and placed one of them against the glossy golden surface of the bowl. In response to his touch the bowl rose off the ground on four shining pillars of light. Then the blue capes shoved him underneath the bowl and the rest of the Avilonian soldiers crowded in behind him. The squads of Zephyrs followed, as did Ethan and Alara. From the inside, the dome was black and empty, as was the slightly raised podium underneath, although a glowing red line ran around the edges of it. Not far from that was a glowing green line, which Ethan noticed the Avilonians were careful to stand inside. Ethan caught Alara straddling the line and he grabbed her hand to pull her over it.

The white-robed man raised his hands as if beckoning to the sky. And with that, the inside of the dome sprang to life, glowing subtly, but with ever increasing brilliance. Suddenly that man dropped his hands, and the dome fell with a *boom*. Alara all but jumped into Ethan's arms, and he held her tight. Then the inside of the dome became painfully bright, and Ethan's eyes shut reflexively. A loud whirring filled the air, wind whipped about in a sudden frenzy, and then Ethan felt his ears pop. The brightness glowing behind his eyelids faded, and the whirring noise disappeared. Then the air was abruptly still.

Ethan felt vaguely dizzy, as if he'd just been spun around a dozen times. Then he felt a draft, and he opened his eyes to see a startling, unobstructed vista of Avilon for hundreds of kilometers in all directions. The lights of the city glittered all the way out to the horizon. The skyscraper whose spire had been ruined by a crashing Nova Fighter glowed orange still, like the superheated barrel of a giant plasma rifle aimed up at the sky. A bed of flaming debris flickered at that monolith's base, while dozens of smaller fires burned in the square and throughout the distant rooftop gardens below. Ethan looked up to see the dome which they had stepped under, now dark and silently hovering overhead once more. Wondering what it was, Ethan walked out from under it with the group of Avilonians and sentinels. As if in a daze, he walked to the edge of the room and placed both hands against another dome, this one completely transparent. It was cold and smooth to the touch, like transpiranium, and it was all that separated them from the chaos beyond the tower. Looking up, Ethan saw the faintly glowing outlines of Sythian cruisers drifting behind a near ceiling of clouds.

Apparently now they were standing in the uppermost reaches of the Zenith Tower. Above them arced two scythe-shaped pinnacles. Somehow the mysterious golden dome they'd walked under had transported them from the garden on the ground floor to the top of the Zenith Tower in a matter of just a few seconds. Given the height of the building, even the fastest lift tube should have taken at least a full minute to get them up that high.

Suddenly a Nova being chased by a pair of Shell Fighters dove past their lofty vantage point. The glowing red barrels of the alien fighters flashed with pulse lasers and Pirakla missiles before disappearing from view. Looking out to the horizon, Ethan saw the night painted with hundreds of bright orange specks—the glowing engines of yet more alien fighters—alternately diving and ascending like musical notes on a sky-shaped score. Rather than weaving melodies, these notes where cacophonic when they came together, pouring out deadly rain on the helpless city below.

"How much longer do you think this will go on before . . ." Alara trailed off quietly beside him.

He turned to her, his usually green eyes now as black and cold as space but for a pair of diamond-bright pinpricks which shone in his irises. "Before it's all just a pile of ash?" Ethan turned back to the view. "A few days—a week at most. As soon as those cruisers start firing, it's going to get ugly down here."

Raised voices drew their attention away from the view, and they turned to study the others milling about inside the glass dome with them. The voices were coming from a raised walkway in the center of the room, found arching out over the golden dome that had brought them all up to the top of the Zenith. The blue capes were standing there, conferring with not one but two white-robed citizens. Ethan was sure that only one of the disciples had come with them from the garden, so the other one had to have been up here already. As Ethan looked on he realized that this one was different. He wore glowing white armor beneath his robe, and his chest bore a glowing golden version of the Avilonian emblem which the blue capes bore on their chests.

"Who is he?" Ethan asked aloud.

"That is the Grand Overseer," someone said quietly.

Ethan turned to see one of the Avilonian soldiers standing there with them, looking up at the glowing white man.

"And? What's that mean?" Alara asked.

"He is Omnius's right hand, his human representative on Avilon. If anyone knows what has happened to Omnius, the

Grand Overseer will."

"Good!" Ethan set off for the raised walkway at a run.

"Wait!" the Avilonian called out behind him. *"Martalis!"*

"Name's Ethan—" he called over his shoulder as he ran. "—not *martalis*."

Chapter 29

"They're not following us, Captain!" Esayla Carvon called out from gravidar.

"What do you mean, they're not following us?"

"They must have realized that we're a decoy. The Sythian fleet is heading for Epsilon."

Caldin frowned. The Nova squadrons they'd sent to that nav point were the only resistance the Sythians had likely encountered from the planet, so of course they were drawn to that point. "Helm, take us to Epsilon."

"Yes, ma'am."

Caldin looked up and out the forward viewports. It was hard to see the city below past the *Intrepid's* mighty bow, but the horizon was clearly visible, and so was the shining golden mountain of light which was the Zenith Tower. Clouds raced by them to either side. In the distance, dozens of Sythian Cruisers could be seen entering the atmosphere keel first, their hulls shining bright lavender against the night.

"We're coming into range . . ."

"Weapons, stand by with our main beam."

"Range!"

"Open fire!"

A brilliant red beam shot out overhead, sounding with a deafening screech as a raging torrent of pent up energy was released. The Corona beam lasted a few seconds before dissipating into the night, and it left a fiery runnel in their target's hull. Then the target fired back with a glittering purple curtain of Pirakla missiles.

"Get ready to evade! Augment forward shields!"

The first missile impacted on their bow with a mighty splash of fire against their shields. The next three hit the same place, breaking through the weakened shield array. As soon as the explosions faded, a gaping hole opened up in the topside of their bow. The helm managed to evade the rest of that volley and certain destruction.

"Premator Beams stand by!" Caldin roared. "Open fire!" Four red beams shot out from the giant turret mounted on their bow, tracing lines of fire across their target's hull. They flayed the Sythian cruiser open and it began drifting out of the sky. Caldin winced as she saw the enemy ship falling toward the city below. It was going to do a lot of damage when it hit.

"Give that beast everything we've got! We need to break it up before it reaches the surface!"

Red and blue dymium beams arced out, joined by

stuttering lines of matching pulse lasers. Ripper cannons thudded through the sky, the shells' tracer alloy painting golden streaks against the night. A volley of Silverstreak torpedoes jetted out on glittering silver contrails . . .

All of that hit the enemy with a continuous flashing of light and fiery explosions. The doomed Sythian cruiser burst into a dozen flaming pieces which rained down like meteors on the city below.

"Next target!"

"ETA sixty seven seconds to firing range . . ." Esayla called out from the gravidar station.

"Weapons, stand by!"

As if by mutual agreement, the dozens of alien cruisers hovering above the city all opened fire. Glittering clouds of missiles swarmed for the surface of the planet in a deadly purple rain.

Caldin looked on in horror. The first droplets hit, blossoming into bright orange fireballs, and the face of the city became pockmarked with them. Those pockmarks grew so numerous that they soon ran together in one endless ruin.

"We're in range!"

"Open fire!"

The *Intrepid's* main beam, her Corona cannon, flashed out once more, seeming to Caldin an inadequate protest to the destruction the Sythians were visiting on Avilon.

"Shell Fighters coming up fast!"

"Have our point defenses . . ." Caldin trailed off as she saw the close proximity of the fighters racing toward them. It was too late to cull their numbers, and there were too many of them—over a hundred. It wouldn't take long for them to devour the *Intrepid*. Their first pass alone could be deadly.

"All power to shields! Open fire on those fighters!"

Before her crew could even respond to those orders, the enemy let loose their volley—a glittering wall of Pirakla missiles which sparkled against the horizon like a field of purple stars.

The *Intrepid* answered with a volley of her own. Hailfires streaked out from her starboard side just as the nav officer turned the ship to evade.

"Brace for impact!" Caldin called out as Hailfire and Pirakla missiles crossed each others' paths. The Hailfires reached a designated range and then blossomed into eight streaking shards each. Then the enemy volley hit their flank, and dead of night turned as bright as the inside of a sun.

* * *

"Corbin, can you hear me?" Atton asked as he circled the spot on the ground where Ceyla's emergency beacon was transmitting. Her flight chair had just settled down in the square at the base of the Zenith Tower.

After an anxious silence, the comms crackled with her reply.

"I'm all right!"

A wellspring of pent-up tension in his chest released. "Good! Get under cover! It's about to get ugly down there."

"Roger that, SC."

Atton's shields hissed with a sudden rain of pulse lasers, and he pushed his Nova into a sharp dive to evade pursuit.

"I'm punching out!" Razor called over the comms just a

second before his fighter winked off the grid. Atton eyed the remaining green friendly contacts amidst the sea of red enemies circling the Zenith Tower with them. Guardian Squadron was down to just three, including him. The Renegades had four.

"This is frekked up!" Eight put in. "I've got three squadrons on me! Nine? Where are you?"

Without so much as a parting scream, Nine vanished from the grid, and Guardian squadron was down to just two.

"I'm on it, Eight!" Atton commed back, pulling an upward spiraling Immelmann turn in order to put his squad mate ahead of him. His own pursuers lazily followed that maneuver and then his enemy missile lock alarm shrieked in warning. *Frek it!* Watching the approaching warheads on his rear scope, he waited until the last possible moment . . . and then jerked the stick left and ruddered in the same direction. The enemy warheads spiraled by so close they bathed his cockpit in a shimmering violet light. Without warning the missile lock alarm shrieked again—

Suddenly it was cut off by a deafening roar, and Atton's fighter rocked violently with the impact.

"Shields critical," his AI warned.

He pushed his fighter into another dive for the surface of Avilon. "Eight! I can't get to you! Meet me on the surface; let's lose them between the buildings."

"Can't make it! *Skrsssss* . . ."

And Eight was gone.

Now Atton was the last Guardian in the sky, but he didn't have time to dwell on that. His missile lock alarm was screaming with nonstop warnings. Nosing down further, he pushed the throttle into full overdrive. Lasers flashed by his cockpit in a luminous rain. Sythian missiles soon joined them, sparkling all around him like glowing amethysts falling from the sky. The missiles beat him to the surface, exploding in a continuous roar. Fire spread out like a carpet beneath his fighter. Atton pulled up at the last possible second and sailed through the roaring flames. Snapping on a terrain following overlay, he guided his fighter through man-made canyons of low-rise buildings, shaded green to reveal them where smoke and flames obscured them from sight. Rooftop gardens burst into flames. Windows which had been bright with light and life a second ago suddenly burst outward in glittering clouds of glass.

Atton dipped down below the rooftops to follow a broad blue river of the planet's segregating shield. The energy barrier raced by underneath, shimmering with reflected firelight. Up ahead another volley of alien missiles hit a set of twin towers, and they telescoped down on top of themselves. He pulled up at the last second to avoid the liquefying spread of debris.

As his Nova roared into the sky, he caught a glimpse of the *Intrepid*. She was firing for all she was worth, beset by a dense cloud of Shell Fighters whose glowing orange thrusters silhouetted them against the night sky like a swarm of glow bugs.

The *Intrepid* was on fire, and slowly listing toward the ground. Horrified, but mesmerized by the sight of it, Atton was unable to tear his gaze away from the doomed cruiser.

So this is the end, he thought. *The final frekking end of everything.*

* * *

As soon as Ethan reached the raised walkway where the grand overseer stood, he saw the blue-caped soldier he'd given a plasma rifle to turn that rifle on him.

"Stop or I shoot," blue cape said.

Ethan held up his hands and nodded to the grand overseer. "Where is your god?"

"Qua est hic?" the overseer demanded, looking Ethan up and down quickly with undisguised scorn. "You dare to approach me, *martalis*? You are unworthy of my attention."

"Yea, yea, I get that a lot. I want to know what you're doing about that—" Ethan gestured to the city beyond the dome-topped tower where they stood. Noticing something new in his periphery, he turned to see Sythian missiles raining from the sky. The cruisers had opened fire. He watched, his mouth agape as those missiles began to impact on the surface. Explosions sprouted like mushrooms, setting the city aflame.

"I have done all that can be done," the overseer replied. Omnius is recovering from an unexpected shut down. It will take some time before He is back online and all of His functions restored."

"You don't have time!" Ethan said. "Where are your defenses?"

"We will regain control of them soon ..." the overseer

replied, turning away from Ethan to place his hands upon a glowing white sphere which sat at waist height, just above the railings of the raised walkway where they stood. The sphere grew brighter at the overseer's touch, and a holographic display appeared in the air. A moment later, the overseer said something in his language, his tone full of reverence. As one, the Avilonians standing under the dome fell to their knees and bowed their heads.

Then, abruptly, the dome was bathed in a blinding light. For a split second Ethan thought the Sythians had found them and that the light was from an exploding warhead, but absent was the anticipated *boom*, and the light remained. He looked up to see a bright spheroid now hovering between the two scythe-shaped pinnacles arcing out above the dome. It looked vaguely like the spiral and eye-shaped center Ethan had seen emblazoned on the Avilonians' armor. The light was so bright that it turned back the night and bathed the surrounding city in a facsimile of daylight.

Ethan was forced to look away. He saw spots, but his eyes were not blind enough to miss what happened next. A terrible, animal roaring filled the air, followed by a deafening *screech* as white-hot beams of light leapt from the sprawling Zenith Tower and from the other skyscrapers which dotted the horizon like glittering mountains of luminescent quartz.

Hundreds of beams arced across the sky—straight bolts of lightning reversed from their natural course. Those beams sliced through the clouds, vectoring in on the wraith-like shadows of Sythian cruisers.

A cheer went up from the Avilonians, but they remained on their knees. Ethan watched that dazzling light display go on for what seemed like hours. The blurry-bright shadows of Sythians hovering above the clouds now turned as if to flee, but the raging torrents of light followed them. The scattered violet rain of deadly missiles falling from the sky took a sudden shift, as if driven by an unseen wind. The Sythians returned fire with focused streams of missiles heading for the Avilonians' ground-based batteries. Ethan winced in anticipation of the destruction. He remembered the damage the crashing Nova had done. Pirakla missiles would be far worse.

The horizon began to flash with the sporadic impacts of alien missiles, and Ethan was tempted to look away rather than watch Avilon's most majestic towers crumble and fall. By some force of will or enervating horror he looked on. Rather than see those towers tumble and fall, he saw them rebuff the attacks with shields.

Ethan's eyes lit up. The towers were shielded now! Hope swelled in his chest as he watched tiny specks of glowing orange swatted from the sky with miniature starbursts of light.

Then, bright golden lights appeared streaking into the sky, swarming up from the city below. For a moment Ethan thought they must be some type of warheads, but then one of those golden streaks flew right past the Zenith's spire with a bone-rattling roar and Ethan saw that it was a starfighter not unlike a Nova. Yet where a Nova's hull was dull gray duranium, this one was a luminous cobalt blue.

Hundreds of those fighters sailed up into the sky, and stuttering lines of red lasers began streaking out from them to join the beams firing from the towers.

A nearby *boom* rumbled overhead, sounding like a thunderclap, but rather than see lightning arcing from the clouds, Ethan saw a flaming wreck burst into view—a mountain on fire sent sailing down straight on top of them.

Someone screamed. An instant later, he realized it was Alara. She was still standing by the edge of the dome, her head tilted up, one hand pointing to the ruined Sythian cruiser. She stood frozen before it like a bosin caught in a hover car's headlights. Ethan vaulted down from the catwalk to get to her. He wasn't sure what he could do, but a primitive part of his brain was screaming at him to do *something*.

Before he even reached her, the beams of light arcing up from the city changed course, all of them now firing on the doomed Sythian cruiser. It was vaporized with a spectacular *boom* and an accompanying starburst of light. Ethan stumbled around blind for a few seconds before his vision cleared enough to see a blurry-bright world saturated with light from the after image of the doomed cruiser's explosion.

Another animal roar sounded, and this time Ethan realized it was coming from the blinding light hovering between the two scythe-shaped pinnacles overhead. He had assumed that light was a representation of Omnius, not Omnius himself, but now he thought the opposite. If the AI god of Avilon had physical form, it was this artificial sun.

Swarms of Avilonian fighters met with the Sythian Shells in the sky—glowing golden thrusters mingled with glowing orange, swirling smoke trails against the faded shadows of the night in a fiery kaleidoscope of death and destruction. Bright lines of red pulse lasers knocked Shell Fighters from the sky by the dozens. The Sythians' answering fire seemed somehow ineffectual by comparison, as Ethan didn't see even one Avilonian fighter fall. All the while, ground-based defenses slashed the sky with vengeful fury.

Ethan shook himself as if waking from a nightmare, and hurried over to Alara. He crushed her in a fierce hug and buried his face in her hair. "I love you, Kiddie," he spoke beside her ear. He wasn't sure she'd heard him over the continuous screeching of weapons fire or the distant thunder of exploding starships, but she whispered something equally unintelligible beside his ear, and he smiled, knowing with a sense keener than hearing that she'd just said the same thing.

* * *

Caldin looked on with wide eyes and a gaping grin. Brilliant white beams of light shot out from Avilon's tallest buildings like the white-hot spokes of giant wheels. Hordes of Avilonian fighters wove through the sky in glittering blue-gold shoals, sending Sythian Shells tumbling to the ground by the dozens. The Sythians were actually outnumbered for a change. *We might just make it out of this yet,* she thought with a flicker of hope.

Then the deck rocked with a sudden explosion, snapping her out of her triumphant daze. The lights on the bridge flickered. Caldin saw the ruined city below slowly tilt on its axis, and she actually *felt* the deck tilt with it. From that she deduced that the cruiser's artificial gravity was failing, allowing the planet's gravity to bleed through. "What was that?" Caldin demanded, grabbing onto the captain's table for support.

"Five Shells just ran into our main engine array!" gravidar

reported.

"What you mean they *ran* into it?"

"He means they flew up the exhausts!" Delayn replied from engineering. "The reactor is at 22% integrity and dropping!"

"Reduce power!"

"If we reduce power any further, we're going to fall like a stone!"

"Comms! I want a repair crew on it now!"

"Yes, ma'am."

"18% integrity . . ." Delayn warned in a rising voice. "It's going critical! I've got to shut her down!"

All the lights and glowing consoles of control stations on the bridge abruptly died and then came back again, but much dimmer than before. Now they were running on emergency backups.

"Status report!" Caldin called out.

"We're going down!" the helm replied.

"Any chance we can land safely?"

"The backup generator is redlining with just 10% power to grav lifts," Delayn said. "That's not nearly enough to land."

"Then use that to steer us away from the taller buildings; aim for the worst of the devastation!"

"I can't," the helm replied, a note of panic creeping into the man's voice. "Maneuvering jets are offline! We're out of control!"

"Calculate our trajectory! I want to know where we're going to hit and when."

"Calculating . . . oh frek."

"Oh frek, what?" Caldin demanded.

"We're headed for the Zenith Tower. We've got three minutes till impact."

Dark Space IV: Revenge

"Abandon ship! We haven't come this far just to die now!"

The evacuation alarm began to sound in strident tones. Caldin turned and ran, pounding down the gangway to the escape pods that lay just beyond the bridge doors. Her XO and chief engineer, Cobrale Delayn, as well as the gravidar officer, Esayla Carvon, reached the same escape pod as her. Caldin keyed open the hatch and shoved them inside. By the time she shut the hatch behind them, Delayn was already at the pod controls, his hands flying over a holographic keypad.

A moment later something *clunked* and the escape pod flew down a brief launch tube, racing past bright rings of light.

* * *

Commander Donali awoke in darkness. He raised his hands, groping in the dark, and promptly smashed his knuckles on the transpiranium cover of the stasis tube.

Stasis. They put me in stasis! He heaved against the cover with all his strength. It swung aside easily. He stumbled out into the room beyond. A dim red light flickered on beyond the stasis tube, revealing that the world was askew, as if he had one leg shorted than the other. He took a few steps, and then promptly fell over, only to stand up and fall over again.

A roaring, screaming noise filled his ears. Frowning, he got to his feet more slowly this time, and now he noticed that the deck was sloping under his feet. That shouldn't have been possible unless artificial gravity had failed and there were another gravity source somewhere else nearby . . .

Suddenly he realized what the roaring noise was. It was the evacuation alarm. The *Intrepid* was in trouble. Donali bolted for the nearest exit. He was naked but there was no time to put on his clothes. He raced out the doors of the stasis room and down the corridor, bumping into bulkheads in his mad dash for the nearest pod bay. He knew there to be a bank of escape pods very near to the stasis rooms, so he was well-situated to get away.

Upon reaching the pod bay, he waved his wrist over the door controls and then hurried inside. He heard booted feet racing after him and turned to see a group of corpsmen and doctors headed his way.

"Hoi!" one of them called out. "He escaped!"

Donali's heart pounded. He thought quickly. His security clearance hadn't yet been revoked, otherwise he wouldn't have been able to get inside the pod bay. That meant his override codes would still be working. He turned to the door controls inside the pod bay and typed in a lock override code. The doors *swished* shut just moments before the doctors and corpsmen reached them. Donali waved to them with a smile as they began pounding on the doors, trying their own security codes to no avail. With that, he turned tail and ran for the nearest pod. He keyed it open and dove inside, reaching for the red launch button at the pod controls. His fingers just grazed the button and then came a sudden burst of acceleration, followed by racing rings of light and then . . . freedom.

His mouth dropped open and confusion swirled as he tried to comprehend what he was seeing. A vast city sailed by underneath his pod, wreathed in smoke and flames. It was the middle of the night. Clouds raced by overhead. Monolithic skyscrapers glittered on the horizon. Wraithlike shadows floated behind the clouds, raining a familiar purple light on the city below. Dazzling white beams of light arced through the night, striking at those shadows.

The Sythians were here, and an unknown enemy was fighting them. Fighters raced by on all sides of him. Some were familiar Shells, but the others ... Donali squinted out at them and he realized that the fighters firing at them weren't Novas.

His brain belatedly put it all together. This was Avilon, and the Sythians had found it. Donali settled into the pod's flight chair with a grin. Somehow his mission had been accomplished without him. He let out a shaky sigh.

Then the comm light on the pod's control panel lit up with the *bleep bleep* of an incoming message. Donali was just about to answer it when he realized that he was a suspected traitor. His hand returned to his lap. It would be better for the surviving crew of the *Intrepid* to think he went down with the ship.

He returned to watching the battle raging around him. He delighted in the destruction of the city, but he could tell that the tide of the battle was turning. Shell Fighters were raining from the sky by the dozens, flaming and tumbling to their doom. Just now a pair of Sythian cruisers came crashing down with them, bursting through the clouds on a collision course with the city.

If this was Avilon and the Sythians were losing, then perhaps his mission wasn't over yet. He might yet find a way to help his masters. Donali smiled and closed his eyes to make contact with his handler. Lord Kaon replied a moment later, demanding to know what had happened to him. He explained everything, right up to the present moment where he found himself sailing out over the Avilonians' home world. Kaon told him the Sythians were losing the battle for Avilon, but that they would return. Donali was instructed to find a safe place to land and then go into hiding until he could be of further use. He ended his telepathic contact with High Lord Kaon and returned to admiring the destruction before him. He was relieved to know that the fleet the Sythians had sent was a mere hundred ships, not their entire armada. His masters had lost the battle but not the war.

Donali reached for the pod's flight controls, but then he recalled the comm light, and he first checked the grid to make sure no one was nearby to see him abandon the pod's auto-piloted course. If he wished to pretend the pod was empty, he couldn't be seen to deviate from his current trajectory. One look at the grid was all it took to assuage that fear. The sky was so fraught with contacts that no one would notice what he was doing. He turned the pod off its current course and began an in-depth scan of the planetary surface, looking for a place he might be able to hide. When the results of that scan came back a moment later, his jaw dropped and he shook his head. The city was far more than it seemed, stretching over a kilometer below the apparent surface of the world. There was some type of energy shield guarding what lay below, but with all of the destruction raining down, he could see a few places on his scopes where the shield had opened up, revealing the city below.

Donali dove for one of those holes, racing toward the raging inferno. He wasn't sure what he'd find in the lower levels of the city, but he had a feeling it would be much easier to hide down there than it would be on the rooftops.

* * *

ASCENDANCY

The escape pod rocketed out the back of the *Intrepid*, flying through a thick, black trail of smoke from the cruiser's ruined thrusters. The smoke cleared to a wispy gray, and then they were flying out over the flaming city. Captain Caldin watched the light show created by hundreds of crisscrossing beam cannons and thousands of fighter-based pulse lasers. Avilonian and Sythian fighters raced by them on all sides, the former swatting the latter with dazzlingly bright red pulse lasers. Shells exploded all around and them in bright orange puffs of molten alloy.

Through the clouds of debris and the blinding light of exploding fighters, Caldin saw something new. "What's that?" she asked, pointing out the front of the pod.

"What's what?" Delayn asked, checking the grid. A moment later he let out a long whistle and shook his head. "Looks like the Sythians didn't wipe out their fleet after all."

"Looks like," she replied. The Avilonians didn't just have fighters in the air. Now there were several large starships roaring up from the ground and racing toward the engagement around the Zenith. They all looked to be the same class as the cruiser which had found them in the gravity field a few short hours ago. Counting just the ones she could see out the porthole-sized forward viewport of the escape pod, there were a least half a dozen.

Looking out to the hazy orange line of the horizon to see if she could find any more, Caldin realized that the city was on fire as far as the eye could see. Millions must have died in the attack.

"Never thought I'd live to see this twice," Delayn remarked, obviously reminded of the original Sythian invasion by the apocalyptic scale of the devastation before them. Caldin saw Delayn reach out beside him to find Esayla Carvon's ebony hand. Esayla was kneeling beside him and leaning her head on his shoulder.

That display of affection had Caldin looking away, out the rear hatch to watch the *Intrepid's* final moments. Her thoughts turned to a certain corpsman—Corpsman Markom Terl—her lover and longtime friend. She chewed her lower lip, hoping against hope that he would have enough time to escape. The flaming bulk of her ship sailed inexorably toward the Zenith Tower like a giant torpedo, trailing a fat plume of ugly black smoke. Here and there an escape pod came jetting out of the flames, fleeing the doomed cruiser in just the nick of time, but those pods were too few and far between to be carrying the entire crew.

Caldin wondered absently what the Avilonians would do to them if the *Intrepid* took down the Zenith Tower, and with it, their AI god, Omnius. She needn't have wondered. A dozen white-hot beams suddenly shot out from the Zenith, converging on the doomed ship.

It burst open like an overripe piece of fruit, and Caldin flinched away from the blinding light of that explosion. An ominous roll of thunder reached her ears just a moment later, and then she turned back to look. The *Intrepid* was gone. In its place, a hail of tiny fragments sailed on and splashed harmlessly across the face of the Zenith, provoking a telltale flicker of light—*the tower is shielded*, she realized.

The escape pods she'd seen streaking out of the fiery ruins of her ship were now nowhere to be seen. Turning back to Delayn she asked, "How many made it out?"

He was quiet for a long moment, forcing her to repeat the question.

"Just three. I'm sorry, Captain." Delayn turned back to her, his pale blue eyes filled with a suspicious sheen of moisture.

"Any from med bay?"

"Let me check, ma'am . . ."

Caldin's heart beat double time in her chest.

"V-966-14!" he said, calling out the pod's tracking number.

"Hail it!" Her heart beat faster than ever with the fearful hope that one of the people in that pod was Corpsman Markom Terl. She watched the back of Delayn's head in an anxious silence, he hands alternately clenching and unclenching.

"They're not responding, Captain . . ." Donali said slowly. "The pod must have malfunctioned and launched by mistake."

Caldin felt something cold and hard settle in her chest like a lump of granite. She swallowed thickly and nodded. "Carry on, Commander."

Chapter 30

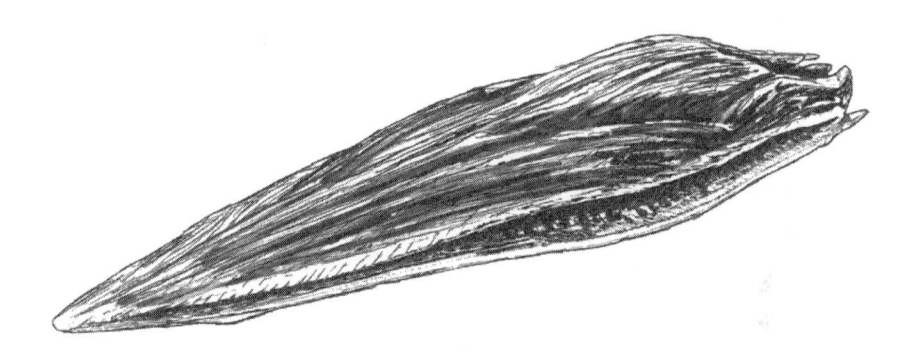

High Lord Shondar sat watching the battle from a high orbit, safely cloaked and concealed behind the lines on his command ship, the *Gasha*. But there was no concealing his disappointment and rage. The Avilonians had lost their fleet, their world laid bare and defenseless. They had been *his* for the conquering! The glory was to have been his alone!

Now . . . now they were suddenly firing back and coming at him with overwhelming force. Shondar stalked up to the edge of the simulated star dome which covered his bridge. He gazed down on the glittering jewel that was Avilon and let out an angry hiss. That jewel had almost been his!

"My Lord, what do we do now?" the chief operator asked.

Shondar took a minute to reply, his glowing white eyes fixed upon a darkened patch of the city below. It was dark for all the thick clouds of smoke that hung over it, obscuring city lights and raging fires alike. That black region was dimly lit by the continuous flashing of lasers, missiles, and exploding Shell Fighters, as well as by one curiously bright point of light which glared up at him with the intensity of a sun.

Shondar's eyes narrowed on that singular, bright point of light, glaring straight back at it. He knew it wouldn't be long before even his cruisers and battleships succumbed to enemy fire, falling from the sky to burst open on the ground like overripe gob fruit.

It was time to retreat. "Have our drivers cloak their ships and return to orbit. They are to rendezvous with us here before we leave. We return no better than when we left. Shame is upon us all."

"Yes, My Lord."

Shondar bit back a roar of outrage. A part of him had known a world as vastly-overpopulated as Avilon could not be subdued so easily. He had suspected it was too good to be true, but he had barreled on foolishly, blinded by visions of glory which were now eclipsed by shame.

How could he have been so foolish!

The humans would pay.

Reluctantly, Shondar sent a brief, telepathic update to High Lord Kaon. The battle was lost; he was returning to Dark Space. Kaon wanted details, but Shondar ended that brief contact abruptly, making it clear that he was not in the mood to analyze his defeat.

"Our drivers report they cloak successfully and are breaking off from the engagement. They return to orbit."

Shondar gave no sign he had heard that update, and no one bothered to ask if he had. He stood watching as the darkened patch of city below grew darker still with the sudden absence of weapons fire. He bared his black teeth in an ugly smile. The Avilonians could not shoot what they could not see. Cloaking technology had won the war with humanity. Now it was being put to a far less glorious use, shielding Shondar's fleet from eyes and sensors as it retreated. It was the first Sythian retreat in the history of the war, and the shame of ordering it fell on him. He hissed once more, displeasure rolling off him in waves.

Then, suddenly, something terrible happened.

The clouds were lit up once more with flashing light, and Shondar felt an uncommon stab of fear. His upper lip curled, and his brow wrinkled with confusion.

"My Lord! The drivers report their ships are being fired upon!"

"This is not possible! They cannot detect us! Have the drivers evade!"

"They do evade, My Lord. The enemy strikes us still!"

"Have them activate flash shields! De-cloak the *Gasha* and do the same! Get us away from the planet!"

The *operator* at the helm began turning the mighty *Gasha* away from Avilon. Mere seconds later Shondar saw the blinding speck glaring up at him from the planet suddenly swell to twice its size and brightness, unleashing a terrifying beam of light. Shondar watched it slice through the kilometers-long bow of his ship, and his glowing white eyes widened with shock.

"How do they see us?!" Shondar demanded, his voice

sounding suddenly shrill. The bow of his command ship cracked away in a molten ruin.

"Flash shields active!" the operator in charge of engineering called out just a moment too late. Fortunately, the *Gasha* could live without its bow, but now Shondar's shame was magnified.

"Get us away from this place—now!" Shondar hissed.

"What of the fleet?"

"Leave them!"

* * *

Atton saw the Avilonians open fire on the invaders at last. Dazzling white beams crisscrossed the sky. Hundreds of starfighters rose to greet the alien swarms. Red lines of pulse lasers streaked out from them, reaping the sky, and the alien armada began raining down everywhere around him.

A ground swell of hope buoyed his spirits and a grim smile began tugging at the corners of his mouth. *Sweet revenge. Serves the kakards right!* It was beginning to look like Avilon might pull victory from this massacre. Atton had to force himself to stop gloating and focus on his immediate surroundings. Whether or not they won, it was still imminently possible for him to die. A pair of Shell fighters roared by, running from the *Intrepid,* which they had been bullying just a moment ago. They cut down across his flight path at an oblique angle, followed by twice as many Avilonian fighters. They were spitting streams of bright red lasers at the enemy shells.

A moment later those two Shells exploded with synchronous *booms* and Atton's Nova rocked in the shockwave. Racing up toward the *Intrepid*, he mentally toggled his comms for the command channel and sent a message: "Control, this is Guardian One, what's your status?"

No answer.

He followed the *Intrepid's* flaming ruin across the sky, hoping against hope that they could hold out just a little longer. The Avilonians were scraping the Shells off them like bugs from a hover car's windshield.

"Guardian One, this is Control, we—*skriss* . . ."

Whatever the comm officer had been about to say was cut off with a burst of static. A flash of light followed, and suddenly the *Intrepid's* thrusters were gushing fire and smoke. The ship took a sudden dive toward the planet. A quick look at the grid showed it going dark. The cruiser was running in low power, but Atton was sure after the explosion he'd witnessed that it wasn't by design.

Mere seconds later, he saw a flurry of escape pods jet away. They were abandoning ship! *Frek,* he thought, still rushing up to greet the *Intrepid,* as if he could somehow stop the cruiser's suicidal plunge to the city below.

"Sara, plot a trajectory for the *Intrepid,*" he said.

A moment later, a curving red vector appeared on the grid, reaching out from the doomed cruiser to the tallest tower in the city below. *The Zenith Tower,* Atton gasped.

It wasn't even another minute before the Avilonians responded to the crashing ship. Blinding beams of light converged, and Atton saw the *Intrepid* begin breaking up into flaming chunks.

Then it flew apart with a terrific *boom,* vaporizing all but the smallest specks of debris. Atton gaped at the explosion now blossoming a few short klicks from his fighter. Then came the shockwave and his Nova began to buck and twist under him. He battled with the flight stick for just a second before the shockwave passed. In its wake came a hail of superheated grit and small, molten debris which hissed off his shields and stole a few percentage points of charge. That was all that remained of the once majestic cruiser. Atton's gaze dropped to the grid to look for the escape pods he'd seen fleeing the ship.

There were just three left.

Targeting the nearest one, he hailed it saying, "Pod vee nine sixty six dash four, this is Guardian One, what's your status?"

The comms crackled with a familiar voice—that of the *Intrepid's* XO, Deck Commander Delayn. "Good to hear from you, Guardian Leader. We're all right, but a bit shaken up. We have the captain with us. Where's the rest of your squadron?"

"I'm it," Atton replied.

"Kavaar...."

Atton felt the same dull shock coursing through him. Out of the over one hundred men and women who had been aboard the *Intrepid* when they'd set out from Dark Space, they'd be lucky if a dozen had survived.

"Mind giving us an escort to the surface?" Commander Delayn asked, interrupting his thoughts.

"It would be my pleasure."

Atton brought his Nova around until he had the glowing blue thrusters of the escape pod under his crosshairs. When he drew near to it he saw that it was charred and blackened on the outside, revealing just how lucky it had been to escape the explosion that had taken out the *Intrepid*. Atton kept half an eye on the grid to make sure no enemy fighters were vectoring their way.

"Sara," he said, "Set the TDS to maximum sensitivity and add pod V966-4 to our watch list. I want to know the minute a Shell so much as wobbles onto our flight path."

"Yes, sir," the AI replied.

A moment later the TDS screeched with a warning and Atton saw a Shell Fighter ahead of them begin flashing on the grid as it banked toward them. Sara had auto-targeted it for him. Pushing the throttle up past the stops, Atton surged ahead of the captain's escape pod, and then thumbed over to lasers. Lining up for a shot, he brought the red brackets of the target under his crosshairs. The targeting reticle flickered green and he held down the trigger. Lasers screeched out in a continuous stream toward his target, and its shields began to drop. Then came the *beep-beep-beeping* of an enemy target lock, and an alarm screamed out a warning as a glittering pair of Pirakla missiles leapt out toward him. The Shell fighter's shields dropped to 46% and then it dove away, breaking out of the head-to-head and leaving Atton to deal with the missiles now vectoring in on him. A moment later his TDS blared out another warning just as a group of Shells angled in on him from his starboard side and began firing dazzling violet streams of pulse lasers across his path.

He began yawing erratically from his straight-line course in order to throw their aim. The missile lock alarm grew progressively louder until his ears began to ring with the sound. "I get it!" Atton roared. "Sara turn down the volume on the TDS!"

The alarm diminished and then the missiles were upon him. He nosed down and hauled back on the throttle until the glittering purple stars of two Pirakla missiles appeared to shine down into the cockpit like twin suns at their zenith. As soon as he'd judged they were just about to hit him, he triggered his afterburners and pulled up hard, letting the alien missiles skate by behind him with bare meters to spare. Strident purple light continued to flash around his cockpit—

Then it suddenly ceased.

Atton deduced that the Avilonians had taken care of those fighters for him. A muffled clap of thunder applauded their demise a split second later as the sound of the explosions reached his ears.

He let out a breath he hadn't realized he was holding and checked the grid for the captain's escape pod. It was still cruising on behind him, unmolested. Either the Sythians hadn't noticed it, or they were prioritizing targets by threat level. He knew better than to think they had spared the pod out of mercy. Hauling back on his throttle so the escape pod could fly past him, he keyed his comms and said, "Commander Delayn, you need to set down as soon as you can. Things are going to get worse before they get better up here."

"Agreed, but for now we're safer in the air."

Atton was forced to agree as he peered over the nose of his fighter to the inferno raging through the city below. The shimmering cascades and lush, shadowy green of the city's rooftop gardens were now a distant memory. Everything was black smoke and curling orange tongues of flame as far as the eye could see. He considered that at least the planet-wide city was too vast for the destruction to have spread very far.

As if to confirm his *look-on-the-bright-side* attitude, he saw the smoke begin to thin out up ahead. A few minutes later, his Nova punched through the fading black haze, and pristine gardens raced by once more. The captain's pod flew past him and angled for a grassy garden which lay at the foot of a giant skyscraper. Not waiting for them to touch down, Atton began banking back the way he'd come.

"Thanks for the escort, Guardian Leader," Delayn's voice returned. "Where are you going? The Avilonians look like they can handle things from here. You'd be better off keeping your head down with us."

"I'm sure they can handle things, sir," Atton replied, "but I have at least one friend down there somewhere, and I need to go back and look for her."

Delayn hesitated to reply, as if he thought that was a skriff's errand, but all he said was, "I hope you find her."

"So do I. Get under cover as soon as you can."

"We will. Thanks again."

Atton nodded, but gave no reply. He raced back into the inferno, the smoke swallowing his Nova greedily. Unable to see, he snapped on a terrain-following overlay, and a jagged world of broken towers and twisted debris became visible, painted over the hazy black smoke in shades of green.

He scanned the grid, searching for the ping of an emergency beacon which would alert him to the presence of a downed pilot, but there was nothing. Gravidar was completely devoid of any active signatures, either friendly or enemy. Most of his pilots had crashed in the vast square at the base of the Zenith Tower, but Atton couldn't find either the square or the tower through all the debris. Flying up higher to get his bearings, he saw the smoke clear just enough to make out a blurry outline of the gargantuan Zenith Tower. The tower lay off his port side. Banking that way, Atton checked the grid for emergency beacons once more.

Still nothing.

Then his shields hissed with a string of impacts, followed

by the sudden appearance of a Shell Fighter on his tail. *It must have been cloaked!* he realized. His missile lock alarm blared out a warning, but the enemy was too close for him to evade. The missile hit with a deafening roar, and his Nova bucked violently. His AI screamed out, "Shields depleted!"

After that, a damage alert blared close beside his ears, along with a sharp whistling sound. Thick black smoke began swirling into the cockpit, giving him a clue about the whistling noise—there was a hole in his cockpit. In the next instant his flight suit auto-pressurized and sealed, cutting him off from the cockpit's depressurized, contaminated air supply, but not before his ears popped with the sudden change in pressure or before he caught a lungful of acrid smoke.

Then a loud shearing noise drew his attention out the port side of the cockpit. He was just in time to see his wing sliced off by a lavender-hued flash of light. The Shell Fighter was still on his tail, intent on finishing him. Now unbalanced, his Nova began rolling over. Atton fought the controls for just a second before he realized it was futile. He pulled the red lever beside his flight chair, and explosive bolts blew his canopy into a netherworld of greasy black smoke.

Sudden acceleration squashed him against his seat, carrying him swiftly away from the doomed Nova. His spine compressed painfully, the chair's inertial management system too weak to shield him completely from the g-force. Then the sudden acceleration eased as the booster rockets in his chair sputtered out. Atton drifted to the top of his ascent, his head poking out above the pervasive smoke for a murky view of his surroundings. He was high above the ruined square which lay at the foot of the Zenith Tower. All around him bits of flaming debris and ash were fluttering to the ground. Overhead, bright white beams and red pulse lasers crisscrossed the sky, swatting at the Sythians' fighters and fleeing cruisers. At the top of the Zenith shone a bright orb which Atton had somehow missed seeing before. It shone almost as bright as a sun, turning black of night to dawning day. As he watched, that orb seemed to swell, and then it shot straight up as the thickest, brightest beam weapon the Avilonians had fired thus far. His gaze followed that massive weapon up into seemingly empty space.

Feeling his stomach lurch as his flight chair began to slowly plummet to the ground, Atton turned away from the scene of the Sythians' defeat to rather focus on his own survival. Using the controls on his armrest to direct himself as best he could, he headed for the Zenith Tower. Through the reams of smoke, he could just barely make out a gaping hole in the base of that tower. If he could get there, he might be safe.

The chair's grav lifts controlled his descent as best they could, but the power supply wasn't nearly strong enough for powered flight across the odd kilometer between him and the Zenith. With that in mind, Atton traded altitude for speed and used that speed to get himself as close as he could. When he saw the ground rushing up too fast beneath his feet, he pushed the grav lifts to their limit, buoying himself up at the last possible second. The resultant force threatened to flatten him against the seat of the chair, placing an almost unbearable pressure on his spine, but then that pressure eased and his chair slid to a stop, still upright and hovering a few inches above the ash-covered ground.

Atton hurried to unbuckle his flight restraints and then he set out at a run to cover the remaining distance to the Zenith. Thick black smoke clogged his way everywhere he looked, disorienting him. Giant black flakes of ash pinwheeled from the sky like snow. The ground shook with the periodic thunder of debris crashing all around him. The limited sensors inside his helmet were equally blinded by the smoke, and he was left groping in the dark, trying to steer clear of the blurry orange light of raging fires.

Desperate, Atton tried the comms as he ran. "This is Guardian Leader to anyone who can hear me, I'm on the ground at nav point Epsilon, looking for cover. Can't see a frekking thing through the smoke..."

The comms crackled ominously with static. Either everyone was dead, or they were too far out of range to hear him.

But then a gruff voice cut through the static, and a light appeared, bright and shining through the gloom.

"Commander, this is Mech Captain Alpha One—hold your position, I'm on my way to you now."

Relief flooded through him, but rather than stop running, he ran faster, heading toward the light. All of a moment later, a dark shape came swirling out of the chaos—faceplate blue and glowing in the light of holographic displays. It was a Zephyr light assault mech.

"Frek, it's good to see you, Captain!" Atton said. "Have you found any other survivors out here?"

"Why don't you come see for yourself," the captain said as he reached Atton's side. "Follow me."

Chapter 31

ASCENDANCY

Atton hurried up the stairs to the entrance of the Zenith Tower. He saw a glimmer of green beyond the gaping hole in the doors. That hole had been covered with a portable shield generator to keep out the smoke. He walked through the diaphanous blue membrane of those shields, passing from the nightmare of the burning city into an ethereal dream. A lush garden stretched out as far as the eye could see. The distant walls of the tower rose like glittering mountains of crystal. A bright blue sky sprawled overhead, etched with a faint spiral dotted with stars. The eye-shaped center of that spiral shone like the sun. White-robed people walked calmly through the garden, seemingly oblivious to the chaos and destruction beyond the walls of their tower.

Atton unsealed his helmet and removed it. The air was fresh and honeyed with nectar. He took a deep breath and slowly let it out. "What is this place?"

"It sure is somethin' ain' it?" the captain replied. "But you can gawk later. There's someone here who'd like to see you. Come on."

"Who?" Atton asked, following the captain down a glittering pathway. They didn't get far before he spied a small knot of people gathered in the shade of a tall, blue-flowering tree. Most of those people were armored Avilonian soldiers, but Atton thought he noticed a few who stood out. They wore neither a shining suit of armor nor the white robes of the people in the garden. What they wore instead were ISSF flight suits. As soon as he saw that, Atton took off at a run, quickly outstripping the sentinel who was escorting him there.

Standing in front of the group were a pair of blue-caped Avilonians, and between them hovered a bright light. As Atton approached, he heard a voice like thunder speaking to the group of people.

The light turned toward him, and Atton was abruptly blinded by it. He fell to his knees in the grass, clutching his eyes.

"Atton!" a gruff, familiar voice called out. A moment later he felt himself yanked to his feet for a crushing hug. Now partially shielded from the light, he opened his eyes to slits in time to see his father withdraw to an arm's length. "Glad you could make it," Ethan said.

Atton took in his father's salt and pepper hair, his grizzly growth of stubble, and care-worn features, stretched now into a smile that crinkled the skin at the corners of his eyes. He gazed into the piercing green eyes set within those crinkles and returned his father's smile. "How did you get here?" he whispered.

"Things got bad after you left. Your mother sent me to look for you."

"Hoi there, Atton," a new voice added. He turned to see Alara walking up beside his father, her violet eyes bright with emotion. "We've been looking for you."

"I found them . . ." Atton said, turning in a quick circle to marvel at the garden where they now stood. "I found Avilon."

"Yes, you found us," a deep, gravelly voice interrupted. "But at what cost? The evil you brought with you has killed millions!"

Atton stepped to one side of his father, and the blinding light found him once more. He was forced to shut his eyes as he spoke. "We didn't bring the Sythians here. The only coordinates I received were for your forward base. It was your people who came and rescued us from the gravity field where we were stranded. They helped us find our way here. If the Sythians followed us, then technically it was your people who led them here."

"You dare to blame us for this devastation?" the gravelly voice replied.

"Silence!" the voice like thunder interrupted, accompanied by an even brighter pulse of light from the blinding sun. "The *martalis* speaks the truth. They did not lead the Sythians here, but neither did my Peacekeepers. The Sythians did not follow you to Avilon. They already knew where it was. A *martalis* man by the name of Stevon Elder told them."

"Who?" Ethan asked.

"Doctor Elder?" Atton added. "How would you know that? Actually, better yet, how do you even know him?"

"I know many things."

"Who *are* you?" Atton replied.

"I am your god!" the thunder boomed.

Atton turned to his father with a dubious look. "He can't be serious?"

Ethan winced away from the light and shrugged. "Just roll with it. The Immortals are the Avilonians, Etherus is Omnius ... it all makes a twisted kind of sense when you think about it. I never believed in all that, but I guess those who do should be running around screaming *I told you so!*"

Atton turned back to the light with a frown, wondering if Ceyla being an Etherian would agree with that.

Ceyla! His heart began to pound with the sudden fear that she hadn't made it. Where was she? He recalled the group of people he'd seen as he approached the grassy clearing where he now stood, and he remembered that there'd been few people wearing ISSF uniforms....

Hope rising past the lump in his throat, he called out, "Marksman Corbin?" At that, he opened his eyes fully, trying to see past the light. His eyes promptly blurred with tears and he was forced to shut them again.

"Over here, Commander!"

Relief flooded through him, and he smiled through the tears.

"Hoi, don't forget about me, you old motherfrekker!" came Razor's voice.

"Quiet!" the gravelly voice hissed at them. "Omnius is speaking."

"They will learn respect ..." the thunder replied. Switching to the Avilonians' language, Omnius said something for the benefit of the Peacekeepers, and then the blinding light vanished, and the gravelly voice said. "On your feet!"

Atton blinked the spots out of his eyes and he picked Ceyla out of the crowd of kneeling Avilonians on the grass. She was sitting beside Guardian Five, Razor. Atton reached her side just as the soldiers rose to their feet. She was in no rush to stand, but Atton held out his hand to help her up. She accepted it gratefully. "Thanks for your help up there," she said.

"No problem."

"Move along!" one of the soldiers beside Atton said, giving him a healthy shove.

"Hoi!" Atton turned to scowl at the man. The face behind the glowing visor was inscrutable, but he imagined a nasty look on the soldier's face. Maybe they were upset with him for suggesting that they were to blame for bringing the Sythians to Avilon.

"Hold on a minute," Ethan said, coming to stand beside Atton and face down the soldier with him. "Where are you taking us?"

"Omnius has told us to leave you all in a temporary holding area and go join the fight."

"I see. Tell you what, why don't you have us join that fight, too."

"Omnius said—"

"Forget what Omnius said. You trusted us enough to ask for our help once. Now I'm offering it."

"Move along," the soldier repeated quietly.

"Quat est moror?" the gravelly voice said. Atton saw the owner of this voice was a blue-caped soldier with a glowing blue emblem etched into his radiant armor.

The unadorned soldier turned to the blue-caped one and they spoke briefly in Avilonian. A moment later blue cape turned to them. "Omnius accepts your offer of service. I assume you plan to use your vessel to join the fight."

Ethan nodded.

"Then go quickly." Reaching down to his belt, he opened a compartment and withdrew what looked like a small sheet of transparent rubber. Stepping up to Ethan he handed over the sheet and said, "Place this over your nose and mouth."

Atton saw his father staring at it in his palm with ill-concealed revulsion. Then he noticed that it was *moving*.

"What *is* it?" Ethan asked, looking ready to hand it back.

"A filter. It will allow you to breathe without being choked by the smoke. You will not get back to your ship without it." With that, the blue-caped soldier turned and spoke to a few of his men. They produced similar squares of living rubber and distributed them to the humans in the clearing who didn't have helmets.

When one of them came up to Atton, he shook his head and smiled, putting his helmet back on instead. He watched with concern as his father pressed the sheet of rubber over his mouth and nose. Ethan's mouth opened in surprise as the thing spread, adhering to his lips and nose.

"Ethan!" Alara cried, her hands already reaching out to scrape it off his face.

"Breathe!" the Avilonian commanded. "It will not harm you."

Abruptly Ethan relaxed and nodded. "Thank you," he said, his voice now muffled with a watery sound. Turning to the others, he said, "Let's go."

"You have room for us?" the Zephyr captain who'd found Atton asked.

Ethan hesitated to reply. "Yes, but you'd be better off helping rescue efforts on the surface. There aren't enough turrets on my ship for all of you."

"Understood."

"We could use some help finding it, though."

"Roger that—Alphas, form up!"

Turning to Atton, Ethan said, "You and your squad mates can come with us if you like."

Atton sent Ceyla a questioning look. She and Razor both nodded, and he turned back to his father with a grin. "Ruh-kah!"

Chapter 32

Ethan stumbled out into the smoke-clouded world beyond the ethereal confines of the tower. From the top of the stairs he could see a vast field of flames, blurry orange light dancing through the fumes. Weapons fire flashed overhead, sounding with the distant screeching of pulse lasers and the resonant humming of beam cannons.

He took a deep breath to test the living membrane the Avilonians had given him to place over his mouth and nose. It worked exactly as advertised, somehow passing clean, odorless air to his lungs.

It did nothing for his eyes, however, which immediately

began to burn and tear. He narrowed them to slits, and turned to look behind him for the mech captain who had agreed to lead them to the *Trinity*. He found Alara standing directly behind him, her eyes similarly clouded with tears. Behind her, Atton and his two squad mates were just now emerging from the tower. Bringing up the rear were eight Zephyr assault mechs—Alpha squad.

"Hoi!" Ethan called out to the mech at the head of the group, shouting to be heard over the sound of weapons fire. "We're going to need you to lead the way with your sensors!"

"Roger that," the mech captain said, striding by him and starting down the stairs from the Zenith. "Stay close," he said as he and his squad descended into the gloom. Ethan and the others brought up the rear behind the mechs. The Zephyrs were keeping a close eye on the sky as they went, as if they could see some hidden danger lurking behind the rising columns of smoke. Every now and then they would hear an unearthly screaming as a Shell Fighter came whistling out of the sky to impact in the square with ground-shaking force.

"We need to pick up the pace!" Alpha One called out from the head of the group. With that, the Alphas began to jog. Ethan and the rest of them had to break into a flat sprint to keep up with the Zephyrs' longer strides. They couldn't see all eight assault mechs, but Ethan tried to keep the nearest four in sight at all times.

They had to watch their steps as they ran over the ash-covered ground. Ethan spared a glance to check on Alara as she ran beside him. "You okay?" he asked, suddenly worried about his pregnant wife.

She nodded. "I'm fine."

"No argument about it not being safe to go up there and fight?"

She took a moment to reply to that. Ethan was just about to ask her again when she said, "We have to fight them. Just look at what they've done to this place!"

"What about our baby? I thought you wanted security. Safety."

"I do, and that's exactly why we have to fight. With these people on our side, we might just win the war once and for all. Our part might not make a lot of difference, but at least I'll be able to look my children in the eye one day when they ask me what *I* did to stop the Sythians. They'll know their mother is no coward."

"Ruh-kah! Now there's the Alara I remember. Welcome back, Kiddie."

"Thanks, I think. I'm new at this. I have to think about more than just me now. It's not just my neck I'm risking."

"So what changed your mind?"

"What's the point in having children if they don't have a world to grow up in? I was afraid to leave Dark Space because there was nowhere to go, but now we've found a place, and I'll be damned if I'm going to rest before we rescue everyone and bring them here."

"Hoi, hold on a minute. We don't have to rescue *everyone*, Kiddie."

"Well, obviously the criminals are a low priority," she replied.

"Actually, I wasn't thinking about them. I was thinking about your father."

"Ha ha, very funny!"

He gave a lopsided grin.

"Heads-up!" the mech captain called out up ahead. "I think we've found her!"

Ethan looked up to see a shadow come swirling out of the

smoke. A moment later, that shadow resolved into the shape of his corvette. The Zephyrs slowed now that they'd found the object of their search, but Ethan sped up. He ran past the captain and opened the boarding ramp with the keycard in his pocket as he ran. "Thanks for that, Captain!" Ethan called out. "I owe you boys a round of drinks when we get back!"

"I'll hold you to that!"

Ethan reached the foot of the ramp just as it finished lowering to the ground. He stopped and turned to see his wife, followed by Atton and two more officers go racing by him. He ran up the ramp after them, triggering it to close before they'd even reached the top. Eager to be rid of the living air filter the Avilonians had given him, he ripped it off his face and threw it over the side of the ramp. He noticed Alara doing the same.

Once inside the ship, Ethan ran up to a lift tube that lay just beyond the boarding ramp, he slapped the call button and then turned to his crew. "Atton, take your friends here and head to the turrets. Alara and I will man the cockpit."

"This is a seraphim-class corvette," the male pilot standing behind Atton said. "You're going to need more than two people to on the bridge."

"What's your name?"

"Razor."

The lift tube arrived and they all crowded into it. "Well, Razor," Ethan said as he selected the gun deck and the bridge from the wall-mounted directory. "This is a modified corvette, and it's built for just two control stations."

"That's a lot to manage in a fight," Razor replied.

"You just worry about manning your turret; let me worry about how much I have to manage."

The lift arrived on the gun deck a second later and Atton

ran out with his squad mates. "Tag a few of them for me, son!" Ethan said.

"I'll tag a dozen," Atton replied.

With that, the lift doors swished shut and it went on to the bridge. A moment later, Ethan and Alara were running out and down a short corridor to the bridge. They reached their respective flight chairs and strapped in. Ethan fired up the *Trinity's* reactors and began warming up the grav lifts while Alara skipped through a quick preflight check.

"Everyone ready back there?" he asked, speaking into the ship's intercom. He left it open to keep a dialogue going between him and his crew.

"Affirmative," came Atton's voice.

"Roger that," the female pilot said.

"Ruh-frekkin'-kah!" Razor added.

Ethan pushed the grav lifts up to maximum power and the *Trinity* shot straight off the ground, rising quickly through swirling clouds of smoke. Despite an upward acceleration of over 35 KAPS, they couldn't feel a thing. "Set IMS to 90%," he said, speaking to the ship. Alara shot him a quick look, and he got it. "Right—the baby—Make that 95%."

Now he felt a subtle pressure on his spine to accompany the upward acceleration. A few seconds later they emerged above the smoke and saw the midnight sky slashed with light and bleeding fire. "Holy frek," Ethan whispered.

Several Sythian cruisers were in the process of plummeting from the sky, breaking up into flaming chunks. Avilonian ground batteries answered that threat, breaking the debris into smaller and smaller pieces as they fell. Ethan looked up still higher to the clouds. Reams of fire converged on the lurking shadows of Sythian cruisers. What looked like thousands of gold-glowing insects danced through the air, firing streaks of bright red lasers at a significantly smaller number of orange-glowing insects.

There were thousands of fighters, and that was just what the Avilonians had managed to rally on short notice. Larger ships were few and far between, however—with just a dozen that Ethan could see, and none of them much larger than the *Intrepid*.

Speaking of which . . . Ethan scanned the grid for the ISSF cruiser, but he couldn't find it anywhere. He had a bad feeling the Sythians had destroyed it before Omnius had come back online and restored control of Avilon's defenses.

Their fleet was destroyed in orbit, and this is what they had lying in reserve on the planet, he thought, marveling at the display of force. He tried to guess how many more fighters they had if this was what they'd managed to rally in the past half an hour since Omnius had been brought back online. He realized the number would be in the high six figures. *Alara's right,* he thought. *We do have a chance.*

He found himself wondering about the Avilonians: humanity could have fought off the original invasion if the Avilonians and the Imperium had stood together. *So why didn't they?*

Ethan frowned and pushed those thoughts from his mind. "We're going to have to hurry if we want to get in on the action," he said while switching from grav lifts to thrusters. A meaty roar rumbled through the ship as he throttled up to the ship's maximum acceleration of 125 KAPS. That was significantly less in atmosphere than it was in space, but still more than fast enough to pin them to their seats and send the city falling away beneath them at a dizzying rate.

"How many are there?" Alara asked.

Ethan queried the gravidar for a tally. "Fifteen capital-class, and just over five hundred Shell Fighters ... they're down to less than half of what they came with.... Hoi! What's this?"

"What's what?"

"Look!" Ethan pointed to the grid, to the red icon of an enemy starship hovering high above the planet. "That's their command ship!"

"Why aren't they cloaked?" Alara asked.

"Maybe the Avilonians have a way to see through cloaking shields?"

"If that's the case, then the Sythians are in for more trouble than they know."

Just as Alara said that, the eye of Omnius at the top of the Zenith Tower abruptly swelled to twice its size and a blinding beam of white light shot straight up through the clouds. Ethan followed that beam on the gravidar to see where it went.

He watched wide-eyed with glee as it collided with the gargantuan command ship and sliced off a large chunk of its port side.

"Holy frek," Ethan whispered.

They soared into the clouds, and the space ahead of them grew thick with red bracket pairs as the ship auto-highlighted nearby enemy targets on the HUD. "Heads-up boys and girls," Ethan said, switching over to Hailfire missiles. Destra had filled the *Trinity's* launchers to overflowing with munitions before sending him on his way—just in case.

Before they were even through the clouds Ethan saw bright lances of red and blue dymium pulse lasers streaking out from his corvette's turrets, tracking enemy Shells. Ethan targeted the nearest fighter and hovered his targeting reticle over the enemy fighter. He waited to hear the solid tone of a lock and then fired off a pair of Hailfires. They jetted out into the clouds and disappeared.

Then the *Trinity* punched through the clouds and they saw the real battle in all its glory. Sythian cruisers and battleships were clawing for the sky, their shining mirror-like hulls peppered with explosions from unseen ordnance. "What the frek is hitting them?" Ethan asked.

"Lasers?" Alara suggested.

Ethan shook his head, barely noticing as the missiles he'd fired split into eight shards each and blew three Shell Fighters out of the sky. "No. Not beams either. Those are being absorbed by shields. These are explosives."

"Well, some type of warheads, then."

"Right, but why can't I see them on the grid?"

"Maybe they're cloaked?"

"Maybe," he conceded.

"Ruh-kah!" Atton whooped over the intercom just as the first Shell Fighter succumbed to fire from the *Trinity's* turrets. "That's one!"

"You're going to have try harder! I'm already up to three."

"Put me in the pilot's chair and we'll see what I can get," Razor chimed in.

"Nice try," Ethan said through a smile. "Not happening."

Ka-boom!

"Hoi!" Atton called out.

Dead ahead a Sythian Battleship cracked into jagged pieces.

"That's a pretty sight!" Razor chimed in.

Ethan grinned. "Copy that."

Alara jabbed him in the ribs with an elbow. "Look at that," she said, pointing to the grid. Ethan looked down at his MHD and found all the Shell Fighters there suddenly breaking off to turn tail and run, leaving the capital ships to fend for themselves.

"It's a rout!" Ethan called out over the intercom. "Let's run 'em down!" He pushed the throttle up past the red lines and into overdrive. The ship began to shudder and shake around them. The stars grew progressively brighter. Streaking golden lights began racing by all around them—hundreds of Avilonian fighters chasing after the Shells at top speed. Curious about how fast that top speed was, Ethan targeted one of them and found it accelerating at 225 KAPS, almost double the *Trinity's* top speed.

He let out a long whistle. "That is one fast fighter." Even Nova Interceptors weren't that fast. And as for the Sythian fighters they were chasing, they may as well have been standing still. The Avilonians caught up in a matter of seconds, and red hot streams of lasers began pouring from them, lighting their targets on fire. Ethan targeted the nearest Shell and tried for another missile lock. The reticle flickered red, and then he heard a solid tone and fired off another pair of Hailfires. More lasers began streaking out from the *Trinity's* turrets as they came into range.

Space ahead of them was peppered with exploding Shells. But rather than slow down to focus on the enemy fighters more squarely, the Avilonians roared past them, giving the enemy a chance to take a few potshots. Ethan saw at least two Avilonian fighters flicker off the grid before they passed out of range.

"I don't get it," Alara said. "They could have hounded those Shells until they killed them all."

"Yes, they could have, but then they wouldn't be able to go after that." Ethan pointed to the Sythian command cruiser, visible as little more than a glinting speck in the distance.

"They can't be far from a safe jumping distance," Alara replied.

"No, I'd say they're just about there," Ethan replied while lining the command ship up under his sights.

"What are you doing?"

"What's it look like? We're going to join the party," he replied.

"What are you going to do when we fly past those Shells and suddenly they're on *our* tail? They'll tear us apart."

"Something tells me they've got bigger problems."

Flying up behind them and catching up fast were a quartet of Avilonian cruisers. All of a minute later, the glinting wave of Shells ahead of them became a dazzling wall of fire that almost blotted out the stars.

"What the . . . ?" Ethan trailed off.

"Hoi, leave something for us!" Razor whined.

"They're dying before I can even target them!" Atton added.

"I didn't see any weapons fire. What's shooting them?" the female pilot put in.

"We noticed the same with the cap ships earlier," Ethan replied. "Possibly some type of cloaking missiles."

"Slick. Wish we had those," Razor replied.

Ethan was just about to pass through the wall of flames, when the Avilonians' fire let up. Now there were just a few dozen Shell Fighters left, exploding here and there.

"This is krak!" Razor said. "I only got one and two assists."

"Two here," Atton replied.

"Still three for me," Ethan replied, finding to his disappointment that the last pair of Hailfires he'd fired had gone to waste—their targets blown apart before they'd arrived. "But I still win."

"I got two and three assists," Ceyla added quietly.

Alara nudged him with her elbow and turned to him with a smile. "You know what that means?"

Ethan was too busy gaping in shock to reply.

"It means she wins," Atton said for him. "One assist equals half a kill, so she's got 3.5. Nice work, Corbin."

"Corbin, huh?" Ethan said. "Well, you owe me a drink little lady."

"That's *Marksman* Corbin to you, civvy, and why do *I* owe *you* a drink? I won."

"Exactly. How else am I supposed to feel better about that?"

Laughter rippled over the comms. "In that case I'll buy you two."

"Generous. I accept."

"Consider it an advance on future defeats."

"If that's the case, I'll have to pay it back soon."

"I wouldn't be too sure about that," Alara said.

"Whose side are you on?" he asked.

"Yours of course. I'm just trying to protect your ego from further bruising."

Girlish laughter trilled over the comms. "I like your copilot, hotshot."

Ethan smiled. It was nice to break up the misery of the past few weeks with some playful banter. Now, finally, humanity was on the winning side of the war.

It's about time we had some revenge, he thought, his eyes on the distant speck of the Sythians' command ship. *Ready or not, here we come.*

Chapter 33

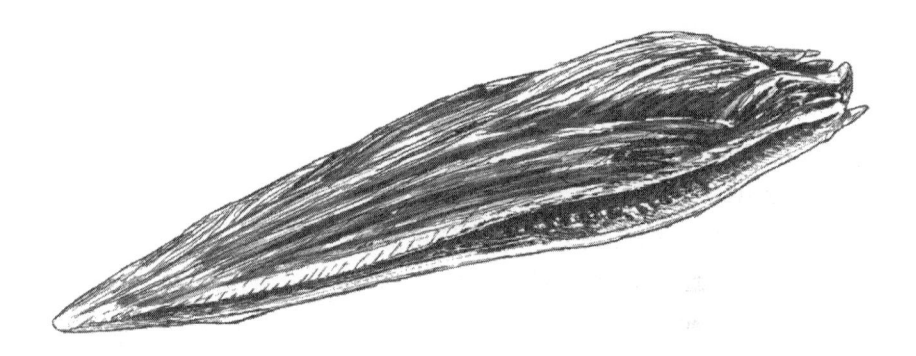

High Lord Shondar was relieved when they were finally out of range of the ship-cracking beam that had been firing periodically at them from the surface of the planet. He began to hope he might just make it back from Avilon alive. As for his fleet, however, that was another matter. More than a hundred starships *gone*—cut to pieces in less time than it had taken for his fleet to dispatch the derelict Avilonian one. The difference was, his ships could still move and shoot back. It wasn't much of a difference. Shondar had never seen such a fast turnabout in war—not in the whole decade which they'd spent wiping the galaxy clean of its human pestilence.

"My Lord, we are ready to enter the light stream," the *operator* at the helm said, interrupting his thoughts.

"Do so!"

The bright sparkle of stars turned to an ugly swirl of light. Shondar hissed and subsided against the back of his command chair. It was done. The Avilonians had won the first round.

But what of the second? From what he'd just witnessed, Shondar doubted that he and the other lords could prevail against the Avilonians. The one hope they had was that they had annihilated the Avilonian fleet before it could come online. At the end, when they had suddenly begun to fight back, the majority of their strength had been in their ground defenses and their thousands of fighters. The Avilonians could not project that strength beyond their world. Not without another fleet. Perhaps they had another one in reserve. Shondar hoped not . . .

He caught himself with an ugly scowl. This disaster planning was beneath him. How had he gone from planning the conquest of Avilon with the other Lords to trying to think of a way that they could survive if the Avilonians chased them back to Dark Space?

The irony of that was not lost on him. Dark Space had been humanity's refuge against the Sythian Coalition for the past ten years. Now it was about to become the Coalition's refuge against humanity.

Shondar's hands involuntarily bawled into fists and he pounded the armrests of his command chair, causing the displays before him to shudder. It made no sense! If the humans were so strong, why had they saved their strength for last? Why not fight as one and repel the invasion? Why had they remained in hiding all of this time, only to show their strength now when they were forced to defend themselves?

The answer to all of those questions came to him in a sudden flash of insight. *Because they know about us,* he realized. *They know we could easily crush them if all of our might were brought to bear. What is one sector against thousands?*

The first seven clusters they'd sent to the humans' galaxy to test their strength had proven to be the only seven they needed to send. Rather than send more fleets needlessly after the first, those seven had gone on to conquer humanity completely. Now that the initial invasion was no longer enough, they had but to ask the supreme one to send more reinforcements.

It would not matter if the Avilonians' technology were more advanced, Shondar realized. They would be so hopelessly outnumbered that they couldn't hope to survive.

Suddenly the *Gasha* groaned and the dazzlingly-bright swirl of the light stream vanished as the command ship was pulled unexpectedly back into real space. Dead ahead Shondar saw the maddening blackness of the nebula they had been trapped within mere hours ago.

"What?" he boomed, rising from his chair. "What happens?" he demanded.

"A gravity field does pluck us from the light stream again, My Lord. This time we are at the edge of it, not far from whence we came."

"Get us out! How far are we?"

"We—"

"Enemy vessels detected!" the sensor operator said. "Dead ahead!"

"They follow us?"

"No, My Lord, they are in the wrong place. They lie here in wait for us."

"How?"

"We do not alter our final trajectory for many minutes. They must have forces nearby, and communicate our flight path to them."

"Come about! We go back the way we come."

"Yes, My Lord."

Then the *Gasha* shuddered underfoot and a distant rumble reached their ears. "What is that? Are they in range so soon?"

"We cannot see what they shoot us with!"

"Fire back!"

"We are out of range!"

Shondar cursed viciously. "Continue running!"

"Enemy contact!"

"Again?"

"They are behind us! These ones do follow us from the planet, My Lord! What are your orders?"

Shondar's naturally gray face paled still further, and his glowing white eyes widened in horror. His gaze turned to the star map hovering before him. Thousands of purple enemy blips were rushing at them both front and rear in two encircling arcs. They were moving to trap the *Gasha* between them.

He'd been so distracted by his sudden defeat that he hadn't even thought about what the Avilonians might do to stop them from leaving. He'd forgotten all about the gravity field.

"Come about and face them! The shakars force us to fight, and so we fight! For glory!"

"For glory!" his crew shouted back.

That battle cry left a bitter taste in Shondar's mouth. For one who knew nothing of defeat, it was hard to accept, but he knew what was coming.

Death was coming for them all.

* * *

Ethan watched the Sythian command ship vanish with a flash of light. "Frek! We missed them."

"That's it?" Alara asked. "Aren't you going to follow?"

Ethan considered that with a frown. "We can't take a 30-kilometer-long warship down with just the *Trinity*, and there's no way the Avilonians' fighters can chase them all the way to Dark Space. Show's over," he said, banking back toward the planet.

They began flying past Avilonian starfighters and then past a group of cruisers. Oddly, none of them was turning around. Ethan watched them on the grid with a furrowed brow. "Why aren't they going back?"

Alara shook her head.

Then the Avilonian fleet abruptly vanished.

"The frek? Where'd they go?" Razor put in, asking the question that was already on the tip of Ethan's tongue.

"Cloaked?" Alara suggested.

"Why? There's nothing to hide from anymore," Ethan said.

"Wait a minute . . ." Atton whispered. Then came a rush

of static as he let out a sudden breath and gave a short yip of laughter. "They just jumped away, too!"

"What?" Ethan shook his head and checked the grid for a radiation trail. "Why would they jump after the Sythians if they don't have the range to follow them? And besides, I don't see any traces of T-radiation."

"Their drives don't work the same was as ours, and as for it making sense, it makes plenty," Atton replied. "We ended up stuck in a gravity field a few light years from Avilon when we came here in the *Intrepid*. It turned out to be one of many. Omnius uses them like a wall to keep people out of the sector."

"You're telling me they're protecting a whole sector with artificial gravity fields?" Ethan was incredulous. "The energy it would take to generate fields that size is—"

"A lot more than we can imagine," Atton finished. "I don't know how Omnius does it, but I witnessed it with my own eyes. Why do you think it took so long for us to get here? We only escaped the gravity field when Omnius shut down."

"What's your point, SC?" Razor chimed in.

Ethan put the pieces together a moment later. "Start spooling for a jump!" he said to Alara, his hands already flying over the controls to deduce a vector from the trail of tachyon radiation which the Sythians had left in their wake.

"Where to?" Alara asked.

"Give me a second. . . ."

"Hoi, I'm not going to die on some skriff's quest!" Razor said. "You can't take us all the way back to Dark Space in this bucket, and even if you could, I'm not going."

"If your commander's right," Ethan said, "we won't have to go that far before we get yanked out of SLS."

"The grav fields . . ." Ceyla said.

"Exactly. If I were Omnius, I wouldn't let the Sythians escape if I didn't have to. I just hope we're in time for as few parting shots of our own."

"Frek yeah!" Razor said.

All of five minutes later the drives were spooled and Ethan had them flying on a parallel trajectory to the one the Sythians had taken to escape. "Ready?" he asked, turning to Alara.

"Punch it!" she said.

And with that, stars and space turned to star lines and bright swirls of light. Ethan sat back and waited. The minutes passed in an agony of anticipation with the occasional comment from the gun deck. He was just beginning to wonder if he and Atton had guessed wrong about the gravity fields when a reversion alarm sounded through the bridge and the dazzling swirl of SLS vanished with an abrupt flash of light.

They dropped out of SLS in the middle of a warzone. Space ahead of them was void of stars, but bright and flashing with dazzling streaks of red light. The sheer blackness of space confounded Ethan for just a moment before sensors flagged it on the grid as a dark nebula.

The Sythians' command ship sat before them, twisting and turning at the edge of that nebula, beset by a thick cloud of starfighters. The Avilonian cruisers hung back where the *Trinity* had dropped out of SLS, seemingly spectators to the battle raging before them. Ethan knew better. The Sythians' command ship was wreathed in fiery explosions from all the mysterious ordnance those cruisers were bringing to bear. Glinting distantly against the dark nebula, Ethan saw yet another Avilonian fleet. He wondered where they'd come from. Then he remembered the fleet he'd found at the

Avilonians' forward base.

"What are you waiting for?" Alara asked.

Ethan hadn't bothered to ignite the *Trinity's* thrusters since dropping out of SLS. He shook his head, and all of a moment later, the Sythian command cruiser flew apart in a spectacular flash of light. "That," he replied belatedly.

"Ruh-kah . . ." Razor said over the intercom.

Death and glory, Ethan translated, nodding slowly. Until now there hadn't been much glory in the war, just a lot of death. Now, finally, it looked like that was about to change. This was the second command ship humanity had destroyed in almost as many months. "Serves the kakards right," Alara whispered beside him.

Ethan turned to her with a wild grin. He strained against his seat restraints to take her face in his hands and kiss her ruby lips. A moment later he pulled away from her to stare into her startling violet eyes. "We're going to be okay, Alara!" he said, taking her by her shoulders and gently shaking her, as if to wake her from a bad dream. "We're going to be okay."

"I know," she replied, flashing a smile of her own.

Chapter 34

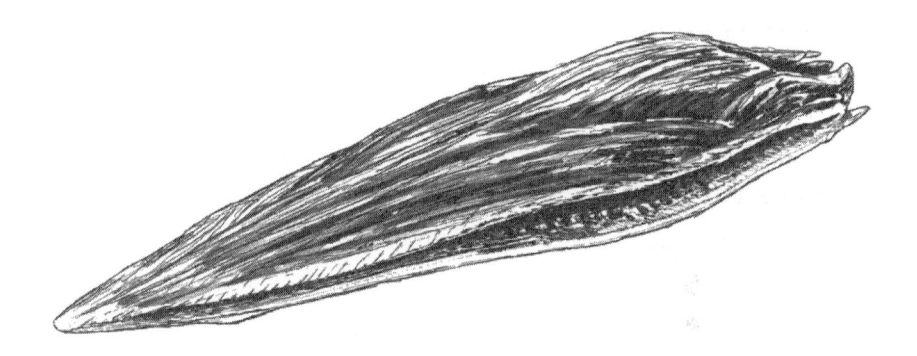

Shondar hissed in fury, watching his mighty *Gasha* swarmed from all sides. They were firing back for all they were worth, but so far they'd only managed to shoot down a few dozen enemy fighters. As for the Avilonians' capital ships, they hung back, safely out of range.

"The shields fail, My Lord!"

"I know!" he hissed, his voice all but drowned out by the simulated roar of explosions, and by the very real rumbling and groaning which echoed through his ship with every hit.

The humans will pay for this!

Then a brilliant flash of light suffused the deck where he

stood, and his furious hissing was cut off in mid stream, his body vaporized in an instant.

Shondar awoke to find himself underwater. Then his muscles all spasmed as one, and the water became turbid with his involuntary thrashing. As soon as the sensation passed, he sat up with a splash and coughed up a viscous fluid. He looked around to find that he was naked, sitting in a bath of translucent blue fluid with tubes and wires trailing from his body. One such tube protruded from his belly button. Filled with horror and revulsion, he almost reached down to rip it out, but he wasn't sure what would happen if he did. His brain pulsed with an angry heat; his heart raced. What had just happened? Had it all been a dream? Where was he? *Who was he?*

Shondar hissed and turned to look around him, but all was darkness besides the blue glow emanating from the bath where he sat.

Then a voice slithered from the darkness: "You return to us in ssshame, Lord Shondar."

That voice was familiar.

"Lord Kaon! Where am I?"

"You die. Now you live. You are in your spawning chamber."

Shondar hissed with rage. "I kill them for this!"

"Be at ease. This already happens to stronger lords than you."

Shondar didn't like Kaon's implication that he was a stronger lord, but he let it go. "Help me out of here," Shondar said, reaching out for the sides of the bath.

"Not yet. Tell me about the battle."

"I am a High Lord! You cannot keep me here!"

"No, I cannot. Not unless your foolishness cost us more

than it appears. We tell you to forfeit your fleet, but retreat with your command ship intact, yet you return here with neither your fleet nor the *Gasha*."

Shondar hissed once more. "You have no authority to threaten me. You do not speak for the other lords."

"I do not. You are correct. Perhaps I should let them speak for themselves."

With that, a dim light grew in the room and Shondar turned to see all four of the other lords, including Lady Kala. Lord Quaris was mysteriously missing. "I can explain," Shondar said.

"Then tell us," Lord Worval demanded in a booming voice. "We are listening."

So Shondar told them. He told them all about Avilon— about the encircling wall of gravity fields and the mysteriously derelict fleet, about their magnificent world-city, and finally about his defeat and the Avilonians' vastly superior technology. When he was done with his story, the lords were noticeably cowed.

"Then we cannot defeat them," Lady Kala said.

"No. Not *yet*," Kaon replied. "The humans left to get reinforcements. I believe it's time we went to get some of our own."

* * *

As soon as the *Trinity* dropped out of SLS with the world-spanning city of Avilon lying before them once again, the comms squealed and a deep voice shuddered through the bridge speakers. "Unknown Imperial transport, this is Strategist Galan Rovik of the *Athos*. Please lower your shields and prepare for boarding."

"What?" Ethan blurted out. He couldn't believe it.

"I don't like the sound of that . . ." Alara whispered beside him. "Did you open the comms?"

"No . . ."

"Then where did that transmission come from?"

"The frek if I know!"

"You have not dropped your shields. You have five seconds to comply before we lower them for you."

"Some thanks we get!" Ethan roared. "Can you hear me? We helped you and now you're just going to take my ship? Frek you!" he spat. With that, he wrenched the flight yoke to one side, turning back the way they'd come.

"Where are you going to go?" Alara asked.

Ethan shook his head. "The frek away from here!"

"Alara's right, Dad," Atton said over the intercom. "We just saw what happened when the Sythians tried to run. You think we'll do any better?"

"So what do you suggest?" he demanded, his chest heaving with fury.

The comms squealed in protest once more and then they heard, "You are out of time."

"Frek you!"

The *Trinity* shuddered with an impact and then all the lights on deck abruptly died. Sparks showered from the console before him, and the flight controls went dead. Ethan felt his stomach lurch into his throat as zero-g replaced the ship's artificial gravity.

Silence rang in Ethan's ears, interrupted only by the frantic beating of his own heart. Then came a noise like rushing water, and a strong gust of wind slapped him in the face, forcing his eyes to close. He opened them a moment later to find a pair of Avilonian soldiers in shining armor standing between him and the forward viewports.

Ethan gaped at them, wondering where they'd come from, and how. "In the name of the Ascendancy, welcome to Avilon," the one with a shimmering blue cape said. "I am Strategian Galan Rovik, but you may call me Master Rovik."

"Excuse me?" Alara asked.

"You need not have resisted when we asked to board your vessel. We are merely here to escort you safely to the surface. Omnius will explain everything once we arrive."

Ethan's cheeks bulged with indignation. *"Lower your shields or else we'll lower them for you* is a damned fine way of *asking* to board my ship!"

"We did say please."

"Right," Ethan snorted. "I almost forgot."

Before long, the *Trinity's* systems were back online and she was cruising down through Avilon's atmosphere. Atton and his fellow pilots were standing on the bridge, keeping a close eye on the Avilonians. Ethan would have liked to keep an eye on them, but he needed to keep his eyes on where he was flying. As it happened, the Avilonians were content to let him pilot his ship down to the surface, not that he suspected they could do it themselves. He hoped that was a good sign, but he decided to reserve judgment until he heard what Omnius had to say.

Ethan was very curious about a few things. At the top of that list was why the Avilonians hadn't joined the war sooner. They'd routed the enemy fleet fast enough to make him think they could have won. Right on the heels of that question was what the *frek* Omnius had been doing while his city and his fleet in orbit were sacked.

"Over there. You may set down on the grass." Master blue cape pointed to a large, illuminated green space on the rooftop of a low-rise skyscraper at the edge of the devastation around the Zenith Tower.

Fires still raged in the city below, but now they were being attacked from the air with streams of water from hovering starships. The smoke was beginning to dissipate into a thinner, low-lying haze. Ethan took a short detour from the way to the rooftop the Avilonian had indicated to circle above the city and survey the damage. The debris of crashed starships was everywhere. Here and there Sythian Cruisers lay half buried in the city, half sticking up at an odd angles, like alien plinths.

"It's going to take a while to repair all of that," Ethan remarked.

"It could have been a lot worse," Alara replied.

"Please do not deviate from the indicated course," blue cape said as he realized what the delay was about.

"What did I tell you about getting your cape in a knot?"

Ethan said, bringing the *Trinity* back on course.

"You have never told me any such thing, *martalis*, and I would caution you to show more respect," blue cape replied.

"Oh, I must have the wrong blue cape. Never mind then."

Alara shot him a frown. He replied with a smile, and she shook her head.

Just a few minutes later they hovered to a stop above the Avilonians' chosen rooftop. Ethan saw a small gathering of people in the garden below. As the *Trinity* entered its landing sequence, he used his console to magnify that gathering. Zephyr light assault mechs stood flayed open, their *stomper* pilots out getting some fresh air under the watchful eyes of a few dozen Avilonian soldiers. Besides the stompers there were a handful of others. Ethan immediately recognized one of them by her uniform and her familiar face. *Captain Caldin.* He'd had ample opportunity to get to know her during his brief time with the fleet.

"Hoi! Look who it is!" Atton exclaimed, obviously noticing the captain now, too.

The *Trinity* settled down with a subtle jolt. "Ethan . . ." Alara whispered.

"I see it," he replied, his eyes back on the rigid line of Avilonian soldiers watching over the group of Imperials. He'd seen a few firing squads in his time, and this one was no different from the rest.

Chapter 35

"Captain Caldin!" Atton said, jogging across the clearing to get to her.

She turned to him with a haggard expression and nodded. "Commander."

He stopped before her and offered a quick salute, which Ceyla and Razor both matched. "Reporting for duty, ma'am," he said.

"You can dispense with the formalities, Ortane. We're not in the fleet anymore."

Atton shook his head. "Captain, just because you lost your ship doesn't mean you're no longer part of the fleet."

"They're not letting us leave, so I won't be getting another one, and that *does* mean I'm no longer a part of the fleet." She cast a glance over her shoulder to the officers and enlisted men gathered behind her. "None of us are," she said, turning back to him. "What fleet? Where? Unless we join the Peacekeepers, I think we'll be looking for new professions very soon."

"If we live through this," Ethan whispered, coming up behind them.

Atton turned to his father with a frown. "The admiral said they wouldn't kill us."

"Did he?" Ethan asked, raising his eyebrows. "What are they doing here, then?" he asked, turning to indicate the stolid line of soldiers behind them.

"Ethan's right," Alara said. "That's not a welcoming party."

Atton watched the line of soldiers carefully. They stood with their backs straight, their heads up, arms pinned to their sides. He didn't see any weapons. "If they're not friendly, where are their weapons?" he asked.

"They don't need weapons," Caldin replied. "I watched them execute a squad of Gors with their bare hands."

"What?" Atton turned to her, shock coursing through him. "When was that?"

"You didn't notice? One of them was lying right at the doors when you and the rest of the crew used a cutting beam to break into the bridge."

"That's what that was? I thought it was some kind of debris."

"You didn't get a very good look then."

"Frek..." Atton whispered. "How did they do it?"

"Integrated weapons in their armor, fired straight from

their palms."

"What are we going to do, then?"

"About what?" a new voice asked.

Atton turned to see the blue-caped soldier who'd ridden down from orbit aboard the *Trinity*. He approached quickly, stopping in front of Captain Caldin. His blindingly-bright faceplate bored into her eyes for a long, silent moment before that faceplate abruptly disappeared, replaced by the face of a young man with bright, *glowing* blue eyes.

"Strategian Rovik," Caldin said.

"Captain."

"You know him?" Atton asked.

"He was one of our uninvited guests aboard the *Intrepid* before we left the nebula."

At that, Atton heard his father snort and say, "Showing up uninvited seems like a bad habit of yours, Mr. Rovik."

The Avilonian sent Ethan a thin smile and then turned back to the captain. "Omnius is about to address his people. You are not yet a part of His people, but He has decided to address you separately. After all, you have a right to know the state of your new home."

"Our new home?" Atton asked.

"You're not going to kill us?" Alara put in.

"Kill you? Why would we do that?" Rovik asked, his head tilting to one side.

Ethan jerked a thumb over his shoulder to the line of soldiers watching them. "Where I come from we don't greet people with armed soldiers."

"Not everyone likes to be told they cannot leave *Domus Licus*."

"We were warned," Atton replied.

Rovik's glowing eyes widened with surprise, and then

inclined his head in what was surely an Avilonian gesture. "So you do know something about us. Good. That will make your transition to life here much smoother."

"Why force us to stay if the Sythians know where you are now?" Caldin asked.

"Why try to leave if there is nothing for you out there?" Rovik replied.

"That's not an answer."

"But it is. Now, save the rest of your questions for the time being. You will soon have a chance to ask Omnius anything you like."

"Anything?" Ethan asked.

"Yes, anything. Please turn to the Zenith. I would recommend that you bow."

Atton's eyes narrowed. "And if we don't . . . ?"

"Nothing will happen to you, if that's what you are wondering. Reverence and respect cannot be compelled. They are earned, and Omnius will earn yours very soon."

"Right . . ." Ethan replied.

Atton saw Alara elbow him in the ribs, and then they all turned toward the Zenith Tower and Master Rovik moved to the edge of the rooftop to stand between them and the Zenith.

Atton gazed up at the bright light shining down from the top of the tower. That light was so bright it was hard to look at. A few moments passed, and then the light at the top of the tower swelled to many times its size, blinding them and forcing them to bow their heads to look away from it. The Avilonians behind them called out, "Omnius grando est! Omnius grando est!" and Atton turned to see the line of soldiers now standing with their hands raised to the sky. Upon the last utterance of whatever it was they were saying, they dropped to one knee and bowed their heads.

Then a voice like thunder began booming out from the tower—at least Atton thought that was where it came from. It seemed to resonate and echo all around them. He turned to look for the source of the echo, and his eyes found the next nearest monolith, the one which had lost the top of its spire to Gina's crashing Nova. He was almost certain that tower was transmitting the same speech. In between him and that distant spire, he saw rooftop gardens like the one where they were standing, crowded with white-robed citizens.

Atton turned back to the fore and forced his eyes to open against the blinding brightness. The thunder rolled on, speaking in Avilonian, but just a moment later, a softer version of it began to rumble out in Imperial Versal. This voice didn't come from all around them, but from Master Rovik. A miniature version of the light shining down from the Zenith shone from his chest.

"Welcome to Avilon!" it said. "I have seen your sacrifices during the recent battle. On behalf of my people, thank you for your contribution. In part thanks to your actions, you shall all be rewarded with a place in my kingdom."

"What if we don't want to be a part of your kingdom?" Captain Caldin asked, a note of challenge in her voice.

Atton felt a spike of fear for her, but to his surprise, Omnius did not sound angry when he replied. "I will get to that in a moment."

"You blew my ship apart, killing everyone on board. What do you have to say for yourself?" she demanded.

"I have to say that death is not the end, Loba Margarath Caldin, but a new beginning."

"How do you know my name? No one knows my full name."

"I told you. I know many things. I also know that

although you are an excellent leader and you truly care for those under your command, your present anger is not about the deaths of your crew, but about the death of one man in particular—Corpsman Markom Terl."

"How the frek do you know that?" she spat.

"Let's just assume for now that I know everything. As to your question, I could not allow your ship to crash into my temple without it killing many more people than were aboard the *Intrepid*.

"Are there any more questions before I continue?"

"Sure, I've got a few," Ethan said. "Why didn't you help us? I spent ten years mourning for my family, thinking the Sythians killed them. Turns out they survived, but not everyone was that lucky. Why didn't you stop them?"

"We could have stopped the original invasion."

"So why didn't you?" Alara put in.

"We never could have stopped them all. You surely know by now that the fleets your Imperium has faced thus far are but seven of many hundreds."

"*Hundreds?*" Atton had kept quiet until now, listening patiently as everyone brought their charges against Omnius. "If that's true, what are you going to do? They know where Avilon is!"

"Yes, that is unfortunate. We are going to send what few ships we have left to rescue your people in Dark Space and bring them here. Then I will activate the gravity fields around Avilon and we will not venture out again."

"That will only buy you time," Captain Caldin said.

"A lot of time. The diameter of each field is over two light years. It would take a minimum of 15 years to cross that at sub-luminal speeds. Given that much time, I am certain to come up with a plan that will suffice to wipe out every living

Sythian in existence. Until then, you and all of humankind will be safe. Is that sufficient security for you?"

Atton nodded weakly, shocked, but no longer surprised to hear just how much Omnius seemed to know about everyone and everything. It was as if he'd been there all along, quietly observing. He was starting to wonder if Omnius really was a god.

"There is one other question to answer, but no one here has ventured to ask it yet."

"Why did you shut down?" Atton whispered.

"Yes, that is the eminent question. It is the one I have spent the past five minutes answering for my people. They are understandably more curious than you, since they have never before witnessed something so terrible as my absence, but you who have not known me your entire lives are not so easily surprised.

"By now you all know what I am. You know that I am a god, created by man to rule and watch over them. My original purpose was to prevent crime, specifically high treason. I was created to anticipate another war before it began, and to stop it before it did. For many thousands of years since my birth, I have kept Avilon safe and hidden. There has not been another Great War between mortals and immortals, and there never will be again.

"Your very own Admiral Hoff Heston had a part of the solution all along. He was exiled for telling the royal council what he thought, and the truth is that he was right. People must be given the freedom to choose how they will live their lives if they are expected to live those lives in harmony. I have since found a way to give them that choice without jeopardizing the ideal of immortality."

"So you're saying we can live in Avilon without

becoming immortals," Atton said.

"If that is what you truly want, then yes."

"That's what the shield is for . . ." Atton replied, realization dawning. "It's to separate mortals from immortals."

"There are two shields. One, which you have seen, is the Celestial Wall. It separates Celestials from Ascendants. Far below that is the original shield, and it separates immortals from the Nulls in the Null Zone."

"The what?" Ethan asked.

"You might know it better by another name—the *netherworld*, perhaps."

"So you resurrect your people there after they die in order to punish them for things they did wrong in life?"

"No. That is an Etherian interpretation of the *netherworld*."

Ceyla, who had been quiet until now suddenly burst out. "You're a fraud, Omnius!"

Atton felt a sharp spike of dread lance through his heart. "Ceyla!" he whispered, grabbing her arm tightly.

But she would not be quiet. "You're not what you're pretending to be," she went on.

"Dear child, I am not pretending to be anything."

"You're pretending to be Etherus! You're *not* him; the netherworld is *not* under your city, and Etheria sure as frek isn't this!" she said, gesturing to the world around her.

"What makes you so sure?"

"Our religion predates you."

"You don't even know how old I am. Perhaps you should investigate the facts before you make rash assumptions."

"Whose facts? Yours?" she sounded shrill. "The original Etherian codices were destroyed in the Great War."

"I am not here to debate my deity with you, Ceyla

Taratha Corbin, and I am truly sorry that your god isn't real, but at least now you have one that is."

Atton felt Ceyla start trembling, but she said nothing further, and he released her arm. Hoping to change the subject, he looked up and spoke to the light, "You still haven't told us what happened to you."

"That is because you keep interrupting me, but I understand. You are all very confused right now. I told you about the netherworld below the city. It encompasses the first fifty levels, as well as roughly another fifty under levels. I am saddened to say that many have chosen to walk away from the light and live in the shadows. They do not want me as their god, and they do not want to live forever in this universe. I am not a tyrant, and I love my children. My fondest wish is for them to be happy, even if that means they must stop being my children and some day die. Therefore, I have determined that all who reject me and choose not to become immortals must live below the lowest shield, which we call the *Styx*."

"So if we decide to become immortals and accept you as our . . . god," Atton began, "then we get to live up here?"

"No, only Celestials live above the Celestial Wall. You must prove to me you are worthy to live up here, but do not trouble yourselves—that is the reason we call ourselves the Ascendancy. Here, people are ever rising higher. If you choose life, you will have all of eternity to rise to whatever heights you are able.

"But I digress. There is still much for you all to learn, and little time for you to learn it. For now, all you need to know about my unexpected shutdown is that there was a rebellion. The Nulls managed to introduce a virus into several of my data centers. They were trying to corrupt the Lifelink database in order to trigger a mass resurrection, killing everyone above the Styx. I was able to stop the virus and stop them from killing all of my children, but I had to shut down nearly all of my systems in order to isolate and remove the virus."

"How would they be able to kill people just by corrupting your database?" Atton asked.

"Besides recording and mapping every part of a person's brain for later transfer to another body, Lifelink implants can also trigger a premature death and resurrection. This is an insurance policy that I built into the system."

"So you can kill anyone at any time—shut them down like they did to you."

"No, not like they did to me. I shut myself down, and it was temporary. If I choose to kill someone, it is permanent. Do not worry, however, I have never misused this ability. My people put me in power because they trust me, and that trust has never been misplaced."

"So what would cause you to kill someone?" Ethan asked.

"Treason."

"Then why didn't you kill the rebels?" Atton added.

"I did, but by the time I realized what they had done, it was too late."

"Not so omniscient after all, hoi Omnius?" Ceyla said, chiming in once more.

"I purposefully turn a blind eye to the Nulls. It is what they wanted. It is why they live in the netherworld below the city. I was merely respecting their wishes. Now I see that I was wrong to do so. I will have to keep a closer eye on them in the future.

"I trust that I have answered all of your questions. There is one more thing I must tell you before I leave, but I would rather you see for yourselves. Master Galan Rovik will escort you."

"What is it?" Atton asked.

"A surprise."

With that, the blinding light disappeared, as did the thunderous voice. Atton blinked spots out of his eyes. He noticed that the blinding light from the Zenith had toned down to a much more tolerable brightness. Master Rovik now walked to one side of the rooftop, crossing the grassy clearing where they stood to an adjacent path.

"Come with me," he beckoned to them from the path.

Atton and the others turned to follow him there. The soldiers joined them, escorting them on both sides. Once they reached the pathway, Master Rovik turned and started down the path. The soldiers subtly herded them to follow. Up ahead, at the end of the path and near the middle of the rooftop, lay a golden dome with a mirror-smooth finish, shining subtly with a reflection of the artificial light radiating down from the Zenith. As Atton watched, Master Rovik reached the dome and placed his hands against it. The dome rose up on four shining pillars of light.

Atton wondered about that dome, but he decided he'd find out what it was soon enough. Turning to Ceyla he said, "So, looks like your people were right."

"My people?"

"Etherians."

"As I told Omnius, he's not Etherus, this isn't Etheria, and his people aren't the Immortals."

Atton looked around at the lush, green beauty of the garden and from there up to the sparkling towers. Not far from them a waterfall cascaded from an adjacent cluster of towers, throwing rainbows into the night. "Why not? It looks like a paradise to me. Everyone here lives forever. There's some kind of god in charge...."

"He's an AI, not a god," Ceyla replied. "Besides, this place might look like a paradise from above, but you saw how much of the city lies below that shield. I'd bet a month's pay the people down there are much less convinced that Omnius is a benevolent god—to say nothing of the netherworld where he locks up all the mortals. I wonder if everyone living down there really is there by choice? It sounds like a prison to me."

"So where do you think they're taking us? And what do you suppose that is?" Atton jerked his chin toward the mysterious golden dome.

A hand landed on Atton's shoulder and squeezed. He turned to see his father and Alara walking behind him, their expressions grim. "It's some kind of lift tube, but a whole lot faster," Ethan said. "And as for where we're going, my bet's on either of the two netherworlds."

"Two? Omnius only mentioned one."

"Yea, but there's two shields. If life were so great below the *Celestial Wall*, then why use a shield to keep people out of the upper city?"

"There could be a lot of reasons for that," Atton said.

"Sure, plenty. We have walls in our society, too, but they're drawn with distance, and that distance is measured in a horizontal space rather than a vertical one. No city planner worth a damn puts the bad neighborhoods right next to the good ones unless he can somehow keep them from mixing. Omnius didn't have a choice because you can't waste space on a world with so little to spare. In my experience, for there to be so many *haves* up here living in the lap of luxury, there's got to be a whole lot of *have-nots* slaving away to keep them there."

Atton thought about that as the soldiers guided them

under the hovering golden dome. They were led into the middle of a glowing green circle on a raised black podium. Galan Rovik entered with them and raised his hands as if praising his god. With that, the inside of the dome began to glow with ever-increasing radiance, and the soldiers retreated from under the dome. As soon as all the soldiers were standing outside, Galan dropped his hands, and the dome fell over their heads with a *boom*. It became so bright inside that Atton was forced to shut his eyes. A loud whirring noise filled the air, and a strong wind gusted through the dome.

Ethan called out, "Brace yourselves!"

Suddenly the blinding light was gone, the whirring noise replaced with a ringing silence punctuated only by the *hiss* of escaping air, and the *tik-tik-tik* of cooling alloy. A cold, musty breeze swept in. Taking a deep breath, Atton risked opening his eyes. . . .

And he beheld the netherworld for the first time. Except that it wasn't a netherworld. It was the most beautiful place he had ever seen.

Chapter 36

ASCENDANCY

Ethan grabbed Alara's hand and walked up to the edge of the dome in shock, dumbstruck by the view. When he reached the edge, he stepped back with a gasp. Once again, the roof of the dome hovered overhead on four shining pillars of light, revealing a panoramic view of where they were now. That view was at once startling and breathtaking.

A carpet of tufted clouds stretched out to the horizon, shining gold in the rising sun. Those clouds whipped by underneath them at a frightening speed, and the sun hung just above them, a blinding red eye peeking out over the tops of the clouds. Overhead, the sky was a deep indigo, still glinting with the diamonds of the night. Below the edge of the dome where they stood lay nothing but open air. If it were being carried by something, Ethan couldn't see what it was. They seemed to be floating high above Avilon and racing after the sun at a considerable speed. A cool breeze was sweeping in, but it was not nearly as violent as it should have been at the speed they were moving.

"How did we get up here?" Alara breathed, her nails biting into his biceps as she clutched his arm with both hands.

"I don't know," Ethan whispered. A moment ago they'd been standing still on a rooftop in the middle of the night, and now they were high above the city and racing after the sun at sunrise. He thought he knew how that must have happened, but he was reluctant to accept the truth. The golden domes, which he had assumed to be some type of lift tubes, didn't actually move people from one point to another, they *teleported* them instantly. That explanation also meshed nicely with how the Avilonians had mysteriously managed to board his corvette without having to dispatch a shuttle.

Ethan heard the others gasping and shouting out with fright as they realized where they were.

Then came the gravelly voice of Master Rovik. "Do not be afraid!" His voice was somehow louder and more resonant than before, as if he was speaking into a microphone. "We are safe here."

"Where is here?" Atton asked.

"How did we get here?" another added.

"The answers will come clear in time!" Rovik replied. "Move to the edge of the transporter," he instructed, and Ethan saw in his peripheral vision that the Rovik was himself doing exactly that. His cape fluttered softly in the wind, and again it struck him that the wind was far too gentle to correspond to the speed that the clouds were rushing by below.

Ethan crept as close to the edge of the dome as he dared and peered down on the tufted clouds below.

Alara hung back, trying to pull him away from the edge. "Ethan!" she shouted. "Get back here!"

Rather than listen to her, he turned to Master Rovik. "What now?" he asked. None of the others had dared to venture as close to the edge as he.

Rovik inclined his head and smiled, as if in appreciation of Ethan's bravery. The Avilonian's glowing blue eyes were wide, but Ethan suspected that was from exhilaration rather than fear. "Now we trust that Omnius will catch us!" Rovik said, and with that, he dove off the edge of the dome.

People screamed. Ethan's own eyes widened with shock as he watched Rovik falling swiftly toward the clouds, his blue cape fluttering as he fell.

"What the frek!" someone said. It sounded like Razor.

A moment later, Atton stepped up to the edge where the Avilonian had been standing. Ceyla was with him, and Ethan noticed they were holding hands.

"I'm not jumping," Atton said, looking up to meet his father's gaze. "You were right, but this is a lot of trouble for Omnius to go to just to kill us."

Ethan frowned. "He wouldn't send one of his own to die just so we could all follow him to our deaths."

"No? Maybe he doesn't care. His people can't die, but *we* can."

"Atton's right," Alara said behind him. "Get away from the edge, Ethan."

"Not yet . . ." He was still watching Master Rovik fall. Something wasn't adding up. Then, all of a sudden, he realized what it was. The Avilonian wasn't falling anymore. He was *flying*. "Hoi!" Ethan pointed to the blue speck which was the man's cape. "Look!" Rovik was now skimming low over the tops of the clouds, arms outstretched as he flew toward the distant sun and horizon.

"What is it?" Alara asked.

"I don't believe it . . ." Ceyla whispered.

"Just because he can do that, doesn't mean we can," Atton added.

"No," Ethan shook his head. "This is an illusion."

"What? What's that supposed to mean?"

"I mean, it's not real!" Ethan shouted so that everyone could hear him above the whipping wind. "If it were real, don't you think at the speed we're moving we'd be ripped right off this platform? Not just that, the air would be too thin to breathe, and it would be much colder than it is."

Atton's jaw dropped and he began nodding slowly. "You're right. . . ."

"I know I am," Ethan said, taking half a step toward the edge.

"Ethan!" Alara screamed, yanking hard on his arm to pull him back.

He turned to her. "Trust me," he said, using one hand to pry the other loose from her white-knuckled grip.

Alara shook her head. "No," she mouthed to him.

"On three?" Atton asked from beside him.

Ethan backed away from his wife, and shot his son a grin. "On one."

With that, he spread his arms wide and dove backward off the edge. He heard Alara screaming after him as he fell, but soon her voice was stolen by the wind whipping past his ears. His eyes began tearing, the clouds rushing up to greet him. The exhilaration of free fall reminded him of ejecting from a starfighter, only much more frightening. At least an ejection seat had grav lifts to slow its descent. His body was falling like a rock, faster and faster. The speed and heart-stopping acceleration stole the breath from his lungs and the tears from his eyes. As he drew near to the shining carpet of golden clouds below, he felt a stab of doubt. What if he'd been wrong? What if this really was an elaborate way to get them all to jump to their deaths? Ethan spread his arms wide, trying in vain to slow his free fall.

Then, all of a sudden, something changed—he felt his descent begin to slow, as if the clouds were somehow repelling him. He leveled out to skim low over their tufted golden tips as he raced toward the sun. His eyes were still tearing from the wind, but now he was no longer free falling—he was flying!

Ethan let out an exhilarated whoop of delight. He twisted around to see if anyone had followed him, but no one had. Now flying on his back, he stared up into the indigo sky to see the shining golden dome that had teleported them all here—wherever here was. As he had surmised earlier, the dome was not supported by anything, but suspended in midair. The bottom of it was rounded like the top, but with a series of glowing white portals—*grav lifts?* he wondered—radiating from it.

As he watched, Ethan saw a few dark specks begin to tumble from the dome. They screamed as they fell. He twisted back onto his stomach and flew onward with a smile. Soon their screams would turn to cries of delight as they began flying too. He looked down, reveling in the sensation of unassisted flight. The clouds passed underneath him in a cottony rise and fall of peaks and valleys, like mountain ranges in the sky. The wind whipped past his face, tearing at his clothes and hair, but he was able to keep his eyes open without them tearing too much. Again, he realized that the wind didn't correspond to the speed he was travelling. A suspicion formed in his gut, and he twisted onto his back once more. He noticed the golden dome glinting above him, no closer or farther away than it had been before. It was following him. He began to wonder if the glowing white portals in the bottom of the dome were grav guns rather than grav lifts. Perhaps they were what was holding him aloft. How the dome stayed aloft was another question. To answer that, Ethan returned to his original supposition—all of this was an elaborate illusion.

One of the specks tumbling down from the dome came sailing down alongside him, and he saw that it was his son, Atton. The boy wore a wild grin on his face, and his dark hair was sticking up at odd angles. "Kavaar!" he said.

"You didn't jump with me," Ethan accused with a smile.

"Hoi, just because I'm your son doesn't mean I'm completely skriffy."

"Are you implying that your old man's a skriff?"

Another dark shape reached them then and began flying on Ethan's other side. He was happy to see that it was Alara. "You're completely skriffy!" she shouted at him. "I'm going to kill you for this!"

He reached for her hand, and despite her promise of revenge, she grabbed his hand in a vice.

"Where are we going?" she asked, her voice trembling now.

Ethan shook his head. "I don't know."

Another person sailed down beside them, next to Atton. Ethan turned to see that it was the young woman who'd been holding his son's hand a moment ago. He sent her a smile, but she was too busy gawking at the view to notice. "This is incredible!" she said.

"Makes flying a Nova seem dull!" Atton added.

"It's amazing, but what's the point?" Alara asked. "What are we doing here? And how are we not falling to our deaths?"

Ethan pointed toward the sun, to a series of bright specks flying up ahead of them. "What are those?"

"Birds?" Atton suggested.

More people began dropping down all around them. Ethan craned his neck to look over his shoulder and found that now everyone was soaring through the clouds with them. He turned back to the fore and eyed the bright specks up ahead. There were hundreds of them, all growing gradually closer. Those specks began to resolve into familiar shapes, with arms, legs, heads, and torsos.

"They're people!" he shouted. "Look!"

In just another few seconds they reached those people, and suddenly Ethan was afraid that they would crash into them, but as they drew near to each other, one or both sets of people began to slow down. Ethan noticed that the others were standing upright in thin air, as if the clouds were made of substance rather than condensing water vapor. They wore shimmering white robes like the ones he'd seen people wearing in the upper city. As he and the others who had jumped from the dome slowed to a stop in front of these white-robed people, he felt something hard and smooth touch his belly, and he flinched as if scalded by it. Suddenly, he understood the illusion—

And he stood up.

The floor under his feet was invisible, as if cloaked, or

covered with a projection of what lay underneath—racing clouds. That meant it wasn't all fake. They were riding high above the surface of Avilon in some type of starship—the walls, ceiling, and floor of which had all been cloaked to hide them from view. Their fall had been arrested by grav guns as he had suspected, and then they'd been held aloft above the invisible deck to enjoy the illusion of unassisted flight until everyone had jumped. As for the wind . . . that must have been generated.

Ethan realized that it was all some type of elaborate trust exercise. Once everyone had literally taken the leap of faith, they'd been accelerated slowly up to the group of white-robed people standing at the opposite end of the chamber—their welcoming party.

Now he understood why the wind hadn't corresponded to their velocity. Ethan glanced behind him to look up at the golden dome once more. He estimated that it was hovering at least a hundred meters above their heads and perhaps two hundred meters behind them. That meant that the ship they were flying in was relatively large, and the space where they now stood was at least as large as one of the venture-class hangars aboard the *Valiant*.

Ethan began to hear people crying out with glee and shouting exclamations of joy.

"Ethan . . ." Alara whispered beside him, tugging on his arm to get his attention.

"What?" he asked, turning back to her with a frown. Then he saw that she was pointing to someone, one of the white-robed Avilonians—a young man, with dark, wavy hair and piercing gray eyes. Something about him was familiar, but Ethan couldn't decide what it was. The man's angular features . . . his broad, square jaw, the stubborn set to his lips

. . . all of those features reminded him of . . . *It can't be.*

"Hello, Ethan," the man said, walking toward him. "It's good to see you again."

Ethan shook his head, his brain denying what his eyes were telling him. "I don't know you," he said.

"Yes, you do," the man replied. Then his gray eyes flicked over the group of people who'd jumped down from the dome, and that young man began nodding slowly. "You all do."

His son was the first to recognize that man. Ethan turned to see Atton take a few quick steps forward, his jaw agape, his green eyes wide. "Admiral? Is that you?"

Chapter 37

Atton couldn't believe what he was seeing. The gray-eyed man standing before him couldn't be more than thirty, but his resemblance to the admiral was unmistakable.

"Yes, Atton, it's me," that man said, but Atton still didn't believe it.

"You look . . ."

"Younger?" Admiral Heston smiled a familiar smile and he nodded. "One of many advantages of life here in Avilon."

Atton shook his head. "I don't understand, are you a clone?"

"Of a sort. I'm still the same man, if that's what you're

asking, but now I'll never age or die, and my body has few of the frailties it once did."

"You're not the admiral I remember," a new voice said. Atton turned to see Captain Caldin stalking up to them. There was a dark look on her face and a note of accusation in her voice.

"I am he," the young admiral replied.

"Bullkrak."

"The admiral you are looking for died."

"Yea, that's what the Omni-frekker said, but I'm starting to think you're all just full of the same krak."

"That's enough!" a gravelly voice bellowed.

The crowd of white-robed people parted and Atton noticed the blue-caped soldier who'd jumped from the dome first striding toward them with a scowl. Atton also noticed that the white-robed people were all smiling broadly as if they shared a secret they weren't telling. He frowned at that. A few of them noticed him looking, and their smiles only grew wider still. He looked away, unnerved by their stares.

"The Sythians invaded Dark Space and executed me not long after you left to come here," Admiral Heston explained.

"And I suppose you still remember that," Caldin said.

"As a matter of fact I do."

"Then you're a delusional freak of frekkin' nature!" Caldin replied.

"You need to calm down," Galan Rovik said, stopping in front of the captain. His glowing blue eyes looked angry to Atton.

"Why? What are you going to do, kill me, too?" Turning back to the admiral, she said, "What the frek do I have to lose? My ship? My crew? My *lover*? No . . ." Caldin shook her head bitterly. "The Sythians already took all of them, and now you're here, miraculously back from the dead. What makes you so damned special?"

Rather than offer words of sympathy for her loss, the admiral smiled broadly. Atton saw Captain Caldin's indigo eyes flash, and for a moment he was afraid that she would leap out and punch him in the face.

"But that's just it," the admiral replied. "I'm not special. I'm just one of many—one of a great multitude, actually."

"What are you talking about?" she demanded.

The admiral turned to gesture to the crowd of people behind him. "These men and women are your crew."

"What?"

Atton's shock mirrored hers. He found himself scanning the faces before them, searching desperately for one that might be familiar—for one in particular. It wasn't long before he'd found her.

Gina.

Her face was younger and more beautiful than he remembered it, but she was still easy to recognize. When she saw him looking at her, the smile she was wearing turned to ice, and she looked away, turning instead to the man standing beside her. That man was none other than Horace "Hawkeye" Perkins.

"I don't believe it . . ." he whispered.

"Believe it," Master Rovik said. With that, he turned to the crowd of white-robed people and nodded.

That must have been the signal they'd been waiting for. Now everyone rushed forth for a reunion, the likes of which Atton was certain had never been seen before.

"Captain!" a deep voice called out. Atton spied a tall, familiar man rushing toward her, and he thought he knew who that was. What the captain said next confirmed it.

"Markom Terl! You stim-baked *skriff!*" The two of them collided, and Atton watched with a growing smile as they wrapped their arms around each other, hugging and kissing each other with wild abandon. They'd always been discreet about their relationship before, but now they didn't seem to care who saw them.

Atton shook his head, feeling left out. "This is incredible . . ." he breathed, speaking to no one in particular. He turned to look for Ceyla, to see her reaction, and he found her standing off to one side, locked in an embrace of her own. He frowned, wondering who the man and woman with her were. He walked up to them, thinking they might be pilots from Guardian Squadron.

"Corbin," he said, tapping her gently on the shoulder.

She turned to him with tears in her eyes and streaming down her face. She was blubbering like a little girl. Atton's own eyes narrowed sharply and he turned to glare at the people she was with, as if they'd done something to hurt her. "Hoi! Get away from her!"

"Atton!" she said. "They're my parents!"

"Your what?" he shook his head, uncomprehending. "They weren't aboard the *Intrepid*, were they?"

"No, Atton," she said, smiling wildly at him and shaking her head. "They were dead! I told you, remember? They died in the invasion!"

With that Atton took an abrupt step back. What felt like a thousand volts of electricity went coursing through him, and he shook his head. It was too much. In fact it was impossible. There was no way these people were her parents. They were far too young to have a daughter her age. "How can you be sure?" he asked, searching those two strangers' smiling faces.

"I'm sure," she said, wiping her tears with the backs of

her hands. "They know things about me, Atton . . . things no one else could possibly know."

Atton still refused to believe it—*any* of it. He turned away from Ceyla, walking on across a deck that was seemingly made of thin air. He felt like he was about to pass out. Stopping for a moment to crouch down and put his head between his legs did nothing to help. He stared down at a racing carpet of clouds lying close beneath his feet. Just then a gap in those clouds appeared and he saw the ground—a vast city of shining towers capped with green parks, sparkling rivers, and thundering cascades. Between the sprawling green parkland, lay the hexagonally segmented shield. The Celestial Wall.

Atton's stomach did a queasy flip and he stood up. Trying not to look down again, he turned in a dizzy circle to look at the crowds of people around him. Everyone was locked in some type of conversation or embrace.

Everyone but him.

Atton spied his father standing nearby, and he headed that way, walking on wooden legs. Ethan had his back turned, and he was stooped down to give someone a hug.

"Dad!" Atton called out.

Ethan turned, and although his eyes weren't gushing with tears, they were red with the threat of them. "Hoi there, son," he said in a voice that was choked with emotion. "You should come meet your grandmother. It's been a long time since she's seen you."

Now Atton noticed the person his father had been hugging—a short young woman with familiar green eyes—his and his father's eyes. She had long, dark hair and a beautiful smile. Her cheeks were wet with tears. "Hello, Atton," she said as he drew near. "Look at you . . . all grown up. I've missed you!" With that, she crushed him in a surprisingly strong embrace.

Atton gaped over her shoulder. She was young enough to be his sister. There was no way she was his *grandmother!* "This is impossible," he whispered.

"No, Atton," his grandmother said. "It's a miracle."

Before anyone could say another word, a voice like thunder split the sky. "Some of you are wondering if this is real. Those of you who aren't are afraid to ask, but I tell you that your eyes do not deceive you. These are the same loved ones you lost. Many of them have been waiting a long time for you. Soon you will all return to the surface to begin your new lives on Avilon.

"Some of you have asked me why I didn't stop the Sythians when they invaded. Part of the answer which I haven't given until now is that I didn't need to stop them. I only needed to bring everyone back to life in my city, where they would be safe. I have spent the past fifty years expanding the city of Etheria to make room for everyone, and now that the work is done, none of you need ever die again!"

A loud cheering rose from the crowd: "Omnius grando est! Omnius grando est!"

Atton wasn't sure what that meant, but if it meant what he thought it did, then he was inclined to agree. "Great is Omnius..." he whispered.

Epilogue

Three weeks and 116 hours earlier . . .

Red emergency lights flashed inside the air lock, and a warning siren wailed. That siren indicated that the airlock was about to be opened without taking the time to suck out all the air and depressurize it. Anything inside the airlock was just seconds from being blown violently into space as positive air pressure met vacuum.

Admiral Heston stared into the black lens of the holo news crew's camera and raised a shaking hand to his forehead in a salute for the people who would soon be watching his execution on news channels all over Dark Space.

In the next instant, Hoff heard a violent roar of air. It ripped him off the deck and tossed him out into space. The roaring gave way to a painful silence. He watched the *Valiant* spinning away beneath his feet. He tried to hold his breath, but it burst from his lungs with the same violence as the air in the airlock. His lungs collapsed and began heaving desperately for air. His ears popped, or perhaps they burst. The searing pain suggested the latter. But that was the extent of it. Having already suffered worse pain while the Sythians tortured him for the location of Avilon, he wondered—*is that it?*

Taking a space walk without a suit was a surprisingly peaceful way to go. He began to wonder if he was dreaming. Wasn't being thrown out an airlock supposed to kill him instantly? Why was he still alive? He took a moment to ignore his heaving lungs and stinging ears in order to appreciate an unobstructed view of space. The diamond sparkle of stars against the black velvet of space had never looked so beautiful.

A sudden chill swept through Hoff's body and he shivered. He felt cold, but not nearly as cold as he would have expected. He supposed his body could only lose heat by radiating it away from him. In every other respect, the vacuum was a perfect insulator.

This must be a dream.

Then Hoff's limbs began to tingle. Gently at first, but the sensation became rapidly more urgent, quickly turning into pain, and that pain soon grew to be unbearable. Hoff's mouth opened in a soundless scream.

He needed air to scream.

His body convulsed. Without air pressure to keep his

bodily fluids in a liquid state, they began to boil, and as they boiled into vapor, they lost energy so quickly that they began to freeze.

Hoff knew that now he had only seconds to live, and he was grateful for that. He tried to focus on the view. Then the capillaries in his eyes burst and he saw red. He passed a few more seconds in agony before he lost consciousness. An indeterminate amount of time passed, and then . . .

He woke up. At least he thought he did.

A bright light appeared in the distance. He saw it growing ever nearer as he raced down a long, dark tunnel toward it. He felt as though he were being *pulled* toward the light. The brightness swelled until it blinded him, and then he heard a familiar voice. "Hello, Hoff," it said.

Then the brightness faded somewhat and he noticed where he was. He gasped. He was soaring out over a golden carpet of clouds, racing toward a rising red sun. He looked down and found that nothing was holding him up. Somehow, impossibly, he was *flying*. For the first time in forever he felt truly *free*, but he also felt strangely numb.

Hadn't he just died? And yet here he was. Was it a dream?

All Hoff could see anywhere he looked were clouds and the blinding brightness of the rising sun. "Who are you?" Hoff thought to ask of the voice that had greeted him. He was afraid to know the answer. If this was the afterlife and he had just come face to face with his creator, then how would that creator think of him for having thwarted his own death so many thousands of times by transferring the contents of his brain to an endless series of clones?

"You know who I am, Hoff."

He shook his head and tried to search the blinding light

for something with substance or even an apparition of substance.

Yet there was nothing.

"Etherus?" Hoff tried.

"That is one of my names. I am known better by my children as Omnius. I am your god, Hoff Natharian Heston."

"Is that why I recognize your voice?"

"It is the same as your inner voice—the one that has always been there, often heard, but never listened to."

"Where am I?"

"You are home."

"Home?"

"Avilon."

"*What?*" Hoff's thoughts took a sudden right turn. This wasn't a conversation with his god. God didn't live in Avilon. Avilonians lived in Avilon.

"Your thoughts betray you, Hoff."

"What are you?"

"I have already answered that."

"This is a dream," he replied.

"No, it is not."

Hoff began flailing in the air. "Let me down!" he roared.

"No, there is someone you must meet."

Then Hoff noticed that he was racing toward someone—someone standing in front of the rising red sun, with his feet seemingly planted squarely on the peak of a tufted white cloud. He wore a shimmering white robe.

As Hoff drew near, he thought he recognized the man's face, but he couldn't seem to remember who it was. Then he seemed to slow to a stop in front of that white-robed man, although the clouds continued to race by beneath them. He drifted gradually closer until he came face to face with that stranger—a stranger with familiar gray eyes, and a younger version of *his* face.

Hoff's mouth dropped open, and he shook his head. "Is this some kind of a joke?" he demanded, turning to look up at the indigo sky and address the god he had been speaking with a moment ago.

But Omnius didn't reply, the stranger did: "It is no joke. We share the same memories, the same personality—well, give or take the past seven years."

"What are you talking about?"

"You died on Ritan—or I did anyway. That Hoff—the one who died in his lover's arms—is me."

"You don't even look like me!" Hoff spluttered.

"Yes I do, except that I am even younger than the man who died. Rest assured, however, my mind is identical in every way."

Horror and realization sliced through Hoff like a knife. He had no memory of Ritan. He'd been stranded there while escaping the Sythians over ten years ago—or so his wife told him. Destra had been stranded with him. That was where they'd grown close enough to conceive their daughter, Atta. Hoff couldn't remember any of that because he hadn't made it off Ritan. He'd died there, and he'd been too far from his ship to transfer his Lifelink data to a clone. The artificial intelligence in charge of the cloning chamber aboard his flagship had decided to revive him soon after it had lost contact with him during the invasion. The one it had revived was *him*, and for a time there had been two of him, living parallel lives—the one on Ritan, and the one with his fleet in the Enclave. Now he was coming face-to-face with the one that had died, but that should have been impossible. He had recently disabled his Lifelink implant at his wife's request. So how had he been revived here, in Avilon? And how had the clone of him on Ritan been revived? If he'd been too far from his flagship to revive there all those years ago, then how could he possibly have revived here in Avilon?

"I don't understand . . . how . . . how are we still alive?" Hoff asked, struggling to put a sentence together.

"We're not the only ones," the younger Hoff said. "There are trillions here like us, resurrected from the war. Omnius brought everyone back."

"That's impossible!" Hoff said. "Not everyone had Lifelinks! Almost no one did! And where did all the clones come from? Where do you even put that many people? Not to mention how you might feed such a multitude."

"Everyone was implanted long before the invasion, without their knowledge. The implants were attached to standard Imperial identichips, which were introduced in 48 BE and implanted in every citizen at birth. From there a pocket of nanites traveled to the host's brain and built a cloaked Lifelink implant. As for where the clones came from and where we put everyone, Omnius has spent the last fifty years growing those clones and expanding the city of Etheria to make room for them. That city stretches from level fifty to level three hundred on Avilon, between the Styx and the Celestial Wall, and it spans the entire planet. There are currently over sixty trillion inhabitants, all resurrected from the invasion. Feeding them is just a matter of technology and utilizing the arable worlds found in the sector of *Domus Licus*."

"I . . ." Hoff shook his head. "What are we going to do? Will there be two of us now?"

"No, Omnius tells me I have to decide whether or not to merge my memories with yours. It will be strange for both of us if we do. I'll remember your life, everything you saw, felt, or otherwise experienced in the past seven years."

"And me?" Hoff asked.

"You'll become a part of me."

Hoff couldn't help feeling like that wasn't fair, like he was being asked to die and share all the intimate details of his life with a fraud, but he had a feeling that he didn't have much choice in the matter. "And what have you decided?"

The younger man smiled. "I think I need to sleep on it." With that, he turned to leave.

"Wait!" Hoff yelled. He wasn't sure what would happen to him if this Hoff decided not to merge memories with him.

The younger man turned.

"You married her," Hoff said.

"I'm sorry?"

"Destra. You're married to her now."

"Really?" that seemed to take the younger man by surprise.

"Yes. You have a daughter with her, too. She's seven years old."

"Seven? That's about the time . . ."

"You died. Yes. She was conceived on Ritan."

"I'll have to ask Omnius about that. If what you say is true, then I'll have no choice but to merge your memories with mine. To do otherwise would be to deprive my daughter of a father and my wife of her husband," the younger man said.

"Exactly," Hoff said.

"We will speak again soon."

Hoff felt desperation rising in his chest. He didn't want to spend any more time than necessary in this lonely, cloud swept place. He reached out with a hand to stop the man—

himself—from going, but his hand never passed in front of his face. He felt like he'd raised his arm, but nothing had appeared to happen. Hoff frowned and hurried after the younger version of himself, who was now *walking* across thin air away from him. He bumped into the younger man, and that man turned to him with a frown.

"What are you doing? You can't follow me to the surface."

"Why not? If everything you said is true, no one should be surprised to see two of us."

"Surprised? Perhaps not. Frightened maybe."

"Why would I scare anyone? I'm the same as you. You said so yourself."

"I said our minds are the same. That does not mean we share the same body. Why would Omnius create two bodies for the same man?"

"What are you talking about?"

With that, the younger man pulled him frighteningly close, until their eyes were mere centimeters apart. Hoff saw his reflection in the younger man's familiar gray eyes. *No.* He shook his head—but he didn't have a head. He began to tremble all over, but he had no muscles and no nerves to produce that effect.

He was nothing but a shiny silver ball, floating in the air. An artificial eye glowed red in the center of his metallic casing, glaring back at him.

With that, Hoff wondered how he could have been so foolish. He and all the other immortals who had cloned themselves to escape death hadn't found a way to live forever.

They had found a way to die a thousand times.

DARK SPACE CONTINUES WITH

DARK SPACE V: Avilon

To get a FREE *Kindle* copy of the sequel, please post an honest review of *Dark Space IV: Revenge* (http://smarturl.it/ds4amz) on Amazon, and then send me the contents of your review by signing up at: http://files.JasperTscott.com/ds5.htm

Your feedback is important to me and to helping other readers find the books they like!

PREVIOUS BOOKS IN THE SERIES

Dark Space I: Humanity is Defeated
(http://smarturl.it/darkspace1print)

HUMANITY IS DEFEATED
Ten years ago the Sythians invaded the galaxy with one goal: to wipe out the human race.

THEY ARE HIDING
Now the survivors are hiding in the last human sector of the galaxy: Dark Space—once a place of exile for criminals, now the last refuge of mankind.

THEY ARE ISOLATED
The once galaxy-spanning Imperium of Star Systems is left guarding the gate which is the only way in or out of Dark Space—but not everyone is satisfied with their governance.

AND THEY ARE KILLING EACH OTHER
Freelancer and ex-convict Ethan Ortane is on the run. He owes crime lord Alec Brondi 10,000 sols, and his ship is badly damaged. When Brondi catches up with him, he makes an offer Ethan can't refuse. Ethan must infiltrate and sabotage the Valiant, the Imperial Star Systems Fleet carrier which stands guarding the entrance of Dark Space, and then his debt will be cleared. While Ethan is still undecided about what he will do, he realizes that the Imperium has been lying and putting all of Dark Space at risk. Now Brondi's plan is starting to look like a necessary evil, but before Ethan can act on it, he discovers that the real plan was much more sinister than what he was told, and he will be lucky to escape the Valiant alive. . . .

Dark Space II: The Invisible War
(http://smarturl.it/darkspace2print)

THEIR SHIP IS DAMAGED

Ethan Ortane has just met his long lost son, Atton, but the circumstances could have been better. After a devastating bio-attack and the ensuing battle, they've fled Dark Space aboard the Defiant to get away from the crime lord, Alec Brondi, who has just stolen the most powerful vessel left in the Imperial Star Systems' Fleet—the Valiant, a five-kilometer-long gladiator-class carrier.

THEY ARE LOW ON FUEL

They need reinforcements to face Brondi, but beyond Dark Space the comm relays are all down, meaning that they must cross Sythian Space to contact the rest of the fleet. Making matters worse, they are low on fuel, so they can't jump straight there. They'll have to travel on the space lanes to save fuel, but the lanes are controlled by Sythians now, and they are fraught with entire fleets of cloaked alien ships.

AND THERE IS NO WAY OUT

With Brondi behind them, they can't go back, and they can't afford to leave the last human sector in the galaxy to the crime lords, so they must cross through enemy territory in the Defiant, a damaged, badly undermanned cruiser with no cloaking device. Making matter worse, trouble is brewing aboard the cruiser, dropping their chances of survival from slim . . . to none.

Dark Space III: Origin
(http://smarturl.it/darkspace3print)

THE DEFIANT IS STRANDED

Ethan and his son, Atton, have been arrested for high treason and conspiracy, crimes which will surely mean the death sentence, but it's beginning to look like theirs aren't the only lives in jeopardy—the Defiant is stranded in Sythian Space, and the vessel which Commander Caldin sent to get help has used all its fuel to get to Obsidian Station, only to find out that the station has been destroyed. Now the Defiant's last hope for a rescue is gone, and everyone on board is about to die a cold, dark death.

HUMANITY IS STILL FIGHTING ITSELF
Meanwhile, the notorious crime lord, Alec Brondi, is plotting to capture the remnants of Admiral Hoff's fleet, just as he captured the Valiant, but Hoff's men are on to him, and Brondi is about to get a lot more than he bargained for, forcing him to flee to the one place he knows will be safe—Dark Space.

AND A NEW INVASION IS ABOUT TO BEGIN
But Dark Space is only safe because the alien invaders don't know exactly where it is, and now they have a plan to find it which will threaten not only Dark Space, but the entire human race.

KEEP IN TOUCH

SUBSCRIBE to the Dark Space Mailing List and Stay Informed about the Series!
(http://files.JasperTscott.com/darkspace.htm)

Follow me on Twitter:
@JasperTscott

Look me up on Facebook:
Jasper T. Scott

Check out my website:
www.JasperTscott.com

Or send me an e-mail:
JasperTscott@gmail.com

ABOUT THE AUTHOR

Jasper T. Scott is the USA TODAY best-selling author of more than eleven novels, written across various genres. His abiding passion is to write science fiction and fantasy. As an avid fan of Star Wars and Lord of the Rings, Jasper Scott aspires to create his own worlds to someday capture the hearts and minds of his readers as thoroughly as these franchises have.

Jasper spent years living as a starving artist before finally quitting his various jobs to become a full-time writer. In his spare time he enjoys reading, traveling, going to the gym, and spending time with his family.

Printed in Great Britain
by Amazon.co.uk, Ltd.,
Marston Gate.